Esra

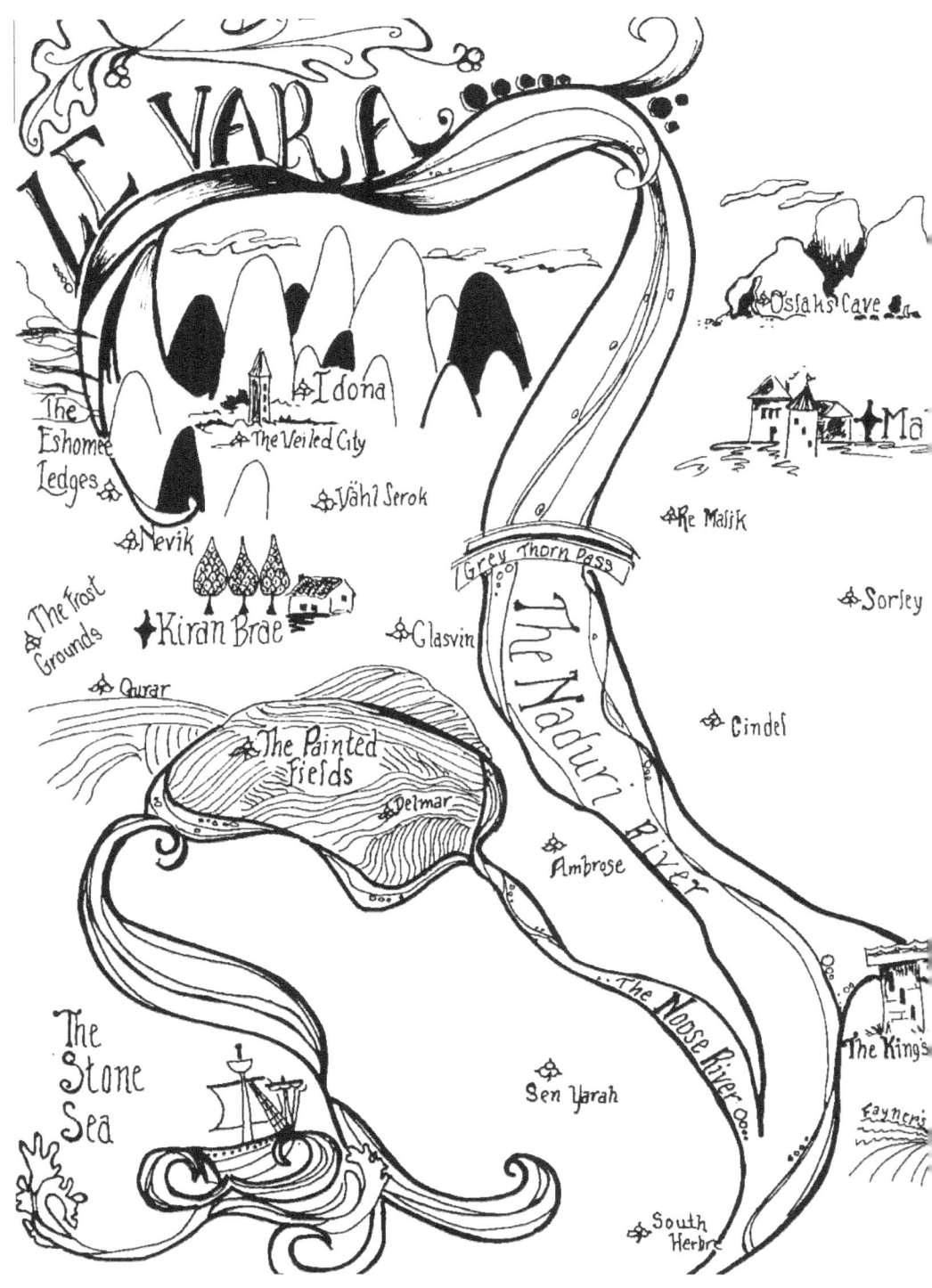

LE VARA

Oslah's Cave

Ma

Re Malik

Sorley

The Eshomee Ledges

Idona
The Veiled City

Vähl Serok

Nevik

The Frost Grounds

Kiran Brae

Glasvin

Grey Thorn Pass

The Naduri River

Cindel

Qurar

The Painted Fields

Delmar

Ambrose

The Stone Sea

The Noose River

The King's

Sen Yarah

Fayneri

South Herbre

Esra

Book One
The Keepers of LeVara

Nicole Burr

DEDICATION

For my family and friends, who have supported and encouraged all of my endeavors, no matter how insane. And to all the books that kept me up until the wee hours of the morning in greedy anticipation.

ACKNOWLEDGMENTS

There are so many people to thank, egads!

To my husband, my Baelin, who inspired me to finally start what I've always wanted to do and who continues to support me through all the long revisions, the joys and obstacles. He tells me to hurry up and get rich so he can retire. I say baby, I'm trying.

For my parents, who always wanted me to think big. And who truly believed in me from the time I brought home smiley stickers on my first elementary school essays. You've listened to my hopes and dreams, comforted me through disappointments. I love you more than you know.

To my brothers, one so passionate and the other so patient, you really inspired much of what I wrote. You also remind me to laugh, and that you can never remember too many ridiculous movie quotes. I am always grateful for your support and honesty.

To my new son Benjamin, who reminds me that to smile and play are more precious than anything else, and that the dishes can always wait. There's a world of fantasy to be discovered! And now I've created one for you.

To my aunts and uncles, who gave me honest criticism with love.

For my grandparents, who remind me of all the good things in life, like laughter, hard work and the power of love.

For my friend and artist, Nancy, who gave life to the characters and world of LeVara. Way better than my stick figures.

To my high school English teacher Mr. Stavar, who never let good enough be good enough. Abandon all hope ye who enter here!

And last but not least, to my Higher Power, the Great Spirit, the Mother Who is Called by Many Names. I follow where you lead.

I

Esra had sensed lately that someone had been watching her, but now she was quite sure of it.

Pushing aside the dense brush with her left arm, she squatted beside the two large, indisputable footprints. Meshok pranced up to the evidence and sniffed it suspiciously for a moment before turning to nuzzle Esra's neck with her wet nose.

"Who are ye?" Esra whispered aloud to the forest, gently tracing her finger around the fresh edges of the indentations. She cocked her head to one side, a habit she had formed as a small child when she wanted to listen very carefully. There was the soft chatter of birds, the dry rustling of crisp leaves, and the raspy panting of Meshok, but nothing else. Brushing off her hands, Esra grudgingly made her way back to the trap where two unlucky rabbits awaited the soup pot.

Carefully unwinding the snare from the first animal's leg, she reset the trap with the quick precision her grandfather had taught her, tucking the end just beneath the loose surface of the ground. Wiping a trickle of sweat from her brow, she continued on to the next rabbit with the same practiced motions. Using her field knife to loosen the snare, she noticed again how dull the blade was getting and vowed that she would sharpen it that night. Finished, Esra slung both animals over her shoulder and began to wind her way through the trees towards the farm.

It was apparent from the size of the footprints that the person was a man. She had a feeling for the last few moons of something being near her at times, especially when she was alone in the forest. But it was as if no matter how alert she forced herself to be, the cause was always out of reach, a shadow fading just as she turned. Esra thought that finding confirmation of her suspicion would cause greater anxiety, but it was in fact a relief. She had begun to think she was losing her mind.

A twig snapped sharply behind her and Esra whipped her head towards the sound. She set the rabbits down gently and scanned the trees with slow deliberation, trying to take in every inch of the forest. Nothing. She laughed at herself for being so childishly anxious. *Get ahold of yerself, Esra. About to get into a full blown panic over a whipbird or a rabbit.*

She turned her head to take a step forward when the smallest glimmer caught the sun in the corner of her eye. Squinting towards the offending spot, Esra could barely make out what appeared to be the corner of a gold trimmed cloak peeking out from behind a tree about fifty paces away. Slowly removing the dull field knife from her belt, she argued with herself over her next course of action. Not knowing if the person was armed, it seemed silly to approach them, especially since they must have a specific reason for not wanting to be seen. Yet she had to know who it was, why she was being followed. Meshok seemed extraordinarily unalarmed by the presence of this man and sat licking one of her paws. Maybe it was just a boy from the village, trying to scare her. Or maybe it was a thief.

Before she could make up her mind, the figure stepped out from behind the tree with the hood of a dark cloak pulled down low over his face. Turning quickly, he sprinted away from Esra at an astonishing speed. Esra blinked her eyes in disbelief and forced her legs to move, stumbling a few steps before steadying herself enough to run towards the intruder. Meshok suddenly took off as well, disappearing just as quickly into the thick mess of trees.

Esra's chest felt tight from terror as she leapt over a fallen log and broke into a full run. Reminding herself to breathe, the branches of thinning leaves tore at her face and clothes. Although she was quite fast, her heart sank as she watched their forms growing steadily smaller in the distance. She wasn't quite sure if she wanted to really catch the trespasser or not, but her body seemed to be in control of her pursuit. Urging herself forward in a final burst of adrenaline, Esra scanned the forest for any sign of the man, but he was gone just as suddenly as he had appeared.

Slowing down to ease the burning in her throat, Esra leaned against a large oak, sliding down the rough bark until she was resting in an exhausted heap against its solid form. Panting heavily, she watched as Meshok came trotting up from behind a tree to lick Esra's cheek with her rough tongue. The Great Wolf sat with a sigh and stared at her with boredom, as if they had not just been frantically chasing down a strange, large man.

"A lot of help ye are," Esra sighed, "Ah well, even if ye saw who it was, ye couldn't tell me anyway." Allowing herself a few minutes to regain her composure, Esra stretched her trembling legs to try and relieve some of the tension from the unanticipated sprinting. Pulling herself up slowly, she tucked the knife back in her belt and scratched Meshok behind the ears before slowly making her way back to where the rabbits lay. She wondered if now that the man had been discovered, that he would leave her alone. Her hands shook as she plucked the rabbits off the ground and walked quickly, wanting to be out of the shade of the forest as soon as possible.

Upon reaching the boundary of the tree line surrounding the low green fields of the farm, the Great Wolf was suddenly ready for another game. She turned around and playfully dipped the front half of her body, tail swaying.

"Ye want to race again, after all that?" Esra asked incredulously. They stared at each other for a long moment, neither moving, until suddenly Esra bolted out of the edge of the forest at full speed. The rabbits bounced clumsily on her shoulder as Meshok spun effortlessly to pursue her with long, full strides. Knowing that she could very easily be overtaken, Esra laughed at the Wolf's generosity as she slammed into the door of the house and burst into the kitchen, claiming her victory.

"My goodness!" Esra's grandmother shrieked as she dropped her basket of vegetables. Meshok plucked a carrot off the floor and swiftly made her way to the hearth rug, her favorite eating spot. Plopping down, she swallowed the prize in a few loud crunches. Esra laughed as she pursued a turnip that was rolling for freedom towards the back door, her grandmother's flustered sigh trailing behind her. "Yer lucky I don't drop dead with fright when ye run through here like a wild banshee."

"Sorry, grandmother," Esra apologized, continuing to gather the runaway vegetables. It was as if they had multiplied upon hitting the floor, and she scooped up handfuls of them into her skirt. Meshok got up with a groan and slinked towards grandmother, rubbing affectionately against her legs in an offering of truce.

"Ah, well. Ye may kill me in the end, but at least ye'll give some color to my cheeks in the meantime," she patted her face and winked at Meshok, whose charm she could hardly resist.

"Esra, please get some water so that I can start noonmeal,' grandmother called over her shoulder as she began to chop one of the carrots with ferocity. There was always an element of resentment in the movements of her kitchen knife. If vegetables ever decided to make war on her town, Esra's grandmother would make short work of it, she was sure.

Esra pulled the bucket out from under the table and slung it over her shoulder. Being careful not to slam the heavy door behind her, she ambled towards the spring that bordered their property in the north, the Great Wolf close at her heels. Just this morning she had taken Meshok for a swim in the cool water. Esra relished the way the streams would press around her body, creating a cocoon of refreshing fluidity. She imagined it felt similar to flying, the sensation of being weightless and free.

Dipping the bucket under the strong current, she looked up in time to see Meshok snapping her jaw shut on a rather large huckfly.

"Well, looks like someone's decided to eat early."

Esra bent forward towards the spring and caught sight of her reflection in the small pool of water that gathered at the eastern edge. It always made her think of her mother.

"Do you think I look anything like her, or that perhaps I take after my father?" Esra looked towards her friend who was now stretched out lazily in the grass next to her. As a child, Esra had spent many long hours at the edge of this very stream, gazing over her face and trying to discern what parts were truly hers alone and which ones were inherited. She could not remember her mother or father, but she had spent countless nights imagining the details of their lives and mannerisms, so that after a while she felt as if she knew their stories almost as well as her own.

"Well, ye know I can't ask the grandparents again. I stopped asking about my parents around the age of five, when I fully understood such questions would avail me naught. *It is not time yet, Esra,* grandmother would gently chide me. She always seemed to say this not with pity or frustration, but with a look that seemed to be a burden of knowing such things and the conflict of needing to protect a young child. It always disappointed me that they never said more.

"I do appreciate the fact that they did not lie to me, at least. How easy it could have been to concoct a story about a tragic death, a dramatic parting of loves. I would have grown up none the wiser." Meshok seemed to cock her head as if she were smiling. "Yer right, the thought of either of them devising such a story is absurd. Although they both have a good sense of humor, grandfather even being quite silly at times, nowhere in all of the Kingdom of LeVara are there two more logical folk than my grandparents. I'd always expected them to hand me a guide to life at any moment, the black and white way to put everything in its proper place."

Esra paused to swat at a particularly bothersome bee as she thought about her grandparents and their consistency. By the time she was ten, she knew all of the dreary details of her parent's untimely deaths by heart. Both had loved her very much. When Esra was only a year old, her mother had fallen ill with a slight fever and chest pain which turned very quickly into The Cough. She was bedridden for five days before she died quietly, her husband devotedly at her side. Only a few fortnights later, Esra's father was thrown from his horse while out hunting vernok in the North Woods, the large, elusive beasts known to feed a family for two seasons. He had died upon impact, before any of the other men could even dismount to help him. Her grandparents were heartbroken over both tragedies, as they were close to their daughter and her new husband, but the presence and energy of Esra pulled them through their grief.

They told her enough details to keep her from thirst, but not, she regarded, enough to fully quench it. Whether they thought that it would be too painful for Esra to hear more, or it was too hard for them to tell, she did not know. They seemed to be comfortable describing the looks and characteristics of each, but not the deeper facets of their personalities or what they really believed in. Now that she was twenty, Esra had learned to accept her parents' fate and appreciate being raised by such wonderful grandparents, even if they decided to withhold some information regarding her past.

"What really amazes me is how I could've grown up surrounded by such order and yet become so chaotic. No matter how much grandmother pins and twists my hair, it will come undone before reaching the bottom of the stairs. Shoelaces triple knotted in the morning won't make it past breakfast. And how I can manage to get an orange stain on my dress when the only thing around fer miles is blankets of soft white Snow, is a complete and utter mystery. No wonder grandfather calls me 'his little vagabond'."

Esra was also unusually tall and towered two hands' breadth above the average woman in town, even surpassing some of the men. Her extreme growth spurts seemed to contribute to her stumbling, though she never quite grew out of her clumsiness.

It did not help that her best friend was one of the most graceful and lovely creatures around. A Great Wolf, she had long, dark grey fur that shimmered in the sun, reflecting a black sheen that gave her a sleek, polished look. A thin line of pure white ran from the tip of her snout and curled behind both ears like an ancient helm. She was tall and solid, the contour of her body reaching Esra's midsection. She had paws that were the size of Esra's palm, and a strong tail that stung like a whip when it joyfully thumped back and forth. When anyone showed an overly-energetic interest in scratching her, Meshok would defy her usual elegancomposure to flop over heavily and squirm from side to side until the designated party would give her the brisk belly rubbing she was owed.

Leaning back from the water's edge, Esra reclined back into the grass as Meshok shuffled over to lay her head on her lap. The Great Wolf stared up into her friend's eyes with a pleading gaze.

"Ye'd like to hear a story, would ye?" Meshok sighed in agreement and closed her eyes, breath rasping noisily from her flared nostrils. "The one about how we met, eh? Well, I suppose I don't get tired of telling that one. After all, ye know I've always been the independent sort, preferring to wander the countryside in solitude. I never found it necessary to have companionship throughout most of the day, although I make friends easily with the townsfolk when I mean to. It was only after becoming dreadfully lost while daydreaming that I had a stroke of luck to give me a dear friend.

I found ye in the forest two springs ago, whimpering by yerself next to a mother dead and cold. The other pups must have wandered off or fallen prey to some other animal. Ye were small, about the size of a fat field rabbit, and yer coat was a much lighter grey. I hadn't the faintest clue that the plump bundle of fur before me was a Great Wolf, only hearing tell of such beasts in old stories and such. I tread lightly towards ye, so as not to cause a fright. I could hardly believe it when my clumsy feet brought me within two strides of yer mother. Ye were just as stunned by my silent and steady arrival as I was. Seconds after bending down to scoop yer little furry self up, ye let out a growl like a Bear and bit down on my forearm like a full grown vernok."

Meshok groaned happily in recognition of the offense, perhaps pleased with her ferociousness.

"Ye think that's funny, do ye? Well, if ye remember, after I screamed to Mother Oak in glorious pain, I pulled back my arm and lifted yer little pup-ness entirely off the ground. Ye were dangling there like a rabbit ready fer the pot. But the skin on my forearm where yer small, sharp teeth had clamped down tore something awful and I shook my arm free. Yer fat little body thudded heavily on yer back and ye were kicking yer legs like a newborn baby Lamb until ye finally rolled over. Ha!

"Anyway, the jolt of pain seemed to invigorate me, and I ripped a piece of my underskirt off and wound it around my bloody arm, more determined than ever to take ye home. We sat there, staring at each other intently, neither moving. After a long moment ye walked towards me with a deliberate and pompous stride, snapping yer teeth in a display of daring. I admired yer audacity, as ye seemed to think ye were a much larger animal. And I can relate to wanting to take on something people think is too big fer ye, I do it often. So I took the opportunity to swiftly pluck ye off the ground with my good arm and quickly wrapped ye in the folds of my skirt. From that moment on, we were an inseparable pair."

Meshok stretched contentedly before gazing up at Esra, willing her to continue on to her favorite part.

"As ye know, I didn't know at first that ye were a Great Wolf, as they were believed to be a dead race. No one had seen one since the age of King Rïvan. But it became very apparent within a few short weeks that ye were no ordinary hound. The size of yer paws were unlike anything I had ever seen. My grandparents warned me against speaking about ye in town, as someone may think themselves clever and try to capture ye. Or do worse, since the hide of a Great Wolf would be worth an indiscriminate amount of coin to a hunter or trapper. But ye did yer part by showing yerself to very few people, as if ye understood this danger. Besides, I always said ye were less a pet than ye were an independent, headstrong friend. I learned after a few short moons never to worry over a dinner not eaten, as my new companion would come and go as she pleased, hunting and wandering, sometimes staying away fer a night. The rest of the time ye spent curled up at the foot of my bed, snoring loudly, or basking by the fire after eating three portions of Lamb. Grandfather and grandmother took a quick liking to ye, even though ye were an inconsistent creature. Although it wouldn't have mattered since by this time I was fully and deeply devoted to my new friend."

Pausing for a moment to let the memory wash over them, Esra could see the fiery little creature in her mind as if it were yesterday. Smiling, she slowly stretched and lifted Meshok's head from her lap so she could stand. Steadying the bucket with her free hand, they began the slow walk back to the house. Esra always had to concentrate when she fetched water, a seemingly simple task. Her lack of grace usually meant that at least a third of the water would slosh over the rim of the bucket on her return, making it necessary for her to make two trips to the cool edge of the stream.

Her grandmother, who always seemed to sense when Esra was near the house, was standing with the thick wooden door propped behind her. "Looks like we'll be gettin' some rain. Better hope yer grandfather gets home in time to avoid the brunt of it."

He had left an hour earlier to make a trip into town for some spices. They had spent the day yesterday drying and wrapping herbs to trade at the general store. Esra looked outside the window at the clear blue skies and tried to understand how her grandmother could always make such unfounded yet accurate predictions. She had no doubt that there would be a storm and that her grandfather would be back before it started.

Nothing, not even an act of nature, could catch her grandparents off guard.

After making the required second journey for more water, she took her place at her grandmother's side to help with the vegetables.

"How go yer studies with Cane?"

"Oh, good," Esra nodded. "We're currently studying Elvish history, which I must admit is very interesting. But I daresay I shouldn't get too involved, fer Cane never does like to stay on any one topic fer too long."

Her grandmother nodded silently in agreement as she poured the second bucket deftly into the cooking pot on the fire. Despite her small, frail frame, she still had the strength and endurance to continue her self-sufficient way of life. She was a woman of structure and habit, finding comfort in completing her daily tasks through repetitive, ritualized movements. Every morning she swept up her long white hair into a tight bun and washed her face with lavender water, patting it dry three times. She took the folded apron from the chair next to her bed and tied the familiar knot at the small of her back before sliding on her boots, left one first. The only hint of deviation from this order and tradition was when her face crinkled into joyous chaos when she smiled.

In spite of all this tenacity, Esra worried how much longer her grandmother's strength would last and each season expected to see the decline begin. She looked at her grandmother, now stirring the pot in steady, circular motions and decided it was as good a time as any to bring up a delicate topic.

"Grandmother, I know that we have discussed this before, but I have been thinking more on the subject, and I wish to make a proposal."

She gave Esra a tired smile, sensing what was coming. "Ye do, eh?"

"Yes," Esra stated, gathering courage. "Ye and grandfather are getting older, and although I enjoy my studies with Cane, it pains me to think that I am not here more to help ye with the chores and the farming. Some of the work that grandfather does in the fields would be difficult fer one half his age and twice his size. However, I realize that my studies are important to the both of ye, although what future it would bring me, I don't know. There is no need fer a teacher in the village and I have no intention of leaving here to pursue knowledge in a larger city. Nor do I have the urge to become assistant to a merchant or tutor fer the wealthy. So instead I will offer ye both a compromise. Why not let me cut my time with Cane in half? I could go there fer three afternoons a week instead of six. I will still be able to have my lessons but I can be here more to help.

"I am not in any way suggesting that ye are unable to do things fer yerself," she added quickly, "but I would like to be able to feel that I pull my weight in this family. And as wonderful as it is to be studying new things all the time, it seems fairly useless."

Esra paused to gauge her grandmother's reaction, who had continued to stir the soup pot in a slow, rhythmic motion.

"And how long have ye been preparing to say that?" Her grandmother chuckled.

"Aye, a few nights," Esra flushed red. "I've been practicing my delivery to Meshok. She's a fair audience but doesn't give much in the way of advice."

Meshok lifted her head from the rug where she was sleeping at the sound of her name and yawned largely to show her disinterest in Esra's sarcasm.

"My dear child," her grandmother said, leaning the spoon against the side of the pot and coming to place her hand on Esra's shoulder. "Ye really needn't worry so much. I am still very capable, as is yer grandfather. Yer studies are very important to us, and they will someday prove to be very useful, whether ye know it or not. Yer right about some of the field work being too hard, but it is also too much fer ye. We have already talked to Baelin, and he will be coming by now once or twice a week to handle some of the heavier work. We offered to pay him, but instead he asked that we allow him the use of our Fariel, since he has no horse of his own. So yer worries are unnecessary and although I applaud yer sensitivity, we are managing just fine. Nothing would make yer grandfather and I more proud than if ye continue yer learning with Cane as planned."

It was hard to argue with her grandmother, especially when she spoke so plainly. But Esra was not ready to concede defeat just yet.

"Then I must ask, at least, what is the purpose of my studies? I am not willing to leave Sorley. Ye and grandfather are all I know. And while my learning…" she tried to think of the best way to describe her feeling, "fulfills me, it is not, as I said, very useful here."

"Well, I regret that ye feel that way," her grandmother dissented with a frown. "But Esra, ye must understand that someday, maybe after we are gone, ye may want to leave this place. And even if ye do not, it is not fair to say that this knowledge is 'useless'. Training of the mind is just as important as training of the body. They may not produce the same visible effect. Sow a crop in a field and ye will have a harvest to show fer it. But the results of wisdom are much harder to see, harder to measure. Ye must trust that yer grandfather and I are doing what's best fer ye. We want ye to have this opportunity, and despite what ye think ye were born fer such things."

Her grandmother took her hand from Esra's shoulder and returned to the soup pot, indicating that the conversation was officially over. Had Esra been more inclined towards stubbornness, she would have argued further. But she was generally open-minded and adaptable, perhaps recompense for a childhood without any parents or siblings, or due to her studies with Cane which forced one to see things from multiple perspectives. There were still many times she wished she could be more obstinate, especially in situations like this, but she had an appreciation for knowing when acceptance would serve her better.

She also recognized that what her grandmother had said was true, especially about her talent for learning. Aside from appearing like a wandering vagrant, Esra maintained a rare grace of mind. She was clever, insightful, and soaked up knowledge without abandon or prejudice. Even though Esra had few friends her own age, all the townsfolk respected her cleverness and foresight. She was especially regarded for her skill in preventing heated arguments between wives and their drunken husbands with a well-timed piece of wit.

But Esra also had a habit of daydreaming mercilessly, her head constantly full of imaginations from books and her own making. This greatly added to her distracted and accident prone state, and it was not unusual for her to be unable to identify a certain tree she passed twice a day or the color of the general store she visited once a week. And the amount of times she had gotten lost on their own property was astounding.

Although she was entirely unobservant of her surroundings, it did not give her the air of being foolish. She simply preferred the unlimited imaginings of her own mind to the boring restrictions of reality. She liked to think that this gave her great creativity and tolerance to change, which had helped her adapt to a life in Sorley without her parents.

Her grandparents had sent her to study with Cane as soon as she could walk. While the other children in town worked the fields beside their families, Esra was learning about mathematics and geography of the Old Kingdom. The townspeople, however, remained oblivious to the true purpose of her visits with Cane and believed, upon the adamant insistence of her grandparents, that she went there each day to cook and clean for the old man. When Esra was younger she questioned the motives behind such secrecy, but her Grandmother told her "to appear humble in this town, ye must ne'er force others to face intellectual ignorance by strutting about yer accomplishments".

Although unsure of what this meant or why it was so important, she trusted her grandmother to understand the workings of the village where she had been all her long life. Most people had a notion that Esra being hired to cook anything, especially when that task involved fire, was absurd for such a clumsy girl. But if they did entertain such thoughts, no one would dare say these things aloud. Her grandparents were well respected people, known for their generosity and kindness. They had managed to help many townsfolk while simultaneously earning the trust of those they helped by keeping such business between themselves.

And even though their household portrayed the epitome of order, they were also a very jovial bunch. There were nights when they would all sit around the fire and in a special streak of silliness, her grandfather would stand before them and pretend to be a Bard. He would devise songs like "I'm richer when I'm drunk because everything seems to double". Esra and her grandmother would be bent over in their chair in a fit of laughter as he tried to maintain a stance of mock seriousness, which eventually would twitch determinedly at the corners of his mouth until he joined them.

They were also some of the wealthiest villagers, but not so much that it separated them unduly from the rest of the town. Esra often wondered where they had gotten such money, and when she asked her grandmother, she spoke of names and places unheard of, and an inheritance that came from distant relatives. It allowed them to live in comfort, and keep a yard full of fat animals, although they still preferred to grow many of their own vegetables and herbs.

When children asked their mothers why Esra, already a strange creature to be twenty and unwed, could do things such as wander about in the forest while they spent every waking moment bent over a plow, they were quickly hushed and told firmly that good people were entitled to the privacy of their own way.

There was a gentle knock at the door and Esra wiped her hands on her smock to let her grandfather in. His hands were teeming with baskets of heavily scented leaves and crisp, paper wrapped parcels. His sparse white hair was sticking up on its ends as it always did, giving him a look of playfulness and mischief that Esra treasured. He stood only as high as her nose and had grown plump with age, with cheeks that seemed to be permanently rosy.

"He is worse to send a'shoppin than a woman," her grandmother chuckled.

Esra laughed under her breath as she helped unload the overflowing pile of goods in his arms. It was true that her grandfather never went into town without returning with something completely unnecessary for his two favorite women. For Esra it was usually a sweet treat to savor, and for his wife something more practical but relatively unneeded. This was the small thorn in their realm of predictableness; her grandfather's ridiculous shopping habits. He handed his granddaughter a small wrapped package which she knew from the smoky rich smell contained sweetened corra nuts.

"And this is fer ye, my lady," Esra's grandfather bowed to his wife as he swept open his coat dramatically, pulling out a wooden contraption. It was short and fat with four protruding, rounded stumps. His eyes shone with pride as his wife took the item into her hands.

"Wonderful!" She exclaimed. There was a pause as she turned the item over. "What is it?"

Grandfather loved these moments for telling what the thing was probably more than the act of giving it. "Why, it's a bread beater, of course!"

Her grandmother turned to Esra with wide eyes, who shrugged to show that she was also quite mystified.

"See," he slid the wooden debacle out of her hands and waved it around in front of his chest. "Ye use it to knead bread!"

"Oh!" Grandmother clapped her hands cheerfully as she watched him flail about. It did not matter that she would probably never use the thing correctly, or if she did, would decide that her own hands were more efficient. He had never failed at being able to surprise them with a preposterous gift. The village was not a particularly large one, but Mr. Sturik, the owner of the general store, had learned to order these strange items for one particular customer alone. No one else seemed to have the desire, nor the extra coin, for such bric-a-brac.

The general store was located at the town center along with the five bedroom inn, alehouse, apothecary, grain mill, and other various small shops. The village of Sorley was shaped like a large "L", with the town center resting comfortably in the crook of the two main intersecting roads. It housed around four hundred families, and Esra had always appreciated that there were enough people to know practically everyone but not so little as to know everyone's business. Her grandparents' farm was located at the eastern edge of one of the main roads, about a twenty minute stroll from the central intersection. It was a small town, but everyone seemed willing to look out for each other and it was generally a happy place. The townsfolk especially prided themselves on creating witty allusions to their village name. "I Sorley need a drink" and "a Sorley boring place" were such common phrases that the people who wandered through the town en route were bound to give a startled look when first approached with such a turn of tongue. In fact, the alehouse held a contest at every spring Trader's Day to see who could come up with the most amusing new idiom. Cane and Esra spent the weeks before the challenge coming up with all sorts of ludicrous sentences.

Like all other towns and cities, Sorley was part of the Kingdom of LeVara, and King Keridon had been the ruler for almost a decade. Although his father before him was fairly popular as a strong and intimidating sovereign, his son Keridon was somewhat weaker willed. Even though the current King was of middle age, he seemed to be more interested in frivolous gaieties such as hunting parties and his Queen's sitting ladies than making progress with the common people. But his taxes weren't abhorrently high, and although he appeared somewhat disinterested and dimwitted, he was not an unkind ruler. His distaste for all things gloomy and resentful assured that he never treated his people too harshly.

The King and Queen had two children, the eldest a son named Bronnen who was about Esra's age, and a younger boy named Samuin. The assurance of an heir with an extra male was reassuring, and luckily Bronnen seemed to take after his grandfather, not his father. The only concern the people of Keridon's Kingdom had was that if anyone were to invade, the army would never be trained or ready in time to even think of defending the realm. But then again, that had not happened for hundreds of years, and there was no reason why it would now.

The Kingdom where Humans resided was split in half by the impressive Naduri River, a massive torrent of water that ran from beyond the northern border of LeVara until splitting into a fork just before the southern edge. Nestled in between the fork of the river was The King's Hold, where the royal family and other nobles lived. The only place to cross The Naduri River's massive berth was by Grey Thorn Pass, located in the relative center of LeVara. Bordering the entire northern expanse were the Eshomee Ledges, the vast mountain range which housed the Elves. Their capital, The Veiled City, was on Idona, the largest and most imposing mountain in the range. The Elves seemed to be secretive people, as Esra had never met one nor knew anyone who had met one besides Cane. And he never said much about it.

Running down the western border of the Kingdom were The Frost Grounds, a barren, cold place that stretched downwards until it collided with The Stone Sea. No one knew how far The Stone Sea continued, for any who had tried to find the end of the horizon had never returned from their voyage. To the southeast was the dense Fira Nadim Forest, which the Unni inhabited. The Jade Gardens bordered the eastern end of LeVara, creeping north from the forest until Fire Lake, the residence of the Shendari. Esra knew very little of the Unni or Shendari people, but was hoping that the topic would be addressed at some point in her learning.

Although Humans were curious creatures at heart, most people knew little of the communities of non-Humans and had never been more than a town or city away. There was not much need for travel, as the town provided for the most basic needs, and Trader's Days allowed for more variety in goods and peoples. Nearly all the inhabitants of Sorley were farmers, and the fields required a most constant attentiveness that did not bode well for unneeded travels. Aside from the traders who visited twice a year, Cane seemed to be the only one in town with extensive knowledge of the world outside and its many different races.

The fact that Cane was an educated man, when most barely knew how to read or write, helped allay the fears of his scandalous pursuit of knowledge into something like avid curiosity. While some people took pity on the lonely status of Cane, others had a faint aversion to him, and superstitious fear ensured that they kept such thoughts to themselves. While most agreed that he was quite eccentric, surely the possession of such knowledge would eventually cause such a thing to occur. His eccentricities were harmless, they decided, and if nothing else he was a quirky, slightly removed old man.

Of course there were always a few in town that would rather be entertained by spinning his situation into a more dramatic story. Last summer, Esra overheard a couple of girls her age discussing their thoughts on the matter. She had to cover her mouth to prevent a forceful burst of laughter from escaping when one girl quite seriously claimed that "Cane and Esra are secret lovers, to be married soon, I'm sure." *If Cane were to marry anything, it would be a book,* Esra thought. He constantly fell asleep clutching a large volume to his chest, like a long time wife he had grown accustomed to shaping himself around at night.

It was times like these that Esra was grateful she cared little for what others thought of her. It was also one of the reasons why many of the other young girls in town were not close friends. They seemed to always be searching for some way to impress someone else. Esra had always lived in a state of proud individuality and independence. If you liked her, that was wonderful. If you didn't, that was your choice. She tried to be kind and helpful, but she was who she was and she was not going to waste her time pretending otherwise. She felt it was a strength of character, but one that resulted in a lonelier existence. Esra often thought it would be easier to gossip and prattle and talk for an hour about lace as if it mattered to her, but she could not bring herself to act as such. The truth was, there were not many things in life she could possibly care less about than lace or if Narvin Glasby meant to wink at Bruna the other day or if it was just the sharp glare of the sun or if perhaps he meant to wink at Tempa, who was standing beside her. How exhausting.

"Esra, yer going to be late," Grandmother turned about suddenly, sweeping the bread beater in a wide arc. "And I need ye to stop by Baelin's house to see if he can come reshoe the horses."

A short moan escaped Esra's lips as she dashed for her cloak and hurried out the door. She felt like this day was shaping up to be nothing but running from one place to another. But at least there was no mysterious, hooded man where she was headed.

II

Esra felt her wavy blonde hair falling in a disheveled mess around her head but she dared not stop to fix it. As if such a thing could be fixed, anyway. As usual, Cane would expect her to be late for her instruction and come stumbling up the steps murmuring apologies. Arriving at the blacksmith's, she went immediately around the house to the back, as Baelin was rarely found anywhere but his workshop. A large stone fire pit stood in the middle of an open area bordered only by four sturdy poles and a tall, heavily thatched roof. A square wooden table stood to one side with various tools strewn across it. Baelin was standing over the blue tipped flames, pounding a long glowing piece of metal on a block of stone with such force that she was amazed to see it was still whole.

Baelin was by far the most reserved man in town, aside from Cane. He said little, went into town even less, and was known far and wide for his superior craftsmanship. Esra sometimes thought that if he didn't need to interact for the sake of his shop he would probably never speak a word. No one knew where he came from, or who his family was. He just seemed to appear two years ago, adapting to his new space with such fluidity that only a few moons after his arrival, not one person could recall who had lived at the house before him.

Men would come from three towns away, sent by richer men to request an expensive sword or a glittering helm, all of which would become cherished family heirlooms. They would stroll up to Baelin, eyes wide as they took in the enormity of the man and the gentle nature with which he silently nodded to their appeals. To say that he was large would be quite the understatement. He towered more than a full head higher than the average man and his arms better resembled tree trunks than Human limbs. Darkened skin and hair added to the threatening illusion, although his mild temperament usually dispelled any fear.

Mischievous, gold flecked eyes were a childish contradiction to the age he really was, which Esra guessed to be in the late twenties.

The people in town joked that he was "a magician of metal, the only man known to make something out of nothing." He did not just shoe horses or make adequate weapons. His intricately carved lockets adorned many a wealthy lady, and the impenetrable yet finely decorated shields seemed to come just as much from artistry as strength or skill. Why he chose to settle down in this boring town, Esra often wondered. Even though he was only a few years older than her, had he lived in a bigger city he could make ten times the amount of gold as a more experienced blacksmith. He could no doubt work for the King himself. But she had an idea that he did not work to make a grand living, but to make a small life in a quiet town. The serene pleasure he got from using his two large hands to create such beautiful things was very apparent.

Although Esra was unaware he had seen her approach, Baelin had been watching her from the minute she trudged out from behind the house. It wasn't hard to hear her crashing through the field. Others thought it a shame, a defect for such an otherwise lovely lady, but he had always found it appealing the way she stumbled after every twenty paces. It didn't seem to bother her much at all. In fact, she barely even flinched anymore. He had decided long ago that she didn't really walk, she twitched, like a spastic jig was raging in her bones, trying to find the beat to a song all her own.

The other young women in town worked out or around the fields all day but took care to smooth every stray piece of hair and wrinkled skirt when in town, batting their eyelashes at each eligible man in sight. Baelin had had his share of young girls coming to see him, feigning a chipped horseshoe or some other small task. He told himself it was only the fact that he was able to earn a good living and enjoyed a responsible lifestyle. The truth is that many of the young women found his silence to be mysterious, and they were intrigued by this man who did not forwardly tell them they looked beautiful in their new dress like the other men did. Some were insulted or took his disinterest as a challenge, trying everything to catch the eye of the man who seemed to not concern himself with matters of love.

Baelin once had a girl come to his workshop, believing to be unseen, who turned around and pinched furious color into her cheeks before she faced him. It was strange behavior that he never quite grasped, and he liked the natural way Esra talked and the easy way she laughed. There was a comfort in such honesty to self, and he greatly respected her for it. Mingling with others was definitely not one of his strong points, especially with women. It seems as though they were always saying one thing to mean another, which may also turn out to be just the opposite. Metal was predictable, at least to a certain degree. Women, well, he'd rather be in the middle of three thousand wild Boars.

Sensing that he was presently enthralled with the stubborn piece of metal before him, Esra leaned against the nearest post and waited patiently. She knew the concentration that such a feat required, as she had encountered this feeling many times in her studies. Not wanting to interrupt, she took the opportunity to watch as he transformed the odd lump into a perfect shape. Unlike most of the young village folk, Baelin was not the type of person who was ever in a hurry. Esra wished this was true for her and her constant struggle with tardiness, since it was already dangerous enough to try and walk a slow, deliberate pace.

She liked Baelin, liked the way he never gossiped or prodded. He also didn't give her the uncomfortable looks of desire the other young men in town quite often bestowed upon her. Romance was an uncertain topic for Esra, and for all her vast learning from books she still never seemed to understand the complicated webs of courtship.

Either way, her grandparents thought very highly of Baelin, and although they generally liked most people, they seemed to hold a deeper respect than customary for this particular man. He also gave the impression that although he was quiet he held knowledge inside him that most do not have. Esra could understand this, as she was not entitled to share what knowledge she gained from Cane with those outside of her grandparents and very few others. It instilled in her a slight curiosity about Baelin and his mysterious, silent ways.

"Good mornin', Esra. Meshok," he greeted them both in a deep, booming voice without turning around.

"I could never sneak up on ye," she laughed.

"Unfortunately, ye could never sneak up on anyone, let alone someone who still has most of their hearing." One of Baelin's favorite things was to poke fun at her blundering gait. And she was never offended at the multiple ways he concocted to do so.

Meshok murmured in agreement and leaned forward in an extensive stretch. The Wolf was a constant victim of Esra's trips and falls, even though she came up to her waist. And she would never allow Esra to visit the blacksmith without her, as she was one of the few people allowed to be in her presence.

"My grandparents would like to see if ye could come to reshoe the horses," she said, resting a hand on the head of her panting friend. Above the clamor he gave a terse nod to show he understood and picked up a new piece of metal from the fire.

"When?"

"Whenever ye can, no hurry," she offered. "Ye know my grandparents, they never actually have a problem with the horses. It's probably just a premonition of disaster that they will succeed in avoiding."

"Aye," he agreed. He knew her grandparents to be the most prepared and level headed people he'd even known. They had already brought in the wash and hung it inside two hours before anyone else even suspected it would rain.

Esra shifted on her feet nervously, debating if it was a good idea after all to discuss her close encounter with the hooded man in the forest. She did not want to worry her grandparents and she trusted her blacksmith friend more than almost anyone in this town. She quickly decided it was worth the risk of him thinking her unbalanced. Besides, she needed to solve this riddle once and for all, and she wasn't getting any closer to the truth on her own.

"Baelin?"

"Aye?" He asked, noticing the slight edge in her voice but not slowing his steady pounding of the hot metal, which glowed fainter with each hit.

"I think that someone is following me. Actually, I know that they are. I'm just not sure why. I don't want to worry my grandparents and as Cane seems to pay no attention to most people in the town, I was wondering what yer opinion is. They're only there when I'm alone in the forest. Today I saw footprints, and then caught a glimpse of his cloak behind a tree. I chased him fer a while, but he got away."

Baelin paused and pulled a square of faded brown cloth from his back pocket, running it along his forehead. "If someone is following ye, it might not be the best idea te go chasing after them on yer own."

"I know," Esra admitted. "I just need to know who they are. I can't understand why someone would do such a thing."

Baelin just nodded as he tucked the sweaty cloth back into his pocket. "Well, do ye get the sense that they want te harm ye?"

"Ye mean ye believe me?" Esra was somewhat taken aback that she did not have to further explain herself. It had sounded a little mad once it came out of her mouth after all.

She recalled the atmosphere in the forest when the man was near, tried to remember her feelings. "No, I don't think they mean me any harm. Besides, they could have done that by now if that's what they meant. It's just making me crazy that I don't know who it is or what they want."

"Well, I'd say fer now, keep yer eyes open. And make sure Meshok's always with ye. I can come with ye next time as well."

"Alright," Esra agreed. "Not that Meshok's much help, though."

The Great Wolf sighed heavily at her friend and inched closer to the fire. Esra felt better just knowing that she had told someone else. And that he didn't think she was unbalanced. Her stubborn independence still didn't want to give up the search just yet.

Baelin glanced up to see the sun still early in the sky. "Tell yer grandparents that I'll be by tonight fer the horses."

With a quick flick of his hand that Esra interpreted to mean goodbye, he turned back to the blue flames as the first drops of rain spattered on the ground beside the shop. Esra picked up the folds of her skirt, even though running would not help the fact that she was late again.

III

Cane's house was in the center of Sorley, tucked behind the apothecary shop. You had to take a long, narrow alleyway to find the entrance, and Esra liked that he was in the middle of town while still maintaining some privacy. For the past two seasons Cane had changed the course of her studies to include more "active" topics, as he called them. Growing up, she had studied history, writing, herb lore, topography, and many other widespread topics in the dusty, thick volumes of books that lined the numerous shelves of his study. Most times she could tell you the name of a city in LeVara, where it was in relation to other towns, what plants and animals were native to the area, and who of note came from that place. She did not know if these facts would ever be of use, but at least she could hold onto the knowledge so that one day she may pass it onto someone who may need it. Perhaps a young girl like herself, eager to explore in knowledge and imagination what lay beyond the confines of a small town.

Cane had studied with some of the best scholars in the Kingdom, and chuckled to say he retired because he "Sorley needed to rest his brain". He was a tall, gangly man, whose entire face turned downwards as if gravity was just too much for him in his old age. His nose, chin, and even his eyelids had a droop to them, which gave him a permanent look of exhaustion mixed with melancholy. Greying hair surrounded a bald circle in the middle of his head, which Esra liked to tease him about.

"Yer brain got so big it just blew the hair right off the top," she had said to him once, causing the downwards force of his mouth to twitch into an amused smile.

Cane was usually found in straight fitting clothing that extended almost to the floor. These elegant garments had sophisticated embroidery around the edges, reminding Esra of a dress tunic. It was not something customarily worn in Sorley, as the men here preferred the basic leggings and loose shirts or overcoats of field workers.

His physical mannerisms were usually methodical and purposeful, like Esra's grandmother. All this order surrounding her and yet she couldn't even keep her boots tied. Esra could predict with startling accuracy when Cane was about to pack a pipe or turn the page of a book. He also had a habit of drumming his left hand on the table when deep in thought, his gnarled fingers creating a steady rhythm. Esra insisted that he needn't make her study music, as the tap tap tap of his pipe and drum drum drum of his fingers would suffice.

It was said that there was a student before her, a young man, but he had moved away very suddenly to Cane's great displeasure. They had never discussed the issue. How he had gone on to adopt Esra as his pupil, she did not know. But her guess was that it had more than a little to do with her sly grandparents. As meticulous as his physical mannerisms were, he taught more like a Jackrabbit in an open field. It was a random way of learning, but Esra had gotten used to it. At first it had confused her, for just when she thought that she might be gaining an understanding of what they were studying, he'd have a book pulled down from the shelf and open to the "next adventure".

"First," Cane explained, "ye need to know a little bit of everything. Then, only after it has all been exposed to ye, may ye find what ye are called to learn. Many scholars make the mistake of choosing a study that they feel is important to others without first learning what is important to *them*."

Esra began reciting back to him the correct pronunciation of Elvish cities when he put his hand up in a request of silence. She quickly scanned the last few phrases to see which one she had botched.

"Esra."

"Yes?"

"It is time we move on."

"Thank goodness," she exclaimed. "I've secretly been peeking forward at the next chapter …"

"No, Esra. I don't mean the next chapter. I mean a different topic altogether." He calmly leaned forward to tap his pipe out the open window. Although he spent a good deal of time carefully packing the leaf and lighting the basin, he rarely remembered to inhale. As good a teacher as he was, there seemed to be something quite distracted about him.

"But I was quite enjoying Elvish history! And we almost never get to talk about the other races," she said sulkily. If it was agriculture or something else equally as boring, she normally wouldn't object.

"I daresay I think ye'll like our next topic even better."

"Really?" Esra asked suspiciously. "Alright then, what shall it be? Geography of the western Kingdom? Or perhaps the reign of Kaldor?" Excitement mounted as she thought of all the possibilities, as there were still many subjects they had not yet breached.

"No. Today we shall begin yer study of the Keepers."

Esra had never heard Cane mention something so fantastical, even in reference. He had always stuck to the more refined and useful lessons, like mathematics and agriculture. He seemed to be studying her, awaiting her reaction to the introduction of this strange subject. "I'd like ye to tell me what ye know of them."

She looked towards Meshok, who was sprawled luxuriously on the thickly braided rug next to Esra's chair, and absentmindedly reached down to stroke her grey fur. "I have seen the ones they call Keepers before, of course. Most everyone has. A group of four or five is bound to come by every year or two to stop in the inn fer a night before continuing on to some anonymous destination. The only reason ye even know they're sorcerers is the strange feeling ye get when walking by. It's something that seems hard to describe, even harder to forget. Like a mixture of power and calmness, an aura of controlled command. Either way, it's always been an unsaid feeling that these people are best left alone.

Esra paused here but he nodded at her to continue.

"When I was younger I expected them to be more like tricksters, pulling flowers out of thin air and making mead appear in their empty cup. I figured that people with such talent would naturally want to flaunt it a bit, if only to entertain townspeople who had so little other excitement. As it turns out, they are never showy nor entertaining, and prefer to keep to themselves. They usually take dinners in their rented rooms and leave before most have a chance to muster up the courage to ask where they came from or where they're headed. Not that they are ungrateful or unkind. In fact on rare occasions a few of them have come to the inn to enjoy an ale and join in the townsfolk's quest for the perfect Sorley quote. No, it's rather like they sense and understand peoples discomfort in their air of magick, and graciously take the opportunity to rest in solitude, so that no one would feel obligated to entertain them.

"I also think it's odd that no matter what the weather, they are always adorned in those dark blue hooded cloaks. And underneath they wear travelers' boots and leggings, even for the women."

Esra envisioned the outfits that were simple but beautiful, with an intricate embroidery of vines swirling in rich gold around the cuffs and bottom hem of the soft blue cloaks.

"I feel like relationships with the Keepers had been one of a mutually distant respect. It's said that they generally band together in small groups and rarely live in places where non-magickal people reside. I've never heard of any of them living in Sorley, even in the old stories. I've also heard that they prefer the more rustic land, having a natural inclination towards all things of the earth. What they do or what kind of sorcery they perform, I don't know. Every so often someone at the Inn will have an ale too many and speculate. There are many stories that fly through the air on these nights, but none ever seemed satisfactory to me. The only thing absolutely agreed upon was that these Keepers are very important, although no one can remember exactly why.

"Is it true that Magick was something that used to be very common generations ago? I've heard tell that almost every family had a relation or two that was gifted in some form of it. Some could use their skills to grow crops, settle arguments, communicate over great distances, or even see into other places and times. I believe they could even heal. And that over the years these sorcerers have become fewer and fewer until hardly any remain."

"And what do you think of sorcery?" Cane asked.

"Well, sorcery is not something that most people are suspicious of, since it seems true that many had ancestors who practiced magick, but it became less important."

"That may be the general thinking, but what do *ye* think?"

Esra brushed a strand of hair off her face as she debated whether her opinion may make her look silly. As much as she didn't care what others thought, sometimes the desire to please her teacher overcame her candor. Then again, he was the one who brought such a topic up, so why should she be embarrassed. "Actually, I used to ask Grandmother about magick incessantly as a child. I had often wished that someone I knew was a sorcerer or had retained a few remnants of magickal ability from an ancestor. On the very few occasions that Grandmother would answer me on the subject, I remember she said that it was a practice that has been slowly forgotten. People no longer spoke about how a great aunt could start fires instantaneously without flint or remedy a headache with a touch. She said that maybe the people of LeVara figured that the inheritance of these skills eventually declined or that the need fer it became unnecessary. There were various herbs to heal and new tools to use in the fields, so that those magickally gifted people simply stopped practicing their craft. This theory always disappointed me, because I found it fascinating that such people had existed, still exist today in remote glimpses like the Keepers. And I can't imagine why someone with such a skill would just stop using it."

Cane looked at her thoughtfully, knowing that Esra had something else to say. What she wasn't telling him was that there was something about the topic of magick that pulled at her, and it seemed more than just her curious nature. Sometimes Esra wondered if other people secretly thought that the adventurous spirit of these traveling Keepers wasn't just a peculiar shame but exotic and appealing. Most of the townspeople were uneasy, but Esra was enchanted. It was as if these people, these Keepers, they called to her in some way when they were near. Esra knew that didn't make sense but the feeling was there, nonetheless. When a group of Keepers were in Sorley everyone would tell stories of the few sorcerers they had known throughout the years. Tales of healings, of people able to control fire and move objects without the need for touch. All of it fueled Esra's interest in magick.

"Is that all?" Cane looked at Esra steadily, taking a small puff from his pipe.

The thoughts swirling around her head seemed like the wild imaginings of a small child, dreaming of fancy adventures. Esra wasn't sure how to explain herself without sounding as if her life and studies here were not enough. "There's something about them that make me wish for something more, something my current way of life can't provide. I don't mean to sound ungrateful or unhappy, I just can't figure out why everything regarding magick has become so lost."

He paused thoughtfully. "That is a feeling I can certainly understand. Either way, it seems ye know vastly less about the topic than I thought."

"Less like nothing," Esra mumbled in surprise. Cane rarely pointed out when she was oblivious to a topic they had not covered yet, as he did not expect her to have knowledge of such things. The people of Sorley were only expected to know farming and basic numbers, many could not even write. But looking back on what she had told him about the sorcerers, it did seem like the idle chatter of a superstitious housewife. Which is where most of her information on magick had come from, it was true. She hated feeling incompetent. Even though Cane was much more knowledgeable in all subjects, Esra took pride in her capacity for learning. A twinge of resentment flared as she thought of these "Keepers" and their stupid mysterious ways. Magick smagick.

Yet Cane did not look displeased as he usually did when his student confirmed their ignorance. In fact, his demeanor hinted slightly at relief.

"Good. I think it easier to teach this subject to those who have not been...corrupted by others' opinions."

Underneath both her forearms a burning itch began, like a bug bite scratched too hard. She turned her hands over to see small dark red dots running up to the elbows. Cane peered down at the strange rash, and

Meshok lifted her head from the rug where she was lounging.

"Is this the first time ye've noticed it?" Cane asked.

"Aye. Do ye think I got into some odd plant?" She hadn't been paying much attention while they were chasing the hooded man through the forest.

He gazed at the spots again. "It won't kill ye. It's not common, but the Witch Hazel leaf is known to appear around these parts every few years. It's rare, that's all."

Esra shrugged and grabbed a clean sheet of parchment, all the while rubbing her arm on the side of the chair. *They should call the stuff Itch Hazel,* she thought miserably.

"We will be on this topic and a few others fer at least a year," Cane announced.

She gaped with an open mouth, unable to hide her amazement that they would stay on a subject for more than a week.

"But ye always say that someone should know a little about everything…"

"Yes, yes," he impatiently scolded. "But I respectfully ask that ye trust my judgment in the matter. We have much to do and not much time to do it."

"What do you mean no time? But…"

"No buts. And there's one more thing," he continued, "and ye may not like it, but it is above all else the most important to remember. Ye may *not* ask any questions fer the first few moons that we study. Ye're to listen, and nothing more."

"The first few moons!" Although Cane joked about her incessant questions, Esra could tell that he was pleased to have someone so interested in the things that had once consumed his curiosity as well. "But why?"

He sighed heavily and leaned back in his chair. "Esra, I cannot tell ye these things now. But I can say that what we will be doing is exceedingly important, and ye *must* be willing to trust me. I can waste no time in these next months with ye asking questions that will soon enough be answered. It is just as much a test of patience and humility as it is of intellect. I assure ye that after that time ye may ask anything ye wish of me. And I do promise to answer every one of those to the best of my ability."

Esra's head was spinning with confliction over this restraining information. She paused for a moment to reflect on this. Surely this is what she had wanted all along, to dive wholeheartedly into a topic. Really master something. She could argue, but she knew that it wouldn't do any good. He had obviously made up his mind, and when Cane didn't want to speak any more on a subject, it was best just to give in. This would be the second argument she lost today after her grandmother, and Esra was starting to feel exasperated at her lack of conviction.

She nodded solemnly and surrendered to his will. After all, she would be learning about sorcery and who knows what else. It would be a difficult task to keep her mouth shut, but well worth it.

Cane gazed at her calmly from beneath his sinking eyelids and understood that she would do as he asked. He did not go to the shelf to get a book nor to the closet where the scrolls were kept. Instead, he sat in meditation, considering his next choice of words. She waited with unsuspecting curiosity, for she did not know these next lessons would change her life, and the lives of those who would never hear them.

IV

Cane continued his instruction first thing the following day with no leniency upon their agreement. After only an hour, Esra found her mouth opening and shutting at such frequent intervals that Cane sternly suggested she take a short break to compose herself, lest Meshok mistake her for a fish and try to steal a bite of her leg. She roamed gloomily around the back garden, disconcerted that she must endure this type of schooling for countless hours more. The excitement of yesterday had somewhat lessened with the reality of her circumstance. She had always been encouraged to question her teacher, and her stubborn curiosity was the only thing that made her return to the large mahogany chair, prepared once again to listen and listen only.

"Sorcerers have not, as most believe, become fewer in number over the ages. Ye do not see them as often anymore, surely, but that is not because the practice of magick has dwindled or its participants died off. Magick has become an art that has moved underground, as secrecy has a growing importance. The Keepers are a special group of sorcerers that have grown from the need to protect the Kingdom from various threats and they have done so in private. There are some who believe that the Keepers have always been here, since the dawn of our age. Sorcerers have, of course, but the special need for a *concealed* society of Keepers was completely unnecessary before the reign of the thirty first King.

"I want to talk about an event that changed our history immensely, even though most people are unaware that it ever happened. At the death of the thirtieth leader, the great King Jythan, the people of LeVara mourned his passing as a just and generous ruler while preparing fer the coronation of his son, Haylore. But one thing the people did not count on was the coming of the youngest son, wrought with fury to claim his brother's birthright, his seat on the throne."

Esra furrowed her brow in concentration as she thought of the name of the next King in succession. "Ye mean King Rïvan? But I did not know he was the youngest! Who is this Haylore? And why did Rïvan gain the throne before his elder brother?"

A sharp glance from Cane caused Esra to wince and rephrase her slur of questions into an apology. "What I meant to say is that King Rïvan, as I had been taught, was an only child and was bestowed the same joyful blessings from his father just as any other whose legacy was with the throne."

"That's what he would have ye think!" Cane exploded as he pounded the arms of his chair, causing Meshok to bolt upright in alertness. He smoothed the front of his shirt, attempting to compose himself. Esra stared at his reddening face, knowing that Cane was generally a passionate man when it came to learning but rarely moved to such anger.

"King Rïvan took to great lengths to see that this lie was all that was known after a few years' time. Anyone who spoke differently faced penalty of death. Although the Prince was barely the age of twenty when he took the throne, King Jythan had sensed the wickedness of his younger son from an early age. Rïvan was thirsty with vengeance and greed, two very large feelings fer such a small boy. In an attempt to stifle such destructive traits, The King sent the child with some of his most trusted associates to an estate in the country. He hoped that a life away from the pressures of court and spending time with good, honest people would help quell the fire within his young son. He still saw the boy frequently and at such intervals became convinced that Rïvan was indeed gaining insight and honor. But King Jythan had underestimated his son's most prominent attribute; manipulation. He did not see that the face which Rïvan turned to his father was not the same when the King's back was turned. He remained at this country estate fer years and years, growing more impatient and cruel over time.

"A few days after King Jythan' s death, Rïvan called fer his brother to dine in mourning at his estate in South Herbre, where he planned to have the rightful heir to the throne assassinated. But Haylore had many that were loyal to him, good men who sensed the brother's malevolence, and they convinced him to send a decoy instead. A gifted woman sorcerer named Yuri was called upon to ensure that Rïvan would not recognize that the man sent in the eldest son's clothes was not actually the future King.

"When the decoy returned dead, Haylore knew the truth of what Rïvan had planned fer him. He beat his chest in grief, fer now he had lost a good father and a wicked brother in the same fortnight.

"Now Haylore had the mightier army and the people's good grace.

and Rïvan knew this. As a last gesture of good faith, Haylore sent a messenger to implore his younger brother forfeit, in exchange fer forgiveness and a life of solitude in banishment to The Frost Grounds, a cold, desolate place in the far western Kingdom. He sincerely hoped that Rïvan would accept his offer, fer he had no desire to wage war in the first year of his reign, especially with one of his own bloodline. And above all, Haylore was a peaceful man, as were all the kings he could remember that came before him. He possessed none of the selfishness or hatred that his brother exuded.

"But Rïvan had used his long absence in the country to make friends with those far and wide who were just like him; hungry fer power. They devised a plan to kidnap the wives and children of those men loyal to King Haylore while their fathers were at court, and brought the captives to his estate. Rïvan knew that his brother-King would now gather an army in an attempt to rescue the captives. But he had also anticipated, long before the kidnapping of the women and children, the place where the battalions would gather, south of the castle and next to the river in Fayner's Field. He ordered his sorcerers to poison the Naduri River where it would border the encampment. I am not sure if ye realize it, but the fork in the southern Naduri River was not always there. Haylore's sorcerers, led by the enchantress Yuri, worked some of the most powerful magick in the history of our Kingdom trying to redirect the poison away from the soldiers and towns that lined the river banks. And so the western fork of the river was formed. It did not happen quickly enough though, and within the first night most of the King's army had died wretched, vomiting deaths. The poison continued its path down the river, killing many more innocents, including plants, Humans, animals, and even some of Rïvan's own allies. But in his ruthlessness, this caused him no great discomfort, as it was to be expected. The weak will have to die in order fer those with true power to come to fruition.

"To show his enemy his true supremacy, and to stay those that would rise against him in retaliation, Rïvan ordered his most favored guards, a secret group of skilled sorcerers and soldiers referred to as the Elites, to kill all of the kidnapped women and children as they slept. With no army left to fight, and no families left to barter fer, the people of LeVara fearfully acquiesced to their new ruler, and secretly hoped that King Haylore had not been slain.

"Unfortunately, the King had not been slain by the poison directly, but he had spent so much time by the Naduri River trying to save his men and tending to the sick that he fell ill with The Cough and perished within a week. Rïvan decided to build his new castle in The Frost Grounds as a mockery of his brother's attempt to banish him there.

There was no army to oppose the younger son and no other heir to claim the throne, so Rïvan took control. By the time a generation had passed most people had learned never to speak of this abomination, and the story of King Haylore's murder was silenced at last. Even our current King Keridon, being a fair but indifferent sovereign, does not sense the trouble that now brews in his Kingdom. Now tell me, what do ye think of all this? Ye have permission to speak."

At this interval, Cane paused, staring intently at Esra. She sat pensively for a moment, absorbing the words of this chronicle. It seemed a great feat that King Rïvan had achieved such treachery and covered it all so swiftly and with such finality that no whispers of the truth remained. But she trusted her teacher, and knew that although he was eccentric at times, dishonest he was not. There was also a twinge of anger in her, to be so deceived by a history she had trusted. The books she had read, the stories she'd been told, now she wondered how much of it was real, how all the people of LeVara had been living a lie. And it was true that King Keridon was a somewhat dimwitted and lazy ruler, though not a cruel one. She wasn't sure what trouble Cane spoke of, but it seemed likely that the King would dismiss any threat against him as nonsense, simply because he was foolish and ignorant. He was a great enthusiast of hunting parties and women, not the welfare of his people. And he certainly had no interest in something as unattractive and hardworking as training an army. Although he did not actively harm his people, his inactivity had the potential to be just as destructive. This Rïvan, however, was a despicable character.

She chose her next words carefully. "Then King Rïvan has achieved a level of deceit and malice unmatched by anything I've thus known. Forgive me, but I am…resentful that someone could get away with such treachery."

"Esra," he said quietly, "I am *very* glad to hear ye feel that way."

Now it was Esra's turn to be surprised. "Of course I would. What else would ye expect of me?"

She hastily rubbed where the Witch Hazel rash was creeping towards her elbows on both arms. Cane shifted uncomfortably in his chair and cleared his throat. He had a habit of clearing his throat when he was struggling with whether to reveal more information to her or not. Meshok, who had been sleeping obliviously throughout most of the lesson, stretched out her back legs and perked up her ears, matching Esra's anticipation.

"Not everyone takes such news with …" he paused, squinting in an attempt to find the right word, "honor."

He could see the confusion in her eyes. "Do ye remember that I once had an apprentice before ye, a young man?"

"Aye, but ye've never said much about him. He moved away very suddenly. I figured it was because he grew older and decided to pursue something other than knowledge, or that ye were unsuccessful in his training. Not that it was yer fault," she added quickly.

"Actually, ye are right in both senses," he admitted, reaching under his chair for the box with his pipe and leaf. He set about the meticulous task of filling the chamber, pinching a few leaves and packing them carefully into the pipe, ignoring his student's impatience.

Esra was beginning to worry that her face would soon carry a permanent look of consternation from this man. "As in…?"

"Well, he decided to pursue things other than knowledge, *and* I was utterly and shamefully unsuccessful as his teacher." Esra tried to hide the surprise that alit on her face at his admittance of failure. Although he jumped around through his topics and could be enigmatic, Cane was a very capable teacher.

He lit the chamber of his pipe, causing Meshok to shift closer to Cane's chair. The dog had proven to be a pipe smoking enthusiast who loved the smell of burning leaf. Cane took the opportunity to rub her briskly behind the ears before he continued.

"His name is Tallen, and ye will probably do well to remember it." Esra saw something flash briefly in his eyes, perhaps disdain, or even hatred. Then she recognized it. Guilt.

"Many years ago, I trained and informed the most dangerous man in the Kingdom. The new leader of the Elites, the descendent of Rïvan, and the most treacherous man alive. Rïvan may have long been dead, but his malice survives on in Tallen, I am disgusted to say."

"But how can this be?" Esra cried. "I have never heard of these "Elites" nor of anyone named Tallen. How bad could he honestly be if no one even knows he exists?"

"Because," Cane leaned forward in his chair, "a struggle that most people are ignorant of has been going on fer centuries. The Keepers and the Elites have been at battle since the age of Rïvan. This war has been waged mostly in locations uninhabited by common folk and in ways unnoticed by them. Fer years the scales have been tipped this way and that. But now with Tallen, the descendant of Rïvan and the most formidable enemy the Keepers have faced since Rïvan himself, I fear it will not stay a battle unseen. We have been able to keep most people uninvolved until this time…"

"What do ye mean *we*?" Esra exclaimed. The itching on her forearms was growing more intense, they were starting to burn.

Cane stood up, pipe in one hand, and went to the window. He

peered out casually as he lowered the curtain with his free hand. Esra's head was spinning, there were thoughts, half-thoughts, racing back and forth. She felt that there was no room for more, that these questions were already crashing into one another.

"Nevermind, we will talk about the rest of that another day. Fer now, our instruction will focus on learning yer true history. Ye must know where ye come from in order to decide where ye will go. We will resume the prior rule about not speaking during lessons." He reached for a large volume that was hidden beneath his chair and handed it to her. "I expect ye to read this in a week so that we can begin discussions."

"What do ye mean by 'we'. What kind of battle? Is my family in some kind of trouble?" He could be so cryptic and mysterious, sometimes it drove Esra mad. Looking at his stone face, she sighed heavily and lowered the heavy book to her lap. With her left hand she absentmindedly traced the white lines on Meshok's head that curled behind her ears and down her snout. It was something she often did when she felt discouraged and her friend nearby for comfort. Why was he being so secretive?

"Alright," she agreed, giving in for what seemed like the hundredth time that day. "Let's continue."

V

After her stressful new lesson, Esra decided to stop by the general store to tease Mr. Sturik about the bread beater. She was greeted by the familiar chime of the large brass bell as she swung open the door to the shop. Mrs. Lara Sturik, who was sweeping with small, jolted motions behind the counter, looked up and smiled genuinely when she saw Esra standing there.

"Esra!" She beamed. "What a pleasant surprise!"

Although it was commonplace for Esra to stop by the store once or twice a week, she was always greeted like a long-lost sister. Lara was in her late thirties, with curly dark hair and a short, slightly plump figure. Everything about her was soft, including the curves of her face and body, the waves of her hair, and especially her lulling voice that seemed to put everyone under a relaxing trance.

The shop owner's wife had moved a great distance from her family in the western Kingdom to put down roots in Sorley, but she quickly made friends with the more honorable townsfolk. The dishonorable would have loved to be friends with Mrs. Sturik as well, with the general store being a center of all the comings and goings of town, but seeing as she permitted no gossip within earshot, it was an empty hope. As such, most people had come to trust her with a fervor that was not misplaced. No secret would go beyond her lips to anyone else, including her own husband. She guarded people and the talk of their lives like a vulnerable child. Even greater than this seemed to be the sense of comfort that one came into when in her presence. It was strange, but being in a room with her was like the moment when you were in your bed and just about to fall asleep; snug and safe. The combination of her aura of peace and reputation for discretion ensured that one could come to her for either a friendly chat or advice on a very private matter.

Mr. Sturik walked in from the back stock room while Lara stopped to lean on her broom. He was the exact opposite of his wife, energetic and as tall and angular as she was soft and rounded, with a great swirl of blond hair in the middle of his head. Lara glanced over her shoulder at her husband and asked Esra teasingly, "So what brings you here? Have you demand for more bread beaters? Perhaps as gifts?"

Mr. Sturik chuckled beside her. They enjoyed the game Esra's grandfather played probably just as much as he did. Mr. Sturik searched and plotted for these odd items like the fate of his store depended on it. Some poor trinket peddler was making out like a King with her grandfather's strange purchases.

"Aye, tis but a shame," he shook his head with a grin. "I sold the last twenty off this mornin'. Demand is very high and the bread beater is quite a nice seller after all."

Lara giggled and swatted him on the shoulder. "Oh, you are a silly old man. Come Esra, sit and have some tea with us," she beckoned to a nearby stool.

"I'd be happy fer some of yer special mitroot tea."

"I think that's a wonderful idea. Besides, it's about time my husband let me have a break," she winked at Esra as she walked over to one of the long wooden shelves lining the store and scanned the various bottles and parcels. She selected a small wrapped package from a middle shelf and made her way to the black stove behind the counter.

"How are yer studies going?" Mr. Sturik asked, taking a seat across from her at the counter. The store owners were one of the few people who knew the truth about Esra's trips to Cane. Although Esra had never divulged this information personally, her grandparents must have, because they'd known for as long as she could remember.

"Oh, quite well," she answered. "Ye know Cane. Just finished hopping about with me through some Elvish history."

"Hopping," Lara mused as she poured the steaming water into small wooden cups. "That is a funny thing to picture Cane doing."

"What a sight!" Mr. Sturik laughed. Esra sipped at her mitroot tea, delighting in the warmth spreading through her bones. She felt a twinge of disappointment, remembering that this loving couple could not have children. They did not seem to mind that a family was not fated to them and were quite contented with each other and their shop. And they had adopted and loved many in town like they would a son or daughter.

Esra could remember that even as a child she had been drawn to the serenity of the general store. She had always been very active, constantly looking for new places to explore and new things to do. Being bored and keeping still were not desirable choices. The townspeople knew she had a reputation for being adventurous, and it was not uncommon to see her trying to climb a tree much beyond her height or venturing into an area of the forest that other children avoided with suspicious fear. If there was one thing that could make Esra sit still, it was a good story about a place or time that she had never been to. Even as an adult her thirst for adventure and knowledge carried her through her studies with Cane. But there was something about the small wooden stools that lined the counter of her friends' store that allowed her to sit peacefully for an hour at a time, listening to stories of the western city of Delmar where Lara was raised. One of her favorites was the story of how the two had met.

Mr. Sturik, it seemed, had gone to the city to collect an inheritance he had received from an uncle. He was planning to use the money to open a store of his own. The wealthy grain merchant he had apprenticed under had paid him fairly well, but the man had a habit of shorting people on their orders and got fairly angry when Mr. Sturik refused to swindle customers out of their rightful share. Tired of working long hours with a less than honest man, he was grateful to hear that he would now be able to start a business of his own, and run it how he saw fit. Lara had just lost both her parents and was looking for someone to take her towards a small town in the eastern Kingdom to find her only brother. When she had taken a risk and asked this bright young man if he would mind escorting her, she immediately regretted offering to travel alone with a man she hardly knew. But Mr. Sturik laughed and said that he himself had just hired a caravan to transport the goods he had purchased for his new store, and that he would be happy to take her as far as Re Malik. As it turns out, Re Malik seemed to come too soon, and the young man decided that perhaps this fine young woman's destination was as good a place as any to start his business, and from that moment on they never parted.

"Are ye preparing yet fer the next Trader's Day?" Esra asked the shop owner. Trader's Days were festivals that lasted for three days and occurred once every spring and fall. It was an opportunity for traders and merchants from some of the large cities, like Mahesh in the north and Hals Arün to the south, to come exchange wares. The merchants also picked up some spices and other goods native to the region of Sorley for selling abroad.

"Aye, I've been saving my coins fer one of those fancy perfumes my wife's been eyeing."

Lara blushed at her husband's disclosure. "I can't help myself, they just smell so sweet and exotic. It is like being able to travel without leaving home. I can just close my eyes, take a deep breath, and imagine the wonderful places those smells come from."

"There are many tempting things at Trader's Day," Esra agreed. She was familiar with the intoxicating pull on one's mind as a result of all the strange and wondrous enticements at these festivals. It was usually a day where walking into random objects was even more likely as her daydreaming took her far away from reality. "My grandparents always find at least one bolt of fine cloth and more than enough delicious treats. We must gain a pig's weight in the few weeks that follow."

"I think most people do," Mr. Sturik laughed. "And I daresay the last few trips there have been an increasing number of merchants wishing to visit our fine blacksmith, Baelin. If he was a man interested in money, he could run most of them home with empty pockets."

"He is very talented," Lara murmured in assent. "I have also heard that he will be coming to help your grandparents in exchange for some riding privileges?"

"It's true," Esra nodded. "I think it will be a good agreement. Baelin is one of my best friends and I am glad that my grandparents will be able to take it a little easier. Our horse Fariel is a fine steed, so it will be nice to see someone ride him properly. I've often wondered if he has some royal lineage, as he is obviously no field horse. He seems to be more fit fer a war."

"I have surely never come upon such a wondrous horse elsewhere," Mr. Sturik pondered, "and I have done a fair amount of traveling throughout LeVara."

Fariel was at least eighteen hands high, much taller than an average field horse, with massive grey flanks that Esra could barely straddle. It was awkward to ride him, so she normally preferred the smaller horse, Breti. But every once in a while she got a flare of courage and took him for a stroll through the woods. He was remarkably agile despite his size and could hurtle over most shrubs and fallen trees. Had she been a better rider, she would have loved to see what he could really do, but as it was, a short ride left her breathless with her heart pounding in her ears. Not to mention that mounting the tall beast usually required the creative stacking of wooden crates in the barn.

"Oh, I almost forgot," she placed her arm on the counter and pulled up her sleeve to show the rash on her forearms. "I wanted to see if either of ye have seen this before."

Mr. Sturik gave a look of perplexity to his wife as he gently took Esra's arm to look at her skin. They were both silent as he turned her wrist this way and that, studying the markings. Suddenly Lara stood up from her stool and went to the stove.

"Nope, never seen anything like it! You, dear?" She implored her husband.

"No," he shook his head. "I haven't any idea."

"Oh, well," Esra sighed. "I was just wondering. I'll stop at Muriol's apothecary shop on the way home and see what she says."

"Good idea," Mr. Sturik patted her hand gently.

"More tea, Esra?" Lara asked as she took her empty cup away.

"No, I must be off. But thank ye. It was delicious, as always." She stood up and walked to the door, covering her arm and giving a wave. "Next time I will bring some beaten bread to share with the tea."

The door clanged shut behind her and Esra squinted in the bright light filtering through a sky peppered with thin, wispy clouds. Cool tendrils of a fall breeze swirled around her and she shivered involuntarily. Walking down a few buildings, she stopped in briefly at the mill to see if her grandparent's grain was ready. After promising to stop by the next morning with Breti and a cart to pick it up, Esra strode past a line of shops and crossed the street to Muriol's. The smell of herbs and unknown plants greeted her a good thirty paces before she reached the front steps of the apothecary shop.

The owner, Muriol Menthy, was an elderly widow who smelled about as odd as her many wares. She had sparse white hair and a face so tough and wrinkled that it gave her the appearance of a roja fruit left in the sun. Her body was just as shriveled, with creased skin hanging loosely from her petite frame. The one youthful trait she retained were piercing green eyes that danced with excitement when someone came in to seek counsel.

The townsfolk could not remember a time when the woman was married, nor anything about her husband, for it seemed that she had been in the town since its founding. Some of the more gossipy folk swore that no one could remember Muriol's husband because she killed him off and made him disappear with one of her flesh eating minerals. Although Esra thought the woman was certainly odd, she saw no hint of maliciousness in her temper nor encountered anything wounding in her balms. She did not doubt that the woman was being unjustly judged, considering what some people said about others in the town that lived outside the normal traditions and expectations.

Another reason she had a strong inclination to like this woman was because Meshok seemed to love her. Besides Baelin and Cane, Muriol was the only other townsperson that knew of Esra's friend. As if on cue, Meshok slunk around the corner and trotted slyly up to Esra just as she was opening the battered wooden door to enter the shop. How she was able to do this undetected, Esra was amazed. Muriol looked up from the book she was squinting at in the darkened room.

"Esra, Meshok, welcome," she greeted them with a wave of her hand, placing a leaf in the book and closing it.

"Hello, Muriol," Esra strode past the long rows of jars and bottles, ducking under long strings of herbs hung from the ceiling to dry. Meshok slunk her way around the counter and appeared next to the herb woman, who was not in the least bit surprised by such an act and tenderly petted the beast behind her ears. "I am in need of yer advice on a rash that has appeared suddenly. It gives an itchy, burning feeling, and seems to be spreading over my forearms."

Esra raised her sleeves to show the old woman, whose sat as still as a stone as she gazed at the dark red dots.

"Oh dear," she breathed. "And it aches, ye say?"

"It feels more like a burning itch. Nothing horrid, but enough to be a constant reminder and a bother."

"I see," Muriol nodded. "I can give ye something to ease the discomfort, but unfortunately that is all."

"What is it? Cane said it might be from Witch Hazel," Esra asked, curious at such a thing that could stump the town's very capable apothecary.

"I know no remedy fer such a thing. Here," she said, taking a small jar down from the shelf. "Place this ointment on yer skin twice a day. And don't worry, it will not spread beyond yer arms."

Esra was confused at the woman's cryptic answer, but relieved at this small victory. At least if Muriol didn't know what it was, then at least she thought it wouldn't get worse. She pulled out the small cloth purse that was attached to the inside of her cloak. "Thank ye. How much?"

"Nothing, nothing," the herb woman chided, waving them towards the door.

"But I must…"

"No," Muriol insisted. "Go home and speak of this no more. The ointment will help until later."

And with that Esra found herself back in the bright light of the street, Meshok panting beside her.

"Well, that was strange," Esra mumbled to her friend, who had already disappeared from the prying eyes of the town. Tucking the jar into her cloak, she began the journey back home with tired, heavy legs. It had been a very long and thoroughly exhausting day. Esra thought about what her grandmother had said, that one day she may leave this town. She wondered if that road would feel much longer than the one she traveled now.

VI

Her studies with Cane had been slowly taking shape for the last six moons. She had watched out the open window during their lessons as a mild fall gave way to a dreary winter that seemed to drag on forever. They had finished with history and moved on to royal affairs, studying how the King had come to be, what his responsibilities were, and all the major players in the Kingdom of LeVara. She could tell you who were the head of mercantile and first apothecary, and even the name of the palace cook. Esra had brushed up on her limited pronunciations of the ancient languages and began to practice reading and writing in Tur, which was immensely hard for her.

All this left little time for Esra to worry about Cane's cryptic warnings about the Kingdom being in danger, and the secret war of the Keepers and Elites. She didn't think she could possibly handle the stress of that topic with all the stringent new requirements for her lessons. And although she had sensed the presence of the man following her in the forest on multiple occasions, Esra never caught sight of him again.

Today she had arrived breathless and late to see Cane perched upon his armchair in waiting, seemingly lost in thought somewhere far away. She plopped down in the chair across from him as Meshok circled on the rug between them. In typical Cane fashion, he began drumming his hands upon the arm of his chair for the next minute, not saying a word.

Suddenly he looked up at her and blurted, "I now want to focus on the other three races, the Elves, Unni, and Shendari. Instead of just studying the history and culture, we will discuss the strengths and weaknesses of each peoples, in battle and in diplomacy. Ye should take care to learn the names and responsibility of their leaders, and what each race desires fer their people."

"What fer?" Esra asked, then recoiled when she saw the stern look on Cane's long face. She couldn't help it. There was nothing besides magick that fascinated her more than the three races. And yesterday he had assured her that from this point forward she would be allowed to ask questions and speak freely, which thrilled her after so much disciplined listening. He continued solemnly, as if she hadn't interrupted.

"We will start with the Elves, since I believe they are the most commonly known and we have already discussed some of their history."

She shifted in her chair in anticipation, accidentally kicking Meshok in the side. The Wolf groaned loudly and lifted her head in irritation.

"Contrary to what most people believe, the Elves are not a secretive people."

"Oh. But then why don't we see one once in a while?" Esra had always thought them to keep to themselves because they did not like Humans, or perhaps because they were distrustful of outsiders.

"Probably fer the same reason most Humans would never make the extensive journey to the mountains. It's a long, hard journey. If a traveler does make the dangerous trek through the mountains to visit, the Elves welcome newcomers with curiosity and warmth," Cane explained. "They are not secretive, just shy. They prefer the shade of the mountains, which provide a startling view of LeVara, fer they have a deep reverence fer the natural world. The Elves are also a people who cherish simplicity and tradition, and enjoy the art of storytelling as much as the written word. As such, they are sometimes quite dedicated to learning about their lineage and history. Their simplicity and respect for tradition, however, does not suggest weak minds or an aversion to original thinking, as they are known to be some of the most intelligent, forward thinking scholars. Most of them speak the languages of all four races and the Ancient Tongues as well."

Cane had recently taught Esra some of the formal Elvish phrases, but had explained that learning the entire language would be quite unnecessary, since all Elves were more than fluent in her tongue. Esra figured the likelihood that she would ever need to use these few sentences would be slim at best. But it thrilled her to know them either way.

"The Veiled City, the Elvish capital, is in the midst of Idona, the tallest peak in The Eshomee Ledges that lay to the northwest, just beyond the Kingdom of LeVara. They are governed by the Elders, a council made up of three of the wisest of their race, who come together once a lunar cycle to discuss important matters. They are the most populous of the three races, with villages and cities scattered throughout all areas of the vast mountain terrain. Elves live, on average, about fifty years longer than a Human."

"Jumping jig," Esra exclaimed.

"Their longevity is mostly due to their practice of meditation and other magicks. As ye know, they are a dark skinned people whose physical traits can vary as much as Humans. And although they are similar to Humans in appearance, they all have small scars on their foreheads, which profess membership in a tribe; an indication of their lineage. The Elves are an impressive people, known fer their skill in sword, spear throwing, and stealth. They also have a naturally strong affinity towards magick in all forms."

Cane paused here to pull out his pipe and leaf and began the slow process of packing it precisely. "Where the Elves are the mountain people, the Unni are the forest people. They reside in Fira Nadim Forest, beyond the southeast border of the Human realm. The Forest is made up of yanquor trees, which are so tall and wide it would take a hundred paces or more to walk around ones base. Their capital is in Shadow Glenn, a large and mysterious clearing in the east forest. They are known fer their talent with blunt weapons and their ruthless determination in war. They are excellent strategists, and all men and women in their tribes are taught to be warriors soon after taking their first steps."

"So they're violent, then?" Esra interjected.

"No, no." The beginnings of a smile twitched at his mouth. It was always a strange and glorious sight to see Cane smile, his lips curving upwards to battle against the downward pull of the rest of his face. One could always guess how happy or angry he was by the position of the lines on his face. If the edges of the mouth were straight across, things were good. But if they made it past the dimple in his chin, watch out. "The Unni are always at war with the Valkor people who live south of the Forest. The Valkors are a battle hungry people who attack the Unni just to be spiteful, and fer nothing more. And so the Unni have become accustomed to war after generations of being made to fight, though ye could not claim them to be aggressive people at heart. They are proud, however, and will defend their homes and families at all costs."

"So who are these Valkors?"

"A tribe of people that live far to the south, beyond the limits of LeVara. I honestly don't know much about them besides the fact that they are very violent, and they haven't much focus as a society other than attempting to destroy the Unni people and often times each other."

"So what are the Unni like?"

"They are large and stout, standing about seven to eight feet on average. They have a yellowish tint to their skin and dark yellow eyes. Their faces resemble that of an ox or vernok mixed with Human. Two great horns curl upwards and out from either side of their head. They use knives to mark notches in them fer each kill. One of the greatest disgraces an Unni can suffer is if they lose their horns, in battle or otherwise. It is a great deterrent fer crime, as punishments are to take off varying amounts of horns in line with the severity of the offense. One cannot fight well without horns, as they are used in basic defensive and offensive maneuvers. The Unni also have a covering of dark, coarse hair all over their bodies, which when paired with the horns make them appear quite menacing. They also can live to be around a thousand years old."

"A thousand! Unbelievable. Have ye ever met one?"

"Yes, I have in fact. Although unlike the mountains and The Veiled City, Fira Nadim is not generally a welcoming place fer visitors. The Unni are not a murderous people, as I have said, but they do not enjoy outsiders. The few times a brave soul ventured into the south Forest, they were…forcibly removed."

"So how did ye meet an Unni?"

"Actually, I am…" Cane took a long moment to light his pipe, puffing gently with his mouth formed in a perfect circle, "familiar with their leader, a chief referred to as the Unni-se. He is a great warrior named Zakai, who carries a flail into battle and is a formidable foe. He is known far and wide fer his skill in battle tactics. Zakai is a strategist unlike any I have ever seen, and absolutely frightening to meet. The Unni-se is not one to be trifled with but can also be an extremely loyal ally and is known to be a fair ruler fer his people."

"Ye know the Unni-se?" Esra exclaimed, astonished that he had never revealed such unbelievable information before. "Wait a minute…what is a flail?"

"A flail is a special kind of weapon with a long handle that has a chain and spiked metal ball attached to the end. It's a rather deadly, messy thing."

"Oh dear." She pictured Zakai, the massive Unni-se letting out a deep roar as he swung the weapon of death around his horned head, smashing in his opponents' skulls. It was a terrifying picture. "They are definitely a people I would want on my side and not against me."

"I couldn't agree more," Cane laughed, sputtering smoke. "Lastly, there are the Shendari, the water people. They live on Ember Isle on the south corner of Fire Lake. Fire Lake, as ye have studied in yer geography lessons, is the enormous body of water on the northeast border of the Kingdom, and although some of the lake in principle resides in King Keridon's realm, no King had ever actively sought to lay claim to this territory. It is an unspoken rule that Fire Lake is off limits to Humans, especially Ember Isle.

"The Shendari are small, probably only three to four feet in height, and although they resemble Humans in their structure, they are covered in a hardened, porous flesh that allows them to breathe under water. They are an orange color when newly hatched, and grow darker red with age. Although they are extremely talkative, their language is indecipherable to the Human ear, and so they are the most mysterious of the races, as communication is very limited."

"So no one has ever spoken to them?" Esra asked.

"Not exactly. There was a time long ago when the Shendari aided the Elves in battle, and the Elves seemed to understand their language as a result, but the two races no longer mingle. And I have heard rumors that once in a while a Human is born who can understand them, but I do not know if that is true. Some of the Keepers can communicate with them, and the Shendari are quite capable of understanding Human speech when taught properly."

"So who is their leader? Is he as fierce as the Unni-se?"

"They do not usually have leaders, but when they do it is a woman, and she is more than fierce," Cane reached up and scratched his half bald head. "They function and make decisions as a community, except in times of war. The Shendari are extremely playful creatures and need no sleep to regain strength. Although they can be underwater fer hours they prefer to reside on Ember Isle. Ye can see their clusters of thatched huts from the shore on a clear day. They do not believe in material goods and so keep only the bare minimum of items around in order to live."

"The only time a leader is chosen is during times of war. The community will convene to choose a chief, known as the Daughter of the Shendari. The leader is always a woman, and in most cases, all of the warriors are women. Men go to battle only if it cannot be avoided as they are the caretakers of the young. The Shendari women are known to be fierce and strong, and the Daughter is the most ruthless and fearless one of all. Once chosen, she is followed without question into battle. She will also prefer to lead her people at the head of battle as an example of a bold warrior, not order them around from a safe distance like many Human commanders. As a result, most wars that included the Elves and the Shendari proved to be victorious. The water people lead a life of leisure during most times, but when called to aide, exhibit abounding determination and skill."

"But they're so small," Esra pointed out. "Ye said only three to four feet. How do they fight then?"

Cane laughed loudly, causing Meshok's ears to prick up in anticipation. "I wish one of them could hear ye say that. They would laugh until their sides ached. The Shendari warriors are known as Water

Riders, who bring creatures known as Pura to battle. The Pura are massive black beasts who resemble Lizards with short, stunted legs and long, flat heads. They are about eight feet long by five feet a breadth, and as tall as Fariel, yer grandparents great steed. The Pura only ever allow themselves to be ridden by the Water Riders. They have long, spiked tails that release venom into a victim when they are punctured, which immobilizes them if they aren't already crushed. The Shendari are not only skilled in riding the Pura, but are immensely gifted in using a bow.

"Now that there are no battles to fight, they spend their time in leisure, exploring the lake or playing games. Interestingly, I must tell ye that the Shendari do not actually die of old age or natural causes. They are believed to have an unparalleled skill in the magick of healing and meditation, making them practically immortal. They can be killed in battle, which is a very difficult task given their natural scale armor, but never by disease or age."

"Immortal!" Esra exclaimed. She never knew there was so much diversity in the races. And yet she was only skimming the surface, like a bird that swoops in to catch a fish on the crest of the water but never gets to dive under to explore.

"I want ye to take these home tonight and study them," Cane walked over to one of his countless shelves and pulled down three thin, battered books. "I know this has been a rather short lesson in comparison, but I think reading these will give ye a greater understanding of the other three races. And it will give ye a bit of a rest before tomorrow's festival."

"Alright," Esra agreed, tucking the books into her cloak. Her grandparents had grown used to Esra bringing home large volumes of this or that. Often, she awoke to her grandfather pulling a blanket over her in the chair where she had fallen asleep reading next to the fire. Even Meshok seemed to be more patient and apt to stay curled next to Esra's side.

"Goodday, Esra," Cane offered, returning to the padded green chair and his pipe.

"Goodday," she called happily as she half skipped in excitement towards the stairs. She wanted to get home and read these books so that she could go to bed early, for tomorrow began the next Trader's Day. It had approached with startling quickness and she was grateful that the next couple of days would afford her some much needed rest. They hadn't even spent any time coming up with the perfect Sorley quote as they usually did the weeks before a festival.

Esra was the type of person who loved to keep busy and was always working on some task or another, but she was beginning to feel run down. She was quite certain that her head would not hold any more information as it was, and attempting to stuff more facts into it would prove very unsuccessful.

She exited the door at the bottom of the stairs and stepped out into the midst of a crisp, cool spring day. It wouldn't be long before she was home and fed and done with her reading, where she would fall into a deep state of dreamless slumber.

VII

Esra awoke to Meshok tenderly licking her arm as it was hanging from the side of her bed, and she felt better than she had in many fortnights. Clasping her hands above her head, she stretched slowly, assessing the weather through her window. The sun was shining brightly from a sky dotted with a few feathery clouds. She gave Meshok a vigorous ear scratching before rising to change from her nightdress and pull on her new leather boots. Remembering that it was Trader's Day, Esra felt another jolt of happiness overcome her. Surely nothing could bring her mood down today.

Bounding down the stairs with Meshok at her heels, she found her grandmother at the table mending an apron and swooped down to kiss her cheek.

"Well, ye seem to be in a pleasant mood today," her grandmother smiled.

"Aye," Esra agreed, spooning herself some Apple and Wheat breakfast from the pot on the fire. "I daresay I'm ready fer a break, as much as I have learned in the last few moons."

"And it is a break ye well deserve, my dear," she patted Esra gently on the arm, motioning toward a small leather pouch with a note attached. "Oh, and that's fer ye today from yer grandfather."

Esra set her bowl down on the table and reached for the letter.

My sweet little vagabond,

Yer grandmother and I are so proud of ye. We know that life has been very demanding as of late, and ye have borne this burden with dignity and acceptance. We wish fer ye to have a wonderful three days of rest, so enjoy this gift. And please do not spend it on yer grandmother and I, fer I assure ye we have plans to treat ourselves on this occasion as well.

With all our love

Esra took the small pouch and emptied it onto the table. There were five gold pieces inside, as well as twenty bronze and many more copper. She gasped at the sight, as she had never possessed so much wealth at one time.

"Oh, my," she murmured, transfixed. "Grandmother, I cannot…"

"Ye will," her grandmother interrupted sternly. "Ye will say 'thank ye grandmother and grandfather', ye will put on yer cloak, and ye will go spend it on frivolous things. If ye do not do as I say, I swear I shall order Meshok to attack ye, and I daresay she will comply."

Esra raised her eyebrows at her grandmother's sudden outburst and laughed, giving her a fierce hug. She sat down at the table and hastily gulped down the rest of her breakfast, leaving a small amount for Meshok. Placing the bowl on the floor, her legs bounced in excitement as she waited for her Wolf friend to inhale the leftovers with a few long licks of her tongue. Esra wiped her chin with her hand and grabbed her cloak, stuffing the pouch carefully into one of its hidden pockets as she stepped out into the early morning. Grandfather was hiding in the stables trying to console one of their horses, who seemed to be very close to giving birth. She kissed his plump cheek twice and darted off towards the main road, feeling light and carefree. Even Meshok trotted along with her tongue lolling about her mouth, sensing that something exciting was about to occur.

The day was rather warm, but there were still cool gusts of air pushing its way across the fields, the last shred of winter feebly attempting to mask the newly green world, and Esra was glad for her cloak. A thick coat of morning dew still clung to the soft ground and she smelled the sweet blooming of Lilacs. There was a plow left unattended in her neighbors' field, as if the excitement of the festival had allowed a frivolous departure from the meticulous and demanding responsibilities of farming.

Esra let her mind wander, as it usually did without her consent anyway, to imaginings of the Shendari and Unni she had read about last night. Daydreaming was a blissful escape for her, where she could be anyone she wanted, go anywhere. There were no limits, no confines like the reality in which she actually functioned. Sometimes she felt guilty for being such a dreamer, as if she were showing that she was unsatisfied with the life she had been given and would do anything to get away from it. And she worried that eventually she wouldn't be able to tell the difference between the fantasy worlds she created and the one that was truth. But the way Esra spun vast stories in her mind seemed to be as natural to her as breathing, so she accepted it as just the way she was born. After all, one couldn't possibly find happiness if they were always fighting the nature of who they were.

After walking briskly in her reverie for only a few minutes, Esra could hear the faint sounds of Trader's Day; the shouts of merchants in the square, children chasing each other with yelps of joy, the music that floated above the town. She took a deep breath and felt her shoulders relax. She was not fully aware until that moment just how hard she had been working. Her physical chores had not increased; in fact, since Baelin was there he seemed to do half of hers anyway. He was now a regular attendant at their house, and even though he was always invited for noonmeal and dinner he rarely came inside. Fariel was growing strong and lean now that there was someone to ride him more regularly, and most days his grey coat shone with sweat.

Lately she had sensed Cane's urgency in the matters of her education, and she knew it was a gravely important matter that she take these teachings seriously and learn as quickly as possible. She was haunted with the thought that maybe Cane meant to leave Sorley soon, and so he was teaching her all he could in the time they had left. Esra tried not to think too much about it, but the idea plagued her. She was torn between wishing that if he was leaving he'd take her along but hoping that it wouldn't come to that. She could not picture a life without her grandparents nor her lessons with Cane. But today was not the day for such serious musings, so she pulled herself back from her reverie and tried to think instead of what she planned to buy at the festival.

Meshok slunk away from the road to avoid the crowds as Esra made her way into town, the noise and colors of the day increasing until she was right upon it, dodging the merchants and their bartering calls and skipping around the children playing in the street. She slowly made her way through the hordes of people to the general store, where Lara was standing on the front steps, tapping her foot along to a jig some musicians were vigorously playing in the center of the gathering.

"Lara!" Esra yelled to her from the bottom of the steps, waving to catch her attention.

"Esra!" Mrs. Sturik gestured for her to come around the back of the steps. By the time Esra arrived next to her, the song had ended and they both clapped enthusiastically. Before the silence could fully settle over everyone, another lively tune began.

"I'm glad to see you out," Lara said loudly over the song. "I feel this winter has been a particularly long one, especially for you."

"Aye, it has." She looked around for Lara's husband and saw him dancing with a young child near the musicians. His cheeks were flushed red with exertion as he bounced up and down, trying his best to entertain his partner, who Esra determined to be a young girl of about seven. The girl could barely dance with her laughing, and was bent over with her hands on her knees. Mr. Sturik smiled wickedly as he continued to jump in circles and flail about like a rabid Chicken.

Lara caught sight of him then as well, and they both laughed heartily.

"There's no controlling him, I'm sure," Esra teased.

"Oh, my dear, imagine me having to dance with such a man at our wedding. I could barely stand for my sides were cramped from all the laughing." Lara dabbed at the wetness that formed in her eyes. "We've decided to take her in."

"Who?"

"The little girl, Treta. She lost both her parents to an accident three fortnights ago and has no other family to speak of."

"Oh dear," Esra shook her head sadly. "I'm so sorry that she had to lose her parents, but I think it's fitting that she will be with ye and Mr. Sturik. Yer both wonderful with children."

"We are very glad to have her. She's a sweet young girl."

They both stood for a moment trying to suppress a fresh wave of laughter as they watched Mr. Sturik crawl on all fours, spontaneously thrashing out his legs and arms. Lara turned to Esra and shouted above the music, "I hope you will stop by later to say hello to us all."

"I will," she promised, turning to make her way back into the overflowing street.

After wandering about for a while, enjoying the energy of the crowd, she found a trader selling herbs and bartered for some mitroot to make tea. Esra had tried countless times to make the comforting drink that Lara brewed, but had no luck with it in the past. It always tasted similar, flavorful and minty, but it just wasn't as comforting. She placed the parcel in one of the pockets of her skirt, hoping to ask the shop keep's wife later that day to help her prepare the herbs, thinking it must be a secret ingredient Lara added.

She wandered farther through the town, looking at the various merchants that had set up tents and tables with their wares. There were bolts of fine cloth, dyed every imaginable color and in every conceivable texture. The smell of delicious roasted sweets and baked goods wafted temptingly through the air and she stopped at a display of sugared Raisins to purchase a treat. There were artists of varying degrees of skill exhibiting their sketches of a wealthy family or a beautiful painting of a landscape. Slender poles had been propped horizontally to string rows of clay and wooden beads in a dizzying array of colors. There were tents for bowls and water jars, readymade clothing, thick woven rugs, hand crafted furniture, even horses and carts. The animated shouts of vendors struck through the air like bolts of thunder, imploring each passing person to stop and have a look at this one of a kind item, specially priced. It was almost too much to take in, and Esra was glad that she still had two more days to explore it all.

Making her way down one of the side paths by Cane's house, she found Baelin carefully studying a massive leather saddle, thinking of Fariel, no doubt. He was so involved in examining the item that he was quite startled when Esra touched his elbow in greeting.

"Esra!" His face broke into a smile after the brief moment of surprise. "How are ye enjoying the day? Finding much te buy?"

"Aye, it is lovely weather fer a Trader's Day, and I think I'm enjoying the atmosphere more than I'm attempting to buy things. Usually I make sure I purchase all that I want and then relax, but today I cannot seem to find the concentration fer that task."

"I think many people are glad te be out after such a rough winter. Did ye see that I am an official merchant, now?" He gestured proudly towards a tent at the end of the path where various weapons and trinkets were displayed on tables covered with a dark velvet cloth.

"Are ye? Ye must show me," Esra exclaimed. "I'm glad that ye have finally decided to set up a space. Ye are in very high demand, on these days especially."

He seemed to blush a little with the compliment, a strange sight for such a sizeable man, and he walked her slowly over to the tent to describe each group of items. There were swords and daggers, other weapons for fighting she had never seen before, shields with battle scenes etched into them, and decorative items like carved goblets and plates. Although Baelin was used to having something to do with his hands when he spoke to others, Esra noticed he seemed to relax a little from his shyness as he spoke of making these things. She listened with true curiosity as he spoke of the difficulty in forging this or that, and couldn't help but think that of all the time she'd known Baelin, this was probably the most she'd ever heard him say. They were good friends, but relatively quiet ones.

She picked up a small knife, only about the length of her hand, with a Great Wolf head carved into the wooden handle. It was improbably light and smooth, as if it may float away at any minute. She carefully pulled it out of the sheath and turned it over in her hands, admiring it.

"Ye like it?" Baelin asked.

"Very much," Esra nodded. "It's so light and soft. I've never touched anything like it. And I didn't know ye carved wood."

"I don' usually," he admitted. "I decided te try it one day after

Meshok had visited me."

Esra looked up at him with surprise. "Really? It's very good then, no excellent fer a first try. When did Meshok come to see ye?"

"Oh, she comes now and again. Quite often, actually."

Esra was somewhat amazed at this revelation. Although Meshok seemed to like her grandparents and Cane, she had never, at least to Esra's knowledge, gone off to visit someone on her own. It made her wonder what else her friend was doing when she wasn't around, what kind of a secret Wolf life she was leading.

Baelin leaned against the table and chuckled. "Though I think that it's the fire she likes more than my company, I'm afraid. She curls up right next te it every time. Once I tripped over her and she just sighed at me like a mother would a tiresome child. "

"Aye, sounds like Meshok. *Ye* were getting in the way of *her* nap," Esra laughed. "So if ye are willing to part with it, I would love to be a buyer of the new Trader's Day merchant and his fantastic assortment of wares. How much would ye like fer the knife? I must say this is good luck, since the other knife I usually carry has been lost somewhere in the forest. Although this one is much more decorative, I trust in the craftsmanship fully. "

Baelin blushed in full now, and took the knife from her hands. He carefully returned the blade to its sheath and laid it back into her hands. "Then I would like ye te have it."

"I would too, Baelin, but I have the coin to pay fer it. And ye can't say no, since ye do so much fer me and my grandparents already."

"No," he declared in his deep voice. "It is a gift. Unless, well...ye feel that it is inappropriate, since, um...well, we are both unwed...err, some people would talk... not that I care, mind ye...I mean, I do care, but not in that way...it is not my intention te make ye uncomfortable..."

Esra interrupted his clumsy rant with a wave of her hand. "Baelin, I know what ye mean. It is a gift to a friend. Thank ye, I will take it, and I am very grateful."

She closed her hand around the knife and tucked it into the sash of her dress. Poor Baelin was more awkward than she, which was quite a hard thing to accomplish. Esra knew he was not interested in her for courting. But she fully understood how some people in town would see the gift as an exchange of more romantic intentions, especially when he worked in such close proximately to her family, now. They had made stories of much less. His discretion in this matter was appreciated, and she hoped he knew that.

They said their farewells and Baelin turned towards a small cluster of new customers as Esra went in search of noonmeal. She decided to go to the inn and sit at a table rather than trying to find a spot outdoors. After a refreshing meal of fresh bread and cheese with a glass of cold mead, she spent the rest of the afternoon wandering around the merchants, sampling some sweets. She was able to pick up a few new books, one of which she was sure would impress Cane, as she had not seen it in his personal collection. She also found a merchant who was selling various bolts of cloths and readymade clothing. Esra selected a handsome blue handkerchief with a small golden sun embroidered in the corner for Baelin. She felt better being able to give him something in exchange for the beautiful pocket knife and rushed back to the stand where he was tidying his merchandise. She pressed the cloth into his hand and turned quickly before he even had a chance to respond.

Before long dusk was beginning to fall, and she hurried towards the general store to see if she could find Lara and her husband. She had also forgotten to ask the couple again about the rashes on her arms. True to Muriol's word the infection had spread from both of her wrists up to the crook of her elbow, but no further. Lately they had almost constantly burned with a ferocity Esra had not encountered before. Strangely, it seemed to be the worst during her lessons with Cane.

After making a quick trip around the shop, she determined that they were indeed still out and decided to begin making her way home before it grew too dark. Most of the merchants were beginning to pack their tents for the day and the musicians had ended their long day of merry making. Suddenly, out of the corner of her eye, she thought she saw Lara down a side path from Muriol's apothecary shop. She called to her and ran to catch up, but when she reached the back of the lane, no one was there.

"Oh well, I'll see them tomorrow," Esra mumbled to herself, turning around. She did have an odd sensation that someone was in fact still there, although she couldn't see anything. She quickened her pace towards the main street, and breathed a small sigh of relief when she came back into the unwinding bustle of town. How silly of her to be so afraid.

There it was again, out of the corner of her eye, a shape. She turned abruptly, but saw nothing but emptiness. Unable to shake the feeling that she was being followed, Esra placed her hand on Baelin's knife as she continued forward. She had never felt unsafe in town, as everyone knew everyone else and it was not a place for serious mischief. A few brawls between the men after too much ale, perhaps. Then again, Trader's Days brought outsiders in, sometimes petty thieves and drunkards who could make small trouble. Maybe someone had seen the coins in her purse and had decided to see if they could catch her off guard. Although Esra was quite capable and spirited for a young woman she did not want to chance the long walk back in the dark by herself if she didn't need to. The best course of action would be to see if Baelin was still there, that he might walk her home.

Just as she turned the corner to where Baelin's tent was, a strong arm grabbed her from behind and shoved her fiercely into a darkened doorway. She gasped with the force of it and struck out at her assailant blindly. Opening her mouth to call out, she felt a warm hand clamp over her face, stifling her scream. Just as suddenly, she was released from the strong grip and a light came shuddering on. After the momentary shock from the change in brightness, Esra blinked hard to see Cane standing over a lamp a few feet away, safe from her flailing fists.

"Cane!" She cried furiously. "Ye nearly stopped my heart with fright! What is the meaning of this?"

"There is no time," he spoke rapidly, in a hushed whisper. "Lower yer voice and follow me to my study, I will explain more to ye there. And Esra?"

"Yes?"

"Please do so very quickly."

VIII

They wound their way swiftly up the two flights of stairs to Cane's study, where books and scrolls were thrown about the room in a careless fashion, as if someone were desperately trying to find a misplaced item. Her arms burned with the rash, and she fought to ignore the sensation creeping up and down her skin.

"There is much I have to tell ye, and very little time, so please do not ask questions. I am about to give ye a moon's worth of lessons in a few short minutes, so ye must pay attention to everything I say."

Esra's head was still reeling from the earlier panic, and she took a couple of deep breaths to clear her head and focus. After a few moments, she looked up at Cane and nodded for him to continue.

"The Keepers are made up of many different talents. Once a commoner begins to show proof of certain markings, or a special ability, they are taken to the Stronghold to be trained by other Keepers in the ways of our old ones. Most commoners have knowledge that sorcery and magick exists, but limited exposure to it. It is such a rare talent that individuals who exhibit this "behavior" are usually looked upon with suspicion. Ye can see evidence of this in the Keepers that have passed through town here. Most people are reluctant, if not wary, of such individuals.

"Once the choice is made to become a Keeper, one cannot go back. The training is secretive, out of necessity of course, and fairly dangerous. It involves magick and weapons, both intellectual and physical, to be used in the defensive and offensive. A Keeper's lessons are broad enough to encompass most aspects of the battlefield and the mind. But each Keeper has a particular "gift", something that they are especially talented in, that we are able to use against the Elites. Ye may have a Keeper of Flame, one accomplished in fire tactics, who can bend this element to their will, control it. And a Keeper of Voice, one who can imitate with perfection the sound or speech of any animal, Human, or even nonliving object. Gifts, ye see. There are countless types of skills; some are more physical, while others have more of a mental or emotional element. And some skills are not as battle focused as others. Fer example, there is a Keeper of Merry, one who has a remarkable knack fer enticing laughter. I have met him, and I must say he is one *very* funny man."

Esra thought of the absurdity of this situation, of this serious man, her teacher, talking about a merry man when he had just assaulted her in the town. *Maybe he has finally lost his mind*, she pondered. The irony of the situation seemed to be lost on Cane, and he continued unaffected.

"Ye will find that five is the most important number to Keepers. There are five Great Keepers, five skills of magic, five skills of war and five people in a group, referred to as an Assembly. Keepers always travel in groups of five to complete their tasks. The leader of the group is distinguished by rank according to how many tests they've accomplished.

"Tests are individual assignments that are only given when a Great Keeper feels that a member is ready fer it. These are different from what we call tasks, which are much more common. These tasks are sometimes highly dangerous, such as entering into enemy encampments to collect information. Other times, tasks are simply to gather a new Keeper when reports are heard of a small girl in a town who is "acting strangely" and causing droughts wherever she goes. She would be the Keeper of Rain.

"Those in training have to pass only one test before they will be given a group, or Assembly, of other Keepers to work with. The Assembly usually stays the same unless one of the members is needed fer another task, or unfortunately, if someone should die. Rank is established by how many tests a Keeper can pass. Most have two or three, with a small amount able to complete four.

"The leader of an Assembly is the one with the highest number, usually a Three and very rarely a Four. If there are two with the same number then a Great Keeper must choose who will lead. This is usually achieved without much insult, as Keepers are encouraged to be humble and respectful. Their only goal is to complete their tasks, and it is never done by harming the innocent or alerting them of our ways.

"The Elites are not so lucky in the sense of natural abilities. They believe that the Keepers skills are hard to train and control, in which they would be correct. They do not seek out those with special talents, only on very rare occasions. Instead, they prefer the method of forced magick, where a non-magick person is infused with the knowledge and power of sorcery. This act was unheard of before Tallen. Normally they would have to make do with whatever natural sorcerers decided to join their cause, or those they could terrorize into it. This 'turning' is one of the things that makes Tallen so dangerous."

"So are they still Human?"

"The Elites? Yes, or at least they were at some point. Now they hardly resemble what ye or I would call a person. They have been twisted physically and mentally by the conversion forced upon them by Tallen. These sorcerers have been imbued with powers unnatural to them, and the soldiers are also given various herbs and overwhelmed with spells believed to build strength and dull pain. But it is also important to know that most of the Elites are skilled warriors, not sorcerers."

"But why?' Esra asked. "Why not make everyone a sorcerer?"

"Well, the process by which one is infused with magickal ability is not an easy one, and it cannot be done on everyone. There are a few simple tests, I believe, to see if they are capable of undergoing the change. It was not always this way. Tallen used to simply try to turn everyone, and most of them perished or went mad. It was then he discovered that he needed to be more selective on who he changed. So there are usually only a few sorcerers fer every hundred soldiers."

"Well, that doesn't sound so bad," she offered anxiously.

"Trust me, the warriors are formidable enough. The effect of all of these castings upon the soldiers, to Tallen's great pleasure, is that their aggression is severely heightened and their sense of pain very low. The Elite sorcerers also have the advantage of numbers and are able to use multiple people to work the same magick, increasing its effect. The advantage of the Keepers has always been that the skills are more varied and creative, so we are sometimes able to catch them off guard with a skill they cannot match or counter."

"What do ye mean *we*?" Esra's voice sounded shrill and small in the large room.

"There are five Great Keepers. They are, I believe ye could say, the Keepers of the Keepers. They are immortal, and are the most revered of any sorcerer. The only way a Great Keeper can perish is if they choose to pass on their responsibilities to another Keeper who has passed all five tests. And that is not something that happens every day. It can be generations, sometimes hundreds of years before a new Great Keeper comes along. Because of their extraordinary power, ye may be wondering why the Great Ones do not just take care of Tallen and the Elites on their own. The truth is, they could if they were allowed. But to directly interfere with the Human world would forfeit the lives of all five Great Keepers forever. Ye can imagine that this would not be an intelligent decision. Instead they choose to pass on gifts and knowledge, in the hopes that our rebellion will triumph.

"It is said that one day a Keeper will come who has a chance to end it all, to destroy Tallen and the Elites and bring peace to the land. The Keepers place all their hope upon this one person, it is what allows them to continue to fight in the face of adversity, when hope seems to have been lost."

Esra's head was spinning. She felt slightly faint at all of this information bombarding her at once. All she wanted to do was lay down and scratch these awful rashes until they bled.

"Ye say that there are five Great Keepers. Who are they? Are they Human?" She was struggling to comprehend.

"Aye, they are Human, or Elvish. There is The Keeper of War, The Keeper of Magick, The Keeper of Strength, and The Keeper of Destiny. All possess different abilities; all assign different types of tests to a Keeper who is ready fer the next step. Once a test is completed, the Great Keeper then bestows a "Gift" upon the member, a contribution to help in their fight. The Gifts are always a physical item of sorts that contain some magical element to aid the user mentally or physically, like a bracelet or stone. And the Gifts are never alike. It is known though, that the better the Gift from one of the Great Keepers, the greater the strength and skill the bestowed upon will be. Usually after the first test we are able to guess who will be a Fifth, or group leader, by seeing what they receive."

Esra's arms were burning furiously now. There were so many questions she wanted to ask. "But ye said there were five Great Keepers and ye only listed four. Who is the fifth? And how do ye know fer sure who is a Keeper and who is not?"

"Ye can tell who is a Keeper by the markings on the inside of their arms. It resembles a rash at first, and represents when the person is being called by the Great Keepers fer their turn, their time to train. And the fifth Great Keeper is The Keeper of Truth, the one who has all knowledge. He goes by the Human name of Cane and has spent the last few years training an important new apprentice fer her first test."

He grabbed a small scroll from his desk and hastily stuffed it into the pocket of her cloak. "And now, my dear Esra, ye must trust me that ye should do and think of only one thing. Run."

IX

The only sound was the pounding of Esra's feet inside her head as she scrambled into the forest behind Sorley. *Run,* he had said, *run into the woods and hide. Do not, under any circumstances, come back here. Do not go to yer home. Run far away and hide in the woods until either I or one of yer grandparents come to ye. Ye are in danger, Esra, and ye must flee like yer life depends on it.*

And run she did. The panic in her was quite real now; she had absorbed that much from the look on Cane's face. Who she ran from or what she needed to be afraid of was unclear. But her teacher had never been more serious than as he spoke those words to her. Run.

The forest was at the time of fading night where everything was grey and Esra's eyes were still adjusting to the dim light. The ground was soft with the excess of spring rain, and the trees were the pale green of new growth. She could hear the high pitched snapping of twigs behind her as she scrambled up the slight incline that would put the town out of sight behind her. The sound of heavy footsteps fell close by, haunting her. The tight muscles in her legs were already protesting against the exertion. Esra's curiosity was almost overwhelming but she could not stop running. A branch whipped across her face and she tasted a faint hint of metal as a trail of blood ran from her cheek to the corner of her open, panting mouth. The ground was uneven beneath her feet, and she was momentarily grateful that she had worn her new heavy leather boots and not the soft soled walking ones.

The forest behind Sorley was not nearly as vast as Fira Nadim, but they were large enough that someone unfamiliar with them could get lost for the better part of a day. Esra wound swiftly through the maze of trees, her footsteps making a steady rhythm in her head, pushing her onward.

There were shouts from behind Esra, who strained to make out exactly what was being said without turning around. The only thing she could comprehend was that they sounded angry. She wanted desperately to look backwards, to see if her pursuers were close on her heels or if she were gaining any ground. Perhaps get a look at one of them, figure out who they were. But she dared not slow. A rabbit darted out from the underbrush to the right of her, panicked by the sudden noise as she shot past.

Esra veered left suddenly, trying to lose her pursuers, when she caught a glimpse of someone up ahead. They were sprinting at her almost as furiously as she was running towards them. Her mind frozen with fear, she could still hear the uneven pound of numerous footsteps behind her, three or four people, maybe more. Panicked, she quickly decided that she would continue running straight at the man ahead and swerve right at the last minute.

The space between them closing in quickly, she realized there was something very familiar in the man's form. Trying to focus her eyes in the glowing dark, it was a moment before Esra could see that the shape in front of her was in fact Baelin. How he knew she was out here, she didn't know, but her gratitude in finding him gave her new energy, and she sprinted towards him with all her might.

The look on Baelin's face was one of fury, and it took Esra only a moment to comprehend that he was carrying a large staff in both his hands, and coming straight at her. *Oh no.* For a moment she wasn't sure if her old friend could be trusted. The sheer terror of his menacing figure was enough to have Esra decide her plan should be administered early and she veered right, aiming for a small gap between two birch trees.

She made it through, but her right shoulder caught on a large branch and whipped her around with such force that she plowed into the ground and bounced heavily. Scrambling to her knees, she heard the scraping of metal against metal as Baelin met with her first pursuer, tearing open his dark breastplate with one upwards sweeping motion. Without pause, he swung around to stab the second man in the chest, pulling out the blade-ended staff quickly to deflect an oncoming blow. Esra was paralyzed on the ground as the first man clutched his stomach in a feeble attempt to staunch the flow of blood. She could see in the distance that more of these men were coming, perhaps ten or twelve more, and they were faster than an average person should be. The soldiers were clad in dark metal armor with a red line down the center of the breastplate, and a helmet that completely obscured their faces. These were certainly no guards of the King.

"Esra, run!" Baelin turned to her and bellowed with such rage that she snapped her head around and forced her legs to pull her upright.

After a few stumbling steps, she found that the panic in her was renewed, and she willed her body on with fervor. With the noises retreating behind her, Esra tore through the forest and put all of her thoughts into one focus. *Run, run, run, run.* Her mind sang in time with the slap of her feet on the ground. Another branch tore across her face, this time catching her in the eye. She didn't stop as the tears flowed down her face, her lungs feeling as if they were about to burst.

A pain suddenly ripped through her right side and there were flashes of dark shapes swirling in front of her. All of the breath left her body in one large gush as she slammed against the forest floor. Esra thought for a moment that she had run into something, and it was a long moment before she realized that it was a well-aimed staff that had hit her. She tried to roll over, knowing she had to protect herself, but she was so dazed that she could not discern which way she was facing. There was nothing but pain; all her senses became dulled as she was overwhelmed with it. Nothing mattered in that next moment besides this pain, and she cradled her arms around her stomach to try and soothe the shock to her body. Esra had the vague impression of someone large looming over her, and she squinted hazily as that one body was joined by a multitude of other blurred shapes. Her head was filled with a steady pounding in her ears, and she wondered briefly if the man standing above her could hear her heartbeat as loudly as she.

We've got her, one of the shapes said. *Feisty little wretch, ain't she?*

Esra tried to form a coherent thought. She knew she was in danger but she could not seem to move anything, or see correctly, for that matter. White flashes of lights floated before her eyes, and the pain in her side took on a new surge of ferocity as she recovered her breath.

Get her up, another one said, *we have to get moving.*

Did ye kill the other one? The first shape asked.

No, we'll deal with him later. Our first order of business is to get this little miss to her master.

Master? Esra thought. *The other one?* A sense of relief flooded over her as she realized that at least for the moment, Baelin was alive and they were not going to kill her. She moaned in anguish as a violent burning exploded over her midsection. It felt like she was on fire.

Ye were supposed to stop her, not break her in half, one of them snapped angrily.

Details, details.

An excruciating pain raked through Esra's body as she was lifted to her feet. The vague shapes began to come into focus, and she watched as two men came to support her from either side. She could feel both of her legs now, and her arms, but she was quite sure that a few of her ribs had been broken. Each breath was causing blinding pain. Giving in unwillingly to exhaustion, she leaned heavily on each of the men.

We need to go. Move, the leader said. She thought furiously of what she should do. But after attempting to take only a couple of steps, it was obvious that Esra would not be walking anywhere. Another man came from behind a tree and reached into his pocket.

Here, this will make things a little easier, he said as he withdrew a small vial from his cloak. The man on her left grabbed her hair and jerked her head back as the other poured a bitter liquid down her throat. She coughed and sputtered violently, but the man held a firm grasp on her hair, forcing her to swallow most of the foul concoction.

Don't worry, by the time I count to three, this little lady will be dead weight, and ye can carry her upside down if ye'd like.

Esra's mind was growing cloudy, her limbs suddenly seeming very heavy. She struggled to hold on to consciousness, but her thoughts seemed to be slipping away.

One...two...

Darkness.

X

Esra awoke to a chorus of raucous laughter erupting on her left. Feeling the sharp poke of uneven earth beneath her, she struggled to comprehend why in the world she was lying on the ground outside and not in her bed at home. Then she remembered. Cane and his frantic warning, the men with the dark armor chasing her through the forest, Baelin and his staff. Everything around her was black, and for a second she panicked, thinking the potion had left her blind. But after blinking hard a few times she could barely make out the stars poking through the thick shroud of trees. It was nighttime and she was still in the forest. Although this was vaguely reassuring, she had no idea just how long she'd been unconscious.

Trying to rotate towards the sound of voices, she felt a restraining pull on her ankles and wrists. *They've got me bound,* she thought miserably. Rocking back, an explosive pain seared through her right side and she gasped in shock. The staff hit had certainly left her with more than just a bad bruise. She wished vehemently for her grandparents, knew that they would certainly be missing her by now. Surely they would send someone to get her? Then again, she was unsure of what was going on, and maybe these people had captured them as well.

Gritting her teeth, Esra was finally able to gain enough courage and momentum to roll over to her other side. A couple dozen men lounged around a fire burning in the center of a hastily built camp. Some were eating, some dozing, but most were listening intently to one man as he waved his hands frantically, telling some sort of a story about hunting vernok. The men erupted into laughter, not noticing that their prisoner was awake. Strewn about the camp were the pieces of dark metal armor with the red line down the front of the breastplates. The helmets that had covered every inch of their faces now lay at their sides, although she could not see much past the glare of the fire.

63

That's pretty bold of them to build a fire, she thought. *Maybe we're far enough away that it doesn't matter if they create smoke. Who knows how long that potion knocked me out fer? Either that or they're too stupid or arrogant to care if someone sees them.*

She was hoping it was the latter. At least then she'd have a chance to be rescued. Her side still had an intense, steady ache, but the shooting pains were gone now that she was lying still. Esra focused on moving all her limbs, making sure that nothing else was broken. Her left eye had practically swollen shut from the tree branch, but she seemed otherwise in good health. A deep rumbling in her stomach told her it was far past supper, maybe more than one of them. The commotion around the fire began to break up as the elaborate hunting story came to an end. Some of the men began to gather around a large black pot to spoon out some brownish, gruel looking mess.

Under any other circumstances, Esra would never consider eating such a foul looking meal, but the hunger in her was growing, and she wanted to keep her strength up as much as possible.

"Um…" Esra cleared her throat as one of the men turned around to stare at her. "Over here."

"Well, well. It looks like our little treasure is awake, boys." A snicker moved through the group and Esra recognized the voice as the one who had forced her to drink the potion. As the man stepped forward into the firelight, Esra gasped in disgust at the revelation of what was underneath the red striped helmet. His skin was a greyish hue that seemed to be completely devoid of any eyelids or hair. His nose and ears looked as if they were melting off his face and the eyes had no color, only small, black pits that sunk deeply into his grey skin. A mouth that was greatly distorted and much too large completed his grotesque facial features. "Hungry, love?"

Esra stared at the man in shock as a torrent of anger enveloped her.

"I'm not, and never will be yer love," she spat angrily, "and yes, I am hungry."

She realized that it was probably a better idea to have kept her mouth shut, but she was in no mood to take any sarcasm from this despicable character. Her aching body and growling stomach reminded her of just what these men were capable of. Not to mention that they might have captured or hurt someone else.

"Ho!" He reeled his head back and crossed his arms, attempting to look offended. Leaning down towards her, he said in a loud whisper. "I'd thought that maybe after what happened a couple of days ago, we'd tamed yer filthy mouth. I can see now that ye may need some more working. How's bout I teach ye what happens to little girlies who say the wrong thing to the wrong man?"

His fist slammed against her cheek with such force that she rolled twice. White flashes flickered across her eyes as an intense wave of nausea seized her. She tilted her head to throw up, and as she did the taste of blood filled her mouth. Turning over, the nausea lifted and was replaced by a severe pulsating pain on the left side of her face. Her eyes throbbed as she resolutely tried to focus back on her attacker.

A rage Esra had never felt before surged through her, and she grinned a bloody smile at the man, mocking him. "Who'd ye say was the girlie?"

His eyes bulged with fury and he raised his fist to strike her again. Before she could regret her quick tongue, a man came from behind and caught the fist mid-swing in his palm, a loud slapping sound echoing from the impact.

"Like I said before, Krune, don't touch the goods." The potion man named Krune gave a last furious look at Esra, spitting at the ground where she lay before reluctantly turning around and heading back to the fire. Based upon the quietness that settled over the camp, it was obvious that this man was one of their leaders. He was the stockiest of the group, and his misshapen face was partially hidden by a black, greasy looking beard that sparsely covered his chin.

"Thank ye," Esra croaked, her voice coming out in a raspy growl. The pain in her face seemed to multiply remarkably when she spoke. "Why have ye captured me and where are we going?"

He bent over Esra and grabbed her shoulders, pulling her up to lean against a tree. She cried out as her stiff muscles revolted against the motion. He leaned towards her face, and Esra could smell the mead on his breath and see bits of dried gruel in his wiry beard. He glared at her with his revolting black eyes and Esra could feel her brief wall of stoicism being punctured. She gasped in disgust as the commander opened his contorted mouth to speak, his foul breath warm on her face. "Just because I didn't let him pommel ye doesn't mean yer allowed to speak. Ask a question like that again and I will make certain myself that ye will never open yer cursed mouth again."

With that he turned and stalked away, leaving Esra to sit against the rough bark of the tree, stomach still growling. What did she do? She didn't understand, was she to be ransomed? Her grandparents were fairly wealthy but certainly not enough to warrant this kind of exchange. Why were there so many of them? Did they need this many men to capture one girl? Or maybe there were other captives? It was still hard to form a coherent thought with the intense pain that pulsated through every vein in her body. It was as if her mind was far away and she could hold on to a thought no more than a stream could prevent itself from washing over the rocks below it. And now that she was fully awake, a savage hunger tormented her weak condition. *I'll wait till they're asleep and I'll run.* Although the men seemed obnoxious and arrogant, she didn't think that they were foolish enough to leave their prisoner unguarded while the rest slept. And it didn't seem likely that she could get out of her bondage or run very fast, given her current condition.

Sighing in resignation, Esra instead turned her focus towards the sky in an attempt to determine their location. Although the night was clear, the trees obscured many of the stars and after a few minutes she was still unable to grasp exactly where she was. They could be anywhere in the forest north of Sorley. The one man had said it was a couple days since they had captured her, so they could be in a different forest altogether by now. Somewhere in LeVara she was unfamiliar with. Had they run all this way? She didn't hear horses anywhere near.

There had been one time when Esra was much younger, before she had the experience and navigational skills of Meshok to help guide her, that she had found herself hopelessly lost in the woods behind her grandparents' farm. She had been daydreaming about The Painted Fields, a most curious place in the far western Kingdom. She weaved slowly through the forest, lost in her imaginings for some time, until she looked up to see that the place she had wandered to was unrecognizable. A brief moment of panic struck hard in Esra's chest, and her breath caught in her throat painfully. Sitting against the side of a tree for a moment to calm herself, she pushed aside the fear and tried to think clearly. Using a combination of the sun's location and her intuition, she was able to direct herself back towards a part of the forest she was familiar with. She never spoke of it to anyone, but the fear that had gripped her so strongly for that moment stuck in her head, and she thought of it any time she came near the place. Funny that she was remembering this now.

Scanning the area immediately around her, Esra searched for something within reach that she could hide behind her back to cut the binding that held her wrists. There were no small flat rocks or anything that looked sharp enough to help her break free. Perhaps she could roll a little at a time until she was closer to someone's weapon, lean against it and try to work the ropes on her hands. After all, she was sore and aching but had nothing but time, especially after sleeping so long from the potion. She would need to position herself without putting weight on her broken ribs. Maybe if she went slow enough the soldier on guard wouldn't notice.

Esra's thoughts were interrupted as something zipped past her head and stopped at the man sitting directly in front of her. Looking down, the man clutched at the slender wooden shaft of the arrow that had just pierced his chest. Before the others could scramble to their feet, two more were struck through their midsections, one by an arrow, and another by a throwing spear.

"Get yer weapons!" The commander howled as he grabbed his morning star from beside the fire. There was a flurry of motion as everyone snapped to their feet and rushed about, calling out directions and sputtering curses. A few of the men snatched up their weapons and ran into the forest, trying to locate where the hidden assault originated. A blinding light erupted at the left side of camp, temporarily stunning a few of the men. In a matter of seconds one of them was on the ground from an unseen assailant, the other two stumbling awkwardly towards the fire.

Directly to her right she could hear a singing clash, like the sound of two swords meeting, but she could not see beyond the wide glow of the fire. Rolling clumsily over to her side for a better view, she saw the outline of a man surrounded by three or four of her captors. He appeared to be swinging a sword deftly and calmly at the center of the circle of heavily armed men. Krune, the man who had just threatened Esra, rushed in towards the swordfighter with his club raised and was felled in one fluid motion. His loud cry broke above the clamor of the camp like a wounded animal's howl, and he clutched the rapidly spreading pool of blood that covered his shirt as he fell to his knees.

The man in the center of the danger appeared unfazed by this sight and Esra was momentarily entranced by the beautiful arcs the warrior's blade made in the night, glinting periodically off the fire's flickering blaze. He swung his weapon like it was only an extension of his arm, no heavier or harder to control than one's own finger. Although obviously outnumbered, the skilled fighter's dark face appeared calm and relaxed, and he steadily cut down his opponents. She had never seen anything like it. No one in Sorley could possibly fight that well. Glancing about quickly, she noticed that most of the camp had been emptied or was engaged in battle at the outskirts of the fire.

Now's my chance. Esra rolled onto her knees with a grimace, the pain bringing tears to her swollen eyes. Taking a moment to recover, she grunted loudly and pulled herself to her feet. The ropes on her wrists and ankles made her sway awkwardly and she fell hard against the tree.

She was not sure if the people attacking the camp were any better than the group that held her captive now, but she was willing to take that chance. One of the men saw her standing up and bolted towards her with sword raised. Another arrow whooshed past her ear and caught the man through the right eye socket. He twitched a few times before collapsing into a heap on the forest floor. Esra wasted no time to see if anyone else had seen her and began twisting and turning away from the fire, intending to try and hide herself in the brush. Every time she moved a sharp pain seared where her ribs had been broken.

Under any other circumstance, Esra would have collapsed and let the agony overwhelm her, but fear for her life seemed to win out over any physical torment. Remembering suddenly that she might have Baelin's knife in the sash of her dress, she fumbled to get underneath her heavy cloak until her fingers closed on the slender handle. There were shouts and clashes coming from behind her at the camp, but she didn't dare turn around. Turning the knife over in her trembling hands she began sawing at the ropes, cutting through them instantly with the new blade. Bending down to her feet, she tore the knot apart and stumbled towards the shadow of the forest. Suddenly a man was upon her, his young face half hidden by the darkness.

"Esra, how's yer holiday going? I bet ye've never seen a Trader's Day celebration like this before."

He paused, swiping two arrows from his quiver and notching them both in his longbow. He closed one eye and aimed the bow with unwavering posture, releasing both arrows with precision. Loud cries rose above the clamor of the camp as he tossed the bow back over his shoulder.

"Can ye run?" The archer asked.

She shook her head in confusion, struggling to find her voice. "I...I don't think so. I think some of my ribs are broken."

"Ok, well then up ye go." The archer grabbed her under the arms and knees and plucked her swiftly off the ground, careful not to grab her side. The force of the impact still jolted her violently and she writhed in pain.

"Sorry," he apologized. "As ye can see we're in a bit of a rush. Love te put ye down later, though. Maybe sometime after we're clear of the stinking, vicious men chasing after us with an assortment of weapons?"

Esra tried to remember if she had seen his face before as the archer turned and carried her into the forest. She strained her neck to see if any of the men were following them, but leaving the small circle of firelight, darkness soon enveloped everything. Although he was keeping his stride fairly steady, the pounding still caused her immense pain every step, and she felt herself growing dizzy with the weight of it. She closed her eyes and tried to focus instead on the labored breathing of the archer, who seemed to be making good time in their escape, mumbling words that she could only guess were some kind of magick. The soft, rolling words relaxed her, and she half-heartedly listened for the echo of pursuing footsteps, but heard nothing.

The sounds of the camp were growing fainter and fainter and she felt herself relaxing on the shoulder of this unknown rescuer. The pain had exhausted her. She couldn't remember ever being so sore and so tired. Against the protests of her side and its shooting aches, she found herself growing drowsy in the steady rocking grip of the archer. For the second time since being in the forest, Esra felt herself unable to keep from falling into the dark depths of sleep.

XI

The smell of food was enough for Esra to be stirred awake from where she was firmly nestled under a soft blanket next to the fire. The young archer who had rescued her was throwing some things into a copper pot, and paused to look over at her with concern.

"Ah, yer awake. Nothing like a good vernok stew te rouse someone out of a lifeless state. Here," he filled a wooden bowl with some of the stew and set it down next to her with three pieces of bread. Placing a hand behind her back, he gently lifted her up, wedging a rolled blanket underneath her for support. They seemed to be in the middle of a small clearing in the forest, hidden safely under the emerging morning. Dawn was in the few precious moments where the night and day collided, creating an array of startling reds and oranges stretching over the horizon.

"Thank ye," Esra said sincerely. She grabbed a piece of bread and ravenously attacked the bowl of stew. The ache in her jaw protested against such motion, but she was so hungry that the pain was easy to ignore. The archer dabbed a minty smelling ointment gently along the side of her face, his forehead creased in concentration. She noticed then that her eye was no longer swollen shut.

"Slow down, Esra," he gently chided. "I've made plenty. In fact, ye can bathe in it if ye'd like. And considering how we both must smell, that might not be a bad idea."

He flashed a large smile at her and went back to stirring the pot. Something about him made her feel safe, even if she didn't know where she was or who he might be. And she doubted that he had gone through all the trouble of carrying and feeding her just to try and kill her. She studied him as he crouched beside the fire, and decided that he was a few years older than herself, maybe around twenty five. Untamed brown curls fell in a tidy mess about his round, kind looking face. Esra could see he was short and his frame was stout, but he looked sturdy rather than overweight. There was also something very mischievous about him, but it was endearing rather than mistrustful.

Esra suddenly remembered the small scroll Cane had given her, and she waited until the archer had turned his back to tend the fire before reaching into her left pocket. She unwound the paper quickly to reveal a few hastily scribbled sentences.

Esra, if yer reading this then hopefully yer with the others. Trust them. They mean ye no harm and will explain everything.

What did he mean the others? Well, she was assuming it couldn't be the last group of dark armored ruffians, they certainly meant her harm. And she didn't feel threatened by this archer, just slightly uncomfortable.

"How did ye know my name?" She asked, tucking the scroll back in her pocket. She swallowed the last delicious bite of stew and set the now empty bowl beside her. The warmth of a good meal invigorated her senses, and she felt herself gathering strength. Suddenly her questions came flowing out in rapid succession. "Do ye know what happened to Cane? To Baelin? Are my grandparents alright? Who were those people? What's yer name?"

"Whoa there, hold on," he laughed, revealing an almost perfect smile that caught Esra off guard with its generous intensity. "First off, my name is Fynnigan, but everybody calls me Fynn."

A figure suddenly emerged out of the darkness of the forest and stepped into the clearing. It took Esra only a moment to recognize the large, looming shape as her blacksmith friend.

"Baelin!" She tried to stand up in her fervor and felt the gentle weight of Fynn's hand holding her down. It was then that she looked down to see that her side was wrapped in some strong, minty smelling leaves. "I was so worried about ye. Thank goodness yer not hurt. Do ye know who those men were? Are my grandparents alright? How is Cane? Do ye know Fynn? Where's Meshok?"

"Give her a little bit of stew and she perks right up," Fynn joked. "Esra here fires questions like I fire arrows, more than one at a time and right on target."

"Aye," Baelin laughed in his deep voice. "She does."

He first went to check on Esra, looking tenderly over her face and side where the minty poultice covered angry purple bruises. Quietly satisfied with her recovery, he stepped towards Fynn and took a bowlful of the breakfast, settling down on a fallen log that lay near the fire.

"We have much te talk about, Esra. First I will let ye know that everyone in Sorley is safe. But now I must eat and ye must rest. Once the others get back we can discuss everything."

"What others?"

"Arland and Nadia. Now sleep fer awhile longer and we'll wake ye fer noonmeal."

"But Cane said he's a Great Keeper. And immortal! Is it true, is he really a sorcerer?"

"Sleep. Now."

Esra began to open her mouth in protest but instead burrowed back under her blanket upon seeing the stern look on Baelin's face.

"Now I truly am worried. This is much worse than I thought," Fynn turned to Baelin, who raised one questioning eyebrow at the archer. "If she listens te a bloke like ye, then she must have a serious head injury."

Baelin shook his head. "Keep talking, plant man."

"Hey, ye don't seem te mind me being the plant man when yer injured, or in need of a delicious stew, fer that matter. Here Esra, drink this," he brought her a small cup of something that smelled hauntingly like Lara's mitroot tea. "This will help ye te sleep a little bit longer. And don't worry about the people who captured ye, we took care of the lot of 'em."

"But there were dozens of them..." her voice trailed off as she grudgingly gulped down the warm, syrupy drink, surrendering to the fact that they were not going to tell her anymore. It was sweetened with Honey and traces of something else, perhaps Gingerroot. Lying down, she closed her eyes and listened to the soft crackle of the fire until she drifted off.

After he was sure she was asleep, Fynn slipped away and sat next to Baelin on the fallen tree. "How much does she know?"

"Not much, I'm afraid," Baelin said quietly, running his hands through his thick, dark hair. "They found her before she was able te finish her studies with Cane. I think that he gave her a quick telling about the Keepers before she ran off into the woods, but that's it."

Fynn raised his eyebrows in surprise. "So she doesn't even know about ye, then?"

"I'm not sure," Baelin admitted, absentmindedly poking at the fire with his staff. "But she'll know everything soon enough."

XII

True to his word, Baelin woke her for noonmeal. Getting a bowl of food in her stomach and some sleep seemed to have had great healing effects on Esra, but she was rather suspicious that Fynn was more than a capable apothecary. She remembered the words he had been whispering as he carried her to safety, and had a strong feeling that magick was involved.

She had also had the most amazing dream about Sorley. She was in the woods with Meshok and they came upon a beautiful stream of water where her grandparents waited at its bank. They drank cool water from the stream, relaxing in the warm rays of the sun as Meshok chased a huckfly in the field. It had seemed so real, like she was really sitting in the damp grass, drinking the sweet fresh water.

Esra stretched luxuriously as Fynn unwound her side from the minty leaf wrap. Bending over tentatively, the pain from her broken ribs was almost completely gone. She looked down to see that the dark purple bruises had faded to only a vague suggestion of a past hurt.

"Jumping jig, Fynn. It doesn't even ache. How did ye do that?"

"Fynn, Keeper of Earth, at yer service." He took a deep bow followed by a playful curtsy. "I am an accomplished apothecary, with the ability te create herbal blends and heal most ills. My affinity lies with nature, so I can track any living thing and navigate all terrains. If it grows from the earth or is a creature of it, then I can do something with it. My favorite ability, however, is that I can communicate with animals."

He put two fingers up to his mouth and gave a shrill whistle. Meshok came trotting out of the forest, tongue lolling.

"Meshok!" Esra exclaimed with delight. She had not seen her friend since they had parted before town on Trader's Day. "So yer a sorcerer then?"

"That I am. And Meshok would like te apologize fer not being with ye in the forest," Fynn said. "She followed ye but couldn't show herself. Ye see, the Elites don't know that the Great Wolves are still alive. It's a widely kept secret that their race has been in hiding since Rïvan's reign."

"Ye mean there's more of them? Wait a minute...the Elites? *That's* who captured me?"

"Aye," Fynn nodded. "They have some very bad manners if ye ask me. That's not the correct way te get a lady alone, if ye know what I mean. Dark potions and breakin' her ribs. Not that ye put up with any bit of their filth. *'Who'd ye say was the girlie?'* Ha! That certainly put a briar in his britches. Anyway, I'm sure ye know about the trouble that has been brewing between the Keepers and the Elites? Yer a very important part of this battle."

"Me? But I'm not a Keeper. Cane said that he's been hiding in Sorley to train me, but I've never had any special abilities or been able to do any sorcery."

"And we've been lucky fer that, we have. It has allowed ye te go unnoticed and unfound fer quite a long time. The Keepers have used this time te gain strength and numbers and te pursue vigorous training. But it has always been key that ye were allowed te grow under the instruction of Cane and the guise of appearing te be a normal Human."

Struck dumb like a slap in the face by his use of "normal" Human, Esra remained silent as she wasn't quite sure how to respond. Of course she was normal. Wasn't she? Meshok plopped down next to her as Baelin threw a few more logs on the fire, glancing over at her with concern. Along the horizon she could see two more figures entering the clearing, small packs hanging casually over their shoulders.

"Nadia and Arland are here," Baelin motioned to Fynn, who turned around to greet the newcomers. It was clear as they approached that the other two people were young Elves, as they had rather dark skin. Esra noticed they were all wearing the dark blue cloaks she had seen on the Keepers who came through Sorley. The Elves and Fynn stood for a few moments, deep in discussion as Baelin took a seat on the ground beside Meshok.

"So yer a Keeper too?" She whispered softly. Baelin absentmindedly stroked the Great Wolf's back as he stared out into space. She waited patiently for him to answer as she tenderly felt the area of her jaw covered by the poultice. Thinking he hadn't heard her, Esra opened her mouth to repeat the question when he finally spoke.

"Esra, I know that this is all very difficult and very confusing, but I want ye te know that everything is alright. What we are about te tell ye is already known by yer grandparents, so please don't worry about them.

They know what has te happen and that ye're with us and safe."

She felt her face flush red with anger. "Aye, I suppose everybody knows what's going on but me. I'm the one captured and almost killed and yet all I keep getting are secrets. Well I must say that I am sick of these secrets and I don't care about these Keepers and Elites. I just want to go home and be with my family."

Esra expected her childish outburst to startle Baelin, but instead he seemed to sit for a moment in agreement. "I thought the same thing when they told me of all these things. I wondered how people could go so long hiding the truth and then expect me te be alright with everything in one quick moment. But everything was not alright, the world was full of all these new things I had no understanding of. Everything was backwards. Trust me, Esra, ye will grow te appreciate what we had te do, what ye are. Ye must have patience and know that all we want is te help ye and help yer family, because the time is soon coming when no family will be safe from the cruelty of Tallen and his Elites."

Esra sat in silence, still vaguely perturbed, but at least somewhat sedated knowing she hadn't been the only one ambushed with all this information. As the other three returned to the fire, her curiosity overcame her anger as she confirmed that the other two were indeed Elves, and beautiful ones at that.

"Esra, meet Arland, Keeper of Charm," Fynn introduced a startlingly attractive male Elf with wavy black hair that fell just below his ears. A small braid trailed down his left shoulder to the middle of a strong chest. Although he was rather dark skinned, his eyes were so light blue they were almost clear. He appeared to be younger than Esra, perhaps seventeen or eighteen, but she was unsure since she knew that Elves lived longer and she had never actually met one. Everything about him was appealing. He had an engaging smile that tilted to one side, a strong jaw, and hair that fell seductively into his eyes. The small markings on his forehead that indicated his tribe and heritage made beautiful, subtle swirls above his eyes that added to his air of exoticism. His body was also flawless, as he was tall and lean, with strong arms and shoulders that highlighted a broad chest that sloped down to a slim waist. A greatsword hung by his side, a large, two-handed weapon that Esra was quite sure she couldn't lift without slicing off one of her own fingers.

"Pleased to meet ye," Arland grasped her hand and kissed it playfully. Under any other circumstance, the forward gesture would have made Esra feel uneasy, but for some reason she could do nothing but smile stupidly back at him. It was a strange sensation, as if he were pulling her towards a carefree state where she would trust him as she would any other intimate friend. "I am forever sorry that ye had to be left alone with the madman, Fynnigan. We've tried to lose him quite a few times, but he always manages to track his way back to us."

Fynn laughed jovially at the jest. "Alright, we get it. Arland is the beautiful one and I got all the brains."

He turned to the young woman who was standing back from the fire and motioned for her to step closer. "And this is Nadia, Arland's twin sister."

"Hello," Nadia nodded at Esra. The way she came forward to greet Esra reminded her of a cat, slinky and sly. It was hard to even keep your eyes on her. As if you were quite sure she was there, but then not really. As she came into focus, Esra took note that if Arland was an example of male perfection, here was his female counterpart. Unlike Esra's wavy, dark blonde hair she usually tried to keep restrained in a knot, Nadia's long black hair shimmered freely in cascading curls down her back, reflecting beautiful hues of darkness. She had large eyes, similarly light blue, and a strongly framed face that gave a seriousness to her expression. Her dark features were less seductive than her brother's, but she was beautiful nonetheless.

The one large difference between the two siblings was their size, as everything about Nadia suggested slightness. Her frame was tiny, but muscular. Esra stood open mouthed before the shimmering form before her, not sure why she couldn't entirely see the Elf woman in solid form. Maybe her eye was not fully healed yet.

"Nadia is the Keeper of Stealth, as ye can probably tell," Arland explained. There was a twinge of an unknown accent in their voices, and Esra nodded in bewilderment as the dark skinned beauty smiled kindly at her.

"I'm sorry if I seem ungrateful or unhappy," Esra apologized. "I've just had a lot of things happen in the last few days. I've been studying with Cane fer a long time and I never once imagined that it may be fer a carefully planned purpose, nor that he would turn out to be one of the most revered sorcerers, a Great Keeper. And immortal at that. I feel like I should have seen something, some clues."

"Cane tried very hard *not* to leave any clues," Nadia assured her. "Let's sit down together and talk, answer yer questions."

"I would greatly appreciate that," Esra admitted. They all took seats around the fire and Fynn passed around bowls of noonmeal, which appeared to be a delicious mix of rabbit, onions, corra nuts, and some herbs she couldn't name.

Where should I even start? Esra wondered. There were so many things swirling in her head, she had trouble even focusing on one.

"Well," she began slowly, "I guess I will start by asking why and how the Elites found me. And in turn, how did ye find me in the forest?"

"We were not sure at first how the Elites found out ye lived in Sorley," Fynn explained, "until we discovered a scout among our ranks. We used some spells te see what we could about their plan, but the only thing we could get before he died was that they knew ye were in Sorley. Cane assumed, and rightly so, that the Elites would want te make a move during the bustle of the next Trader's Day. He called us all here, and the 'rashes' on yer arms started getting worse. It was a sign that ye would soon need te be taken te the Stronghold te begin yer training, so even if the Elites didn't show up, we were planning on taking ye there after the festivities anyway. We found ye because I tracked the Elites in the forest. That was only after Baelin went all 'save the Kingdom with my mighty staff' and made them scatter, which made my job a little harder."

"Sorry," Baelin mumbled. "At least I killed some of 'em."

"So how did a scout know about me? And ye say that ye tortured and killed him?" Esra asked. She was slightly appalled that the Keepers would resort to such tactics, even with an enemy. Cane had made it seem as if they were a force of good, and held themselves to a high moral standard.

"No," Nadia assured her. "We just held him prisoner while we were questioning him. But we have ways of getting information without needing to torture someone. Unfortunately Tallen has no problem with disposing of one of his own to keep his secrets."

"But how could he kill him if he was with ye?"

"Well, because Tallen leaves his mark on all the sorcerers he turns. All he had to do was say the word."

"That's awful." Meshok sighed heavily in agreement and began licking Esra's shin. She had no idea that Tallen could be powerful enough to kill someone over a great distance. It was not encouraging information. No wonder most of the people of LeVara were wary of magick. "So how long have ye been Keepers? How many tests have ye passed?"

Arland took to answering this question. "Well, we are all Fours, so we have passed all tests but one. Baelin has been a Keeper the longest, and Nadia and I have been Keepers since we were very young, perhaps about seven or eight. So we have been training fer almost a decade. Fynn is one of the more recent additions, coming in about five years ago. He was already in his twenties. A late bloomer, ye could say."

"I'll show ye a late bloomer!" Fynn shook his fist playfully at his friend. "Mature, that's what I was. Practicing advanced herbal medicine when ye was just a bop in his skivvies."

"But isn't passing four tests very difficult to do?" Esra asked. "Cane had told me it was extremely rare, and that usually a Three of Four was the leader of an Assembly of Keepers."

Arland smiled proudly, "Aye, it is very difficult, and equally as rare. Usually we would be split up among various Assemblies as leaders, but we were put together with a special purpose. We always knew, or hoped at least, that ye would be the last one to join us."

"But I don't know any magick!"

"Sure ye do, ye just haven't tried it yet."

"How can ye be so sure?"

"I'm not."

Esra stared at him incredulously. "So who is the Fifth of yer Assembly, the leader?"

"Baelin."

"And what happens if ye don't pass a test? Do ye ever get to try again?"

"Aye, but ye must wait five years," Arland explained. "Tests are not something that are handed out lightly. They are a great honor, a symbol of advancement. As fer that rash on yer arm, it does have a purpose. It's not actually a rash, but the markings of a Keeper. It's how we communicate, a language ye have already learned, called Tur. Look here."

He put his forearm palm up in front of her as she studied the rash. The markings began to move on his skin, and a faint glowing came from behind the black shapes. It was like they were insects, crawling around to arrange themselves into lines of glowing black script. Esra was astounded as she began to slowly read the newly formed text, pulling the language from her lessons with Cane.

Arland, Keeper of Charm.

"Bumbling huckfly. Does it hurt?"

He smiled cheerfully, "Good reading! No, it doesn't hurt. I believe that it felt the worst when it was first appearing, burning and itching like mad. That's why many people mistake it as a rash. Ye can't get into the Stronghold without these markings, or Tur. A spell protects the fortress so that one who is not truly a Keeper can never find it."

"But ye said ye use these to communicate?"

"Yes," Arland continued. "That is the more complicated part. A Keeper can store information with their Tur like they could writing on a scroll. We often use Tur to collect maps, new spells, and other details about a task before we leave the Stronghold. But there is another reason that Keepers always travel in groups of five. By putting together our Tur, we can perform much more powerful magick. We can communicate directly with the Great Keepers, but only when there are five of us. We actually used Tur to talk with Cane just before ye were captured on Trader's Day."

Esra nodded. She had never looked at her teacher's forearms before. Then again, she had never had the opportunity since he always wore long tunics, no matter what the weather. To think that he could have been receiving a magickal Tur message during one of their lessons was odd. "So ye put yer arms together and communicate? Sounds very strange."

"Ye don't know the half of it," Fynn joked. "Ye haven't seen strange 'til ye've been with all of us."

"So who was the fifth?" Esra asked. "Ye said ye need five, but there are only four of ye."

"Very perceptive," Arland commended. "Ye listen well. The fifth Keeper was actually Lara. She came into the woods a few times to help us."

"Lara!" She exclaimed. A hint of betrayal brushed against the center of her chest at the thought of her friend's secret. "I had no idea."

"Well, Lara doesn't actively work with the Keepers on tasks anymore. She had chosen to move to Sorley with her husband to try and watch out fer ye."

"Mr. Sturik is a Keeper, too?"

"No, but his brother is one, which is why Lara could marry him without much explanation or trouble. He already knew most of what happens. And Lara is the Keeper of Tranquility, so I daresay she reassured him through any of his fears."

Esra thought back to all the times she had felt a calmness settle upon her when entering the shop. The mitroot tea that brought such serenity that she could never duplicate. How people trusted Lara with their deepest secrets and desires. It all made sense in a new way. Esra felt a lump grow in her throat as she was overcome by a feeling of great sadness. "So many people in my life are forced to keep secrets, to hide who they are. How awful to have to fight against one's nature, deny yer true self. But part of me is proud that the people dear to me, people of Sorley, have such talents. These are remarkable skills. If only they would be able to share them openly again."

Esra turned towards her old blacksmith friend. "And what are ye the Keeper of?"

"Actually," Nadia offered, "Baelin is the only person ever known to be a dual Keeper. At first he was called forth to be the Keeper of Arms after completing his first test. That was fairly obvious to everyone. I'm sure yer familiar with some of his work. His craftsmanship is unmatched by any in the Kingdom. He can work with any metal, any wood, any element, to create weapons and armor in perfection. "

Esra lightly touched the Great Wolf blade that was tucked safely inside her boot. She wasn't surprised by this one revelation at least. "I see."

"The things ye've seen at Sorley are only a few of the items I can make," Baelin explained. "I also had te be very careful that my skill wouldn't bring too much attention. I make weapons fer all the Keepers, except those that receive them as a gift, like Fynn and Arland."

"That's true," Arland pulled out his greatsword and offered it to Esra. She stroked the flat surface of the sword hesitantly, the cold metal sending a chill down her spine. The blade gave off a subtle reddish hue, almost a glow like fire.

"So ye are the one I saw in the camp, surrounded by a group of Elites?" Esra thought back to the beautiful arc of a blade in the firelight, the calm warrior overcoming his attackers with ease.

"Aye, that was me," Arland confirmed. "This is the Greatsword of Narajuv, which I received as a Gift fer passing my first test."

"Yer very skilled in yer weapon of choice, I must say. Ye should have been a Keeper of Sword."

He must have noticed the slight pause as she said this, for he offered her an explanation. "It does seem strange at first when ye hear that a Keeper of Charm would be in such an esteemed Assembly, I agree. Especially when ye see such battle ready skills like a Keeper of Arms and Stealth and even Earth. What is the use in being Charming, ye must wonder?"

Esra blushed at his forwardness, but was inwardly thinking the exact same thing. He was undeniably charming, but she didn't see how that could aide much in a tight situation. Unless you could woo an Elite soldier while one of the others clobbered him.

"Well," he continued, "to state the more obvious of my abilities, I can attract or distract people. That can certainly be an advantage, especially when I work with Nadia to get into or out of somewhere we shouldn't be. As twins, our skills work together very well. But although Fynn will claim, jealously of course, that I am nothing more than a pretty face, that isn't quite true. I have the ability to not only charm people, but influence them, and objects as well. I can bend something's purpose or will to me as Baelin bends metal. I am also extremely lucky, so ye will find that just being near me will increase yer chances of success at most things."

"Sounds like very good skills to have handy if ye ask me," Esra nodded, impressed.

"Aye, I keep trying te get him te go gambling at the pub, but he ne'er will," Fynn complained. "Claims it isn't fair or such nonsense. And that Keepers should be honest. Blah blah."

Esra chuckled and turned her attention back to the greatsword as she ran her hand along the smooth blade, the intricately carved inscriptions running down its length. Although it was obvious that Arland was very fond of this weapon, it showed no signs of wear. She had not known a piece of metal could be so beautiful. "What are the carvings on the blade and hilt?"

"They are the markings of my people, similar to the ones I carry on my forehead. As fer the rest of us here, Fynn is a skilled archer. The Longbow, as ye've already seen. Baelin likes to use a staff of his own creation. It has a dagger-like metal tip on one end and a spiked metal ball on the other. I daresay it is a heavy and difficult weapon to wield, but he has mastered it, and it makes him a formidable and intimidating opponent. I use the Greatsword of Narajuv and Nadia uses lances, or throwing spears. She also keeps a dagger fer up close encounters, but it's rare that she is seen when she doesn't want to be, or that she'd miss a target with her spears in the first place."

Esra had a flash of a man in the camp being pierced by a spear-like weapon. "Yer all very good warriors, then?"

"The best, actually," Nadia said proudly. "We have been training fer this fer quite some time."

Esra sat in awe that she was surrounded by such skilled sorcerers and warriors. Surely she had never met anyone like them. And to think that there were so many more of them. "But how am I supposed to be a part of an Assembly when I've exhibited no better talent than proficient reading? It just doesn't make any sense. And Baelin, they said ye were a dual Keeper. So what is the other thing that ye are to keep?"

He stared at her unwaveringly. "Ye, Esra."

XIII

"Me?" Esra exclaimed. "Why do I need a Keeper?"

"Well," Nadia started, "he was in Sorley to protect ye. He's yer guardian."

That explained why Baelin had arrived so suddenly in a town where he had no family or other reason to be there. Why a skilled blacksmith would want to hide away in the middle of nowhere. Esra could not keep her frustration from growing once again. Everything was becoming a lie. Was he even really her friend?

"But why do I need a guardian? Why are Tallen and his Elites even after me?"

"Maybe it's easier if we show ye," Nadia suggested. She held out her arms palm up to the center of the group. The others joined her, placing their forearms up against one another to create a wavy row of skin. They looked to Esra and she reluctantly turned her arms palm up and added them to the line. As she did, she felt a tingling sensation as the shimmering black text began to snake itself across her arms.

"Although we must all concentrate on Cane, only one of us should be the main speaker so as not to confuse everything. Focus yer thoughts on trying to communicate with Cane. Baelin will tell him that yer alright." The peculiar script felt like a spider that was slowly making its way across her skin, and she fought the urge to brush it off. This time the Tur seemed to be different from what Arland had shown her. The script was brighter, like a light shone from behind their skin, illuminating the dark moving lines. The lines soon came together, and she began to read the message:

Hello, Esra, it's Cane. I'm glad yer safe. I am also pleased to see that our studies of the Tur are coming into good use. Please trust yer new friends and make it back to the Stronghold soon. Yer mother and father cannot wait to see ye. And Esra, please do not be too angry.

She jerked her arm away from the group and the writing disappeared.

"Is that a joke?" Esra spat angrily. "My parents are dead."

"No, they're not," Baelin said quietly. The other three looked uncomfortably at the blacksmith, then back at Esra. She did not wait for an explanation. In one swift movement Esra was on her feet and running towards the forest. She was not sure where she was headed, but she did not want to be anywhere near those people and their lies.

She ran hard, feeling the rage gain strength every time her foot hit the ground. She wanted to stay angry, to refuse to believe their ridiculous tales. But the running couldn't erase what they had said. The words haunted Esra, and she ran even faster trying to escape them. Her breath came out in great heaving gasps and her legs trembled beneath her, whether from anger or the exertion she wasn't sure. The space behind her eyes seemed to ache with this knowledge, and she resented not running back to Sorley the second she had awoken next to the fire. They were all liars.

Stumbling in her exhaustion, she fell to the ground, drained, as Meshok emerged from behind a tree. The Great Wolf always seemed to know when she was upset. Esra buried her face in her one true friend's fur and let out a muffled sob. Meshok tenderly licked her salty face, trying to calm the frantic mess on the forest floor.

"I'm sorry, Esra," she looked up to see Baelin standing over her with a pained expression. "I wanted te tell ye, but I couldn't. Yer parents, they are Keepers. I understand how ye feel…"

"Go away." She turned her head so that he could not see the streaks of tears that were running down her face.

He hesitated, as if unsure if he should go to her, then finally turned and walked away. Esra could hear his footsteps retreating and she had a momentary urge to chase after him and tell him that it was alright, that it was all just a big mistake. But although this day seemed unreal, it was happening, and Esra could barely hold on to who she thought she was.

If they all knew her parents were alive, then this meant her grandparents probably did as well. And that hurt her more than she thought she could bear. The story about her mother's illness, her father's hunting accident, it was all a lie. All this time her parents were alive. And waiting to see her. What were they like? Did they know she thought they were dead? Did they leave her with her grandparents because they didn't want her, didn't want to be parents? What were they doing at the Stronghold? What were they Keepers of?

All these questions. She thought that they had begun to answer some of them earlier, but they had just created more. Esra lay down on the ground and sprawled out, breathing in the crisp air mixed with new plants and old trees, trying to clear her head. Meshok curled up beside her patiently. *I am Esra, and I am strong.* She repeated that phrase in her head, willing herself to believe the words. She was still Esra and she was still strong.

Reluctant to move, she lounged under the canopy of Moss covered branches until her breath slowly started to steady. Unknown animals scurried about in the brush, gently rustling the dry leaves. Taking another deep breath, Esra thought about how long it had been since she had been alone like this. She usually enjoyed spending time in the forest behind her grandparents' home, sprawled about in the middle of so much life. It was as if she were watching it grow right before her eyes, could see the leaves of each tree stretch out to claim its place in the air. A great deal had happened in the past few days, and she was afraid the forest would never be the same. That nothing would ever be the same.

She tucked a stray piece of her long hair behind her ear and opened her eyes. Esra thought carefully about all of the things she had been told today, about how everything was starting to fit together with Cane's long winded teachings. She would never have imagined such things had happened in the world, were still happening. But in truth, she was glad to be a part of it. In many ways she had always felt restless in Sorley, like there was more for her than life in a small town. She loved her grandparents dearly, but she sensed that they too were out of their element, like birds in cages that were too small for them to fully stretch their wings. It had never crossed her mind that they could have lived a different life before, one far more exciting and dangerous than the one they had steadily and purposefully built for their granddaughter.

Esra turned towards Meshok, who looked at her with concern. "But I've never done anything that would indicate I was skilled in magick. Then again, I've never tried anything resembling a spell. How does one even cast a spell? Had my...parents... known when they were my age that they were sorcerers?"

Meshok groaned in answer to her friend's inquiries. "Then there's Lara. I thought that her serenity was just a strong character trait, not a force of magick! And what about Baelin? He's been my closest friend besides Lara and ye. Does he know all that I do, everywhere I go? And more importantly, is he kind to me simply because I'm his "task", an assignment that has to be completed?"

Her heart knew that Baelin was a good man, that his words to her had always been honest and true, but her head fought against the notion that he was tainted by his training. Esra was an important package that needed to be delivered safely, and that was all. No, she could not believe that. She *would* not believe that.

"What terrifies me more than anything is the thought of my parents I know ye'd expect that news of them being alive would thrill me There'd been so many nights that I'd lain awake imagining what I would do if I awoke to find my mother and father sitting at the kitchen table. how happy it would make me. But in reality I feel fairly angry. If the Keepers are so powerful and the Stronghold so secretive, then why couldn't they have kept me there? Are the demands of a Keeper too much to have the time or energy to raise a child? I'd thought I wanted to know all about my parents, really know what they were like. But what if I don't? What if they're arrogant or cold or selfish? Or worse, what if they don't like me?"

She pushed these thoughts away for the time being, Meshok staring up at her with a reverent look. "Ye're right, I need to remind myself that above all else, the Keepers seem to be a force of good. Cane wouldn't lie to me about that. If he meant me harm, he's had plenty of years to do it. And as much as I'm reluctant to admit it, I sensed it with the Assembly just now, their good intentions. As they were talking to me I was beginning to respect what they're trying to do, even though we know little of their ways. Or at least we can certainly know from personal experience that the Elites are up to no good. They weren't the friendliest bunch. And Cane's a good person, isn't he? My parents can't be awful. I don't think that a Keeper could be someone who is cruel or uncaring. And until we know more of the story, I'll try to have an open mind. That's what Cane would tell me right now, and my grandparents, too. Don't worry about things ye can't predict or control, it will only consume ye. Ye can only control yerself. Besides, I'm tired, and it just takes too much energy to stay angry."

After a long while, the light started to fade in the forest and she knew that darkness would soon force its way past every opening in the trees. She woke Meshok, who was snoring contentedly at her side and they both rose leisurely to make their way back to the camp. Birds called out greetings to one another, signaling the end of a long day. *It was a long day fer me, too,* Esra thought tiredly.

Reaching the edge of the clearing, she saw that Fynn was cooking supper as Nadia and Arland were in a discussion about what animal they would like to talk to first if they were Fynn. Baelin sat quietly across from them on the other side of the fire. Esra walked towards him with Meshok trotting expectantly behind. No doubt the smell of stew had reached her nostrils.

"I'm sorry," she took a seat beside her friend as the Wolf went to investigate supper. Baelin gazed at her with a look of relief and wonder.

"I wasn't sure ye would ever come back," he admitted. "And I couldn't say I'd blame ye. I lied te ye, Esra. When I told ye that I understood. Of all the things I had te learn, all the truths that were uncovered fer me, there was never anything as heartbreaking as being told that my parents were dead. Yer probably wondering who they are, why they left ye, why everyone would lie about it. I can't even begin te understand what yer feeling, I'm sorry."

"It's not yer fault. I just needed some time alone. I know ye think that news like that should make me want to dance fer joy."

"No, I'd think it'd be confusing and upsetting. At least at first." They sat for a long time in silence before Baelin began to speak again, this time so softly that Esra had to lean towards the fire to hear.

"My mother died when I was a baby and a few years later my father knew he too was dying and sent me away te the Stronghold. The Jade Gardens are all I've ever known as a home. My hands were holding small tools before I could even walk, and it was soon clear that I would be a Keeper of some type of craft. There was nothing I loved more than taking my hands and making something. I remember that even though I was surrounded by people jest like me with special gifts, I still felt alone. Many people had their families with them or they would leave te visit. I had a family in my fellow Keepers, but it wasn't the same. Fer many years I vowed never te have children of my own. I wouldn't risk putting them through the sorrow that I had experienced. I felt like someone who was on a path but still had no inclination of which direction I was headed, only that everyone else was going this way and that I was supposed te follow."

"I didn't know," Esra whispered. Strange that she had never thought to ask him about his family. He was her closest friend, and yet they had never breached such a topic. It was as if all this time they had avoided any serious discussions because of the unknown power it held. Esra had always been one to guard her secrets, her feelings, even when she was just a small child. Strong emotions confused her. She was never quite sure if she was feeling the way she ought to, or if she shared a small sadness or heavy thought with someone else, they might find her gloomy or petty. It was part of the reason why she refused to make many friends her own age, why she preferred to be alone. But the shadows of loss would still overcome her at indiscriminate moments, making her feel as if she could barely breathe. It frightened her, for she had not known her parents, and couldn't possibly miss anything particular about them. She shuddered to think how she would deal with losing someone she knew well, like her grandparents. But growing up without her parents had still left a certain feeling in her, an emptiness. She didn't know how to fix it, this feeling. And she was used to being able to solve problems, like a conundrum Cane plucked out of a book. But if she was experiencing an emotion she didn't understand, she would rather ignore it than brood over it. To think that all this time she had someone to really confide in, someone who was going through the same thing. She looked at Baelin with a newfound sense of closeness. "I'm so sorry. I thought yer parents were jest in another town somewhere, perhaps where ye had lived before coming to Sorley."

"It's not something I speak of often. Not because it is too painful but because it's in the past. I respect it fer shaping me into the man I've become. I know my parents would be proud of the things I've done and the things I hope te do. Looking back, I feel foolish that I didn't speak te ye about this sooner. Even if ye never said anything about yer parents and how difficult it was, I should 'ave known. I went through it too and I could have helped ye, talked te ye about it."

Esra was silent as Meshok flopped down heavily beside her.

"When I was about eight years old I passed my first test and was given an Assembly. In them I found my first true family. They would have done anything fer me and I fer them. Nadia, Arland, and Fynn joined my Assembly much later, but they too are like family te me."

"What happened to them? Yer first Assembly? I thought that once ye received an Assembly it didn't change."

"They don't normally. The four Keepers in my first Assembly died."

"Oh," Esra swallowed, not wanting to ask more. They both sat and watched the flames jump aggressively around the wood it was slowly consuming. Somewhere behind them a bird made a loud shrieking call and took off towards the sky.

"Esra, do ye remember how ye came te me that one day while I was working and says that ye felt someone was watching ye in the woods?"

She thought back to that day at his workshop, a lifetime ago, and groaned. "Don't tell me that was ye? The hooded man in the forest?"

"Aye. I wanted te make sure that the Elites weren't following ye. Cane and I agreed that was how they'd try te capture ye, in the woods when ye was alone. Could blame it on ye gettin' lost or killed by a beast. No one would get too suspicious. Especially since yer known fer being, err...lost in fancies."

Esra thought about all the times she was in the woods with Meshok. She hadn't realized that she was in danger, that all of this chaos and plotting was going on without any of her knowledge. Then she thought about all the conversations she'd had out loud to herself or Meshok, thinking she was alone. Her cheeks grew redder as she slowly understood he had heard all of it. Thank goodness she had never said anything regrettable about him.

"I wasn't scoutin' on ye, Esra," he reassured her, noticing her embarrassment. "I only wanted te protect ye. Keep ye safe. And trust me, it was a difficult task te hide a big lug like me in the forest. And try te get Meshok not te give me away!"

She laughed as she pictured his gigantic form trying to run from tree to tree. "It is a wonder I didn't see ye. I must be deaf or blind or both."

"Well, I may be large, but I'm quiet. Nadia has helped me learn some stealth. And it also helps that yer so oblivious and daydreamy."

"No wonder Meshok didn't seem to worry the day we ran ye down in the forest. She knew who it was. I always thought it rather odd that she gave up chase so easily."

They sat enjoying the warm crackle of the fire while Fynn danced about, throwing herbs into the pot as he sang some song about rabbit stew.

"He's a much better cook than a musician. Is he always like that?" Esra asked.

"I'm afraid so," Baelin admitted with a smile. "Worse, actually. I think he's actually behaving with some restraint since ye arrived."

They both laughed heartily as Fynn hit an extraordinarily high note.

"Sounds like he's trying to talk to a squealing pig, eh?" Nadia smiled at Esra as she and Arland joined them.

"Well, I'd rather hear the pig," Arland jabbed Esra in the side with a mischievous grin.

"Me too," she admitted. They had been nothing but kind to her, and she felt a hot flash of guilt spread up her cheeks at her earlier behavior. Being an independent sort, she had not had much dealings with others her age, so she struggled to find the words for an apology. "I'm sorry I ran off before. It was all just a little too much at one time."

"Esra, ye needn't worry," Nadia assured her. "The Elves are much more open about the Keepers from a young age, so it is not quite the same. Humans don't speak much about magick, whereas we grew up hearing all about it. But had I been lied to about any of it, I can assure ye I would have been very, very angry. The only time my parents lied to me about anything was when they told me that my grandmother was just sick with a stomach ache when they knew she was dying. They had wanted to protect me, but I didn't get to say goodbye and she died a week later. I packed a bag full of dried meat and an extra set of clothes to run away, planning to go to the great Human city of Kiran Brae. It took them three days and the talent of multiple sorcerers to find me. That's actually how we found out that I was skilled in stealth. Trying to find me when I didn't want to be found proved to be a much greater challenge than they thought. But I will never forget how angry I was at being lied to, even though I understood their intentions were good We're just happy ye stayed."

Esra nodded, appreciating the fact that Nadia could relate to how she was feeling. She pictured a young girl with long dark curls running down the side of a mountain, a pack full of supplies bouncing at her side. Suddenly Fynn's song broke through her thoughts as his voice warbled across the clearing.

Rabbit stew, rabbit stew.
Eat it raw, it'll make ye spew.

"So fer starters, I'd just like to tell ye that I know fer a fact that one of the hardest things yer parents ever did was give ye up," Nadia seemed to read Esra's mind. "So don't fer a second think that ye were raised by yer grandparents because they didn't want ye."

"How do ye know?"

"Well, we all know them. They live at the Stronghold."

"Oh, right. Do all Keepers usually live there?"

"Many of us do. We have to be there fer training and afterwards most of us find it easier to set up our permanent homes there. We travel and see our families, and some of us choose to live outside, like Lara. But most of us are gone so often that it just makes sense to make it our home. And it's a wonderful place filled with beauty and all different types of people, each with unique outlooks and abilities. The reason yer parents are there, Esra, is because they are both Great Keepers. Yer mother is the Great Keeper of Destiny and yer father is the Great Keeper of War."

"Oh," a surprised gasp escaped Esra's lips. She sat in silence for a moment, contemplating this revelation. "Both of them? But I thought that only happened very rarely, sometimes hundreds of years apart."

"That's true," Arland confirmed. "If a Keeper passes all five tests, which almost never happens, a Great Keeper can choose to pass on their knowledge. It is only then that they are able to leave their physical bodies. The Great Keepers do not do what they do fer the power or the immortality. They pass on all of their knowledge to the new Keeper in the hopes that they will add to it. And I'd imagine that most of them are ready fer a break after centuries of work."

"So my grandparents…"

"They're not Keepers, strangely enough. But they both had family very gifted in the arts of magick."

Esra felt a weight lift off her chest in relief. She was glad that at least someone in her life wasn't hiding their identity.

"So how long has Cane been a Great Keeper?"

"He passed all his tests centuries ago. Not sure how many exactly. I do believe he was around to see Rïvan's treachery."

"Jumping jig..." Esra murmured. "I'd always joked that Cane was an old man, but I had no idea how true that really was. To think that he has seen LeVara hundreds, maybe thousands of years ago. No wonder he loved history lessons. He had probably lived through much of what he taught."

"Yer parents," Baelin explained, "they both passed all five tests. It had been unheard of until then, two people doing this at once. Actually, the last test yer father passed was yer mother's. She had become a Great Keeper just before him."

"Yer mother found out she was with child right after yer father finished his last test," Arland continued, "and they were both thrilled. Ye were conceived by two Great Keepers, and yer mother gave birth to ye as a Great Keeper. Once again, this has never happened. No one knew if ye would be Human, immortal, or a little of both. But the one thing they did assume is that ye would be an extraordinary Keeper, someone who could possibly end the war fer good."

"Has a Great Keeper not ever had a child with a Human or Elf?"

"No, they were usually fairly old by the time they passed their fifth test, or already had families. And a new Great Keeper came along so rarely, you can imagine the chances of this occurring. It had never been tested before."

"I'm like, some freak, then?" Esra was astounded at this new piece of information. She was honestly surprised that she could continue to be surprised at this point, but the strangeness just kept coming.

"Not a freak, Esra, a gift." Nadia took her hand and held it for a long moment. "Ye give hope to a people who have been fighting fer hundreds of years. It has always been said that a Keeper may come along who can end the war and bring harmony to our land. Ye have been a beacon of light in the last twenty years through the dark times of the Keepers."

"But I'm not a beacon, I'm a farm girl," Esra insisted with a sigh. It was as if they weren't hearing her. "So how does someone find out what they are a Keeper of anyway?"

"Well," Nadia looked from her to Baelin, "usually ye don't find out until after yer training, when yer first test is completed and ye attend yer first Gifting Ceremony."

"That's right," Esra remembered, "Cane told me that the Keepers receive Gifts. He said they're a contribution to help with a skill and no two are alike. And they're always an item of sorts that aid the user mentally or physically."

"Yer right," Nadia said. "My first Gift was the Stone of Awareness. I am able to sense others over great distances, know if an enemy or friend is approaching. I then received the Ring of Haste, which makes my speed increase tenfold, followed by a Necklace of Stunning, which makes any melee attack I use that doesn't kill my opponent stun them temporarily. My fourth Gift was the Bracelet of Evening Eye, which allows me to see in complete darkness. Very useful tools fer someone dedicated to stealth."

"Bumbling huckfly," Esra whistled, impressed. These Gifts were very useful indeed. Too bad she didn't have anything like it when the Elites were chasing her through the forest. "So what about the rest of ye?"

"Well," Fynn chimed in, "my first Gift was the Ring of Tongues, which allows me te speak any language, including Shendari."

"Can't Elves also speak every language including Shendari?"

"Some languages, yes," Nadia answered. "But not nearly as well as Fynn. He has a natural affinity fer all languages, he can speak them fluently without even hearing them beforehand. Ours is a learned skill, one that we study fer long hours as children. If Fynn ever met someone outside of our Kingdom we would have no knowledge of their language but he would be able to communicate with them perfectly."

"Then I received the Bow of Many," Fynn continued, "which allows me te shoot up te three arrows at a time. A nice trick fer the ladies, I must admit. Then there was the Listening Stone. Before that I had te touch an animal directly in order te speak te it. Now I can communicate over great distances with any creature. My fourth Gift was the Earring of Recovery, which allows me te heal from any physical wound without the need of herbs or poultices. I am also immune te illness and disease but still vulnerable te magickal attack."

"So ye can't be injured?"

"I can, and it still hurts like it would any other, but I will heal without any outside help and much more quickly."

Esra had an impulse to ask Fynn to show her, to cut his hand so that she could see if what he spoke was indeed true. But she was too shy to ask such a thing, and besides, he said it would still hurt.

"Baelin?" She turned towards her blacksmith friend.

"My first was the Hammer of the Shendari, which is the only tool that is able te shape Shendari scales. The Knife of Piercing, my second Gift, is able te cut through any material, and I do mean anything. Wood, stone, metal, it will slice through it like a cooked carrot. I forged it onto the end of my weapon."

He grabbed the large wooden staff from where it was leaning on the ground and showed her the end with the spiked metal ball and the other end with a metal casing that held the knife. He took off the covering and pressed a spot on the wood until the knife slid easily off the end and into his hands.

"The metal casing is made from the same material. Otherwise I might cut through everything I touch. The third Gift I received was the Amulet of Resistance, which makes me immune te all influence magick. Tayen, the Great Keeper of Magick, was quite impressed with that one, as it is very rare te have total immunity te any type of magick. My last Gift was the Ring of Esra, believe it or not."

"A ring of me?" She asked incredulously. "What is *that* fer?"

"It is the reason I came te Sorley. It wasn't just that I was asked by the Great Keepers, although I would have gone had they done so. It was when I discovered I was a dual Keeper, fer the title became known te Cane as he was Gifting me the ring. It was a very confusing moment fer him, as he is not used te being surprised at his own Giftings, I'd imagine. But I am always...drawn...te where ye are. It's like a mother who has lost her child in the woods and can't explain why she knows which way te go, but she won' stop looking until they're found. I can't quite describe it. I can sense when yer in danger, when yer afraid. Sometimes the pull te be near ye was so strong I would come find ye just te make sure ye were safe, like all those times in the forest," he admitted sheepishly.

"Oh," Esra said softly. She wasn't sure how to feel about this. How strange to be drawn to someone like that, to be practically unable to stay away from where they were. Strange for her and him both. Esra hoped it had nothing to do with their making friends, that it had been as much an act of free will as it had been a force of magick. The thought of him not truly caring for her filled her with a heavy feeling of dread, and she swallowed hard. Their relationship had always seemed so natural, so fated. Her brain suddenly alit with a thought, as if she had just solved a riddle she had been brooding over for months. It was quickly followed by a strong emotion and she shuddered inwardly as she recognized the feeling. Although she could identify it, Esra was not ready to deal with it. Not yet. She turned hastily towards Arland in an attempt to lead her mind away from the swarm of thoughts. "And what about ye?"

"My first Gift was the Greatsword of Narajuv, as ye've seen. Narajuv was a remarkable warrior from the lost tribes of the north, beyond the Eshomee Ledges of my people. His sword had been shattered in a great battle, with only small pieces of the blade remaining and the hilt, which had been preserved at the Stronghold fer generations. Baelin re-forged the sword with a mixture of Elvish metal and a small amount of Shendari scale, which gives the blade its reddish color. It increases my sword fighting skills immensely. It's almost like having extra intuition when I'm wielding it. Then I received the Bracelet of Dreams, which allows me to alter another person's dreams. I can do this to influence them perhaps, or calm them, or warn them. There are many different reasons."

"Alter their dreams?" Esra thought back to the dream of Sorley she had after her rescue and how realistic it had felt. "My grandparents by the stream. That was ye?"

"Aye," he smiled, "I thought it would be refreshing fer ye to have a night in familiar surroundings."

Esra nodded slowly, confused by the intrusion into her mind but grateful for the gesture. He held out his arm for her so that she could see the bracelet, which was thickly woven with a strong black material. In the center, woven into the dark threads was a cloudy silver stone. It was flat and round, about the size of her thumbnail, with the Tur word for dreams carved onto the surface of the stone. *Pyrthoria.*

"My third Gift," Arland continued, "was the Armor of Deflection. This repels most attack spells back to the caster."

"But I've never seen ye wear any armor."

"It's not a full chainmail suit," he smiled. "Since it is to defend against magickal attacks, I wear it as a talisman."

He pulled out a leather cord that was tucked into his shirt and showed her the small metal charm shaped like a starburst. "My final Gift was the Rock of Memories, which allows me to alter the memory of anyone I touch."

Esra raised her eyebrows suspiciously at this revelation before he quickly explained. "Not that I do it every time I touch someone. I have to be holding the rock and it requires a lot of concentration. It's not something I use very often."

"I see," she said in relief. Although if he was changing her memories, she supposed she'd never know the truth anyway. Maybe they had already had this conversation. No, that was too strange for her to think of. "These are all very powerful Gifts. What happens if ye lose it or someone steals one?"

"The Gifts are meant to be used by one person alone, so it would do ye no good to steal one. And if they are lost, they will always find their way back to their owner. Almost like magickal tracking."

"I see."

"Many at the Stronghold believe, Esra, that ye are destined fer great things," Arland admitted.

"Ye keep saying that," Esra sighed dejectedly.

Fynn plopped down next to her, winded from his dancing and cooking. "Destiny, shmestiny. So, I take it they told ye all ye needed te know?"

"Not nearly, but it's good enough fer now. I have a lot to think about," she smiled.

"Esra, we also want ye to know that becoming a Keeper is a choice," Nadia offered gently. "We are not here to kidnap ye like the Elites and turn ye against yer will. If ye choose not to join us, we will escort ye to someplace safe in the morning. Unfortunately, it will not be safe in Sorley, but we will find yer grandparents and take ye somewhere else."

It was quiet for a long moment as Esra pondered this decision. If she choose to, she was actually going to see her parents. That seemed to be the scariest thought of all, even worse than Tallen and his Elites. "Although it frightens me, I cannot in good conscience deny that if I might be able to help in this fight in any way, I will. Even if I end up sweeping the floors of the Stronghold. I had no idea that everyone I knew had been taking fer granted the peace that we have enjoyed all these years. The experience of being kidnapped still hangs heavily in my mind, haunting me. I can still see their twisted faces scowling in the shadows whenever I close my eyes. All of the people in LeVara are in danger, including the people of Sorley that I love dearly. Mothers, fathers, children. I can't turn my back now, not if there is even the slightest chance that I could help end it, strange as that thought is. Even if I can't do a lick of magick, I will certainly do my best."

It was hard for her to believe that most of all, that she gave people so much hope. But underneath the terror of leaving all that she knew behind, there was excitement to venture out and see some of the grand sights that had so far only been described to her in books. To discover who she really was.

Esra looked around at her new friends, her Assembly. They would now become the people she would trust her future and her life to. "I will come with ye. I highly doubt that I will be the great sorcerer that everyone expects, but I will do what I can to help."

"Great," Fynn reached over and slapped her leg with his wooden spoon, as everyone gave each other glances of relief. "Better eat up good tonight and get some sleep. We need te wake early."

"Why, what are we doing tomorrow?"

"Tomorrow," he winked at her, "we leave fer the Stronghold."

XIV

The sun was barely peeking over the horizon when Esra felt herself being gently shaken from sleep. She gingerly pulled herself onto her elbows, leaning over to rub Meshok's stomach vigorously. The Wolf let out a long, low groan and rolled over to get a better belly rubbing. Fynn placed a small plate of cooked Eggs in front of Esra and started to pack away the remaining dishes. The others were already up and ready, with the welcome addition of five horses already laden with the rest of their goods.

"Why didn't ye wake me sooner?" Esra protested, shoveling the Eggs into her mouth. "I could've helped with the packing."

"Sorry, love," Fynn apologized. "I was all fer waking ye up, as I'm quite lazy by nature and would've swindled ye into doing all my work. But alas, Baelin here insisted that we let ye get yer rest."

"What is he, my grandmother?" Esra complained loudly.

"Aye, and a big hairy one at that!" Fynn agreed.

"Very funny, the both of ye. Just wait 'til this big hairy grandmother squashes the brains from ye like a ripe roja fruit." He held his hands out and slapped them together in an imitation.

"Eek!" Fynn made a high pitched squeal and hid behind Esra. "I surrender te ye, oh large and meaty one!"

Esra shook her head at them in disbelief and started rolling up her blankets. At least her new friends seemed to be a jovial and entertaining bunch. Which she was sure would come in handy during the dark, bleak possibility of the Kingdom being taken over.

The day smelled fresh and cool, perfect weather for traveling. Esra noticed that one of the colossal horses was Fariel, her grandparents grey steed from the farm. So there were others like him after all. He appeared to be truly Baelin's now, and she was glad for it.

Nadia approached and pointed out a large white horse to the right of the pack. Most of the time Nadia looked as real and solid as the next person. But there were instances when she appeared to be there and nowhere at the same time, like a shimmering shadow. It would take some time getting used to it, Esra assumed. They walked over to the horse with his long white mane and Nadia leaned over to stroke his strong flanks with her small hands.

"The saddles were crafted by Baelin especially fer these kinds of horses. They are made with less restriction than a traditional saddle, since it is helpful to be able to lean forward very far when riding. Sometimes ye will even find it preferable to lay down fer longer rides. So the saddles are mostly fer holding various objects at the sides, but not primarily to restrain yer movement."

Esra nodded as she tied the last bundle to one of the straps, noting the strange shape of the leather. There were not even any stirrups for mounting.

"Yer horse doesn't have a name yet since we were waiting to give him to ye. He is bred from the Great Keeper of Strength's own stock of horses. All of these were. His line was a gift to the Keepers from the Elves. We call them skycatchers, because the Elves say that when ye ride one, it seems as if ye are going fast enough to catch the sky. Fariel and this white one are brothers," she motioned towards the group of horses, quite a majestic collection. Esra had never before seen any other horses like Fariel. She took note of how truly massive they all were. Each one had to be at least eighteen hands.

"He's beautiful," Esra murmured, rubbing the broad white face gently. Meshok trotted up to them from where she had been laying and stood beside Esra, staring up at their new friend. Although Meshok was higher than Esra's waist, the horse stood well beyond her own chest. Slightly panicked that the sudden appearance of a Wolf would spook the horse, Esra held her breath in nervous anticipation. Her fears were unfounded, as the skycatcher appeared to be unstartled by the Great Wolf's approach, and barely paused a moment before leaning down to greet her. Esra stood by in awe as Meshok returned the salutation by touching her nose softly to the horse's cheek.

"Great Wolves and skycatchers are longtime friends. It is said that they fought together with the Elves, Unni, and Shendari long ago when our Kingdom was first formed. This one here is mine." Nadia motioned to a dazzling light brown female standing next to Fariel. "I call her Meda. The larger brown male next to her is Arland's horse, Errol."

"And this," Fynn said, appearing suddenly next to a black mare, "is my one true love, My Lady."

"I daresay it is the only lady ye will ever have hope of riding,"

Arland called from beside Errol.

"Ahoy! Did ye hear that My Lady?" Fynn tilted his forehead into the skycatcher's neck. "We will punish him later when he is coughing behind us in the dust and we are leaping easily towards the Stronghold."

"I'll take that bet," Arland announced confidently.

"Oh, dear," Nadia rolled her eyes at Esra. "Those two are *always* competing at something. I swear if I didn't have Baelin to knock some sense into them once in a while I would have surely whacked their arrogant heads off myself."

Esra chuckled as Fynn strutted by to grab the last of the satchels. "Not that I will like te be so far away from ye, my Nadia. But alas, I must constantly defend myself from being labeled a weakling by the other two burly males we traverse with. A real man will fight fer what he wants."

Fynn cocked a flirtatious eyebrow towards Nadia and snatched up two bundles before she could react, carrying them back to the horses. A red flame shot up Nadia's cheeks, appearing partially from anger as well as embarrassment.

"Are ye two courting?"

"Courting!" Nadia sputtered. "Certainly not."

"Then I must say, I think Fynn has taken a liking to ye," Esra observed with a smile.

"Fynn has always had a liking fer me," Nadia sighed. "Of that he is not shy about."

"Oh, I can't believe he means any harm in it. Besides, he is quite handsome, don't ye think?"

"Handsome!"

Esra didn't know she had stumbled upon such a sensitive topic and laughed at the wide eyed look Nadia was giving her "Ye look like I just admitted I'm actually the Keeper of Carrots. Ha. Don't ye like him? He seems to be very nice, and funny at that. No one can resist that smile. Besides, I'm sure that he can write yer very own rabbit stew love ballad."

"Oh, Esra!" Nadia groaned.

"I think we're ready," Baelin called to them as he swung himself up easily on Fariel's back. Nadia gave a quick nod at Esra and with stunning dexterity, leapt upon Meda as if it were no more than jumping atop Meshok. Fynn and Arland mounted My Lady and Errol in similar fashion as Esra looked from face to face and back to her horse with disbelief.

"Is that some kind of spell? And how do ye propose I get up there? There aren't even any stirrups!"

"Esra, ye are stronger and faster than ye think. Just jump and don't think too much about it," Arland encouraged her from atop his massive beast, Errol. Meda and My Lady began to circle around impatiently, eager to stretch their legs after a few days' rest.

Esra stayed rooted to her spot, unwilling to accept that she could perform such a feat. Even the few times she took Fariel for a stroll on the farm involved the clever stacking of wooden crates. It was as if they had just asked her to jump over the trees in the forest. Although she did consider herself to be healthy and strong, this was beyond any physical limit she could imagine, especially for someone as clumsy as herself. Even the thought of it seemed mad. Then again, they had all done it without difficulty.

The white horse leaned down to nose Esra's shoulder, encouraging her. She shrugged in submission and decided to trust her new friends, backing up to prepare for the jump of her life. A picture played in Esra's head where she smashed into the side of this enormous white beast and trickled down the side into a pathetic, crumpled heap. She shook the image from her head before pushing off the ground with all her might, racing forward to gain momentum before springing upwards.

She made it, but barely, and landed awkwardly on her stomach with the saddle knocking the breath from her in one quick rush. She scrambled to throw her leg over the side of the horse, and dangled there for an uncomfortable moment, recovering from the shock of the occurrence. The skycatcher did not move throughout the entire ordeal. Most horses would have been extremely unhappy with such an attempt at mounting and thrown her off almost immediately. The others cheered loudly and Esra grinned at them wearily, pulling herself upright and grasping the reigns. It wasn't pretty, but it would do. She patted the horse's neck in gratitude, leaning down to whisper in its ear. "Thank ye. I'd imagine that wasn't the most graceful display ye've ever experienced. Ye really are a catcher. And I must say ye are a very comfortable horse to sit astride, considering yer great berth."

The horse whinnied, tossing its head up and back, nodding in agreement. Esra laughed at her playful friend and sat back for a moment, relishing in her unlikely accomplishment. On the top of the left shoulder of the horse was a large black birthmark, the only blemish on the otherwise pure white skin. She traced the mark with her finger. It was about the size of her palm with six curved edges like a roja fruit.

"That's what I'll name ye, Roja!" She exclaimed, tapping the shoulder where the birthmark was. "They're my grandfather's favorite."

"Roja? Like the fruit?" Nadia asked.

"Like the thing that Baelin was about te squash our heads like?" Fynn joked. "No, no, ye should give him a good strong name, a manly name. How about He Who Makes Pulp of Yer Pathetic Human Body or perhaps Elite Death Bringer Served with a Large Helping of Pain."

"Says the man on the lady horse," Arland called loudly.

"True, true," Fynn agreed. "Besides, those are all too long winded. By the time ye announce yer horse's name yer opponents will have hacked both yer legs off. Roja it is!"

They all cheered as Esra took hold of the reins to urge her newly named friend forward. It was then that she noticed that the small leather straps were not connected to any bit or bridle. They were short and tied to opposite sides of the saddle. Seeing her confusion, Nadia trotted over to explain. "Those aren't really reins, they're extra straps fer tying supplies."

"So then how am I supposed to ride?"

"When ye want to go, lightly press yer finger here," she indicated a spot between Roja's shoulders. "When ye want to stop, touch here."

Nadia pointed to a spot only a few inches down from the first. "If ye want her to speed up or slow down, the harder or softer ye will touch. Fer turning ye touch her on either side of her shoulder. Ye needn't press hard, they respond to the softest tap."

"This seems complicated," Esra remarked nervously. "I've never ridden in such a way before. What if I steer us into a tree?"

"Don't worry, Fynn spoke to Roja and told her this would be new fer ye. He'll take it easy today. Ye'll also find ye don't need to steer much when we are traveling somewhere. The skycatchers know their way around LeVara very well."

Still uneasy, Esra gently touched above the center of the mare's shoulders and Roja lurched forward to join with the group.

"Just the lightest touch," Nadia reminded.

Esra nodded and tucked the non-reins into the sides of the saddle. It felt odd to be sitting astride a horse with nothing to hold, so she curled her fingers under the front of the saddle. "So where exactly is the Stronghold?"

Baelin turned towards her as Fariel stomped heavily on the ground. The tone of the morning turned more serious as the rest of her Assembly waited patiently for their Fifth to answer. "I needn't remind ye the importance of keeping all of this information secret. The Stronghold is in the Jade Gardens. They are northeast of Sorley and just south of Fire Lake. It will take about four days te travel there. Normally it would take six, but chasing the Elites took us two days east already. With slower horses it would take much longer. We will stop in the town of Tirbaz te rest briefly, which is a little over a day's travel from here. There is someone there we need te speak with, but we must keep hidden from the rest of the townsfolk. I'm unsure how far-reaching Tallen's guards are, but ye can be certain that he has eyes on the lookout fer us in every town surrounding Sorley, perhaps in all of LeVara by now. We would not normally stop in Tirbaz, except we need te speak te this person fer Cane regarding an important matter."

Esra nodded once to show she understood, and then leaned forward to stroke the mane of Roja. "So just how fast can these horses go? They're so large, it's hard to believe…"

No sooner had she spoke the words then Arland and Fynn shot forward on Errol and My Lady, disappearing from the clearing before Esra could even open her mouth in surprise.

"Very, very fast," the blacksmith grinned. Baelin gave a loud shout and took off after the other two at an incomprehensible speed. Esra glanced down at Meshok, who was sitting uninterestedly on her haunches, licking her paw.

"Don't worry," Nadia assured her, "Great Wolves are just as fast. Meshok will probably be waiting fer us at nightfall when we stop to set up camp."

Satisfied that her friend would not be left behind, Esra gave Roja a soft tap with her finger. The horse responded with such force that Esra pitched backwards violently and had to grab frantically at the saddle. Tightening her fingers around the edge of the seat, they began winding through trees at an unbelievable speed. Large oak and birch trees flashed by her in a blur of color and motion as they went tearing through the forest.

Esra clenched her thighs tightly against the horse's broad sides, terrified that she might fly off or run into a branch. She was used to a Human steering their steed, but obviously no one had told the skycatchers this. wind whipped at her face and pulled her long blonde hair out of its carefully tended braid. Her eyes watered with the intensity of the wind so she leaned lower into the horse's neck.

Feeling the steady rising and falling of Roja's strong muscles underneath her, she slowly loosened her hold on the saddle just a bit. Her legs were tiring already from the panicked grip she was maintaining and she felt them inadvertently loosen as well. Leaning onto her stomach, Esra tried to flatten herself against the horse instead of using only her legs to hold on, adjusting herself against the saddle. She could see how a more traditional saddle would have been too awkward and constricting rather than this smooth adaptation that let her lay forward.

Feeling somewhat more secure after surviving the first few minutes of the ride, Esra let herself look around a little at the forest. Roja's stride was surprisingly smooth, and she jolted around less than she did when riding smaller horses. All the trees burst by in a flash of greens and browns, and she tried to focus her attention on an individual tree up ahead. After a few moments her eyes seemed to adjust and she could make out the more definitive shapes of leaves and twisted branches, the large round trunks. The air was fresh and crisp, and Esra couldn't remember ever feeling more alive.

"I hope that ye know where yer going," she shouted above the wind rushing past her face. "Because I've lost any sense to navigate and our Assembly is nowhere in sight."

Other than a flick of his ears, Roja made no motion that he heard her or attempted to slow down. Since he seemed to be confident in their direction, Esra reluctantly loosened her grip on the saddle and let him lead. Inclining forward even further, Esra took a chance and threw her feet behind her so that she was lying flat on her stomach along the horse's back. After balancing for a moment, she sighed and closed her eyes, enjoying the invigorating sensation of wind raking over her body. She remained that way for quite a while, thinking that if anyone could see Roja running now they would not know there was a rider on his back. The hazy colors and shapes of the forest soon became a sleepy blur.

Perhaps it was the thrill of her first ride, or the calming sensation of being rocked on the horses back, but Esra was genuinely surprised when Roja began to slow, waking her from her hypnotic state. Sitting up, Esra noticed that the other four had stopped ahead at the side of a stream where the horses were drinking deeply. Sauntering next to them, Roja lowered his head, dipping the front half of his body so that Esra could jump off.

"Is it time to stop already?" Esra asked.

"Already?" Arland chuckled. "We've been traveling fer hours. It's time fer noonmeal."

Esra looked up and saw that the sun was indeed straight up in the sky.

"And everyone knows we cannot let a big beefy man like Baelin miss a meal," Fynn patted Baelin's belly as he started to unload the pots from My Lady. "Specially if he still wants te pop me head like a Roja fruit."

Nadia rolled her eyes and began to take off her boots, motioning for Esra to do the same. They pulled off their stockings, walking to the edge of the stream and stepping into the cool running water.

"That feels delicious," Esra moaned happily. "I didn't realize how exhausting it is to ride a horse all day, even if yer lying down."

"Yes, and we still have a good bit of traveling ahead of us," Nadia acknowledged. "It will get easier though the more ye do it."

"Makes me wonder how the horses feel. After all, they're the ones doing all the real work." Esra waded further into the water, relishing the refreshing feeling of water flowing around her. It reminded her of all the times she had taken Meshok down to the stream at the farm to swim, and she felt a momentary pang of homesickness.

"Have ye seen Meshok?" Esra remembered, looking around.

"Over there in the water. I think she's having a glorious time swimming about." Nadia pointed over to where the Great Wolf was panting heavily as she paddled deftly across the stream. Whenever water was near, Meshok was in it. It was something they did often together. And despite her size, the Wolf was a very efficient swimmer. "She was waiting fer us here, just like we guessed."

"Oh Ladies!" Fynn called out from a hastily built fire he was tending farther back from the water. "And I don't mean ye, Arland."

Arland, who was brushing down Errol, let out a mock laugh and whispered loudly to his horse. "That's right, he's the crazy one."

"Yes, Fynn?" Esra called back.

"I'll gives ye all my love if ye just find me some good corra nuts te mix in with this stew."

"In that case, I think we'll be drowning ourselves." Esra took a dramatic pause before diving into the water.

"Oh ho, Fynn! She's catchin' on to ye!" Arland laughed.

"She's just playin' hard te get. Who can resist this?" Fynn began pumping his arms up and down maniacally in a spastic dance.

"Dear King Keridon have mercy," Nadia mumbled as Esra laughed violently beside her. They both began to slosh out of the cool water and onto the fresh green shore.

"Maybe ye should take Arland with ye just in case," Baelin warned. "The forest here is unfamiliar and may hold some unknown beasts."

"Nothing could possibly be scarier than that," Esra motioned towards Fynn as she linked her arm into Nadia's and started towards the trees.

XV

They had traveled hard though the second half of the day and it was well past dinnertime when they decided to stop again. Esra watched with curiosity as the forested rolling hills of the Kingdom near Sorley morphed into a flat, open plain. The air here seemed hotter and heavier, as if it were a living thing of its own. If it was so different only a few days away from her home town, she wondered what it might be like farther away. Would she even still recognize the land as LeVara? Dismounting wearily to catch a quick supper before reaching Tirbaz, Nadia came over and sat down next to Esra.

"Are ye ready fer yer first lesson in stealth? I'll show ye how to catch a rabbit with yer bare hands."

"Really? I mean, yes, of course."

"Good, because it's about time ye had a proper lesson."

"Ye sure ye don't want to take Fynn?" Esra teased.

"Tempting, but I'd rather offer my own arm fer the cooking." She stood up and starting walking towards the center of the field that bordered a small grove of trees.

"Don't ye want to go hunting first by those trees?" Esra asked, perplexed. "Ye won't find much out in an open field. At least not much ye can catch."

"True, but then again I need to show ye how my gift really works, and I can do that much better out here. Besides, it's hard enough to see me in the open, let alone a dark forest." A moment later she appeared on the other side of Esra, who could've swore that she didn't even see her move.

"The Ring of Haste, my second Gift. There is a Keeper of Speed named Humi at the Stronghold. She is fast in everything she does. She can chop vegetables or tie a saddle in the blink of an eye. My Gift only makes me quicker on my feet, but I can't perform tasks any faster like

Humi can. Don't worry, ye don't need my speed fer this lesson. Come on, then."

They had been attempting to stay as close to the shadow of the forest in their travels as possible, but the closer they got to Tirbaz, the thinner the trees became. Esra felt strangely exposed, as if the surrounding forests in Sorley had sheltered her somehow. It was hard to believe that someone could be stealthy in this open terrain. They both walked in the fading light towards the center of the field while Nadia explained the basics of stealth.

"A person is usually detected by four distinct ways. The first is touch. Even if ye were deaf and blind, ye would obviously know that something is there if ye can feel it. The second is smell. This is usually not a problem fer most Humans, since our sense of it is very dulled, but fer animals this is especially important. The third is sight and the last is sound. My gift gives me the ability to conquer all of those things when I so chose."

"Ye mean, the way ye get all shimmery sometimes isn't all ye can do?" Esra asked, genuinely surprised. Although Nadia tried to appear in solid form when Esra was around, there were other times she didn't. It was as if she was in a place neither here nor there, like the flickering waves on the ground of a hot summer day.

"Actually, I prefer to be in the 'shimmering' form as ye call it when I am alone or with others I trust. It is just more natural to me. But I realize this may make ye uncomfortable so I have been more conscious of my solid form." She wavered and Esra squinted hard to try and grasp her shape, not able to follow the flickering ghost of her friend. Instantly Nadia snapped back into focus, becoming as real and sturdy looking as Esra had ever seen her.

"Can ye go completely invisible?" Esra's mouth was open in astonishment.

"Not completely. And it is harder fer me to go undetected around advanced sorcerers. They may not get a good solid picture like ye are getting right now, but a vague glimpse."

"One of the things that drives Tallen mad, fer example," she continued, "is that there is no spell that can stop me from being like this, even temporarily. That is the advantage of the Keepers, of having these natural gifts. Because Elite magick is forced and identical, we are able to directly counter their spells but they cannot do the same. They may be able to put other spells around to keep me out of somewhere, or alert them when I enter a place, but they cannot remove or counter my powers of stealth directly. And many times I can get around those other spells as well. Tallen once had an Elite magnify his hearing to try and discover me sneaking into one of his camps, but it didn't work very well because he heard *everything* ten times louder, including the wind or a buzzing fly. They've really been frustrated with me. Imagine the information I've been able to gain on tasks to penetrate the Elite camps. It has been immensely useful fer the Keepers lately and it is certainly keeping me busy. Especially since my fourth Gift, the Bracelet of Evening Eye, allows me to see in the dark as well as I do at midday. That combined with my speed and stealth has been called upon fer many tasks as of late."

"So what does it feel like?"

"Kind of like when yer in water. Sort of weightless and free. Or maybe even a little like the water itself, fluid and smooth, uncommitted to a specific place or time."

Esra pondered what Cane had said about Tallen trying to turn people against their will and about the difference between natural and forced sorcery. What Nadia did seemed very much a part of her, an extension of her being. She could imagine it would be very different if it was some type of a spell forced upon her.

"So yer going to try to teach me, the loudest, clumsiest girl in the Kingdom, some of that? Hasn't Baelin told ye? I couldn't sneak up on a stampeding herd of vernok."

"Well, we've no time fer a true discussion of magick but we can start with the basics. I can at least give ye some advice so ye can make it with the stampede, but I don't recommend trying to break into Tallen's fortress after just one lesson."

"Deal," Esra laughed.

Nadia placed her finger to her mouth as she pointed out a rabbit in the center of the field.

I know she's talented, Esra thought to herself, *but I doubt that she can catch a rabbit in the middle…*

There was a brief flash and Esra saw various waves of what resembled Nadia racing across the grass. Suddenly her ghostly form was upon the creature and she saw the rabbit's realization. It crouched down into the earth, preparing to bolt, but it was too late. Nadia grabbed the animal firmly by the scruff of its neck and held it up proudly. She came back into full focus as she walked back towards where Esra stood.

"Jumping jig!" Esra clapped her hands as Nadia took a well-earned bow. "I thought ye were going to try and take me with ye this time."

"Then I fear ye wouldn't have had a true appreciation of my skill," Nadia teased as she set the rabbit on the ground and watched it hop quickly away.

"Why didn't ye keep him fer dinner?" Esra said with confusion as she watched the rabbit disappear into the brush. "I don't think I've ever let an animal go once I've had him good and caught. Although with yer skills ye can probably catch a hundred."

"We don't need him to make meat fer eating. Keepers don't eat animals, we just replicate their taste by magick," Nadia explained.

"Replicate? What do ye mean?"

"That's a discussion fer another time." Nadia waved the question away and continued with the lesson. "Now I want ye to try to sneak up on me as best ye can. I'm going to close my eyes and cover my ears out in the field."

Esra pondered how she could best rise to this challenge. She knew she was not capable of anything near what her Elf-friend could do. That was not even a consideration. As Nadia started back out into the field, Meshok trotted up to them, sensing something of importance was about to occur.

"Aside from Cane, this is my first real lesson from a Keeper," she said to Meshok, rubbing her vigorously behind the ears. The Wolf flopped over with a grunt and smiled blissfully as Esra massaged her exposed belly.

"Ready!" Nadia called.

"Here goes nothing," Esra whispered. Tensing her body in nervous preparation, she lifted her left foot stiffly and gingerly placed it on the ground. Trying to keep her breathing low, she followed with the right foot, taking very small steps. Her body was rigid with the knowledge that every movement she made could be detected. *Not too bad,* she thought. Continuing her slow journey, she was ecstatic to find that a minute later she was only five feet from Nadia, and had only snapped two twigs in the process.

Nadia pulled her hands from her ears and turned about suddenly. "Ye have taken thirty four steps so far, and I have heard every single one of them like a galloping vernok."

"And here I thought I was doing so well," Esra sighed.

"The problem is that ye are trying too hard to be quiet. Yer body is all tense. Loosen up and think about being fluid. Close yer eyes and imagine that ye are not stepping on the ground but rejoining it, as if ye are the same. There is a force that connects ye and all living things. Imagine that force as a line between ye and the ground, as if yer foot is really still attached in some way, even when ye lift it."

Esra did as she was told and imagined herself made of earth, her feet covered in soft, lush grass. She could feel her muscles loosening, her body becoming more like it was when she was riding Roja or swimming with Meshok.

"Keep yer eyes closed and trust that ye will meet softly with the ground. Join, not step," Nadia urged. Softly, Esra joined the earth with her left foot, swaying against a sudden gust of wind, fighting to keep her balance.

"Don't fight the wind or anything else that may change yer course. Let it be what it is." Esra focused on letting her body move with the wind, forcing her muscles to relax even further. It was a strange sensation to give up control. A bruncabird called in the distance, his low cry echoing hauntingly through the open field. A sudden burst of Honeysuckle filled her nostrils, and she sighed pleasantly. Esra fought the desire to open her eyes, to see where she was going, but she knew to do so would break the spell of trust she was experiencing between the earth and her body.

"Much better!" Nadia encouraged. "Just a few more steps."

Esra moved peacefully towards the sound of her friend's voice. Opening her eyes, she saw that they had traveled half the length of the clearing.

"Oh," she exclaimed in surprise. "That felt brilliant."

"That's a great job fer a first lesson, much improved. Let's head back to the others and get something to eat."

"I agree," Esra walked proudly back towards camp as Meshok came to congratulate her.

"And ye thought I would be a disaster," she bragged to the Wolf. Suddenly Esra's foot caught on an upturned root and she watched the sky tumble before her eyes as she fell crashing to the ground. Sitting up to rub her skinned knee, she looked up into the panting face of Meshok, who seemed to be grinning as she gave her friend's face a long, wet lick.

"On second thought, maybe the stampede is still wishful thinking."

Nicole Burr

XVI

Baelin decided that they would take a longer than usual dinner break in order to arrive at the city under the guise of nightfall. Esra was grateful for the extra rest and took the time to give Roja a well-deserved rub down. She picked up the soft brush Fynn had given her, which was made of some strange Elvish material, and began to massage the tall white haunches of her new friend. Roja swung his neck back in happiness, his long mane whipping fiercely about his head as Esra tried to shield her eyes from the assaulting tendrils. They had begun to follow this playful routine each time they stopped, with Esra attempting to brush Roja while he danced about in a mischievous diversion. It was obvious that the horse needed little attention, if any, as his white coat never seemed to get tangled or properly dirty given their surroundings. But Esra felt obligated to tend to him as she would any other animal she cared for, especially one that was made to carry her halfway across the Kingdom.

She also wanted to take this time to check thoroughly for any injuries. It was hard to imagine that the horse was free of bruises after all the thumping and poking and kicking included in one of her mounting attempts. So Esra took care to brush the light hair with much more care than she gave her own. Roja seemed to find this attentiveness amusing and continued to tease her caretaker with his prancing evasions, but settled after a few moments to enjoy the attention. Even a toughened skycatcher could not deny the refreshment of such attending, especially after such hard riding. After their few minutes together Roja left to gather with the other horses for some food and water as Esra settled down for a quick nap. Before long they were up and clumsily mounted again, riding smoothly east.

By the time they had reached the outskirts of town there had been no trees for a couple of hours except for the occasional orchard on a

108

farm. Tirbaz was fairly larger than Sorley, although not considered one of the three large cities, and had a vast grey stone wall that encased its inhabitants and various buildings.

"We can't risk taking the skycatchers into town. One massive horse will be suspicious enough, but a group of five would be simply begging fer trouble." Baelin explained as they dismounted. "We'll proceed or foot te the Vernok Inn and then meet our charge."

Approaching the town in the dead of night, Esra was fairly disappointed that the first place she had ever traveled to she would not be able to properly explore. Sensing her fallen mood, Meshok came to give her friend's dangling hand a good sloppy licking before taking off to the west. Too many people, Esra knew. The Great Wolf would not risk being seen.

Barely able to keep herself awake on the long evening's journey, the anticipation of their arrival began to give Esra renewed energy as they came within sight of the main entrance. It was a huge stone archway, flanked on either side by life size sculptures of roaring Lion heads. Esra had never seen a Lion, but knew from some of Cane's picture books that they existed somewhere far east of LeVara. The heavy wooden doors were held open by two thickly braided ropes tied securely to the standing wall, ready for removal should the entrance need to be sealed off suddenly. It was a different atmosphere from her home of Sorley, where everything was open and inviting. Esra noticed that there were two guards with long spears posted at each end.

"I hope that there won't be any problems fer us," she offered nervously.

"Aye, me too," Baelin agreed.

Passing through the entrance, the inn was one of the first buildings on the left. It was a sad, dilapidated looking structure with a thatched roof and worn, empty furniture scattered on a small front porch.

"Is this the only place in town to stay?" Esra asked with displeasure.

"No, but tis closest te the entrance and so the best spot fer us. The less we are seen here, the better," Baelin explained. "It is already a great risk that we have come here at all."

"So who are we meeting here that we would risk such danger?"

"Her name is Maeve. She is here on business with a group that doesn't know of her true identity."

Baelin walked back towards the entrance, as if to leave, then turned abruptly right to slink along the grey stone wall bordering the edge of the town. Esra and the others trailed behind, staying as close to the cold, weathered stone as possible. Continuing along the wall, Esra noticed after a few quiet minutes that a hooded figure awaited them in the distance.

As they approached, she could see that the person underneath the cloak was an old woman. She was standing casually, as if waiting for a familiar friend, and looked up expectantly at the advancing group. Relief washed over her face as she recognized Baelin at the head.

"I'm glad you made it. In here," she spoke quietly and motioned for them to go inside a small shed that appeared to be a stockroom for an alehouse. "We haven't much time."

The Assembly filed in and Esra followed, pulling the door shut behind her. The woman took a small lantern that was sitting on a barrel and lit it. The room flooded with light as she pulled her hood down, revealing grey hair that was curled tightly and streaked with dark brown. Her skin was a darkened hue, but not quite as dark as Esra's Elf friends.

"Baelin, Nadia, Fynn, Arland," the woman nodded in greeting at each of them. "And you must be Esra."

"Aye," she answered.

"Let's get right to it, then," she sat down on one of the ale barrels and the rest of the group followed her lead. "Esra, I will explain quickly. My name is Maeve and I am a descendant of Cane."

Esra's mouth opened in shock as the old woman continued. "I know that I must appear at least as old as him, but remember that he does not age. One of my ancestors, Padri, was Elvish. She was a member of the Elders and died many years ago. Before he became a Great Keeper, Cane was married to Padri and they had a child."

Looking at Maeve more intensely now, she could see how the woman vaguely resembled Cane with her thin, serious face that seemed to pull down just a bit at its corners. And her curly hair was very similar to Nadia's, which she guessed was an inherited Elvish trait. She spoke with an accent more akin to the western Kingdom, and it reminded her of Lara.

"I am a secret informant to the Elders, and have been for many years. Being part Human has allowed me to penetrate into certain groups to gain information on the movements of Tallen and his Elites.

"I bring you news of Tallen and the state of LeVara, and I'm afraid it isn't very good. Tallen has already overtaken Kiran Brae, our great city to the west, and will be using it as a supply base for his army. It is the closest great city to The Frost Grounds, and so we knew it would be his first move to take it. After he becomes fully settled in Kiran Brae, which hopefully will take some time, he will move towards conquering Mahesh. Hals Arün remains untouched, but I daresay not fer long. He knows it is the closest to the Stronghold, and he wants to be well prepared before he attempts to capture it."

A gasp escaped Esra's lips as the realization of war settled in the air. "Kiran Brae, captured? It can't be."

"It's true, it has finally begun. The King is taken entirely unaware and his army, if one can even call it that, is in complete disarray. Some of the people in Kiran Brae made a feeble attempt to rebel but they were quelled almost instantly. Almost half of the men were killed and the other half are being forced to work in the quarry, mining for rocks to reinforce Tallen's new fortress. Any boy or girl that was left alive and old enough to walk is being made to do the Elite soldiers bidding. And the women, well I suppose you can guess that's just as bad. I heard that he's also taking babies from their mothers, to grow as fresh new additions for his army. Anyone who so much as gives the wrong look to a soldier is slaughtered immediately. Having such an indifferent King has cost everyone. No one is prepared. Most people outside of Kiran Brae do not yet know of the falling of the great city. But it will not take much longer for news to reach the Kingdom east of The Naduri River.

"You will need to tell Cane and the other Great Keepers about the true state of LeVara when you arrive back at the Stronghold. I also need to inform you that the Elders are preparing to leave, and the War Council will commence in two fortnights."

"Two fortnights!" Esra exclaimed in a loud whisper. "But that's so far away! People are dying, and in the meantime Tallen may try to take over Mahesh."

"Not likely, but it's possible," Maeve stated simply. "A War Council has not occurred for hundreds of years and we will need time to gather all the races. Esra, we are hoping to have the Unni and Shendari in attendance as well as the Elves. The King is also sending his son, Prince Bronnen, as a representative for his Kingdom."

"The King knows about the Keepers?" Esra asked.

"Kings have always known about the Keepers. They have just known how important it is to keep any information about them hidden. And to be quite honest, King Keridon has another reason. He simply has never cared enough about the condition of LeVara to worry much about them. And now he is going to pay for his disinterest, for the Kingdom is falling into the hands of a madman."

A silence settled over the small, cramped space as the dreadful news became a reality in each person's head. Esra's thoughts were slow, as if her mind were trapped in thick mud. Suddenly she felt a heat rise up in her chest.

"Taking over the Kingdom? How could this happen? A man I never even knew existed, no one did. And now the three glorious cities of LeVara; Kiran Brae, Hals Arün, and Mahesh. Already controlled or about to be taken over by Tallen and his Elites. Everyone I know will fall victim to his treachery. Be made a slave or die in the process of opposing him. We have to stop him. We have to…"

"Esra, how goes your training?" Maeve's voice broke through Esra's agitation and the worrisome trance everyone was brooding under. "The Keepers have been looking forward to your return to the Stronghold for quite some time. Actually, for the entire twenty years since your birth. We have all let ourselves dream that the daughter of two Great Keepers would be the end of the threat of Tallen."

"Esra's been studying under Cane since childhood," Baelin answered softly. "But only the last two seasons have her studies intensified te include more…useful topics,"

"Then you have not yet used any magick or passed any tests?" Maeve leaned forward with her grey eyebrows raised.

"No, not yet," Esra admitted. "And I now fear that there will not be time."

"There's always time," Arland reassured her, placing a soft hand on her arm. A warm sensation swelled over her body, and Esra grudgingly allowed herself to be calmed by his charm.

"Well," Maeve stood up suddenly, brushing off her dress. "I wish you all luck, but I fear I must be getting back to my room. Wait here for a few minutes to make sure we're not seen together before leaving."

"Aye," Baelin stood as well, offering his hand to the old half-Elf. "And be careful. We will need ye when the time comes."

Maeve nodded and opened the door, giving one last look at Esra before disappearing into the dark veil of night. Baelin returned to the barrel he had been sitting on and rubbed his temples, forehead scrunched in deep thought. Arland whistled softly and rocked back in his seat. "So it's finally happening, then."

"Aye," Nadia agreed, flabbergasted. "I mean, I knew this day would come fer a long time, but now it just seems so sudden."

Esra felt as if her skin was about to come off her bones in agitation. All she could think of were her grandparents, alone and vulnerable at their farm. All the people of Sorley, Lara and Mr. Sturik, their new daughter. They were all in danger.

"We have to leave now," she jumped up. "We have to warn them."

"Nay, not tonight," Baelin interrupted softly. "We get a good night's rest and leave at dawn. If we run off now in the middle of the night after only just arriving it will cause suspicion, which we cannot afford. B'sides, none of us will be much good after travelin' all day."

"He's right," Arland assented. "Tomorrow we will ride long and hard, but tonight we should get some well-earned rest in a real bed."

"What's a bed?" Fynn teased. "It's been so long since I've lain in one I think I've forgotten. I also have te warn ye, I'm scared of the dark. So if I jump in with Nadia, just know…"

"Just know I'll be slicing yer head off," Arland scowled dramatically as he drew a line along his throat.

"Alright, alright, sword boy. Save it fer the Elites." Fynn cracked open the door as Baelin blew out the lantern. Esra followed her friends as they slipped out of the storage shed one at a time, slinking along the wall towards the inn. If it hadn't been under such dismal circumstances, perhaps she would have enjoyed meeting the descendant of her favorite teacher.

Coming upon the side entrance of the inn, Baelin held the door for her as she ducked inside the damp smelling building, her eyes adjusting to the dim light. A group of men and women in the far corner were singing a raucous drinking song around a table, swaying and sloshing ale over the sides of their glasses. The abrupt change in mood stunned Esra momentarily, like stepping out into the vicious cold after being beside a warm fire. It seemed impossible that people would be celebrating right now, going on with their lives as if the world was not ending. But she knew that soon enough the news of Tallen's treachery would reach Tirbaz and even the atmosphere of this bawdy inn would change. She envied their ignorance and wished for a moment that she were one of them, and that none of this was happening after all.

"Come on, Es," Fynn took her elbow gently and led her towards the stairs. "Didn't know ye were a fan of drunken songs at a questionable alehouse."

"No, it just reminds me a little of home."

"I see. So yer grandparents are drunkards, then."

She gave him a look of resignation and he put an arm around her shoulder. "Aye, it must be hard. I forget sometimes that yer life is not at the Stronghold like ours. That ye are moving farther away from yer home while we get closer te ours."

She smiled weakly before turning to ascend the long row of stairs. Their meeting with Maeve and her destructive revelations had left Esra exhausted, and she was suddenly grateful that their Fifth, Baelin, had had enough sense to insist they stay the night. She couldn't wait to collapse into a deep sleep in a normal bed.

"An besides, maybe after spending some time with yer parents it will begin te feel like home," he suggested cheerfully. "I think ye'll really like it there."

She hoped for everyone's sake that he was right.

XVII

Esra had been under the impression that they had been traveling hard on their first day to Tirbaz, but it was nothing compared to the pace they maintained for the last three nights. She had seen Fynn talking softly to the horses the morning they had left the inn and questioned Arland about it. He had explained that the horses were in fact quite interested in the course of events in LeVara and were grateful when Fynn was able to communicate any progress to them. The skycatchers had strengthened ties with the Keepers since Fynn's ability to speak with them had reinforced their bonds.

Whatever he had said to them, the horses attacked their journey to the Stronghold with a determined ferocity. Their riders returned the fervor and pushed the skycatchers on relentlessly, stopping only for brief periods a few times a day to rest or eat. Esra had intended to ask more questions about her parents in preparation of meeting them, but her exhaustion was overwhelming. She figured that maybe it was better this way, she had less time to worry. In fact she could barely stay alert long enough to eat or cling to Roja's back. Even Fynn had not sung any funny songs about dinner.

The landscape had gradually been changing from the flat, virtually treeless terrain to deep green rolling hills. Plants and animals that Esra didn't recognize sped past her as she rode towards the Jade Gardens, towards her parents. By the time it had reached dusk on the third day, Esra watched as the flashes of open countryside began to grow more populated with thick, lush trees and plants. Fynn, who was naturally skilled in navigation and had been riding at the front of the Assembly, held up his hand in a signal to slow the horses. Esra pushed herself up from Roja's back where she had been lying and took notice of her first real view of the Jade Gardens. She watched in wonder as they crossed the threshold of the trees, and it seemed as if the earth gave a satisfied sigh of approval as they passed.

A perpetual mist blanketed the entire area, creating a mysterious and sedated atmosphere. Esra felt immediately calmer as she let herself be enveloped by this mist, and it covered everything around it like a soft blanket of Snow. Birds called out to one another loudly, creating a cacophony of varying lengths and tones.

"I didn't know there could be so many different shades of green," she breathed. The plant life had become so dense that the only remaining slivers of light were barely able to penetrate the canopy of trees. Orange flowers with petals the size of Esra's hand were scattered about in a dizzying display, punctuated by large stalks of what appeared to be glowing pink Corn. A group of small purple and blue flowers turned as she rode slowly past, until Esra noticed that they had a small black eyes blinking towards her from each petal. She ducked as a large yellow winged beast flew past her right side, trailing five foot long feathers in a soft floating wave behind it.

"It's as if the plants in this place not only have unexpected colors, but textures as well," she said to Roja. "Some leaves look more like fur or liquid than vegetation."

The thick undergrowth was a bluish hue, giving the impression that the forest floor, if one could even call it that, was an undulating sea of plant life. The trees grew in all different directions; some hung as if they were weeping while others had branches that climbed straight up towards the sky. Vines tangled themselves around the trees and plants, small white flowers covering the thick tendrils. Esra had known that the outside world was indeed alive, but nowhere in her experience was that more startlingly apparent than here. A small orange lizard hissed at her, sauntering slowly along a branch of fern-like leaves.

"And how is Fynn able to lead the way? There's no path, or if there is one it's entirely indistinguishable. It looks as though no one's come through here fer a hundred years."

Turning around, she thought that they would certainly be leaving a dense trail of trampled undergrowth behind them for all to see, but the plants seemed to spring slowly back into their upright position after only a few moments. It was as if they were bowing down in greeting to the travelers and rising to bid them farewell as they passed. She had never encountered such a phenomenon before. Not only was it mesmerizing in its beauty, but the Jade Gardens took care to leave no trace of Human disturbance. It was no wonder that the Keepers chose to live here.

"Beautiful, eh?" Arland pulled Errol up beside her and Roja, motioning to the forest. It seemed that the Gardens also had a powerful effect on him. Looking at the Keeper of Charm against the backdrop of such rich hues did not belittle his beauty, but rather made him appear even more striking. It was hard to get used to someone that attractive, those piercing light blue eyes that seemed to see into the soul of a person. It was vaguely distracting to be around him, although Esra knew that it had something to do with her own awkwardness around others, especially young men. But Arland's handsomeness seemed to be just as natural as a leaf growing on a tree. He had a gentle way of easing tensions, it reminded her of Lara. She wondered briefly if her shop keep friend had had been just as speechless as Esra was right now when she first laid eyes on this place. Arland absentmindedly pulled at the long braid trailing down his left shoulder as they rode on quietly.

"It's unbelievable," Esra admitted.

"Aye," he brushed a stray wisp of wavy hair away from his forehead. "It seems like it is a living, breathing thing of its own. The Jade Gardens have a way of entrancing all who venture here. And trust me Esra, there is so much more ye will get to see. Fira Nadim Forest of the Unni, Fire Lake of the Shendari, The Frost Grounds and Painted Fields to the far west. And best of all, The Eshomee Ledges where my people live, and our great fortress The Veiled City. The Kingdom of LeVara is eternally vast in its landscape."

"I can barely wait," Esra confessed. "Although I fear it may be awhile before I get to travel fer pleasure."

"Aye, it may be," he agreed. "But ye'll get to see much in yer lifetime, Esra, Keeper of Unknown Powers."

She blushed gently at the compliment and looked up at the sound of distant voices. Squinting, she could scarcely make out the shapes of what seemed to be dwellings straight ahead of them. She had expected to see a towering edifice with tall white citadels, a fortress fit for a King and the greatest sorcerers in LeVara. A castle for the last defense, complete with battlements and a drawbridge. It greatly surprised her that the area before her appeared to be the opposite of grand. She couldn't see much, but it was vividly apparent that no grand estate awaited them. As they approached, a flurry of muffled sounds and motions erupted as people began darting in and out of places, calling out to one another.

"They are excited at our arrival and have assumed from the addition of a fifth member that we have managed to bring ye back safely," Arland explained.

"Oh," she said softly. It was amazing that people who didn't know her could rejoice in her coming. "I wish I could feel their excitement, but the truth is I'm nervous. Nervous that the people here won't like me, that I'll prove to be a failure. Or more specifically, that my parents will be disappointed in who I have become, which is basically a plain, clumsy farm girl from a small town."

"That," Arland stated simply, "is utterly untrue. Ye are far from plain, even without any magick."

Esra tried to let his encouragement seep into her. "At least my education with Cane may prove to be of greater worth here. Last summer I had a conversation with my grandmother in our kitchen about how she had claimed that my knowledge would be needed one day. Maybe those endless hours of studying may finally come of use."

"That's the spirit. Ye know, this place was a result of the four races working together. Can ye see some of the dwellings over there? The Unni of Fira Nadim Forest brought the massive trees that comprise the basic structure of the buildings, called yanquor trees. These are trees that have lived fer hundreds of years and grow to an extraordinary size."

She watched as the shapes before them took on a more solid form, revealing long, low, earth colored dwellings. Arland was right about the trees, they were massive. If her Assembly stood next to one another and spread their arms they would not even cover half the width of one trunk. A flowering Ivy covered a good portion of the wooden structures, blending them seamlessly into their lush surroundings.

"The Unni are extremely skilled in carving, a skill they developed from their cleverness in weaponry and blacksmithing. Ye will see that all of the furniture here; the tables, chairs, beds, everything is hand carved in intricate patterns and forms. This was the Unni's contribution to the Stronghold."

"What do ye mean contribution?" Esra asked.

"Well, every race gave something to build this place, both in matter and ability. The Stronghold was not built in a time of war. It was created hundreds of years ago when the four races lived and worked together in peace. They had wanted to build a place fer training, where the different peoples could share their skills and traditions."

Esra could barely imagine a time when she would be working side by side with an Unni or Shendari. "It makes me happy that it was not war that brought the peoples together, forcing a bond, but rather a common good. There had once been a time when the races wanted to share fer the sake of learning and community."

"It was a glorious age, yer right. Not something our generation has ever been able to attain, unfortunately."

"What else did the races give?"

"Although the Unni were the woodworkers," he continued, "ye may notice the roof has a...fishlike quality."

She focused her attention in the waning light to the roofs of the dwellings. They seemed to be made of overlapping plates of varying red sheens, indeed like a fish.

"The work of the Shendari, the water people. They shed their skin about every twenty years, so ye can imagine how long it took to collect all of it, and how precious the material. The scales that their bodies are covered in are not only water repellent but nearly indestructible. Ye will see many suits of armor and shields made from them. And the only person alive now that can forge them is Baelin."

"His first Gift, the Hammer of the Shendari," Esra recalled as she gaped open mouthed at the roofs, which shimmered darkly. The structures, although made entirely of material foreign to this region, seemed to blend perfectly into the backdrop of the Gardens. "It looks like the people who built these had obviously taken care that they didn't disrupt the tranquil forest atmosphere. I was expecting something more like The King's Hold, but this is a pleasant surprise. So then what about the Elves?"

"My people," Arland smiled proudly, "brought the stone of the mountains. Ye will see our craftsmanship in the floors of all the dwellings, the pillars of the grand halls, and sculptures placed throughout. We are also responsible fer the marble fireplaces in each room, although they have never been used in any real sense."

"What do ye mean?"

"Well, there is no true winter here. It does become somewhat colder in the change of seasons, but the Keepers have ways of maintaining fires without actually burning anything. There is a fire and flames but wood is not consumed."

Esra did not understand how one could have a fire without burning wood but she listened quietly as he continued.

"Ten years ago, when Nadia and I first came here, I did not take it as good as ye. I remember Nadia sitting in front of me on a skycatcher as her form shimmered in excitement, but all I could do was sulk. I did not want to leave the mountains of my ancestors nor did I understand why I needed to come here. The Eshomee Ledges were my home. Nadia and I are from the Hyvva tribe, as ye can see from the markings on our foreheads. The Hyvvas are some of the oldest Elves in Idona, and have had more Keepers in their line than any other.

"I was not originally sent here to become a Keeper. I came because the only way my mother would let Nadia travel to the Stronghold at such a young age was if her twin brother went with her. I was to stay with her fer the first few moons until she was comfortable here and then return home. The Great Keepers had agreed to this, of course, since they were used to some of the Keepers coming as mere children. My sister was delighted, of course, but I was bitter. I would never admit it, but I was jealous of her skills and resented that she was starting an adventure that I could not join."

"So ye didn't know ye were a Keeper then?" Esra asked.

"Nay, I was much like ye in that respect. I understand how ye feel, not knowing what ye are or if it will be enough, or what yer purpose is. My skills were very subtle at first, and they were not of a physical nature. At home I was able to convince people of practically anything. I could 'charm' my way out of trouble. But there didn't seem to be any magick in that. And being handsome is not a thing of sorcery, or so they thought at first. I also had no evidence of the mark of Tur, or the rash, as Nadia had. It was only after I was here a few fortnights, watching Nadia being introduced to the way of Keepers, that Talitha came to find me. She looked just as puzzled as I when she told me she had my first test.

"It was then that Nadia's teacher gave me a few simple spells to try, and they found I had an enormous talent fer influence magick. At once I understood what my powers were and how to tap into them; I did not even need spells to make objects move around or convince people to do my bidding. Ye have to understand, I could not use a simple influence magick spell on an advanced sorcerer, but to common folk I can make them say or do almost anything I desire. The only exception is that I must be in fairly close proximity to them, and the more advanced the request, the less people I can affect. So I can make an entire crowd of people feel generally happy or angry, but I could only make a few people stand on their head.

"I could see the apprehension in Talitha's eyes as she told me gently that this was a great responsibility, that I had the ability to bend people to my will. I must never use it against anyone or fer my own gain. It was then that they introduced me to the Five Laws of Keepers and asked me if I wanted to stay at the Stronghold and become one of them. The next day the markings of Tur began to appear and I made the decision to stay."

"Bumbling huckfly," Esra murmured in surprise. They sat in silence as Esra passed two small purple birds hopping on a low branch. The one seemed to be holding a large Grub, trying frantically to keep it away from the other by jumping about. She tried to picture Arland as a child, his piercing blue eyes and temptingly crooked smile. How difficult it must have been to know you could practically control someone else. Esra's thoughts were interrupted as they entered the lush field in front of the Stronghold, the skycatchers' hooves gently clomping on the padded ground. She continued forward with a mixture of excitement and nervous anticipation, eyes darting around for any sign of her parents.

Her friends leapt down from their horses as a large group of people rushed forward to greet them. Feeling fairly awkward and not quite knowing what to do, Esra lowered herself from Roja's back and stroked the horse briskly down his flanks. Were her parents here among the excited chatter of welcoming friends and family? She dare not look up to see as her heart pounded loudly in her ears.

"Thank ye, my dear Roja," Esra whispered. "Ye travel faster and more graciously than anyone I know."

"Esra!"

She heard a familiar voice call out to her from the front of what appeared to be the main dwelling, as it was the largest and seemed to be at the center of the rest. The crowd of people became abruptly silent and parted slightly as the person made their way slowly towards Esra. Narrowing her eyes in the failing light, it was a few moments before she recognized the tall, long figure and ceremonial composure.

"Cane!"

She rushed towards her old teacher, catching him around the waist in a relieved embrace. She was not normally so emotional or affectionate with him, but the strange events of late had caused her nervousness to finally explode at the sight of something familiar. The crowd behind her laughed as he patted her head gently.

"Hello, dear girl," Cane said softly before peeling her tenderly away from him and looking her over. "All in one piece, that's a good start."

"Aye," she spoke breathlessly. "I have so much to ask ye. So much to tell ye! Do ye know how my grandparents are? I met Maeve. How come ye never told me about yer wife? I was kidnapped by the Elites. Did ye know Tallen has taken over Kiran Brae?"

"Oh dear," Cane raised his eyebrows in typical teacher fashion. "Has she been like this the whole time?"

"Worse," Fynn teased. "I kept a large rock in me pocket te knock her out with, but it still didn't stop her, she babbles even when unconscious. *'Why'd ye knock me out? What kind of rock is that? Are we there yet?'* Plain stubborn if ye ask me."

"I see," Cane chuckled. "Myself or someone else will be happy to answer all of yer questions after ye get a good night's rest. To answer the most important one, yer grandparents are alright. They wanted me to give ye this as a token to prove they doing well."

He pulled a long wooden item from the pocket of his cloak. Esra took the bread beater into her hands and laughed in relief. Only they would think of sending such a foolish thing, and she was immensely grateful for it.

"Alright," she agreed. Exhaustion washed over her then in a heavy wave and she swayed on her feet.

"We will have yer horse and things taken care of," Cane grabbed her elbow to steady her. "Nadia, can ye show Esra to her room please?"

"Of course," Nadia stepped forward and took her elbow from Cane guiding her through the whispering crowd and around the right side of the main dwelling. Esra had not realized how much her body ached from the stress of everything that had happened in the last few weeks. She also had to admit that she was alternately relieved and disappointed that her parents were not there to greet her.

"Where were my parents? After almost twenty years, I'd assumed they would want to see their long lost daughter. At least everyone made it sound as if they truly missed me. Maybe they were very busy, the Kingdom being taken over and all. Then again Cane had been able to come."

"I'm sure there's a good reason," Nadia assured her. It was all Esra could do to keep from collapsing as her friend steered her towards a cluster of small circular houses. These were also made from the large yanquor trees, but unlike the long, rectangular structures of the main dwellings they were round like a tree. The houses were spaced fairly well apart, about fifty paces, affording privacy to the ones who resided there without losing their sense of community. She couldn't tell how many houses were actually in this area from the dense forest and darkening sky, but she was guessing it was quite a lot.

"Ye'll be in the same dwelling as me. Depending on the size of the house, there are two to eight people in any given one, but always five rooms."

"Ye mean ye don't live with yer brother?" Esra asked weakly.

"When Arland and I were younger we stayed in one of the family houses over there in the middle of the Gardens. Now that we're older, however, we both wanted a little more privacy. I still see him practically every day. Sometimes an Assembly will decide to live together fer a period to bond. And if I choose to live with my brother, or another man fer that matter, it would be perfectly acceptable. There are no real rules here, just general principles we use to guide our decisions. We follow a set of morals that we know as the Five Laws. We enforce no more or less."

"Oh," Esra nodded. "Arland mentioned those."

The spell of dizziness that had overtaken her had begun to subside slightly, and to her relief they walked towards a house near the front at the far right. She wasn't sure she would have made it much farther. Willing her heavy feet up the steps, she arrived on a small porch area that wrapped around the entire house. Esra watched, too tired to be stunned as Nadia whispered a few words to open the door before they approached. The inside of the corridor was as round as the outside, with two doors on each side and an open entryway directly ahead of them. Nadia lit a few candles on the entry table with a flick of her wrist and handed one to her friend.

"There is room fer three here, but one has since gotten married and the other has been...well, killed unfortunately," Nadia explained. "So it's just been me fer the past two seasons. I must say, I'm glad to have a roommate again, although I'm not here much, especially as of late."

Esra was glad as well that she would be allowed to stay with Nadia, as it was one less adjustment she would have to make in this new place. And she had to admit that the two of them had grown closer than she had expected over the last few days, closer than any female friends she had ever had in Sorley. There was a quiet understanding between them already.

"The first door on the left is the washroom, and the open area straight ahead is the common room. My room is the first one on the right." Nadia walked over to the second door on the left and swung it open. "And here will be yer room."

Nadia walked around the room and flicked her wrist again to light the five circular lanterns on the wall, illuminating the small area. A long bed was pushed up against the right wall, and Esra was surprised to see that her meager possessions were already at the foot. A nightstand with three shelves was next to the bed and a small desk sat underneath the one large window overlooking the porch. At the other end of the room was a dresser and tall shelf, both with rounded corners. There was an absence of straight lines in the house's structure, with the ceiling sloping upwards towards the center of the dwelling. It was very different from the sharp corners and square angled Human furnishings she was used to. If she had not been so tired, Esra would have enjoyed studying the intricate craftsmanship of the Unni. She smiled and thought of Arland's proud lesson as she looked at the floor of the room, a beautifully polished blue stone.

"If ye need anything, please come get me," Nadia assured her. "Otherwise I will leave ye to get some rest, and I daresay I am in need of some myself."

"Thank ye," Esra placed her hand sincerely on her friends arm, "fer everything."

"Well, after all they are paying me to be nice to ye," Nadia teased, exiting the room in shimmering, stealth-like fashion. The door shut softly behind her, leaving its occupant alone for the first time in many, many days.

Esra sighed and sat down on the bed, folding her hands in her lap. Now that she was alone, the infinite questions came swirling back into her mind. She decided, against the weakness in her bones, to unpack a little to clear her head. Groaning as she lifted herself up, Esra reached for the nearest bag and dumped it on the bed. There wasn't much there, as she had obviously left Sorley in a bit of a hurry. The things she had bought at Trader's Day comprised the majority of her possessions, along with three generously donated tunics and one thin cotton skirt from Nadia. She would need to find some clothes of her own, maybe tomorrow, since her friend's small Elvish frame was not meant to be covering Esra's tall, lean one.

After sorting everything into piles and moving it into the dresser, she reached for the next satchel and placed the bread beater on the nightstand next to her bed. Examining the beautiful Unni furniture, she discovered a small hidden chamber in the desk, where she hid a few of her more private items, including her coin purse and Baelin's knife. A soft knock at the door pulled her from her preoccupation with the desk and she went to see what Nadia wanted.

Opening the door briskly, Esra began to explain her discovery, "I really like the secret compartment in the desk! I think that once I get a chance to explore this place, I'm going to really…"

Looking up at the shadow in her doorway, Esra noticed with a jolt of shock that the figure was not Nadia's small, slight frame but rather a tall, slender woman. She wore a formal gown of pale lavender, with her auburn hair twisted up in an intricate knot with glimmering gems. The lady was looking at her with eyes wide as if she too was surprised at what she found when the door had opened. A smile crept over her kind looking face, revealing two straight rows of white teeth. Maybe this was Nadia's old roommate that had just moved out, coming to say hello.

"The desk was always one of my favorites as well," the lady said in low tones, stepping a little further into the light. Although she physically appeared to be in her late thirties, there was something about her eyes that suggested she was much older than that. "Esra, welcome to the Jade Gardens, the Stronghold of the Keepers. I hope that I am not disturbing you, and I know you are absolutely exhausted, but you see I could not wait another moment to come see you for myself."

"Oh," Esra was a little leery of the thought that everyone in this place would approach her like this. Then again this woman seemed very genuine and warm in her welcome. "I certainly am very tired, but I'm pleased to meet ye and very grateful that I made it here."

"And I am immensely grateful as well."

There was something in the woman's countenance that reminded

Esra of a Queen. She spoke very formally, not like the casual dialect Esra was used to nor the rougher accent of Fynn and Baelin. They both stood for a moment as the woman stared at her with unhidden admiration.

Esra finally broke the silence. "Do ye live here as a Keeper too? Are ye a friend of Nadia's?"

"Yes, I do live here. I have been here for quite a while. And a friend of Nadia I am as well. Most of the people here know me as Talitha, or the Great Keeper of Destiny. But to you, Esra, I am your mother."

XVIII

Esra, for yet another time in the last chaotic week, had been stunned into silence. She nervously gestured for the woman, her mother, to come into the room. A million thoughts swept through her brain like a stampede of anxiety, and she tried not to let her disquiet show. Talitha swept in with a graceful fluidity that almost hid the apprehension in her slightly furrowed brow. She took a seat at the chair in front of the desk, leaving Esra to plop down onto the bed.

"I had wanted to be here when you arrived, Esra. I'm so sorry," she apologized. "You see, I could barely stand the waiting, and after making everyone crazy with my pacing, I had decided to take a long ride in the Gardens. I was expecting that you were all staying away another night and would be here in the morning."

Esra nodded, still bewildered as she stared at the woman with the long face and dimpled chin that reassembled her own. This was it. The moment Esra had been waiting for her whole life. And yet she wasn't quite sure how she felt. The tension of anticipation and the sudden release as the moment arrived had overwhelmed her. She was ill-equipped to sort out her emotions for much smaller occasions, let alone something of this magnitude. Esra noticed that Talitha sat with her back in a rigidly straight line, and wondered if she always had such impeccable posture of if she too were nervous at their meeting. A brief look of uncertainty passed over her mother's face as she continued.

"Adonis, your father, wanted nothing more than to be here, you see, but he was sent away on a matter of the greatest importance. It killed him that he had to go now, after almost twenty years of longing to see you. But you know all about the state of LeVara. Cane tells me you bring confirmation that Kiran Brae has been taken over by Tallen. It is unfortunate that our meeting must be under such disastrous circumstances. That is also why I was so upset that I was not here when you arrived. You must forgive me again for that, and for coming to see you at such a late hour when you should be resting."

"No, it's alright." Esra sputtered, regaining some of her composure as she began to process the information. So that was her father's name, Adonis. "To be honest, I was very nervous to meet ye and so tired I may have fainted."

"I'm glad at least Cane was there to greet you," Talitha sighed. "He is a wonderful man. That is one of the reasons we felt it bearable to leave you in Sorley, knowing your grandparents and Cane would be right there."

"Why didn't Tallen find me through Cane?"

"Cane was actually not his name before he moved to Sorley, he was known as Zariq. And he was able to maintain his secrecy with some cloaking and influence spells. It also helped that he was pretending to be an eccentric, removed old man, which is not so far from the truth."

"How long has he been here at the Stronghold? How old is he? When did he become a Great Keeper?"

Talitha laughed at the steady barrage of questions. "Very long, very old, and also very long ago. So how is Meshok?"

"Ye know about Meshok? Did Cane, I mean, Zariq tell ye about her?" It was strange to think of Cane being anything except Cane.

"Not exactly. And don't worry, Cane prefers his current name, so you needn't refer to him as Zariq. Cane was the new name he chose for himself, which means "scholar". Very fitting. Do you remember how you found Meshok on your eighteenth birthday? It was your father and I who had arranged for you to find her, as a gift. She was a pup from a Great Wolf that often stays near Adonis and I."

Her mother got up and began pacing the floor, twisting her hands into the folds of her skirt. "We didn't think we could do it, leave you like that. But I knew that it was for the best, that the Kingdom was in danger, and that to keep you with us would put everything at risk. Tallen would have stopped at nothing if he had found out there was a child. It is amazing he did not find out sooner. Only the last year has he had any suspicions. Luckily you had not been using any sorcery and Baelin was able to watch over you. All could have been forfeit, including your life. But your father and I gave up twenty years of our only child's life, forced you to give that up. Please forgive me."

The woman buried her face in her hands and Esra sank lower into the bed. The tension in the air was so distinct it seemed to reverberate throughout the room.

Esra thought long and hard about all the times she had wished for her parents, of the pain it had caused her. She was torn between accepting this woman and her sad tale and being angry that she was ever being asked to consider accepting it. There had been no time to digest this information. Why couldn't they have just tried harder? Fought to keep her no matter what? Who gives up their only daughter? Hot tears gathered in her eyes as she tried to control her frustration. Why couldn't her childhood have been normal? Great Keepers and secret armies, it was all ridiculous. And they had lost so much time together. Could they now go on living like a family when so many secrets were in their past?

But a part of Esra knew that Talitha spoke the truth, or that at least they had done their best with what life had dealt them, which was an unfair situation for a young couple in love. She stared at the graceful woman who now stood in her room trembling with vulnerability. Esra decided that even though she didn't understand everything just yet, she was willing to meet her mother half way to try and forge a relationship. She had many things to fight in the upcoming weeks. She did not want this to be one more of them.

"Even though it has been the most…shocking revelation of my life to know that ye are both alive, I can't honestly say now that I regret the news. It may take a while to get used to all this, but I am going to try."

Talitha stood for a moment longer as she wiped a tear from her cheek and kissed her daughter on the head. "Thank you. I had dared to hope you would not be entirely resentful, at least not for long. And you must assure me that if you ever feel uncomfortable or if things become too much for you to handle, please just let us know. Adonis and I cannot even begin to try to understand what you are feeling right now."

"I must admit, to say all this was a surprise would be a vast understatement."

"Yes, and I'm sorry we had to lie to you. But if you knew we were alive, would you have tried to come find us? Never given up until you had the truth?"

Esra thought about that for a moment. "Aye, I would have. I would have wanted answers. Besides, I'm not sure that thinking I was abandoned would have been much better than thinking ye were dead."

"True," her mother agreed sadly, taking a seat at the desk again. "I am so proud of you. You are in a new world now, one filled with magick and Keepers, Tallen, the Stronghold, the four races. Learning these things cannot be easy."

"It hasn't been," Esra admitted. "I just worry that I will not be what ye need, that I will prove to be no more able at sorcery than Meshok. I don't know what ye think I have been doing fer the past twenty years, but it has not been sword fighting or casting spells."

"And that was just how we intended it to be," Talitha leaned over to pat her hand reassuringly. "Don't worry. You needn't be anything besides yourself. I know that people may look up to you or expect certain things, but I will love you even if you decide to become a cook for the Great Hall. And we intend to defeat Tallen either way."

"Trust me, ye do not want me anywhere near a cooking fire."

"Oh?" Talitha raised her eyebrows questioningly.

"Um...I'm a little clumsy," Esra admitted shyly. "Actually a lot clumsy. And after seeing how gracefully ye carry yerself, I'm assuming I got this trait from my father?"

Her mother's high pitched laughter trickled throughout the room. "Oh dear, I daresay you have. He can barely mount a horse without a mild disaster."

Esra pictured her own recent skycatcher mounting encounters and smiled to herself in amusement.

"Well, I must let you get some rest," Talitha declared, rising from her seat. "Your father will be here tomorrow for the celebration feast and you could probably sleep until dinner."

Nervousness twitched again in Esra's chest at the thought of her father. She tried to gain courage from this brief but promising reunion with her mother.

Pausing in the doorway, Talitha looked upon her daughter's face for the first time in twenty years and tried to take every detail in. The thick, dark blonde hair that fell in wild cascading waves down her back. The pale skin and high cheeks, her thin lips which curved into an endearing smile, the soft blue eyes that would surely turn an incandescent color like the purest spring water when they caught the light. The Great Keeper of Destiny decided right then that of all the wondrous things she had seen in her lifetime, this was by far the best.

XIX

As her mother predicted, Esra did not stir until well after noonmeal the next day. She awoke momentarily confused by the strange smells and sights around her, then remembered that she had indeed made it to the Stronghold and was safe and sound in her new room. She would have probably been able to sleep for longer was she not driven by an intense hunger that forced her out of bed. After a quick visit to the washroom, she went to Nadia's room to see if she was still there. A note on the door greeted her before she had a chance to knock.

Good afternoon Esra!
I slept late myself. I'm meeting with some of the other Keepers for a quick discussion about our journey and what Maeve has told us. If ye go around to the front of the main hall where ye saw Cane, there is another large dwelling to the left of it. In there is the Dining Hall. Come get something to eat when ye feel ready.
Nadia

Her growling stomach guided her towards the door without any further thought. Jogging down the porch stairs and over the lush grass, she was once again taken aback by how vivid the Gardens were. She noticed the tangles of ivy whose vines enveloped a good portion of the dwellings, easing their shape into the green backdrop of plants. Sprinkled between the dwellings were beautiful stone fountains that towered over Esra's head, displaying skycatchers, birds, and many other animals perched in threatening or regal positions. To her left was a towering carving of what she guessed was a Shendari, a subdued smile resting beneath the three small slits resembling a nose on their strange, flat face. Everything seemed to take on a renewed beauty in the bright light of day.

Esra thought then about her meeting with her mother and tried to determine her feelings about the situation. She always needed to make a concerted effort to sort through her emotions, as they were often confusing and convoluted. She could grasp intellectual concepts with ease, but judging her true mood was more difficult. Feeling the looseness in her shoulders and the absence of a knot in the back of her stomach was encouraging. Sorting through her mind was more difficult than reading the signs of stress in her body, but she knew the two were inextricably connected, so it was a good sign that she felt a release of physical stress. Esra tried to look into the depths of her being, organizing her feelings like she would a drawer full of mismatched goods. There didn't appear to be any lingering deep resentment, but there was still a loose fog of apprehension hanging over her thoughts. She decided that it was a good first meeting overall, but that only time would tell if they would be able to have a true relationship. Her adaptability to change would help alleviate the transition but there was no guarantee. She would just have to wait and see.

In her musings, Esra barely noticed when she passed the place where Nadia said the Dining Hall was and had to double back to the large curved entryway. Passing through two grand double doors, she entered into a tall, luxurious foyer. To the right was a room that appeared to be a library, and on the left the foyer opened up into the Dining Hall. All the woodwork and various stone statues had elaborate carvings of every imaginable picture and symbol. Everywhere she looked, it was like an artist had imbued their craft over every inch of the room. The beautifully polished marble floors had varying colors of green, white, and grey, and shone like the surface of water. Centered between the two rooms was a large stone fireplace in a deep green shade with curling grey accents. Looking up, she noticed that the underside of the Shendari scales which made up the roof looked just like the inside of an Oyster shell. The colors reflected in the sun made the ceiling look as if there was a sky full of shimmering gemstones. The amount of time and skill it must have taken to make such things made her head spin.

Esra turned towards the now empty Dining Room, which contained five rows, each of which was five tables long. *They weren't kidding about liking the number five,* she thought. The tables and chairs were made out of a wood so dark it was almost black. Esra had never seen such craftsmanship. No two chairs carried the same design, but yet they all seemed to complement each other. It was as if they were telling a story, from the beginning of time, for all of the races. Through their struggles and triumphs, until the creation of the Stronghold and the unity of the Kingdom. She noticed that the floors in here were almost exclusively light grey and purple, which brought out the color of the tables expertly. Once again, the light that reflected off of the high ceiling cast a mesmerizing glow over everything.

"Don't worry, Es, I saved ye some." A head popped out of one of the doors at the far back of the hall.

"Fynn!" She walked over to greet her friend, who was setting out a small feast for her at the end of one of the tables. "Thank goodness, I'm starved."

"I thought ye might be," he said, handing her a spoon. "Unfortunately we were all out of brengard stew so I had te use Meshok. Gives new meaning te 'Wolfing' something down, doesn't it?"

Fynn sat down in a chair across from her as Meshok ironically trotted in from the foyer.

"Oh no! My secret ingredient has escaped!" Fynn feigned distress as the Wolf yawned at him, circling the floor. Esra shook her head and laughed as she started in on the first dish, which seemed to be some type of broiled fish. It tasted strange and light, almost as if the texture was but a figment of the imagination that dissolved upon hitting your tongue. It seemed to Esra that all her meals with her Assembly thus far had tasted as such. The vegetables were hearty and full, but the meat was always lighter, almost like a dream. The flavor was real enough and fulfilling, but the weight of it was evasive.

"This is the false meat Nadia was talking about. She said that Keepers did not eat animals, but rather were able to replicate meat by magick."

"Aye, it is a strange thing, I know. But once ye become more familiar with our Laws, ye will understand why we do so. It's a difficult piece of magick, one that took a Keeper decades to figure out. So how are ye finding yer new quarters?"

"They're great," Esra admitted sincerely. "Everything here is so unimaginably beautiful. And I'm glad to be rooming with Nadia, even though I'm sure everyone here is very nice."

"Then I must say I'm quite jealous," Fynn sighed, "because *I* have been attempting te be Nadia's roommate fer more than a few moons. She keeps refusing me, the stubborn beauty. Good thing I like te spy on people. And now that yer there, there's twice the loveliness te violate with mine eyes. Ye don't mind, do ye? "

Esra laughed, choking on the piece of bread she had just bitten off. "Oh, Fynn. So what are the plans fer the day? I hear there is going to be a celebration feast tonight."

"Did yer mother come te visit ye, then? I've never seen the woman so untied. She's normally the most practical, graceful woman ye'll ever lay eyes on. Besides my Nadia, of course. Now ye can see the similarities tween yer mum and yer grandparents, so orderly and composed. But Talitha was very nervous te meet ye, she was."

"Yes, she came briefly. And I think it went fairly well. Or as well as it can go fer meeting someone ye thought was dead fer a couple of decades."

"True," Fynn conceded.

"What are yer parents like? Do ye have a family?"

"Aye, four sisters," he smiled. "And I daresay my father was not a happy man when I left him alone with all them women."

"Did some Keepers come to get ye?"

"Baelin, actually. He said that there were three already in his Assembly, including twin Elves, and that the Great Keeper of Destiny had a dream that I was te be the fourth."

"What did ye say? I mean, did ye know that ye were going to be a Keeper?"

"Not in the least. My family and I lived in the far northeast Kingdom, in a small town near Bynthia. We were fairly poor, having five grown children and none of us yet married. The town we lived in was a poor one, so it was not something I was embarrassed about. My sisters were so scrawny that they were not much good fer working the fields, and my mother was sickly so she needed looking after. So it was up te my father and me te take care of most of the planting and harvesting. I have te admit, though, te say that I had an unusually strong affinity fer the fields would be a drastic understatement. Everything I touched seemed te grow twice its normal size and our crops were never less than overflowing despite long droughts or drowning rain. Many times it was the only way my family and the other townsfolk survived. It was normal fer our neighbors te come harvest portions of our crops fer storage. We didn't mind, as it was just my father and I and otherwise the food would go te waste if there was no one te gather it. I had also become the official herbalist of the town, giving cures fer sickness and relief from pains.

"As I was a Human and did not know much about the Keepers, the appearance of the Tur rash did not disturb me. It irritated me that I couldn't cure the itchy mess, but I liked the challenge. When I began te hear the voices of the plow horses I was brushing or the neighbor's dog that I was petting, that was a different story. I went te the town elder te see if I was indeed going mad, but she could offer me no explanation except te wait and 'see if I was summoned'. Of course, that cryptic answer did not sit well with me, especially when a few days later a seven foot tall Baelin appeared at my door. I remember sitting at my kitchen table, offering him a cup of my delicious brewed tea as he told me about the Stronghold and the Jade Gardens. I was fascinated, especially at his description of the plants and animals that I had never even heard of, let alone had the opportunity te see. But I knew that I could not leave my family or my town, that if I were gone the crops may not be enough te feed them. In fact, knowing that I had this skill with the earth only proved te me how much I was needed there. So I thanked Baelin and told him that although I would love nothing more than te come with him, I could not.

"My parents, who had been not-so-secretly listening in the next room, burst in and said that it was nonsense, that they would find a way te make everything work, that I could be of more use elsewhere. That is one of the things I am always grateful fer, that my family taught me that no matter how little we had, there was love and happiness and we always had what was needed. We stood there arguing fer a few minutes until Baelin politely interrupted. He said that there were some spells he could cast te improve their crops and increase the yield of the harvests. Then he offered them livestock, enough fer three of our towns. He also said that the Stronghold would be happy te assist in any other way fer my services, and all they need do is ask and it would be taken care of. "

"Bumbling huckfly. It sounds like he came prepared."

"Aye," Fynn laughed. "When the Great Keeper of Destiny dreams of someone joining their most important Assembly in generations, they want te make sure it really happens. So we sat and talked a bit more before I accepted his offer, satisfied that my family and townspeople would be taken care of. Five years later, here I sit with the fifth and final member of our group."

"Does it always take so long before ye get an Assembly?"

"Sometimes, aye. An Assembly is not some mismatched group of people thrown together out of chance. It is an organized, powerful force of the Keepers, made up of sorcerers whose skills best compliment and aide each other in their tasks. Because it does take so long te find that special group of five, it is common te be assigned te a temporary Assembly fer training and basic tasks. Ye'll not need te worry about that, as yer the final piece te our group. What ye will need te worry about, however, is how te get around here fer yer training. If yer up fer it, I'd be happy te give ye a show of the place before dinner tonight."

"That would be great."

"Alright then. I'll let ye finish eating, then ye can make yer way back te yer house...do ye remember which one it is?"

"I think so."

"Good. I'm not sure if Nadia told ye, but each dwelling has its own plant or animal marking on the front te help ye find them. Yers is an ostrich, which I believe is a very large, fluffy bird from the northeast with gangly legs and a long neck. Although I'm not sure why it's feathered like a bird when it can't even fly. Seems more like an ugly horse. Anyway, each dwelling has a carving next te the front door. Arland and I live in the Elephant house. So get changed into some pants and meet me on the porch."

"Pants?"

"Well, ye didn't think the ladies spend their time fightin' in big bushy skirts, did ye? Not very practical. Then again, there may be a strategy in big skirts. A man could get lost in there, suffocated maybe. If it was Nadia's skirt, I'd be one very happy dead man."

She reached over and punched him hard on the shoulder.

"Ow! Alright, I'm sorry!" He cried, getting up from his seat. "I'd be happy if it was yer skirt too, Es."

She made a fist at him as he took off down the Dining Hall, his maniacal laughter echoing in the empty hall. She grabbed the last bowl, a mixture of chopped fruits, and shoveled it into her mouth. Table manners were never her strong point, especially when she hadn't eaten all day. Gathering all the dishes, she made a neat pile before leaving the Dining Hall, a feeling of contentedness settling in her stomach. She was finally going to see the Stronghold. Get to know the place that held her long lost parents, her recently made friends, and hopefully her new home.

XX

By the time Esra had made it back to her assigned ostrich house she realized that she didn't actually own any pants. Taking a chance, she entered her room and pulled open the heavy wooden dresser. Sure enough, the drawers where she had not placed anything last night were already filled with varying articles of clothing, including four new pairs of pants. A lightweight, dark blue cloak with gold vine trim identical to what the other Keepers wore was folded neatly on the chair of her desk. Underneath it was a similar, heavier cloak, for colder weather. She quickly threw on the trousers, which fit perfectly, and fastened the lighter cloak around her neck. Meshok appeared in the doorway, panting heavily.

"What do ye think?" She asked, twirling around. "They certainly make my legs feel free."

She had never thought about how cumbersome it was to have all of that cloth around her legs, how inhibiting. Then again, although Nadia was sometimes hard to see, she did usually wear trousers instead of skirts. Maybe with all the other strange things that had happened, it just never occurred to Esra that a lady wearing pants was one of them. Going out into the round corridor, she opened the front door and did a hitch kick to one side.

"I saw that," Fynn said, chuckling.

"These feel great," Esra admitted. "Too bad I didn't know trousers were so comfortable back when I was running around in the forest and trying to do my chores."

"Skirts were probably good fer holding things, though. Ye can make yer own little basket fer gathering."

"Aye," she agreed. "So I remember a little bit of what Nadia told me about the dwellings, but not much."

"Well, there are over two hundred houses in the Stronghold, all with five rooms. So there are about five hundred people who live here on a permanent basis and another couple hundred who come an' go," Fynn motioned for her to follow him back towards the Dining Hall. "There are many Keepers who have chosen te live in other areas of LeVara or who are on long term assignments like Baelin was. So we estimate that all of the Keepers make up over a thousand people. Not bad, eh?"

"I never dreamed there were so many. It doesn't seem like there are that many houses, either," Esra marveled. "All of these Keepers with all their different Gifts and yet Tallen still poses a threat?"

"Well, as far as the houses go, they were intended that way," he explained. "We did not want te take over the Jade Gardens, we wanted te live with it. So it is a little deceptive. Every care was taken te blend in with our surroundings, not conquer them. As fer Tallen, his army of Elites is in the tens of thousands and growing. And although we still maintain certain advantages, capturing Kiran Brae will enable him te gain valuable supplies and force people te work or fight fer him."

"How can we expect to win against such evil?" Esra asked sadly.

"Well, hopefully the War Council will help with that. If we can get the other three races te help, we may actually stand a chance," Fynn said encouragingly as they approached the earth colored structure to the right of the main hall. "We'll go into this one first."

Pushing the heavy wooden entry doors open, they arrived in a chamber not unlike that of the Dining Hall. There was a large granite fireplace immediately across the round foyer, but the colors of the room were yellows, oranges, and reds instead of the greens, greys and whites of the Dining Hall.

"This is referred te as the Training Hall," he guided her into the room on the right. "This room is fer weapons training only. It's called the Battle Room. There are also areas behind the hall outside that we use fer archery and sparring if it's not suitable te be inside."

The room was massive and probably over two hundred paces long by a hundred paces wide. The center of the room was empty, providing plenty of space for lessons. Large, high windows reflected brightly off the Shendari scale roof and allowed the entire room to be well lit despite its size. Two younger men were sparring aggressively with shortswords in a corner, sweat glistening on their foreheads. The right wall held wooden stands with various types of swords, bows, morning stars, spears, staffs, and other weapons. The border of the wall to the left was lined with bookshelves holding armor capable of covering every inch of a warrior's body. At the back of the room were sturdy round tables with cushioned chairs positioned around them. Scrolls were opened up on some of the tables with small colored stones about the size of fingernails scattered across them. A group of six or seven people was gathered around one of the tables, listening to a woman in a dark red robe as she pointed to various areas of the map.

"What are those fer?"

"We use them te teach war tactics. Each color stone represents a different type of warrior, like red fer archers, blue fer sorcerers, and black fer commanders. The scrolls represent different landscapes or battle situations, such as a castle defense, mountain attack, or river fight. By presenting these different scenarios we're better able te direct our armies. This is something the Unni taught te us, as they are master strategists."

"But I thought that this place wasn't built fer war?"

"It wasn't built fer it, no, but that doesn't mean it was never used fer it. Mostly these were friendly competitions, opportunities te share knowledge and challenge one another. Unfortunately there were times when it was necessary te fight, either with people and races outside of LeVara's Kingdom or within."

"The weapons in this room are fer practice only," Fynn continued. "We try te ensure a Keeper can fight with all the basic types of weapons. Which has come in very handy fer me a few times when I didn't have a bow or got too close to an Elite. Sometimes ye need te be able te improvise. Once a person finds a weapon or two they are particularly fond of, they go te Baelin or another one of the blacksmiths te have one made. There are times as well when a Keeper will get something Gifted te them fer passing a task, like Arland and the Greatsword of Narajuv or my own Bow of Many. And once in a while a weapon can be passed down from someone who dies. We train in the five skills of war, which are offensive and defensive battle, stealth, strategy, and endurance. Do ye have a preference as te which weapon ye'd like te learn? Maybe try a ranged weapon like me or Nadia, the bow or throwing spears?"

"Nah, not if ye actually want me to hit something. If ye think I'm disastrous in close proximity, wait until I get thirty strides away. There's more room fer me to make a mistake."

"That bad, eh?"

"I tried to shoot a friends bow a few times. Can't hit the broad side of a barn. Managed to hit his younger brother's foot though."

"Ouch. Alright, well maybe a blunt weapon like a morning star?"

Esra paused to think about this, tried to picture herself swinging a club. That didn't seem quite right either.

"I'm not sure."

"May I make a suggestion?"

"Aye, please do."

"I think that ye would be perfect fer a shortsword. It's a one-handed deal, so ye can carry a small shield with it. I think ye'd do well with it."

"A shortsword. That sounds good."

"Well, ye can still hack off someone's foot, but at least we can try and control who's foot ye'll be hacking off."

They exited the Battle Room and crossed the chamber into the room directly across. It was the same size and shape as the previous room, with a similarly large open area in the center, except there were more bookshelves and tables scattered around the perimeter. The shelves held various bottles, stones, herbs and scrolls.

"The Magick Room," Esra guessed.

"Correct. This is where we train in the five types of magick. Restoration, or healing, as ye saw when I mended yer side after yer capture. Resistance, which is also known as defensive magick, strike or offensive magick, influence, and sight."

"And do all the Keepers know all five types of magick and war?"

"Aye, we all try te know the basics of each. But everyone has weak and strong skills. Fer example, I am very adept in the art of restoration but fairly horrid at offensive magick. I am talented with my Bow of Many, so I choose te use that more often te strike an opponent, but there are some Keepers who can do with their minds what I do with an arrow."

"I have so much to learn," Esra admitted, dismayed.

"We all felt overwhelmed at first. The difference is that we had time te practice. Ye may be a wee bit more hurried, but I believe it's possible. Let's go te the Dining Hall next."

They made their way out of the building and across the thick grass, passing the Great Hall and entering into the green and grey foyer of the Dining Hall where Esra had eaten earlier.

"The room on yer left is the Dining Hall where everyone takes their meals, which ye've already seen. It was fairly quiet when ye was here te eat, but normally it's full of other Keepers. The celebration feast will be here tonight. This room over here is the Library, as ye can probably guess from the hordes of bookshelves."

He guided her through the foyer and into the room on the right, where dark wooden shelves bordered the entire perimeter of the room and ran in rows throughout its middle. They were very tall, almost four times as tall as Esra, and there were wheeled ladders attached to the shelves at various locations. Small two person tables and stuffed chairs were scattered in the back of the room, surrounding an immense stone fireplace. A few people were lounging about, faces buried in thick volumes.

"Let me guess, this is where Cane lives?" She teased.

"Right ye are!" Fynn laughed. "See, I said that ye was smart."

She scanned the long corridors of shelves, stuffed full with books of all sizes and colors. Stacks of scrolls were tucked neatly between the volumes, breaking apart the darker rows with splashes of white. She felt a sudden pang of guilt knowing that her scholarly teacher was away from a room full of his life's passion for so many years. Sorley certainly had nothing like this.

"There's so many," Esra gaped openmouthed. "I've never imagined there were so many things to be written about!"

"They cover nearly every subject ye could imagine in all different languages," Fynn explained. "There are maps, books of history, poetry, herb lore, cooking, mercantile, imaginary tales of adventure. It would take a lifetime te read them all."

"I bet Cane is willing to try."

"Aye, and considering he's immortal, he may be the only one with the time te do it. Let's move on te the last building, the Great Hall of Keepers. It's the largest one centered in between the other two."

They made their way back into the open air and turned sharply left. Approaching the front of the main building, Esra noticed that the structure was preceded with long, low stairs. Walking slowly up the stairs, they arrived at an entrance that was similar to the others but on a much grander scale, with two giant doors that peaked in the center. The entire front of the structure was a map of LeVara carved into the massive yanquor trees and inhabited by scenes of the four races. The Eshomee Ledges to the top left beyond the door depicted a view of the great mountain of Idona. A group of young Elves were surrounding an older one who appeared to be telling a story.

"Cane had told me that the Elves treasure storytelling as much as the written word. The detail in these carvings is unbelievable. There are crinkles in the corner of each smiling person, each blade of grass has been outlined with precision."

The top right was a scene of the Shendari people enjoying a day in Fire Lake, lounging on the shore of Ember Isle and chasing each other in the waves. The black Pura beasts ran in a herd, their great spiked tails swaying. The far bottom right was Fira Nadim Forest, where the Unni were crafting various tools at an intricate workshop. Another picture depicted the Unni-se teaching children how to wield a weapon in what Esra supposed was Shadow Glenn, surrounded by a thick shroud of trees. At the bottom left were images of the Humans working the fields and dancing around musicians in a festival. Perhaps they had Trader's Days or something like it long ago.

The two main doors were a portrayal of The Naduri River, the great body of water that separated LeVara into the east and west Kingdoms. She could not fathom what material the doors were made of, for the surface glinted and gleamed like water. As you walked towards them, it mimicked the appearance of flowing water, an undulating sea of silvery blues and greens. It was an extraordinary sight and Esra stood there for quite some time taking it all in.

"It's beautiful, eh?" Fynn said softly. "The only thing that could improve upon it would be my big glorious face as the door knocker right in the center."

"I must say I would enjoy pounding a heavy metal knocker against yer forehead."

"That's what they all say," he pushed open the left door, which swung fairly easily considering its massive girth. They stepped into a round, bright foyer about three times the size of Esra's entire dwelling. The ceiling above was a clear element Esra was unfamiliar with that allowed an uninterrupted view of the sky. She had never seen anything like it. The floors in here were the same dark blue as their cloaks, with light gold walls reflecting the sun richly. In the center of the room was a fireplace that shone in a sparkling, darker gold trimmed in dark blue.

Unlike the other two buildings that had two rooms on each side, this room had four entrances. Two of the doorways appeared to lead down long corridors bordering either side of the fireplace and the usual two were positioned on the immediate left and right.

"The Great Hall includes the Council Room and Ceremonial Room, but officially the Great Hall is the enormous foyer we stand in right now. Foyer is probably not the right word fer it, as ye can see. It's called the Great Hall because of the convergence of five, the outer door, two Halls on either side, and two corridors, representing the revered number of Keepers. The room on the left is the Council Room, which I must show ye quickly because it's being prepared," he pushed open the door gently so that Esra could peek into the room where a few people were bustling about, washing floors and arranging lights. Chairs were positioned around a long table shaped like a 'U' that took up almost the entire room. A substantial grey stone statue with Tur writing towered in between the open space and a small stone podium was perched on the table directly across from it. There seemed to be a small child dancing about in the far corner of the room. Squinting at the strange sight, Esra was shocked to see that the dancing child was actually a broom that appeared to be sweeping on its own. A woman in a light green robe sat at the U-shaped table and flicked her wrist this way and that every few moments as the broom mirrored her motions.

"This is where all the meetings and War Councils are held," Fynn explained. "The statue in the center represents The Five Laws of Keepers. Ye will get te know these soon, as we must practice them at all times."

He closed the door quietly and they moved directly across the foyer to the door on the right side. They entered a large blue room with the same high ceiling and long windows but with rows upon rows of carved wooden benches. At the far end of the room were marble steps leading up to an open platform with ten golden marble chairs bordering the sides and a larger, more elaborate one in the middle.

"This is the Ceremonial Room. It's where we perform all Gifting Ceremonies after a Keeper passes a test, and where all our other formal celebrations are held. If the occasion is informal or accompanied by a feast we use the Dining Hall. The eleven chairs are fer the five Great Keepers, the three Elves from the Elders, the Unni-se, the Daughter of the Shendari, when there is one, and the King. The speaker or presenter fer the event sits in the middle. Fer Gifting Ceremonies that is always the Great Keeper who is bestowing the reward fer passing the test. All eleven chairs have not been filled fer a very, very long time."

They backed out of the room, their steps echoing in the loud, empty chamber. "The two corridors on either side of the fireplace lead te many different rooms, including the living quarters of the Great Keepers and representatives from the other races. I honestly don't know what all the rooms are fer. We don't venture back there. I have heard that there are supposed te be some hidden rooms that no one knows about except the War Council members."

Peeking down the long corridors, Esra was again reminded of the sea. The walls were made of the large rounded yanquor trees, but instead of cutting them flat like the rest of the rooms the Unni had left the trees in their naturally curved state, giving the hallway the appearance of rolling waves.

"So that's the short of it," Fynn walked her out through the foyer and the large river doors. "Ye will get te know more about everything over time, but at least now ye won't be gettin too lost."

"Thanks, Fynn."

"My pleasure, Es," he said as he took her hand and gave it a playful kiss. "Time te get ready fer the celebration. I'll see ye back at the Dining Hall in two hours."

XXI

After a much needed bath and a few botched attempts to pin up her hair, Esra called in the aide of Nadia.

"It's impossible," Esra groaned. "I should just cut it all off."

"Nonsense," Nadia laughed. "Ye just need the help of a Keeper of Hair."

She twisted a few chunks of her friend's thick blonde hair deftly and began to fasten it. "So do ye like the dress?"

Esra glanced over at the dark blue gown laid across her bed. After she had finished with her bath she had come into the room to find it waiting for her.

"Well, whoever is secretly giving me clothes does seem to know my taste," she admitted. The dress was of a simple cut, with plain gold trimming around the bottom of the skirt and long sleeves that peaked downwards at her wrists. The neckline was rounded and less conservative than the dresses she normally wore, dipping to show the tops of each shoulder. It was a smooth, light material that Esra had never felt before, and the sheen caused the dark blue to shimmer with lighter shades. A gold cord to tie around the fitted waist and gold ribboned shoes completed the ensemble.

"It's yer mother," Nadia confessed.

"What?" Esra asked distractedly.

"The one who has given ye all the clothes. She has been sewing them fer many years. She took a chance that ye would be tall and slim like she was at yer age, and it turned out to be a good guess."

For some reason this struck Esra as a tender scene, the Great Keeper of Destiny sitting in her room, sewing a dress for her lost daughter. Although it would be the fanciest thing Esra had ever worn, which made her a little uneasy, she was thankful for the gesture. And also that her mother had known enough not to sew on hordes of lace or bows.

"I always hated having my hair done when I was a girl," Nadia admitted, gathering Esra's hair into her hands.

"The only time I would tolerate it without complaining was when my grandmother did it. She had such an engaging and clever way of storytelling, she enraptured me. Everyone, really. Elves are known fer their passion of the oral traditions but even the elders had to admit that my grandmother had a special gift. I would sit by her lap as she would tell me tale upon tale of the history of the Kingdom, about the Unni and Humans and Elves. There was no topic she would not breach, no territory she would not try to explore with words.

"There was a story that was my favorite, I would beg her to tell it to me over and over again until it was practically a reality to me. I would say I had it memorized, but that was the thing about my grandmother, she never told a story the same way twice. It was about a young girl named Anaya who was born half bird, half Elf, with soft brown wings that stretched farther than her open arms. She could not fly, so the birds did not accept her, and the people of her village shunned her because of her wings. She was too different. Anaya was stuck in between two worlds, belonging to neither.

"There was an accomplished sorcerer in the village, and each day she would go to him and beg fer a cure to her malady. Something magickal that would make her either Human or bird, but not both. And each day he turned her away, saying that it could not be done. After a particularly difficult day of eating noonmeal alone again after being tormented and teased, Anaya was desperate. That night she snuck away to climb the mountains and seek the bird chief, who was rumored to be at the highest peak. She climbed fer days, eating nuts and berries she found along the way. Finally, at the end of four long days, Anaya reached the highest peak of the mountain. She could hardly believe her eyes when she saw the bird chief sitting atop a rock, regally smoothing his feathers. She stumbled forward and fell before him, tears streaming down her face. Anaya told him the story of her birth, of her inability to be accepted by the people of her village or the tribes of birds. She cried fer him to help her learn to fly or else take pity on her and drop her off the mountain top so she would be gone from this in between world forever. Fer a long moment the bird chief stared at her with a mixture of compassion and confusion. He said to her, 'Anaya, you have always been able to fly. You are born of both worlds, and have been given wings. All you need to do is accept this gift.' Mystified, Anaya stood up from the rocky ground and finally understood. She ran from the highest peak of the mountain and jumped, flying off into the clouds."

"That's a beautiful story." Esra said softly. "I'm sorry that I never got to meet yer grandmother."

"She would've loved ye. There," Nadia stated with satisfaction as she stood back to admire her work. "I put yer hair half up so that it's not so heavy and ye'll be more comfortable."

"Thank ye," Esra hugged her sincerely. "I'll be out in a minute after I put on my dress."

"Alright, I need to get dressed as well."

As Nadia shut the door softly Esra pulled the supple material over her head and wiggled it downwards. Just as she had suspected, it fit perfectly. She tied the cord around her waist, laced up her shoes and went into the wash room, where the only mirror stood. Looking at her reflection, she was startled to see that the young woman in front of her appeared, well, lovely. It was not often that she looked in mirrors, vaguely thinking it was a waste of time and energy. Her hair and clothes would do what they wanted anyway. But looking at herself now, she noticed a woman who was flushed pink with anticipation, someone who appeared mature and confident.

"Ready?" Nadia called from the hall.

"Aye." Esra stepped out to look at her friend, who was wearing a similar material but in a beautiful golden hue that contrasted superbly with her dark skin. Her curly hair was pinned up with several locks dangling down at various spots, resting on a dress that was well fitted to her petite frame. It was fuller on the bottom than Esra's and had dark blue trimmings. Her shimmering stealth form added to the overall sparkle of her attire.

"Ye look stunning," Esra said truthfully.

"Thank ye. I must say ye look quite beautiful yerself. Ye'll notice a lot of blue and gold outfits as these are the official colors of the Keepers."

They stepped out into the cool night air and picked up their skirts to keep the dew from moistening the bottom edges of their gowns. Esra laughed out loud.

"I have *never* acted so dainty and ladylike. Give me just a few more minutes, I'll fall on my face, I swear. Do ye normally get to wear things like this in The Veiled City?"

"Sometimes," Nadia answered thoughtfully. "The Elves are a people who love tradition and customs, so there were many celebrations and official gatherings. As much as I love the freedom of wearing trousers, I always enjoyed getting to be a real lady on certain occasions. I was scolded more than once when I was young fer wearing my mother's gowns and prancing about the house."

"Do ye miss it? Yer home, I mean?"

"Aye, sometimes. The Jade Gardens are a thing of beauty, but there is also something to be said fer the strong stature of the mountains. They were like a protective guardian, always watching over me. As children, Arland and I would love to explore the rocky hillsides and deep caves. But I know I belong here. And I visit when I can. This is not a prison, we can see our families as we please. Ye will have a bit of an advantage on that end, since both yer parents are already here."

Esra gave a nervous smile and Nadia touched her arm in sympathy. "Don't worry, they're good people. And ye'll get to see yer grandparents again soon."

Esra tried to believe in those words as they continued through the thick grass. To her right two Squirrels suddenly appeared, leaping and twirling with each other, their high pitched chatter piercing the air as they played. A Mondeer doe walked out from behind one of the dwellings, ears perked in anticipation as the white tip of her tail flashed in the fading light. The animals here did not seem to mind that they were surrounded by Humans. In fact, Esra thought that perhaps they regarded her with the same mild curiosity as she bestowed upon them. Just another creature of the Gardens.

As they approached the main building, their arrival reminded Esra of Sorley on Trader's Day, the noises and laughter greeting them far before reaching the entrance of the Dining Hall. Standing outside waiting to greet them were Baelin and Fynn, both in velvety tunics embroidered with swirls of rich vines, appropriate for a representative of the Garden. Baelin wore a darker gold against his tanned skin and Fynn had opted for the blue with his pale complexion. Peeking out of Baelin's left coat pocket was the blue handkerchief with the small golden sun embroidered in the corner, the gift Esra had given him at Trader's Day.

"Oo-da-lah-ly!" Fynn whistled, taking each of their hands to kiss. "Ye ladies both look absolutely astonishing."

"Thank ye," Esra curtsied playfully. "And both of ye look mighty handsome as well."

"I agree," Nadia confessed. Baelin looked over at Esra then back to Fynn, then back to Esra again. He opened his mouth for a moment and then closed it, turning back to Fynn with a slight look of panic.

"See, ye've made the big beefy one speechless!" Fynn teased. "Not that he talks much anyways. May I?"

He offered his arm to Nadia, who took it after a pause as they stepped into the hall.

"Looks like even Fynn will get a lucky break tonight," Esra chuckled. Baelin swayed on his feet as he awkwardly offered his arm to Esra, who smiled kindly before linking her arm into his. She was grateful her old friend would be with her tonight. Beyond the entranceway awaited many people she had never met, including her own father.

A wall of noise hit her as they walked into the overflowing Dining Hall, the tables littered with silver goblets and pitchers. A few people turned to wave or shout a greeting at Baelin, who steered her towards a table at the back left. Catching a glimpse of Cane, Esra called to her teacher, who nodded back at her pleasantly. A group at one of the tables in the front started singing an upbeat tavern ballad, causing the merry energy in the hall to swell.

Nadia and Fynn had already found seats next to Arland, who stood up and beckoned to Esra and Baelin. He looked striking in a lighter blue tunic that brought out the color of his eyes, his hair falling seductively into his dark face. His strong jaw softened into a smile as he looked over the young woman before him.

"Ahoy, Esra!" He came around the table and gave her a fierce hug. "Ye look ravishing!"

"Thank ye," she said, blushing for what felt like the hundredth time. "And ye look charming, as always."

He laughed at the pun and pointed out a middle aged man at the front of the Dining Hall who was bouncing up and down in an excited fashion, thick blonde hair in a jumbled mess.

"There's someone who's very excited to meet ye."

At that moment the man caught her eye and rushed forward with an eager grin, stumbling over a chair leg. He hopped on one foot a couple of times, grimacing, then continued to dash towards Esra clumsily. He encountered some trouble maneuvering around one of the tables, as he appeared to be a stout man, and by the time he reached Esra his cheeks were flushed pink with the exertion.

"Esra!" He exclaimed, gathering her up into a strong embrace and kissing her head four times in quick succession.

"Hello, father," her words were muffled as he squeezed her into his chest, laughing.

"I can't believe it's ye!" He released her from his iron grip but continued to hold onto both her hands, swinging them erratically. "Yer even more wonderful than I imagined."

"Err…thanks."

The room quieted as Esra's mother Talitha entered and took her place at the front of the room. An intricate gown of blue velvet trailed behind her like soft waves of the sea. She looked briefly towards her husband, who was still grinning goofily, and laughed softly before continuing. Her voice echoed hauntingly in the now hushed room.

"I would like to extend a warm welcome to all of our residents of the Stronghold and favored guests. Tonight we will dine to commemorate a long lost Keeper who has finally come home, our daughter Esra. And knowing what difficulties lie ahead, we offer all Keepers these few brief hours as a sanctuary from their worries. Please remember that all of the Great Keepers are extremely proud of each and every one of you. And now, please enjoy your meal!"

A cheer rose up in the hall and the noise began to climb again as platters upon platters of steaming food spilled forth from the kitchen. Adonis took a seat next to his daughter and poured her a cup of mead.

"So, yer mother tells me that ye've inherited some of my clumsiness."

"Aye," Esra laughed.

Fynn leaned over mischievously. "Then yer probably wondering how such an awkward man became the Great Keeper of War. Well, they figured it would get him into a meeting room and off the field of battle, where he was bound te trip and skewer one of his own feet. Or someone else's."

"Tis shamefully true," Adonis smiled as he shook his head sadly.

"Don't worry, I'm not afraid of ye," Esra assured him. "I have my own foot skewering to attend to."

Plates piled high with a wide assortment of food, more variety than anything Esra had laid eyes on appeared before them. Actually, landed would be more accurate. Esra watched with a gaping mouth as plates soared in from the front of the room above their heads and came to rest solidly on the table before them. There were mounds of magickally created rabbit and vernok, many different fishes that had been broiled, fried, or roasted, fresh fruits, potatoes, carrots, hyntrus, and other vegetables, both raw and cooked. There was warmly baked bread of all different sizes and colors, cheeses that crumbled and others whose stringy texture seemed immune to breaking. These dishes were swiftly followed by three different colored gravies, also floating bravely, a large bowl of hairy, strange looking yellow fruit, and multiple plates of brightly colored candies, some as small and round as a pebble and others long and thin as rope. It was overwhelming, the sight and smell of it.

"Are all these foods native to the Gardens?" Esra noted that although all the food appeared normal in shape and texture, it was much larger than anything she had ever seen. She used both hands to pick up a Tomato that was almost as big as her head and looked questioningly at Fynn.

"Chef's secret. We grow our food fairly large around here."

There was an interlude of silence as everyone gathered food onto their plate, reminding Esra that the beautiful feast before her was indeed intended to be eaten. The distinct sound of multiple feet tapping at a far corner was closely followed by the low hum of instruments. She wondered briefly what to say to her father and if this had been as strange an experience for him as it had been for her. Then again, her parents had twenty years to imagine this moment. She had only a few short days.

The silence was interrupted by another burst of singing from the next table, startling Esra back to the present. Talitha went to join Cane at his table, leaving her husband to enjoy the company of his daughter. Esra continued to rack her brain, trying to think of something to talk with her father about. "So how did ye and Talitha…I mean, mother, meet?"

"Well now," he took a moment to swallow a mouthful of boiled potatoes. "I accidentally knocked her out with a turnip."

"Oh my." Esra's eyes opened in surprise as everyone around the table hooted and leaned in eagerly. She waited a moment for the punch line, but Adonis just smiled at her goofily. "You're not kidding, eh? Not quite the romantic story I was expecting. How did ye ever manage that?"

"Funny story, that is. Well, maybe not when it happened. I had been eyeing yer mother fer quite some time and she knew it. Just the summer before, her family had come to my town from somewhere far away that I'd never heard of. Everyone thought I was a bit too…err…awkward fer a young man. Prone to accidents, ye see. Yer mother was the exact opposite, elegant in every sense of the word. Talitha spoke differently than the others in town, acted different. I thought she was so beautiful and exotic. So ye see, just like every other week I was taking a cart full of vegetables fer my father to the market in town. It just so happened that I was lifting a crate of turnips out the back of the cart when I slipped. The box flew through the air, smashing into a hundred pieces on the ground next to me. Somehow one of those vegetables had escaped and soared through the air to hit Talitha square in the forehead as she was walking by. Knocked her out cold. Scared I killed her, I was. So I was sitting there in the middle of the street cradling her when she woke up, big red welt on her face. Slapped me good once, and then kissed me immediately after. She says that's when she fell in love with me, lying there in the dirt with a big ole turnip bruise on   her   head."

Esra paused, speechless, as everyone at the table burst out laughing. Adonis' face reddened as he chuckled jovially. "So don't say that it isn't lucky sometimes to be a little clumsy. I got a good wife out of the deal."

"I'll remember that," Esra said with a serious look. "Whenever I want to find a man, all I need is a good hard vegetable."

"Are ye sure ye didn't just knock her brain loose?" Fynn cried. "Maybe she's just damaged."

Everyone roared as Esra piled more abnormally large food onto her plate, finally hungry after all of the nervous anticipation. Her father seemed to be very easy to get along with and didn't mind doing most of the talking, which relieved her mood greatly.

The dinner continued, punctuated by various funny stories and sudden outbreaks of tavern songs. Her father told a bit more of the time before Esra was born when he was courting her mother. Everyone ate well beyond their fill, yet still seemed to find room when heaping platters of desserts came soaring out.

"Where are the Great Keepers of Magick and Strength? Did they not attend the festivities?" She asked Baelin over the noise.

"The Great Keepers dine with the rest of the folks of the Stronghold, so they're probably scattered about somewhere."

Esra thought it a good gesture that they did not have special seating in the front to mark their superiority like a King or Queen would. How different things were here. She had never visited the palace before, but she was more than certain that the royalty did not mingle as such, even at special occasions.

Leaning back in her chair, Esra gave a contented sigh as the empty plates and bowls before her lifted up and flew back towards the front of the room. It was a strange sight, the serving platters zipping through the air, everyone talking as if it were a common occurrence. Then again, it probably was, for them at least. The room grew slowly quieter as everyone's stomachs grew fatter, and by the time Adonis walked to the front to talk to the people of the Stronghold, the noise in the hall had lowered to a lazy hum.

"My good friends," his voice boomed across the massive hall, "I hope that ye've enjoyed yer feast!"

There was a surge of noise as everyone cheered and banged their fists on the tables in agreement.

"Unfortunately, we must end the night on a sadder note. We have received word that Kiran Brae, our great city to the far west, has already been taken over by Tallen and his Elites. It is only a matter of time before they continue over Grey Thorn Pass to Mahesh in the northeast."

Gasps and whispers swept through the crowd as Adonis held up his hand for silence.

"It will take time to get everyone assembled here so that we may begin our counterstrike. Regrettably, we cannot attempt to reclaim Kiran Brae at this time, so we will focus our efforts instead on the defense of Mahesh. If we can keep Tallen out of the east Kingdom fer the time being, it will buy us much needed time fer further preparation. The good news is that Tallen believes the threat of the Keepers is nonexistent. We have not opposed him thus far as he took over one of LeVara's great cities, so what has he to fear?

"We must focus our energies upon preparing fer battle and gathering the support of all four races. I fear that Tallen and his army have grown too powerful over the past few years fer the Keepers to fight this war alone. Everything depends upon our unity, everything. If we do not gain the strength of each and every race, the Humans, the Unni, the Shendari, and the Elves, then I fear all will be lost. It seems to be a simple task, to have all the peoples stand together against such treachery, but it is not. A War Council has not been held fer hundreds of years, and the community that once existed between the races has almost vanished. Tallen and his Elites will not be our only obstacle."

More rumblings swept through the hall as Esra leaned over to Arland. "I didn't know it would be so difficult to have a War Council."

"Aye, not only are they worried about conducting the meeting but even getting everyone to attend will be a challenge," he whispered back as Adonis continued.

"And so I want to leave ye with this before we go to sleep tonight. Let yer one focus in the coming weeks be unity, and remember that each and every race is essential to our fight. The Elders are currently on their way to the Jade Gardens and tomorrow an Assembly leaves to employ the Unni-se. We have already sent envoys to the Shendari and King. In less than two fortnights we hope to hold the first War Council in generations, attended by all four races. And I tell ye this, that no matter what happens at the Council meetings, the Great Keepers have decided that we will wage war on Tallen no matter what the cost, even if we stand alone. The people of LeVara count on us to bring them freedom. Let us hope fer nothing more than an open heart and mind fer those we seek to bring to these discussions. We must relearn how to celebrate our differences and share our strengths so that we may triumph in this dark time."

Adonis stepped back and off the small platform as the room erupted into heated conversations. The Keeper of War certainly had a way with words. Esra sat in silence and worried that if the War Council was unsuccessful, many more people would die because of it. Baelin must have noticed her concern for he motioned for her to leave the Dining Hall with him. They wove through the crowds of people until they reached the doors, bringing a sudden quietness as they were shut.

"Don' worry, Esra. I have faith that all will be well."

"I hope yer right."

"I am. Now ye need te get yer rest because we have a big day tomorrow."

"That seems to be a trend lately."

"Aye, it tis," Baelin chuckled deeply. "Ye heard that there's an Assembly leaving tomorrow fer Fira Nadim Forest te talk te the Unni?"

"Oh dear. Don't tell me it's us."

"Afraid so. I'll see ye in the morning. Cane wants te speak te us before we leave."

Esra groaned as she shuffled down the steps towards Nadia, who was already waiting for her at the bottom. For some reason she had the sense that getting a day off for leisure was something that wouldn't happen for a very, very long time.

XXII

The bright light of morning shone in Esra's round window much too soon, but she forced herself up and dressed before Nadia even knocked at her door.

"Morning," she greeted Esra cheerily. "We won't be leaving until this afternoon, as there are a few things we need to take care of before we go. Namely meeting with Cane and giving ye a quick lesson in Tur."

"Alright," Esra sighed, trying to get excited that she would at least be going on an adventure to someplace new. She had dreamt about the Unni-se chief Zakai and his deadly weapon, the flail with chain and spiked ball. He had swung the long metal handle around his head as he ran towards her, screaming like a charging vernok. She had tried to move, terrified, but her feet seemed stuck to the ground. She awoke in the middle of the night with the thin blankets plastered to her body in a cold sweat.

Cane was waiting for them in the Magick Room at one of the round tables. Baelin, Arland, and Fynn were already seated, as was a man Esra didn't recognize. She tried to appear unnerved as she approached, giving her old teacher a tired smile while she took a seat.

"Esra, this is Nor, the Great Keeper of Strength," Cane motioned towards the small man at his left, who was sitting calmly with his hands folded in his lap. She was unsure of how to greet such a person as a Great Keeper, but he bowed his head slightly and she returned the gesture.

"Hello, Esra." Nor spoke very evenly and quiet enough that Esra needed to lean forward slightly in her chair to hear him. He was small for a man, a good head shorter than Esra, and had little tufts of white hair sprouting from assorted places on his scalp. He appeared to be very old, well beyond Cane's age, although she didn't know exactly what that meant since Great Keepers were immortal. Wrinkled skin hung loosely from his arms and Esra wondered how this man could be a portrayal of strength.

"Looks can be deceiving," he answered her thoughts, causing her to blush deeply. He smiled kindly at her and paused for a long moment, appearing contented to sit and take his time. "I have your first test."

"Oh," Esra exclaimed in surprise. "Already?"

"Yes," he nodded. "I know that you have only just arrived, but it is time."

"What must I do?"

"As you well know by now, the War Council will convene in two fortnights. The Elves have already sent their representatives and the King will be sending his son, Prince Bronnen. We have an Assembly on their way to plead our case to the Shendari. I must say our relations with them have been greatly improved since Fynn has been able to communicate with a few of the members. We have high hopes that they will be able to select a Daughter to send to our Council. The trouble, Esra, will be the Unni. There has not been a Human allowed in Fira Nadim Forest for almost a hundred years, since Baelin was born."

"Since…what?" Her breath caught in her throat as she tried to swallow. She must have heard him wrong.

"Since Baelin was born," Nor continued. "He is ninety eight, you know."

The look of astonishment on Esra's face must have been very plain, as Baelin looked away in embarrassment. "Ninety eight? But that's impossible! He can't be more than thirty!"

"Nay Esra, it's true," Baelin replied softly, meeting her eyes. "I am a fourth Unni. My grandfather was chief when he took a Human wife, my grandmother. She gave birth to the half Unni that was my father, who also married a Human."

Esra's head spun as she tried to follow the chain of events almost a century ago and what this meant. His massive stature, gold tinted eyes, even all the soft, dark hair that covered his body now made sense in a new way. And since the Unni could live for hundreds of years, it was no wonder he appeared to be so young.

"Do ye remember how I told ye my first Assembly died?"

"Aye," she thought back to their night by the fire when Baelin had opened up to her for the first time about his past.

"Well, they died of old age, not in battle."

"Oh my."

"Looks good fer an old man, don't he?" Fynn jested.

"I'll say," she agreed. Looking back at Baelin and the pained look on his face, she had a sudden urge to let him know it was alright, that this news did not change the fact he was her best friend. She reached under the table and took his hand, gently squeezing it for a moment before letting go. Esra saw his shoulders relax slightly and she turned to the Great Keeper Nor.

"So why is this a problem? Shouldn't the Unni make an exception fer such a time?"

"It's not entirely that simple. The Unni are naturally inclined to privacy and do not appreciate visitors in any sense of the word. They are wary of Humans and their ways, and even more so since the unification that once existed between the races has collapsed. They have become more and more independent and secretive, and are virtually impossible to contact or communicate with. There was also a bit of an…incident…that caused some of the Unni people to shun Humans. But that is another story altogether, one which we will leave for the journey."

"But what could I possibly do about all this?" Esra asked, still confused.

"Your first test is to bring Zakai, the Unni-se, here for the War Council."

"Bring him here?"

Esra sat for a moment in stunned silence. Not only was she supposed to accompany her Assembly to Fira Nadim Forest, but she was expected to bring back the Unni-se himself. Had she not been so utterly terrified of this prospect she would have burst out laughing.

"Zakai is Baelin's uncle, so we are hoping that helps to smooth things over a bit, or at least allow you a council with the Unni-se." Nor rose to leave, bowing at the others in the group before turning again to Esra. "The Great Keeper of Destiny has seen our fate if this does not come to pass. You must find a way. Good luck."

He exited the room before Esra could fully absorb what had just occurred. She sat staring open mouthed at the people around her table.

"What just happened?" She asked croakily, blinking away the dizzy feeling behind her eyes.

"Ye've just got yer first test!" Arland squeezed her shoulder encouragingly. "I must say it's a big one, but have no fear. We'll all be with ye."

"With me? *With* me?" The hysteria was spreading through her chest as her dream replayed itself over and over in her head. "With me to where? To the land of slow, painful deaths?"

"Esra, get ahold of yerself," Cane said firmly. "Ye may have gotten the sense that the Unni are very…fierce…and although they may fight as such, they are not an uncivilized people. They are simply different from us."

He was right, but the fear in her was nearly overwhelming. More than anything, Esra was someone who could not tolerate people who judged others unfairly, who could never see beyond their own small world. The combination of the vivid nightmare and the enormous amounts of stress she was under had created this image of the Unni as a frightening, barbaric race, just as Cane had guessed. It was disappointing to her that she felt this way, but she could not deny it. She wanted to believe in the strong people who brought yanquor trees from across the Kingdom to help build this fortress of learning.

The Elves, the most similar to her own race, had not frightened her in the least. Especially now that she knew a few of them. She was conscious that they had many differences but had nonetheless been ready to accept them. Even the Shendari of Fire Lake had intrigued her as a secretive and eccentric race. Yet for some reason the thought of going to meet the Unni horrified her. Maybe because they were known as 'the war people' or were physically intimidating, with horns and yellow eyes. But no matter what the cause, Esra knew she was being unfair. Cane and her grandparents did not raise her to be so intolerant, so prejudiced. Isn't this what she was fighting against, intolerance and injustice? After all, Baelin was one of them, or at least partly, wasn't he? And although he fought with great power, wasn't he a very gentle man? And one of Esra's best friends?

"I'm sorry, I'm just frightened," she apologized, looking towards Baelin then back over to Cane. "Ye have not taught me to be so narrow-minded. Of course I will try to do what I can to bring the Unni-se back to the Jade Gardens."

"Well, ye know what they say about fear," Cane said mildly. "If we never had fear of anything, there would be no need fer courage."

XXIII

The Assembly met in the Magick Room for a lesson on Tur after checking that the skycatchers were being readied for their journey. In the interest of time, Humi, the Keeper of Speed, was packing Nadia and Esra's clothes into carefully tied bundles for the horses as they practiced. They all took a seat around one of the round tables in the back of the room as Arland reviewed the basics of Tur.

"When ye hear the word Tur, it refers to both the language and the magick that a Keeper uses to communicate or access knowledge on various subjects. So if ye remember, Tur is how Keepers speak with one another. We can even use these spells over great distances. Also, ye cannot get into the Stronghold without it, as a spell protects the fortress from outsiders."

"A Keeper can store information with Tur like they could on a scroll, maintaining maps, spells, and details about our task. It comes in very handy in cases like today, where we do not have much time to prepare. When five Keepers come together we can communicate directly with the Great Keepers."

"There are two ways to use Tur. One occurs at the beginning of a task or lesson when the information is 'written' on our arms by the spell. We can use this Tur independently. It would be very difficult if one of us was captured and we could not use Tur to complete our task or guide ourselves home. We will all see the same map no matter where we are or who we are with if we call upon it. The other form of Tur takes no preparation and deals with communicating with each other. We do this as needed during a task, especially if we need to split up or stay quiet."

"So how does one get a map or other knowledge onto their skin?" Esra asked, turning over her arm.

"A Great Keeper must do this fer any new information or when we receive another task. Remember, a task is different from a test. A test is a specific challenge fer a particular Keeper which will result in a Gift when complete. Tasks are what Assemblies are given to complete together fer various reasons."

"So we don't need all five of us to say, look at a map?"

"No, only to speak with a Great Keeper."

"But what happens if someone is captured or dies?"

"We can still communicate with each other, just not the Great Ones Also, Tur is invisible to all of Tallen's forces. This has been one of the greatest defensive spells ever created by yer father, Adonis. Tallen gives off a specific magickal aura, as all sorcerers do. Similar to how each animal has a unique scent. He has left his 'mark', ye could say, on each of his minions. Adonis was able to use this to devise a way to block the discovery of Tur around those associated with Tallen."

"Very useful. Cane told me that most of the Elites are soldiers, not sorcerers."

"True, many are skilled warriors but possess no magickal abilities Of the group that captured ye in the forest, only two were able to cast spells. Natural sorcerers in LeVara are few and far between, especially when most of them reside at the Stronghold. That is why we are so concerned that Tallen has found a way to 'convert' a non-sorcerer."

"So do ye keep the old Tur information even when ye receive a new task?"

"Some of it. We keep some spells that we don't use very often, but not much else. And to be quite honest, having Fynn around with his superb navigational skills means there is not much need even fer maps. We have found that it is too risky to walk around with all the other knowledge, even with protective spells in place. Ye can use one arm or both to read Tur. I think it's easier to see a map when ye use both, but I only use my left arm to accept messages." Arland spoke a few soft words and placed his strong arms palm up on the table as she watched the snaking black script become slightly illuminated. The lines came together after a moment to reveal the familiar "L" shape of Sorley, the houses small dots among the hilly landscape. He uttered a few different words and the map changed, focusing now on the area around Esra's house. The woods, barn, fields, house, everything was detailed accurately. The dark lines were even raised slightly at the higher elevations, giving the map a textured, dimensional look. It was as if one were looking down at the town from a hundred miles above.

"Every square inch of LeVara has been captured in this form by the Keepers."

"Amazing," Esra leaned forward to study the softly glowing picture before her. She had never seen her grandparent's farm laid out like this.

"What were ye saying to make it appear?"

"Tur is a form of insight or sight magick, one of the five types. Cane has already taught ye most of the language, correct?"

"Aye," Esra nodded, remembering back to their long lessons over the last brutal winter in Sorley. "But not how to use it."

"If ye already know the language that will be the easy part, trust me," Arland assured her, brushing a wisp of stray hair out of his pale blue eyes.

"Sight magick includes all spells and sorcery related to divination, communication, and insight into other places or times. Tur is the most common and widely practiced form of sight magick, as all Keepers use it. There are very few of us who can use the more prophetic sides of sight."

Nadia, who had been shimmering next to Esra in her chair suddenly became a solid form and leaned in to join the conversation. "All insight spells are started with the Tur word fer sight."

"*Orro?*"

"Right. Tur spells are structured from the most general piece of magick, which are spoken first, to the more specific pieces spoken last. Let's say I wanted to look up a map of yer farm again. I would say *Orro* first, indicating that I will be using sight magick. Then I would say *Wey*, the word fer knowledge followed by *Sim*, the word fer map. In other words, ye are saying a spell of sight magick to gain knowledge from a map. Then ye would say yer general location, *LeVara*, followed by the town's original name, *Sorley*."

"So I would say *Orro Wey Sim LeVara Sorley?*"

"Perfect. And that would bring up the town map."

"So how do I see the farm?"

"Tur can only store information however we tell it to. If we want to get a closer look at any part of the map, we must tell it what we want to see. So I would say the most specific part of the spell last to show yer exact farm. If yer farm had a name, I could use that. Otherwise I would use a combination of words such as the home of Esra, or *Yana Esra*. That would bring ye to the picture ye saw. If I wanted to go directly to the map of just yer farm, I would say all those words in succession. Ye can also use the general words for east, west, north and south to move the map towards where ye want to see more, if ye aren't sure of the specific location."

"So how many maps are there?"

"Well, really there's just one fer all of LeVara, which Cane will be giving ye. It's just that ye can look at very specific parts of that large map depending on which words ye say in succession."

Esra absentmindedly rubbed her hands together while Nadia placed her arm in the center of the table. "Let's talk with Cane together like we did the other day in the forest. Remember, only one main speaker at a time so he doesn't hear a jumbled mess of five people talking at once. Tell him we're ready fer him to meet with us."

Esra absentmindedly put her arms forward before jerking them back. "He's not going to tell me I have any more family members, right? Brothers or sisters?"

"Nope, no siblings I'm afraid," Arland laughed.

"Alright then."

The others joined in, placing their forearms next to one another and closing their eyes. Esra shut her eyes and tried to picture the long, thin face of Cane, the droopiness of his features, the crinkles around his eyes. Slowly she felt the familiar tingling sensation as the shimmering black text began to snake itself across their arms. As Nadia suggested, she focused on only the words she wanted to say to him. *We're finished.*

I'll be right there.

Esra jumped as she felt a hot jolt of energy suddenly flare through her body. Just as before, the words emerged across all five arms in Tur script. The light behind the words was much brighter with Cane's reply than it had been with her words. He was obviously much better at this.

"Good," Nadia smiled, pleased. They all sat back as Cane appeared in the doorway a moment later and stalked heavily towards their table.

"I assume ye have begun teaching Esra the basics of Tur?"

"Aye, and I've already explained about the LeVara map," Arland offered.

"Good, good." Her teacher pulled a chair up from another table and plopped heavily into it. "I must say I am rather exhausted from all this excitement. But no bother. Esra, yer arms."

She put forward her arms as requested and Cane grabbed a hold of her wrists tightly. She felt a powerful rush of energy, as if she were about to explode if she didn't begin sprinting and jumping and screaming simultaneously. It was more powerful than anything she had ever felt before. The center of the table filled with a bright light that seemed to burst from where Cane maintained a steady grasp on her skin. She had a strange sensation, almost like being filled with something, with light. But that didn't make any sense. One couldn't be filled with light. Esra shook her head, trying to clear the cloudiness that slowed her thoughts, making her suddenly weary. The others took hold of Cane's arm for a brief second and the light grew even stronger for a moment. He released Esra and everyone dropped their hands to their sides. The intense light vanished instantly.

"It's a bit overwhelming the first time, I know," Cane said apologetically. "I also gave ye much more information than the others, to aide in yer training on the journey to Fira Nadim. Ye now have the basics of magick and war to reference. The others will show ye how to access this information."

"Thank ye," she whispered, the woozy sensation lingering between her eyes.

"Good luck, all of ye." Cane stood up and paused for a moment before turning to her. "And Esra, do be careful."

"I'll try," she said weakly as he marched out of the room. She blinked her eyes hard a few times, trying to clear the fogginess that had settled before them.

"Don' worry, it'll be over in a minute," Arland assured her. They sat for a while longer as Esra rubbed her temples gently. The disorder in her head began to clear as it was replaced with a dull, throbbing headache.

"What happened?"

"Cane just happened. Try to say the words to bring up the Kingdom."

Esra took a deep breath and watched her arms as she spoke. *"Orro Wey Sim LeVara."*

She watched with curiosity as her skin remained unchanged. A shot of frustration burned quickly through Esra, who was not used to the taste of failure. Trying again she said the words louder and the illuminated script appear dimly and shortly, fading before a true picture could form. She refocused, closing her eyes and speaking the words slowly and softly. Esra opened one eye tentatively to see the picture morph indecisively before disappearing yet again.

"What am I doing wrong?" She sighed in exasperation.

"Jes focus on the words, clear yer mind of everything else."

Esra arranged her thoughts around the words of Tur, seeing the letters in her mind. Slowly, the script on her arm began to form itself into an overview of the entire Kingdom of LeVara. She could see the Eshomee Ledges to the north, Fire Lake to the east and Fira Nadim forest to the south.

"Unbelievable," she murmured.

"That's great Esra," Nadia encouraged. "Once a map is called up it will stay there until ye tell it to do something else. Now focus all of yer attention on yer town as ye say the word."

"Sorley."

The image morphed slightly before returning to the same map of LeVara.

"It's difficult, I know, but ye have to block out every other thought except fer the location ye want to see."

"What if it's a place I've never been to before?"

"If ye've never seen it, just focus on the name of the place. Or you can use the directions of east, west, north and south to 'move' the map towards someplace."

Esra closed her eyes and tried to concentrate only on the image of her L shaped town. The farms lining the north and east, the shops at the crook of the intersection. She spoke the name again and when she opened her eyes, the town map was before her.

"I did it," she said with surprise.

"Ye're a quick learner," Nadia agreed. "Now fer the final location, yer farm."

"*Yana Esra*." After two more tries, the lines took a long moment to refocus back to the detailed map of her farm, dimensionally perfect in every way.

"Once ye practice a bit more and yer concentration is better focused, ye will be able to do that in one spell." Arland held out his arms again as he spoke the words in rapid succession.

"*Orro Wey Sim LeVara Sorley Yana Esra*."

His arm went from smooth dark skin to a brightly glimmering image of Esra's old house in one quick moment.

"Nice," she murmured, impressed.

"Now fer the other type of spell that allows ye to speak with others," Nadia continued. "Ye'll still begin with the word *Orro* fer sight magick but yer second word is *Ken* fer communication. Ye will often hear Keepers refer to the two main types of Tur as *Orro Wey* or *Orro Ken*. Tur of stored knowledge or communication. To send a message to ye, I would say *Orro Ken Esra*, followed by whatever message I would want to appear on yer arm. I can speak the words aloud in Tur or Human speech, whichever I prefer, but it will always appear on yer skin in Tur. Once again, this is a protective measure, as most people outside of the Keepers do not know the language."

"But I must always say a spell out loud?"

"No, but only a strong sorcerer can perform magick without speech. It's a limitation sometimes, I know. All of us here can perform most magick in our heads but not the more complicated spells. And it simply requires more energy and concentration to cast a spell without speech. Keep in mind that one need not speak loudly to cast, though."

"We'll be going over all of that later, on the journey south. Are ye ready te walk over te my shop te get yer first weapon?" Baelin asked softly.

"Weapon?" She asked over the beating of her headache. "I already have a weapon?"

"Aye, I made it fer ye. I think ye'll like it."

"Alright," she agreed tentatively, swaying briefly as she stood. "But I must warn ye all that Baelin here is giving a real weapon to the clumsiest girl alive. Ye better hope that Fynn has brushed up on his healing spells."

XXIV

The blacksmith shop at the Stronghold was much more grand than the simple one Baelin had used back in Sorley. Pulsating waves of heat from the fires greeted them before they reached the wooden beams edging the shop. There were multiple fire pits of varying sizes scattered around an open structure, which was covered by a tall canopy of Shendari scales. Five large stone blocks for shaping the metal stood at various heights and lengths, two of which were currently occupied by Keepers.

"The Shendari scales covering the shop are immune to fire," Baelin pointed out.

"Well, they are the water people," Esra mused.

Wooden stands and tables were populated with a mixture of different weapons needing to be repaired or given to their new owner. Huge chunks of metal, wood and stone leaned against the tables, waiting for their turn to be forged into the next deadly staff or blade resistant shield.

Baelin walked her towards a table at the front right, away from the thrashing intensity of the flames. He picked up a long object that was wrapped in a light brown cloth and began to unfold it, revealing a newly forged shortsword. Offering it to her with both hands, she took the sword cautiously and ran her hands along the smooth blade. The grip was made of a strange kind of white leather which was a perfect fit for her long, lean fingers. Encased in the dark gold metal of the pommel was a large, sky blue gemstone that shimmered brightly.

"I picked out the stone te match the color of yer eyes," Baelin stated simply. Suddenly realizing what he said, he looked down and nervously shifted his weight.

"It's beautiful," Esra remarked truthfully, politely ignoring his discomfort. The blade itself appeared unremarkable in shape, with a simple straight double edge that came to a sharp point. Yet she had never seen such a metal, if that's what it was. The color was an unbelievable incandescent white that reminded her of the insides of the Shendari scales.

She swung the blade in a large arch and listened to it sing in a high pitched whine through the air. It was perfectly balanced and fit her hand like a well-made glove. She had never thought she would be comfortable swinging a weapon, no matter how much she practiced, but this beautiful blade gave her hope. Drawing her fingers along the smooth side of the blade, Esra noticed that there were small inscriptions running along the length of them on both sides, which she recognized as Tur.

"What does this mean?"

"They're the Five Laws of Keepers. Ye may have seen them on the statue in the Council Room."

"Yes, I remember. Fynn said that the Laws were very important."

"Aye, that they are."

She turned the blade over slowly until she found the beginning of the text and began to read it aloud.

"As one sworn to be a Keeper of LeVara, upon these principles we place our lives:

One, We Strive Above All Else for the Peace and Unity of All Races and Peoples.
Two, We Believe in the Freedom of All Creatures.
Three, We Encourage the Sharing and Learning of All Skills and Traditions.
Four, We Shall Not Use Our Skills of Magick or War for Personal Gain.
Five, Although We Seek to Do No Harm, We Will Oppose Those Spreading Tyranny and Injustice Until Our Lives, or Theirs, be Forfeit."

"It's inspiring," Esra said truthfully. She had been expecting something else, something less selfless. Maybe more like the endless laws of the King. But this was everything that Cane had tried to teach her in his lessons, beautifully worded in five simple guidelines.

"Aye," Baelin agreed. "That is the code we live by. Have ye ever noticed we don' tie up the horses?"

"What?"

"The second Law, the freedom of all creatures. We never tie up the skycatchers or any other animals that live here, not even the ones we use te work the field. Everything and everyone is here by choice. No one is ever forced te stay."

"That's incredible," Esra admitted. "What happens if someone wants to leave?"

"Yer welcome te leave at any point. The only thing we must do is have Arland modify yer memory so that ye have no idea of where the Stronghold is or the specifics of what we do."

"That doesn't sound pleasant. So ye can't have any memories of being here?"

"Just nothing that we would consider dangerous if it got into the wrong hands. It's as much fer yer safety as it is fer ours."

"I see. But wait a minute…the horses, they don't run away?"

"Nay, not often. They're here at the Gardens te help, they understand our cause. I didn't quite believe that myself until I went with Fynn te talk with one of them."

"Fynn said that the fake meat that Keepers eat took decades to magickally discover. That it was because of yer Laws, too, that ye don't harm anything."

"Aye."

Esra ran her hand over the smooth surface of the blade again, not quite believing in what she felt, tracing her fingers around the gemstone. "How did ye become so skilled?"

"Well, this old man has had a long, long time te perfect his craft," Baelin smiled. "I had always been able te do uncommon things with my hands. Every attempt at carpentry or blacksmithing showed a new talent, another item I could shape. There seemed te be no material that would not become what I needed it te be. It has always been this way fer me, and so I am not sure how te describe it other than te say it seems te be a natural part of me."

He reached for another item on the table, a buckler about four hands across. It was engraved with a scene of Roja, Esra's skycatcher, rearing on his hind legs. Next to him was Meshok, perched in a vicious position with her sharp teeth bared, ready to pounce. Esra took the shield in her other hand, finding it surprisingly light and thin. She swung the sword again, attempting to find a balanced position.

"Ye should learn te fight with a buckler if ye can. I go without one since I've learned te use my staff fer defense as well as any shield. But it will protect yer hands and help ye deflect attacks. Ye can also use it te attack by hitting yer opponent with the edge or face of it. I'll be making ye a full suit of armor, but it won't be done 'til after the War Council."

She swung the shield in a large circle, then practiced lurching forward, thrusting the buckler into her unseen foe. "I love it. The sword, too. Ye made everything a perfect fit fer me. I actually believe I could learn to fight someone now. Bring on the five skills of war!"

"Now don't get too ahead of yerself, Esra," Baelin laughed. "Better learn some basics fore runnin' out onto the open battlefield."

"Bah! Now that I have yer wonderful blacksmithing gifts, what's the worst that could happen?" At that she made a quick jump forward as a demonstration of her newfound confidence, frantically swinging the shortsword upwards with a loud "Hi-yeeee!" Losing her grip on the hilt, Esra watched in horror as the blade flew twirling through the air, sticking in the ground between two blacksmiths who were standing unaware on the other side of the shop. Their conversation halted abruptly as they both turned with perplexed faces towards the offending warrior.

"Err, sorry!" Esra called to them as Baelin doubled over in laughter.

"Dangerous ye are, that's fer certain. Danger te yerself and yer kinsman."

Esra blushed in embarrassment as she joined in his laughter.

"Thank goodness ye don' have a turnip," he roared. "I'd be a dead man!"

After shamefully walking over to retrieve her weapon and apologizing profusely again to the offended parties, Esra gathered up her new sword and buckler and headed back to the stables. She wanted to finish packing Roja with her new weapon and shield. The others were already there, straightening their saddles and tucking in stray leather straps. A young boy of about eight was patiently brushing Roja's thick white mane. Esra strolled up to the skycatcher and started rubbing his long, lean flanks. The rest of her things had already been packed and tied to the horse by Humi, the Keeper of Speed.

"Are ye miss Esra?" The young boy asked, looking up at her with wide brown eyes. He was missing his front two teeth, which caused a slight whistle when he talked.

"Aye. An what's yer name?"

"Yarmon, the Keeper of Foresight."

"Pleased to meet ye, Yarmon."

"Don' wear the helmet, miss Esra."

"What helmet?" She tilted her head in surprise and bent down to face the young boy who was staring at her with deep concern. "I don't have any armor yet."

"The bad man does. Don't wear it. Promise."

She stared at him for a long moment, expecting him to say more. The furrowed brow on his young face helped her understand that he had said all he could and was waiting for her answer.

"I won't. I promise."

He nodded in satisfaction and took off running towards the Dining Hall.

"I see ye've met our Yarmon," Arland appeared suddenly beside her. "What did he tell ye?"

"Not to wear the helmet."

"Hmm," Arland frowned. Even with a sulky look on his face he continued to be endearing. Esra didn't think there could be any circumstance that made him appear less attractive. "Wonder what he meant."

"I'm not sure," she mused.

"Well, whatever it means, keep it in mind. There's been quite a few times when he's helped us to avoid disaster."

She nodded and took a few steps back, preparing to attempt another run and jump mounting. Just as she leaned back to propel herself forward, a strong hand landed heavily on her shoulder.

"Ah!" She shrieked and hopped forward clumsily, turning to find her mother and father standing behind her.

"Sorry, dear," Talitha apologized. "We've come to say goodbye and good luck."

"Tis a shame it's so soon." Adonis hugged his daughter fiercely, kissing her forehead. "I will miss ye all over again."

Her mother stepped forward to embrace her, whispering lowly into her ear. "Have faith, Esra. It is always in our darkest hour that we prove we are capable of a courage we did not know we had."

They both stepped back and watched their daughter clumsily mount the tall white skycatcher and straighten herself in the saddle. The others had finished saying their goodbyes and stood waiting atop their own steeds, My Lady, Meda, Fariel, and Errol. They were a glorious sight, the five young travelers atop their majestic skycatchers. As they took off across the green lush grasses of the Gardens, Esra took a last glimpse towards the place that would become her home, and swore that she would return to it with the Unni-se, no matter what.

XXV

Knowing that the War Council would be held in less than two fortnights and that it would take almost half that time to reach Fira Nadim, they rode hard under the black cover of night. It was approaching mid spring and the increasingly hot days meant that they preferred the cooler air of darkness, both for the horses as well as the element of protection it provided from Elite trackers. It was a strange schedule to keep, and Esra found it difficult to sleep in the midst of the high noon sun until Nadia showed her how to fasten a cloth around her eyes to keep out most of the light. They continued to use cloaking spells for the fires so that they could enjoy fresh meals while remaining hidden from danger. The last thing this group needed was to draw attention to itself. And just as Arland had said, they did not collect any wood but continued to burn their smokeless fires from some magickal source.

They also rode hard because they needed to have breaks to train Esra in the five skills of war. It was necessary to know at least the basics of each if she were to have any level of respect approaching the Unni-se, as battle skills were the most highly regarded ability in Fira Nadim. Not to mention the fact that her Assembly may actually be engaged in battle at any moment. It terrified and excited her at the same time. Esra was more than ready to learn how to fight, her confidence boosted by a weapon and shield she felt she could manage. And she found herself becoming increasingly angry at Tallen and his wicked followers, disgusted that she had to learn such things to defend the basic liberties of the people of her Kingdom. Yet here was an opportunity to bring together the races and reinforce the First Law of the Keepers, and she tried to focus on using that anger to fuel her training.

On the second day of their travels, Arland woke Esra to the last few hours of evening for her first lesson.

"The main skill ye need to learn is defense, because all the other skills are no good if ye can't stay alive long enough to use them. But ye will also need to understand basic attacking maneuvers to defend yerself well. Ye'll gain endurance as we are training and I will give ye some exercises to complete when we are between lessons. Some ye will even be able to do while riding Roja. Strategy is something that will have to wait until we get back to the Stronghold, as time won't permit a thorough study. And all four of us will be contributing and giving ye lessons, as we are all strong and weak in different areas. There should be some information on yer Tur from Cane about the skills of war. We will show ye how to access that information shortly. Hopefully this will give ye a well-rounded knowledge in the basics of war."

"Agreed."

"And I know that Nadia continues to work with ye on stealth, correct?"

"Aye," Esra nodded. Every day since the rabbit in the clearing a short week ago they had been spending a few minutes here and there trying to improve upon what she had learned, namely how to stay quiet and unseen. It was proving to be a challenge for Esra, but she was making slow and steady progress with a very patient teacher.

"Well then, let's begin. I want ye to have a seat on that log over there, because yer first task is observation. Ye need to study us as we spar, try and make sense of how each of us approaches defensive and offensive maneuvers, how we use our different weapons."

She did as she was told as Arland called to Fynn, who reached eagerly for his bow and quiver. After some convincing he instead took up Esra's shortsword and buckler to demonstrate a duel between two blades. He muttered something under his breath and she wondered if he was cursing his luck or casting a spell.

"I am a master archer and much prefer te shoot my foes from a distance, but if ye feel better beating me te a pulp so I can court yer sister, then swing away."

At that Arland charged forward with a grin, swinging the Greatsword of Narajuv with both hands in a wide upward motion. Fynn parried the blow with the buckler and was knocked back a step as Nadia took a seat on the ground next to Esra. Fynn spun quickly to the left, swinging his blade around and over Arland's shoulder, who deftly ducked out the way. Both of them prowled around in a circle and the archer turned swordfighter taunted his foe with an impromptu jig, causing Arland to lunge again. Fynn blocked the first swing with his blade, stabbing under his buckler as the second swing met with his shield.

"They certainly are competitive."

"Aye," Nadia laughed. "Don't worry, we use a spell so that they can't kill each other. At least fer now."

"So that's what Fynn was doing. Have they ever hurt one another?"

"Aye, but nothing serious. Or at least nothing that Fynn couldn't heal."

The two continued to spar for a few minutes as Esra studied their movements with quiet intensity. Arland was certainly the more skilled swordsman but Fynn was very quick, avoiding disaster on more than one occasion by a mere hair's breadth.

After they tired, Nadia and Baelin decided to showcase their talent with his staff and her throwing spears. Nadia explained that she had to be very careful since receiving the Necklace of Stunning as her third Gift. If she forgot to take it off before sparring, everything she hit with a weapon or shield would be knocked senseless for a few minutes. Esra took the thin chain into her hands, rubbing the flat orange stone with its four square sides. It seemed so harmless, beautiful even. It was hard to believe this small ornament could cause such destruction.

Nadia used two of her throwing spears like small staffs, something Esra would have never thought of. The two were a comical sight, the seven foot tall monstrosity battling the tiny shimmering Elf woman. But neither of them held back as they darted and spun, clashed and grunted. Nadia was much quicker, but Baelin seemed to possess a skill for anticipation and was holding his own defensively. A few times he knocked her so far back with a mighty swing that she appeared like a glistening ghost at the other side of the battle ground before recovering swiftly to take the offensive. At one point Baelin struck one of her throwing spears from her hands and she pulled out a small dagger. Esra remembered Fynn saying she used them as a backup weapon for close encounters. In a few moments Nadia had evened the score by landing a fierce kick in the center of Baelin's stomach, knocking the breath from him.

Esra could not believe the skill level of the members of her Assembly. She was even more bewildered that they could ever expect her to fight like this. A farm girl who studied books all day. A clumsy farm girl at that. She was lost in worried reverie, forgetting her earlier confidence as she imagined an Elite soldier spearing her with one quick thrust.

"Now, Esra," Arland called to her, "let's begin with the skill of defense. Grab yer sword and shield and get out here."

She struggled to her feet, the muscles in her legs protesting in their stiffness. Reaching for the soft white leather grip of the luminous shortsword, she picked up the weapon that was slowly growing more familiar in her hands. The night before she had been studying the light blue gemstone encased in the dark gold pommel, tracing the stone's smooth surface as she relaxed by the fire. Esra had tried to think of how she could possibly approach the Unni-se with the proposition of attending the War Council. *Um, excuse me large, hairy sir. Would ye mind traveling halfway across the Kingdom to have a talk with us Humans? No? Alright then, sorry to trouble ye.*

She picked up the buckler lying on the ground next to the sword and studied the picture of Roja on reared legs with Meshok beside him in a threatening stance. Esra tried to absorb the courage and intimidation that they exhibited in the engraving. Sighing in resignation, she could not deny the fact that even though she was looking forward to this training she was already tired from riding. "I have no misconceptions of how much work this is going to be. Then again, any advice that may help me avoid getting my head hacked off by an Elite is most certainly welcome."

She ambled to the center of the space that her friends had been fighting in and gave Arland a weak smile as she swung the blade a few times in an attempt to loosen her muscles. She slid the buckler through her left arm as the rest of the group took seats around the area to watch, heightening Esra's nervousness. Then again maybe it was better that they knew how terrible a warrior she was, so that hopefully they knew to aide in her protection as much as possible. She would take all the help she could get.

Arland got the extra wooden shortsword and buckler that they had brought along to practice with and met her back in the field to begin their instruction.

"Ye will eventually learn how to use yer sword to defend, but fer now we will start with yer buckler only. The most important thing yer shield is fer, is to protect yer sword arm. If ye are struck in the hand that ye are holding yer weapon in, it will be very difficult fer ye to fight. Therefore, a good defensive stance is one that puts the shield in the front of the body and the sword arm towards the back of the body." He demonstrated by taking the defensive position and Esra attempted to imitate him. Arland walked over and manually adjusted her shoulders, lowering her shield arm to cover the center of her body.

"Widen yer stance and bend yer knees fer balance. Good. The second most important thing is to use yer shield as a deflector. Yer buckler is light but strong and the slightly curved shape will make it easier fer ye to defend against a sword attack. Ye will learn how to deflect a blade as well as catch an arrow in its path or turn aside a well-aimed staff hit. Now, I want ye to put yer shield down fer a moment and try to attack me."

"Attack ye?" Esra asked

"Aye. Just take a few swings."

Esra shrugged and took a position she thought suitable for someone about to commence a sword fight attack. Stepping forward, she swung her blade in a large arc around her body. Arland easily parried the blow with such force that she stumbled backwards. Coming forward again, she swung and stabbed a few more times as he effortlessly defended her attacks, driving her quickly backwards.

"Great. Now did ye see how I used my shield? And how I barely moved from this spot? Ye want to keep yer knees bent at all times so ye can be on yer toes and ready. Ye will be able to shift position quickly and with little movement. Now I want ye to put down yer sword and try to deflect a few of my blows."

"I want ye to know," Esra admitted, "I'm embarrassed but very grateful that ye had thought to bring a wooden practice sword. It would not look good if the daughter of the Great Keeper of War lost her arm on the first day of battle training. And I'm not quite sure if Fynn has the ability to regrow limbs, talented as he is."

She took the defensive stance that they had just practiced and bent her knees slightly in preparation. Arland came towards her with a wide swing and she turned to the left to block the attack. He spun quickly and jabbed at her right, but she shifted her buckler in time to parry him. After deflecting the next couple of attacks, her elation deflated as she realized he was being easy on her, even with a wooden sword.

"Ye needn't take it so light with me," Esra paused to scold him, slightly out of breath. "If ye want me to be fighting like a true warrior in a few fortnights, we had better hasten the intensity of our lessons."

"As ye wish," Arland gave her one of his appealingly crooked smiles and peeled off his sweaty shirt. His perfectly formed chest glimmered darkly as Fynn let out a whistle and shouted.

"He intends te distract ye with his glistening man chest. Skewer him through!"

Arland laughed and looked at her determinedly. "Let's try it again."

Esra took a few steps back and lowered into her stance as he came towards her. This time his sword hit her left side before she had even considered moving her shield. He caught her right shoulder with a quick jab and spun around, his blade singing with victory as it found her thigh. Esra tried to regain her composure as she lifted her arm to deflect his next swing but he struck her hard against the hip.

She gasped in pain and held up her hand in surrender as red welts began to rise all over her body. "Alright, ye win. I thought that ye were supposed to be good luck to have around."

"Aye, but only if I intend fer it. Otherwise every opponent I fought would have the gift of fortune with them at all times, which would prove very unlucky fer me."

Esra nodded as she leaned over and tried to catch her breath.

"Another advantage to having a light shield and sword is that ye will be able to move rapidly and yer buckler can be used to hide yer sword arm's position. This will make it harder fer yer opponent to anticipate what ye will do next.

"There are also certain offensive advantages to having a shield, as ye can use it to directly attack yer opponent. The face or rim when thrust at someone can be a heavy hit. There may also be times where ye are able to use yer shield to bind yer enemy's sword hand against themselves or another object, preventing them from striking. Or, when ye get very skillful, ye may even learn how to catch a blade and disarm someone."

After taking a few more minutes for Esra to recover, they all took turns attacking her with the practice sword as she tried to defend against them. Most of the time she could not deflect their hits, but she could feel herself growing somewhat more comfortable with using the shield. By the end of a long and grueling hour she was swollen and bruised in almost every part of her body from being hit repeatedly with the blunt wooden blade. But she continued fighting, bending low in the defensive stance as each person came towards her swinging.

The light began to wane and Arland finally held up his hand in a signal to stop.

"Fynn," Esra panted, "I have a feeling I'll be needing yer healing hands in a very short while."

"Bah, what's the fun in that? Don't ye fancy looking like a rotten, bruised potato?"

She smiled as everyone collapsed around the fire in exhaustion. Esra devoured two bowls of vegetable stew before falling asleep almost as soon as she lay down, full of warmth and food. She was shaken to consciousness less than an hour later and groggily made her way to Roja, where it took her three attempts to mount the steed. As she clenched herself against the skycatcher with her bruised legs, she hoped only for the mercy of a smooth and gentle ride.

XXVI

This would become the pattern of Esra's next days, waking a few hours before nightfall to practice with vigorous intensity for as long as she could stand it before collapsing in their temporary camp, attempting to steal a few moments of sleep before they continued their ride towards Fira Nadim Forest. Almost every inch of Esra's body was covered in angry purple bruises. Fynn made her various herbal remedies, which he would heat in a small pot by the magickally invisible fire before dipping strips of cloth into the mixture and wrapping the poultices around her sore limbs. Esra was infinitely grateful for these sometimes foul smelling concoctions, as they did much to ease her pain and allowed her to endure the long ride through the night.

On days when they were severely pressed for time it was dried, magickally imitated meat and cold stews. Esra didn't mind much, as Fynn's herbs kept it flavorful. And Meshok usually appeared at meal times, devouring any scraps left behind and rolling over to let everyone rub her eagerly exposed belly.

They would also practice Tur before beginning their journey, having Esra call up certain maps and locations using the ancient language. A few nights before Fynn began to instruct her further on the use of Tur for communication.

"Instead of *Orro Wey*, which are the words fer sight magick and knowledge, ye need te say *Orro Ken* fer sight magick and communication. This is followed by the name of whoever ye want the Tur te be sent te. The other thing about using Tur te communicate, as if squiggly little worms on yer arm ain't creepy enough, is that the person receiving the words must say *Alor Etta*, which is the spell te accept the message. It doesn't jes show up on yer arm."

"And ye said before that I could speak the message out loud or in my head in Tur or my language, right?"

"Aye, but the message will always appear in Tur."

"How do I know when someone is sending me a message?"

"Ye know that strange itchy, burning sensation ye get when ye call up a map, jes before the lines appear? Ye will feel that."

"And how do I know who it's from?"

"The person's name will appear in the top left corner."

"Alright," she said slowly, remembering the awful sleepless nights last winter she spent scratching and rubbing the insatiable rashes covering her arms.

"Ye'll get used te it in time. Let's practice. First I want ye te accept the message I'm going te send ye. Remember, ye can use one arm or both."

Deciding it would be easier with one, Esra held up her left arm and remained still for a moment until she felt the familiar burning itch. She was relieved that it was much more subtle, like a map was trying to appear, just as Fynn had said. She whispered the words he had taught her. *Alor Etta.*

Slowly the script snaked its way across her arms to reveal a short sentence in Tur. *Arland is a Bug eating scoundrel...*

"I can see it," Esra exclaimed, proud her first attempt was successful. "Yer a scoundrel."

"If I want te send a long message, it will appear in multiple phases. There will be a symbol that looks like a sun at the end of the line te indicates there is more. Ye will need te say *Terna* te continue reading. It's almost like turning the page of a book. In fact, that's how ye can remember the word, Terna fer turning."

"I see it. *Terna.*" As she spoke the black words disappeared and reformed into a new illuminated sentence.

...who doesn't know I've poisoned his stew so I can marry his sister.

"Fynn!" Esra reprimanded him with a playful swat on the shoulder. She focused all her energy on sending him a message, saying the spell lowly under her breath. *Orro Ken Fynn...*

He looked up at her and grinned, realizing that she was trying to communicate with him and whispered the acceptance spell.

She'll never say yes to a brute like ye.

"Ah, yer breakin' me heart, Es." He held his hand over his chest in a mock swoon. She continued to practice, whispering the spell to speak with the others in her Assembly. Over the next few nights Esra would be interrupted by their communication attempts as they tried to teach her to recognize the subtle tingling sensation of the spell. That was proving to be the hardest part, especially if she was distracted by some other task.

In addition to her lessons with Tur, Esra continued to practice using her shield as they moved on to defending with the sword and hand to hand combat. The days became blurred together as she fought against fatigue and aching muscles, overcoming them gradually to gain strength and endurance. It was a different strength from what she had acquired working on the farm and she could feel it steadily growing.

As her skill level improved they continued to add new lessons, moving on from defensive maneuvers to offensive exercises. The shortsword that Baelin had made for Esra could not have been a better fit. It was as if the sword itself had an influence on her training, willing her to learn and adapt at a steady pace. Soon she was able to deflect a few of their attacks with her shield or sword and could occasionally land a blow herself. Rotating through the different sparring partners and their various weapons helped her gain new perspectives on how different warriors fought and kept her from getting too comfortable with one opponent or fighting style.

As they moved south towards the forest, the rolling hills of the Jade Gardens had gradually morphed into a flatter terrain. The lush dark green grass was beginning to be replaced by thinner, lighter fields with less vegetation. Under normal circumstances the hunting would have been sparse at best, but thanks to Fynn's expert gathering and the magickally created meat, they had no worries over food. Esra watched with interest as the new land exposed itself before her, trying to burn the images of the countryside into her mind so that she would remember them later. If she ever did get to see her grandparents again, she couldn't wait to tell them all about this.

Even with her heightened attentiveness, it greatly startled Esra one morning to see the vague horizon of a tree line as she was dismounting Roja.

"Is that Fira Nadim Forest?" She asked Nadia with surprise.

"Aye. And it's likely the Unni already know we're on our way."

"How?"

"As ye recall, the Unni are not fond of visitors and keep their boundaries well-guarded. They've probably already sent a scout back to the main camp at Shadow Glenn to warn of our possible arrival."

"Is that good?"

"I'm not sure," Nadia answered mildly. "Let's hope so."

After falling asleep under a small cluster of shaded trees for the day, Esra awoke at dusk to the low rumbling voices of her group members. She pushed herself up and stretched, reaching for her sword as Baelin called to her.

"No need fer that tonight, Esra. Come join us."

She nodded and approached the low fire, grateful for one night's respite from her lessons but curious as to why they should cease with such little time left. Plopping down between Arland and Nadia, Esra yawned largely as she waited for them to continue their previous discussion.

"We'll be at Fira Nadim in the early morning," Baelin explained "So we'll sleep a little later tonight te gather our strength, as we will probably not be able te rest during the day tomorrow."

"Alright," Esra nodded drowsily. "So what's the plan?"

"Well, there will probably be a scout or two before we even reach the tree line. I think we should approach unarmed, with our weapons tied te the horses in plain sight but out of easy reach. This will hopefully give any awaiting Unni scouts the impression that we come in peace."

"Hopefully?" Esra raised her eyebrows.

"Yes, hopefully. Ye must remember that we have not attempted te communicate with the Unni in almost a hundred years, so we must be very cautious, as they will most certainly be suspicious. In the event that anything should go wrong, please don't say anything and just follow my lead. I will most likely be the one able te exchange a few successful words with the scouts since I am part Unni. And Arland will do what he can te help ease the situation with his skills."

Esra glanced over at Arland who was looking at the ground, deep in thought. She remembered that Nor, the Great Keeper of Strength, had told her there was a story behind why Humans were now shunned by the Unni people.

"What happened?" She asked tentatively. "A hundred years ago, I mean? Why do they hate us so much?"

Everyone was silent for a long moment before Nadia began to speak.

"Hundreds of years ago, when the Stronghold was still being used by all the races fer learning, Baelin's grandfather was the Unni-se, chief of his race. His first wife was a strong Unni warrior who had borne him a son they named Zakai. After her early death the chief fell in love with a Human woman and decided to take her as his second wife. Marrying a Human was something that had never happened before in the history of their kind, at least not fer a chief. Marriage is considered a spiritual as well as physical journey, so once an Unni takes a wife or husband, they very rarely ever take another unless they are widowed. Most did not mind the mingling of the races, as this was still a time of peace and sharing, when the Stronghold was being used fer the exchange of knowledge. And Baelin's grandmother was a greatly respected Human among the Unni, even before she was married to the chief. But there were a handful who were angry at the Unni-se fer what they saw as a weakening of the blood lines. Baelin's grandfather also knew that his Human wife would not live nearly as long as an Unni woman, who as ye know can live to be almost a thousand, but he loved her very deeply and accepted this fate.

"The chief's Human wife gave birth to a half-Unni son who would later become Baelin's father. The full blooded older brother Zakai resented this new addition to his family, but this was due mostly to grief from the loss of his own mother, not hatred fer his new family. At about this time the thirty first King came into his reign, King Rïvan. I assume that Cane told ye about his treachery and how he stole the throne from his older brother Prince Haylore?"

Esra thought back to the vivid account of LeVara's history that Cane had told her a lifetime ago. The story of a vicious younger brother, about the murdering of women and children. The poisoning of The Naduri River that killed an entire army and its peaceful King.

"Yes, he told me."

"Well, King Rïvan had been able to kill off most of the Human army and end any resistance when he poisoned the river. But there was still the Stronghold. He knew that the races had come together fer centuries now to learn from one another, and that this unity was the one thing that could destroy him. Not wanting to risk a direct attack so soon, he instead devised a plan to cause trouble in these harmonious relationships. He would destroy them from within. And the first step was to capture the Human wife of the Unni-se.

"Baelin's grandfather was so distraught about the kidnapping of his beloved new wife that he called upon the aide of the Humans, Shendari and Elves to free his love. Sensing a trap, a War Council was hastily assembled to discuss the matter, with representatives from the four races in attendance. There was much debate on whether a rescue should even be attempted, which greatly upset the Unni-se. The Elves believed we should not rush in to Rïvan's lair to save one person, as the fate of the entire Kingdom now depended upon our cohesive action. The Daughter of the Shendari felt that a small group of volunteers should be sent to try and recover the Unni-se's wife while the rest of the Stronghold members planned fer a war. And the Humans, angered at all of the murders and treachery that had recently plagued LeVara, wanted revenge.

"It was normal fer the War Council to disagree. Healthy debates were always encouraged and there had been battles before, mostly minor ones between tribes. What *didn't* normally happen, however, was that the Humans grew tired of waiting and convinced the Unni to join them in launching their own attack on Rïvan before the Council could reach a unified decision. Many warriors died that day, including the great Unni-se and his wife. Stricken with grief at the loss of their leaders, the Unn resented the Shendari and Elves fer not aiding in their cause. The Elves and Shendari were upset at the Humans and Unni fer not respecting the laws of the Council and ruining any chance of a unified attack. The Humans and Unni continued fighting amongst themselves, as the Unn also blamed the Humans fer convincing them to go. No matter that it was the Humans who fought alongside them at the attempted rescue. Some took it even further and decided it was the treachery of a Human wife that had brought this disaster upon their people. In their blind anger they claimed that the wife of the Unni-se must have used sorcery to seduce their leader, intending all along to lead him to his death. And wasn't it also a Human that was causing such chaos in LeVara? This attitude of mistrust began the slow dissolution of the unity of the races. Eventually, all of the races returned to their respective homes, full of resentment and mistrust. And the Keepers emerged in their stead. They were those who decided to stay at the Gardens and work together."

"How did everything go so wrong?" Esra asked with sadness.

"They lost track of their true goals. One mistrust and wrong word led to another, until it grew into something so big that no one could stop it. It was like a runaway horse. That was why the Keepers wrote The Five Laws. We hope to rebuild what the four races used to share and reclaim the hope that once lived in LeVara."

"So what happened to yer father?" Esra turned to Baelin, who looked up slowly. The small fire crackled loudly and he absentmindedly stirred it with his staff.

"My uncle Zakai decided te take up a wife, a strong Unni woman known fer her unmatched skill in war strategy. It allowed him te avoid the brunt of the resistance that came from a few of the members who disliked his father's second marital choice. Zakai became chief and my father went te live at the Stronghold te become a Keeper. About five hundred years later the half-Unni that was my father fell in love with a Human woman and decided te take her as his wife. They were very happy together fer a long time. Like my grandfather, he was a very dedicated husband. Tallen killed my mother many years ago when she was discovered te be part of an underground scouting group among his ranks. She was young then, as I was only a child myself, but she had managed te penetrate deeper into his forces than anyone before her. My father died a few years later from an illness our most talented healers could neither name nor cure. I believe it was from a broken heart as he never truly recovered from the loss of his love."

"How awful," Esra admitted bitterly. She thought of Baelin as a child, first learning that his mother had been killed so senselessly, and then watching his father slowly succumb to the same fate. "Did ye ever live at Fira Nadim?"

"When I was a young lad we used te visit. But once my parents died that stopped."

"So that's why it's been a hundred years since a Human's been there."

"Aye."

"But all this would make Tallen very old though, over a hundred?"

"Actually, he's almost two hundred now," Arland offered. "No one is quite sure what kind of sorcery he's using to do it, or if like Baelin he has ancestry in another race. There are different rumors, one of which is that he was able to capture a Shendari, who as ye know are immortal, and somehow adapt their longevity to his own body."

"So then Rïvan murdered yer grandparents hundreds of years ago and then his ancestor, Tallen, killed yer mother? Ye must want to avenge them. And how is it that Tallen is a descendant of a King and yet we've never heard of him? Is he related to King Keridon? "

"No, yer current King has none of Rïvan's blood in him, thank the stars," Arland answered. "King Rïvan ruled fer many years, but he was cursed by another fate. In his greed, he decided to take as Queen the most powerful woman in the country, a great sorcerer named Yuri. He thought that this would show the absolute power he had over the Kingdom of LeVara."

"Wait a minute…Yuri. That sounds familiar. She was the enchantress that split the Naduri river into the southern fork when Rïvan poisoned it. She was a great sorcerer."

"Aye, that she was. The greatest."

Fynn leaned over to spoon some stew into his bowl as he chimed in. "What Rïvan didn't plan fer, was that Yuri was not a woman to be tamed. Reminds me of ye, Es. A feisty one, Yuri was."

"That would be putting it mildly," Arland laughed. "Instead of opposing the marriage, Yuri welcomed it as an opportunity to keep an eye on Rïvan and achieve revenge fer her people. The King was so conceited that he barely wondered why this beautiful sorcerer that had fought against him so fervently was now so eager to be his wife. And I daresay the spells she was using helped blind him further.

"Although Yuri was very powerful, the King had many advisors and scouts in her midst, and she feared she would never have a chance to enact her revenge. Many moons went by until the Queen finally announced that she was with child. The Kingdom mourned silently, thinking that Yuri had finally given up and all had been lost. The King was overjoyed at the news that two of the most powerful sorcerers in all of LeVara would bear a child. In his vanity he never questioned Yuri's devotion to him. While the Queen was giving birth, she allowed no one but her most trusted maidens and midwives in her private birthing chamber, which was customary practice. The moment the child was born it was exchanged fer another, the newborn of some simple farming folk with absolutely no magickal background. And Rïvan's son was taken far away with another family to be raised in seclusion, never to know who his real parents were. Yuri had briefly contemplated killing the child, as the threat of him was still so great, but unlike Rïvan she had faith in Humanity and the power of true love. She hoped that the child would grow to be more like herself than his father in the care of loving people."

"So the child that Rïvan thought to be his son was really from common farmers?"

"Incredible, isn't it?" Fynn laughed. "Now only the Keepers know the truth, and te this day all the people of LeVara have no idea that their King is of no more royal blood than ye or I."

"Jumping jig," Esra whistled.

"Yer telling me," Arland continued. "Rïvan raised his son zealously, not understanding why he could not perform even the simplest of magick when he was the product of two such great sorcerers. Yuri ensured that the child looked exactly like him, so there was no doubt who was the father, an accusation she anticipated would come to surface otherwise. After a while it was apparent that the boy had no magickal abilities at all, so Rïvan decided to devote himself instead to having another child. But Yuri had already ensured that the King would not bear another child, neither with her nor any other maiden. She had secured her place as Queen with an heir to the throne that had no drop of sorcerer's blood in his veins. Rïvan's most trusted advisors, the Elite Commanders, who were also sorcerers of varying skills, whispered to him of treachery, but the King was too proud to believe that his beautiful wife would betray him. He was the most powerful sorcerer in LeVara. He had killed a King, slaughtered an army, and taken the throne. What could one woman do against such a man?"

"There's his blunder," Fynn interjected. "Every man knows not te underestimate the plotting and scheming power of a woman. 'Specially a pretty one."

"So then what happened to Rïvan's real son?" Esra asked Arland.

"Well, the King lost interest in trying to teach a son who could not learn magick, and focused all of his attention on the fruitless task of producing another heir. He became obsessed with it, his frustration growing as time passed. Luckily, this left most of the child rearing to

Yuri, who had ensured that the child's nursemaids were of her own choosing, her most trusted apprentices. This was not a happy time in the palace, as the King was rageful at his bad luck. The Elite Commanders suspicions were heightened, as they were sure that the Queen was deceiving them, but they could find no proof. Although they rarely left the mother alone with her child, Yuri was able to steal small moments to try and teach her adopted son of honor and truth and compassion. Far away in the country, Rïvan's real son grew older feeling that there was something out of place in his life, that he didn't quite belong. His parents were simple people, kind and loving, but he knew that there was a power in him they could not explain. A darkness that threatened to overcome him.

"Years later the King finally perished from an unknown illness, Yuri's doing if ye ask me, and Rïvan's loyal advisors mourned his death. Frightened that this would signal the end of their claim to power, as it was apparent to them that the Prince could be no son of Rïvan, they went in search of a common man they had heard had been experiencing strange and powerful bursts of magickal abilities. They found him, a farmer planting fields in the hot sun, and he hesitantly explained to them the nature of his uncontrollable magickal events. The resemblance to his father was indisputable, as if King Rïvan himself stood before them. There was a mixture of excitement over finding their beloved King's heir and contempt fer the woman they knew had deceived them fer many years. The Commanders then attempted to explain to the boy the nature of his history. Wanting to believe he was a great sorcerer and heir to the stolen throne but unconvinced by the babbling of old men, the advisors went about to prove his heritage and magickal skills.

"Queen Yuri heard of what was happening and that her plan had finally been uncovered. She moved quickly to crown her adopted son, knowing that fer the time being LeVara would be safe under her watch and its new King. The Commanders could not make it known that they had been fooled, they would look weak, and they needed time to train their new sorcerer. They also could not risk an open attack on the throne with a King loyal to Yuri. Her adopted son now commanded a large and powerful army; the army that they knew should have belonged to Rïvan's true son. The people of LeVara were none the wiser of the King's common bloodline, as they were overwhelmed with gratitude that he did not take after his father. Eventually Rïvan's loyal advisors, the first Elite Commanders, convinced their new apprentice of his rightful place. They went into hiding to train him in the magick of shadows, which he would practice until death. He would pass on all of his knowledge and power to his son, who would later become the great great grandfather of Tallen."

"So why did the descendants of Rïvan wait to take back the throne until now?"

"The Elites did not want to be outwitted again, so they decided that patience would be their greatest strength. They would become such great sorcerers that no one, man or woman, could ever oppose them. By passing on their knowledge of the magick of shadows to their sons, they would grow in power through the generations, eventually becoming unstoppable. They invented new spells, each son growing more crue and enraged at his stolen birthright. They were angry and dedicated. choosing the path of patient determination. Until now, since Tallen has accomplished the unthinkable by turning non-magickal Humans into sorcerers."

"Cane said that he had once been Tallen's teacher."

"That's true. Cane once thought that he could save the boy, keep him from the shadows. Although it's not his fault that Tallen turned to such treachery, as guilty as he feels. Tallen was simply born to do evil things."

"Oh dear," Esra sighed. She looked down at her empty bowl, not quite remembering eating, and set it down by the fire.

Baelin stood and nodded to his Assembly. "I think it's time we all get some rest. We leave in three hours."

Esra made her way back to her makeshift bed and pondered this new information, the story of Yuri and Tallen and switched babies. It seemed so unbelievable. But this nightmare of the past was certainly real enough now. She was proud of Yuri and hoped that she would demonstrate the same fearlessness when it came time for her to have courage. If only she could be a great sorcerer and save her Kingdom. But she was only one person. She would just have to do the best she could with what she had been given, which included some very talented friends at least.

"*Orro Wey Sim Fira Nadim,*" she whispered the words for sight magick as the lines snaked around the soft flesh of her inner forearm. As the map took shape, she traced the outline of the field they were camped in and noted the short distance to the edge of the trees. Shadow Glenn was just a small clearing in the midst of the dense forest, shrouded in darkness. It was almost upon them, the meeting of the great warrior people. Her first test, a desperate appeal to the Unni-se. Esra just hoped she'd stay alive long enough to meet him.

XXVII

It seemed like only moments since Esra had lain down on the carefully rolled blanket before she was pulled from her dreams by Meshok's long, wet tongue stroking her face. Her sleep had been troubled and full of glimpses of mysterious terrors. She dreamt that as soon as her Assembly had crossed the tree line of the forest the world was covered in darkness. There was some type of invisible wall that would not let them pass, and she could feel the dancing shadows of demons slowly overcoming them. Suddenly the Unni-se appeared, raising his flail with a menacing glare. Esra awoke in a cold sweat, wishing she had Arland's ability to change where her mind went in the night. Perhaps later she would ask him for the favor of another refreshing dream. She gathered her things swiftly while the impatient stamp of Roja's hooves churned the dry ground. As she tied the last of her things to the horse's saddle, she remembered what Baelin had said and made sure that her shortsword hung in its scabbard barely within reach and in plain sight.

Wanting the reassurance of her friend, Esra turned to Meshok, giving her one good ear scratching before the Wolf departed. They all quietly mounted their skycatchers and followed Baelin's lead, trotting slowly towards the tree line. It was a drastic change from the frantic pace they had maintained the past few days. The Assembly was still and pensive, the only sound the slow clicking of hooves and the rhythmic clatter of weapon against saddle. Esra tried not to think about what lay ahead of her. *Stay in the moment. Where are yer feet right now?* She repeated the things Fynn had told her to help stay out of her head and stop worrying. *Let this exact moment be yer focus.*

As Esra focused her attention on the gentle rocking of Roja's strong hips, the Keepers made their way slowly across the wide field. The sun was close to rising, casting an eerie orange glow over the travelers and their path ahead. The slow, rhythmic sway of riding comforted Esra, and she noticed the forest line was becoming less of a horizon and more like the shape of its individual yanquor trees. They would be at the border of Fira Nadim within minutes. She wanted nothing more than to finally arrive, to have an end to the ridiculous anticipation that had been engulfing her more each day.

Esra was alarmed to see a handful of small figures burst from the shelter of the forest, running swiftly towards them. She looked anxiously at her friends, who continued forward slowly with composure. Esra wondered if they were indeed that calm or if it was a learned skill of all Keepers, such determined restraint. Or maybe she really was just making too much of it all, tainted by bad dreams and fear so that she could not see their situation clearly. As the forms came into better view, she counted eight Unni warriors. Her throat was dry as she watched the scouts slow to only fifty feet away, forming a single line directly across their path. Esra noted that the figures were massive, unlike any Human she had ever seen, much bigger than even Baelin. The puffs of their breath in the cool air were barely visible under the brightening morning sky. No one spoke as her Assembly continued forward undisturbed.

They stopped only twenty feet from the line of Unni warriors as Esra's eyes frantically darted about, trying to stay on guard. The scouts were large and stout, she guessed somewhere between seven and eight feet tall. Even atop a skycatcher it didn't feel like the extra height was any real advantage. Two thick, dark horns bowed out from either side of their heads, curling out and upwards from their faces. There was a yellowish tint to their skin, and their bodies were covered in coarse, brown hair, which contrasted menacingly with the dark yellow of their eyes. Aside from the color, their eyes were surprisingly Human, even though their faces resembled a Lion, especially at the mouth and ears. A few of them had varying lengths of their horns cut down as punishment for crimes. They wore little armor, as if the massive breadth of their chest was enough protection. Leather skins were tied about their waists and Esra noticed that none of them wore shoes. She found it hard to believe that the crafty people could not make them, but perhaps their soles were so hardened it did not bother them to be barefoot. They had long hair that some pulled back and others let fall as it may, but the lack of clothes and dark appearance did not give them a disheveled look. No, it seemed as though they knew they looked intimidating and preferred it that way.

Some of the scouts held staffs, some morning stars, others had axes or clubs. Esra noticed with relief that there was at least no archer or ranged weapon. It gave her a momentary sense of comfort that she wouldn't be picked off unawares by an arrow until she realized that any archers were probably just hiding in the trees. And the warriors in front of her were certainly strong enough to throw their weapons with great force towards her anyway, twenty feet away or no. There was probably no need for a ranged attack.

For a long moment no one spoke, the two lines at a standstill. It must have been a strange sight in the middle of an open field, eight Unni warriors silently facing five Keepers atop skycatchers. It was then that the deep, booming voice of Baelin cut through the space between them.

"Mighty Unni warriors, guards of The Forest, we come te ye in peace. I am Baelin, Keeper of Arms, Keeper of Esra, and nephew to Zakai. Unni blood runs in my veins. We are Keepers of the Stronghold seeking council with the great Unni-se."

The line of warriors appeared slightly taken aback by this declaration but continued to hold up their weapons. An Unni with a club who stood on the end of the row leaned forward and let out a long, low snarl. Some of the others pounded their chest and howled in a display of aggression. Esra, unable to hide the terror on her face, looked towards her friends for a sign to flee. Her heart pounded loudly in her ears, marking time with steady rhythm. *Ta thump, ta thump, ta thump.*

Suddenly the Unni at the center, the only one silent and motionless until now, held up his fist. The others fell immediately quiet, lowering their weapons slowly. The center warrior took a step forward, sweeping his gaze over the five trespassers. Roja whinnied softly under Esra, sensing the discomfort in the air. She noticed that the one who appeared to be the leader had the most notches in his large horns. A chill ran down her spine as she remembered that Cane had told her these were marks earned for kills. When the leader finally spoke, his voice was even deeper than their blacksmith friend and slightly raspy.

"Baelin, Keeper of Arms and Esra, travelers of the Stronghold. It has been many years since yer kind has been allowed te enter Fira Nadim Forest. I know ye are not here te claim a noonmeal chat with long lost family. What business have ye with Zakai, the great Unni-se? Speak and be plain or we shall cut ye down as ye stand."

There were roars from the line of warriors behind him as Roja stepped about nervously, waiting for the cue to retreat. The center Unni raised his hand impatiently once again and the warriors fell silent. Baelin appeared unfazed as he answered the threatening intrigue.

"Great warriors, as I have said, we come in peace. LeVara is under attack and soon the Kingdom will be controlled by a more formidable foe than Rïvan himself, his descendant Tallen. We seek counsel with the Unni-se on matters of war."

The center Unni maintained a stone face amidst this revelation. "Yes, we are aware of Tallen. Yet this appears te be a war between Humans, not one that involves the Unni."

"Perhaps fer now," Baelin stated simply, "but I fear that Tallen's appetite fer power is far too strong te be satisfied by conquering one race and only part of the Kingdom. Soon all of LeVara will fall victim te his curse. This situation has not been been forced upon the races in a long time, and it is one that surely merits at least an audience with the Unni-se."

Esra swelled with pride at the courage of her blacksmith friend, the Fifth of their Assembly. The Unni warrior paused, looking unconvinced as he contemplated Baelin's words. "An' who are the rest of yer friends?"

Baelin nodded towards the Assembly as everyone introduced themselves.

"I am Arland, Keeper of Charm."

"I am Nadia, Keeper of Stealth."

"And I am Fynn, Keeper of All the Pretty Ladies in the Kingdom," he said, taking off his cap and swirling it downwards in a fancy bow.

Baelin gave a stern look, causing Fynn to straighten. "And Keeper of Earth, of course."

Esra wondered how he could be joking at a time like this as she looked towards the center Unni. Her voice came out at a somewhat higher pitch than normal and with a slight waver. "And I am Esra."

The Unni stared skeptically at the outsiders, brow creased in concentration. Esra worried that they had come this far only to be told it was impossible, that they could go no further. He looked towards her and bent his head slightly. "And what are ye the Keeper of?"

"Um, I'm not sure yet," she mumbled. "I mean, I'm not, um…"

Baelin interjected quickly. "Esra is in training. She is the daughter of two Great Keepers; Adonis, the Great Keeper of War and Talitha, the Great Keeper of Destiny."

Rumblings made their way down the line of Unni warriors. The commander looked mildly uncomfortable as he struggled with the difficulty of this decision. Esra held her breath as he took a long moment of quiet deliberation.

"Ye will dismount yer steeds and surrender yer weapons te us. All of them. We will then escort ye te Shadow Glenn where ye may seek council with the Unni-se. We will let him make the decision of what te do with ye."

A couple of the warriors growled in protest but were quickly silenced by a burning glare from their leader. "Search them."

Esra and the others leapt to the ground and were swiftly surrounded by the scouts. Before she could object she was being patted down by large hairy hands and stripped of all her weapons, even the small dagger she had carefully tucked into her boot last night. The bright rays of the morning sun cast a strange glow in the warriors' dark yellow eyes, causing them to dance with golden flecks. It was an unnerving sight, such Human traits in their beastly forms. But something about it reminded her of Baelin, and suddenly Esra wasn't so overwhelmed by fear.

They were herded into a cluster as the Unni encircled them, nudging them forward. Two of the scouts took a strap from the horses and guided them to the rear of the group. She opened her mouth to tell them the Great skycatchers need not be herded like livestock, but thought the better of it and kept her mouth shut. Besides, the skycatchers didn't seem to mind. In fact they whinnied a little in excitement. Esra took a stumbling step forward, willing her feet to move with the others. After a few tense minutes they came upon the forest line where the enormous yanquor trees stood as if fiercely guarding the entry to their home. There was no turning back now.

No one spoke as they crossed the border into Fira Nadim. As she had suspected, a few archers climbed down from their perches and joined the escorted group. Although Esra was fairly tall, the Unni had a much longer stride and she had to jog at frequent intervals to keep from falling behind. They continued this way at length, the breath of the Unni scouts coming out in swift gusts as their Lion-like nostrils flared. In her nervousness, Esra tripped clumsily over a root, scraping her knee against the rough bark of a tree.

After what felt like hours of silent traveling to her fumbling legs, Esra began to hear the faint sounds of life far ahead of them. They continued steadily through the forest, weaving around the large trees and stepping over the protruding sea of roots. Distracted, Esra stumbled once more and felt a large hand roughly grab her arm, keeping her from falling. She looked at the Unni next to her and smiled weakly in thanks. The townspeople of Sorley would never believe this story in a million years.

All at once the noises grew drastically louder as they exited the confines of the forest and entered a great open field. Even though the clearing was immense, the towering trees gave shade to much of the area and Esra immediately understood why it was called Shadow Glenn. Surrounding the open space were houses carved into the massive trees, smoke rising from chimneys jutting out from the side of the dwellings. Everything was a variation of brown or green, a hundred different shades. Spiral staircases wound around the outside of the yanquor trees. and it took a moment for Esra to realize that they were not structures affixed to the side of the bark, as Human staircases were built, but actually a part of the tree, carved seamlessly into the wood. Triangular lanterns made of a substance that resembled paper were scattered all over the clearing, casting a soft white glow.

In the center of the glade were round, open structures with fern covered canopies, a natural variation on Human blacksmith shops. The shelters were used for various purposes; some appeared to be stands for traders and merchants, while others were open aired taverns, with tree stump chairs and tables. A group of Unni gathered in one of the taverns gaped unabashed at the intruders, one holding a mug suspended a few inches from his open mouth, frozen in place.

In a large structure to the left, children were sitting quietly, watching a grown Unni give some type of lesson using a large wooden board with stones. Esra noticed that all of the canopies were covered in a soft netting which hung to the ground, perhaps to keep out Insects. And each side of the shelters had a roll of fabric tied to the fern covered roofs, protection that could be let down when wind or rain decided to appear.

One of the scouts must have gone earlier to the Glenn to tell news of the visitors, for there was already a crowd of Unni men, women, and children gathering near the tree line. Some of them looked angry, others curious, and some of the smallest children were dancing with excitement over the strange intrusion upon their normal Unni life.

The Unni children were much smaller than their parents but relatively large compared to Human children. They did not yet have their horns and the soft hair covering their bodies was not yet darkened. The strange yellow eyes and Lion-like face was more endearing rather than intimidating on the small ones. A man caught Esra's eye and spit at the ground with vehemence. She closed her eyes, wishing she had learned the magick of invisibility during her stealth training with Nadia.

The scout commander cleared a way through the crowd and towards the center of the clearing where a large fire was burning. Waiting there were hoards of Unni warriors with their weapons ready, glaring at the oncoming trespassers. Esra unconsciously drew near to the Unni that had saved her from falling and he turned his head to give her a puzzled look. *I hope they're not planning on eating us*, she thought anxiously, then scolded herself for being so silly.

The crowd swarmed around the area to get a better look as the intruders approached. Behind the fire was a raised wooden stage with an elaborately carved chair in its center, and sitting upon the chair was the most frightening thing Esra had ever witnessed. Even her nightmares about Zakai couldn't compare. His chest was as broad as three Humans, his hair thick and dark. Multiple scars covered his body, leaving jagged patches of skin where no hair would grow. A long braided beard hung down from his chin and his horns were longer than most of the other Unni, with notches covering almost every inch. The flail that Esra had dreamed about hung at his side, the huge spiked ball swinging tauntingly in his powerful grip.

As if he wasn't menacing enough, the eight foot tall figure stood up on the platform. All the other Unni froze in place, and there was a pulling tightness in Esra's chest. Her throat was so dry it felt swollen and raw. Willing her heavy legs to move closer, they stopped only a few feet away from the Unni-se, causing Esra to crane her neck upwards to take in the beast in front of her.

A wave of dizziness swept over Esra, who thought very seriously that she was about to faint. Wiping her clammy forehead with the back of her trembling hand, she hoped the helpful Unni would catch her again if she did fall. There had been brief periods during their journey from the Stronghold that Esra had been able to maintain a sense of optimism at her first test. Looking at the monstrosity before her, she now seriously doubted her powers of persuasion. The only hope left in Esra's mind was that the Unni-se would take pity on her weak soul and let them leave with their lives.

XXVIII

Zakai said nothing as he returned to his seat, looking down at them with a mixture of scorn and disbelief. The hot breath leaving his flared nostrils was the only movement on an otherwise still face. Esra's friends stood beside her unwaveringly and she turned to them for encouragement. Unable to catch anyone's gaze, she closed her eyes briefly before turning back to the Unni-se. The rough sound of his voice was so loud and deep that Esra thought she could feel her bones vibrating from within her chest.

"Humans of the Jade Gardens, what is yer business here? Speak quickly, fer I am a busy man."

At this Baelin took a step forward and bowed low, gesturing to the Assembly beside him. "Fearless Unni-se, we come te ye and yer people in peace. This is Arland, Keeper of Charm, Nadia, Keeper of Stealth, Fynn, Keeper of Earth, and Esra, daughter of the Great Keepers of War and Destiny. And I am Baelin, Keeper of Arms and Esra, and yer long lost nephew."

Growls swept through the crowd as shouts of anger and suspicion punctured the air.

"Silence!" Zakai snarled, raising his flail slightly. An uncomfortable stillness settled over everyone as they awaited their chief's next move. He cocked his head towards Baelin and gave a slight nod, allowing him to continue. Baelin turned to Esra, indicating that it was her turn to speak.

She tried to swallow but her throat was too dry. Racking her brain, she tried to remember all of the things she had prepared to convince the master of the forest that he was needed at the Stronghold. But her forehead felt clammy and she shivered violently as a bead of sweat trickled down the center of her spine. Esra could not remember the last time she felt such dread. Not even after being kidnapped by the Elites or waiting to meet her birth parents for the first time. It was as if she were never more aware of her body, every twitch of every muscle felt intensified.

She wished vehemently that her grandparents were with her. Sudden memories of the farm where Esra grew up flooded through her. She saw Lara and Mr. Sturik, their newly adopted daughter, Muriel Menthy and all the people in her town of Sorley. She thought of the people of Kiran Brae who were terrified and mourning and now being forced to work for the very souls that had killed their friends and family. The mothers whose babies had been torn from their pleading arms. If they could endure Tallen's treachery thus far, then surely she could think of something to say. Esra stepped forward and tried to hold her head up, although she could not stop the slight waver in her voice.

"Great Chief, we come to ask yer help. Tallen and his army of Elites are taking over the great cities of LeVara as we speak. Kiran Brae has been captured and Mahesh and Hals Arün will soon fall under his grasp. The Keepers wish to hold a War Council in little more than a fortnight with all representatives in attendance. We request yer presence so that the races may once again come together in order to defeat the evil that plagues our lands."

Shouts rose again in the crowd and this time Zakai did not try to silence them. "What makes ye think that the business of Humans is of any concern te my people? The unity that once existed has died long ago and fer good reason."

Flustered, Esra felt her face redden. Her Assembly had caused no trouble, not shown any aggression or hatred. The least he could do is be civil to them. They were rude and unwelcoming, and she felt a twinge of annoyance. "This may be the business of Humans now, but not fer long. Do ye think that Tallen will stop when every Human is under his rule? He is a wicked man and the threat is much greater than ye think."

"Don't talk te me as if I was naive of Tallen's abilities," Zakai snarled. "Perhaps he will try te war with us, perhaps not. I only wish he would be so stupid. Either way I don't see how we can trust a Human or the Council again after all this time. Ye are foolish te come here and hope fer such things."

Esra felt her face grow even hotter with aggravation. Instead of being frightened by his words she was very quickly becoming infuriated. She had felt the same way towards his people, the fearful apprehension, but she was working past it. Why couldn't he? "But that was hundreds of years ago! Are ye really so intolerant? There was a time when all the peoples came together in peace and sharing. When the Unni-se was married to a Human and that was respected. Don't forget that ye had a brother that was half Human. Besides, when did the Unni turn down the opportunity fer vengeance? Even if he chose not to come here, which isn't very likely, Tallen and his ancestors have already killed many of yer people."

Zakai leaned towards her with his yellow eyes narrowed. "Many people here believe it was the Humans who lead my people te slaughter trying te rescue a woman who bewitched our chief. If ye Humans consider yerself so informed and skillful, why do ye need the help of the Unni?"

"That's ridiculous, and it's exactly what Tallen wants ye to think. We need yer help because Tallen has already succeeded in conquering one of our great cities and in turning non-magickal Humans into sorcerers. He has an army of Elites as despicable as him who will stop at nothing to infect this land. He has found a way to make himself live far beyond the limits of Human age. He kills innocent men, women, and children who oppose him, and those left alive are made to do his bidding. Although the Keepers are strong, we cannot take the chance of fighting him by ourselves. We are LeVara's only hope. We must defeat him or the entire Kingdom will fall. I thought that ye were defenders of free people, the greatest warriors of our time. Perhaps I was mistaken."

Protests bellowed through the crowd as the Unni-se cocked his head at Esra. She could not read the emotion on his face as he raised his hand for silence. He turned and sat down in his chair, tugging at the long beard on his chin. After a long moment, he spoke with a voice so deep and soft that Esra had to lean forward to hear him.

"I believe in the skills and hearts of my people, know that they are the fiercest warriors. I also believe ye are right when ye say that he will not stop at a few cities. Tallen aims to conquer everything, that much is plain. Even from the shelter of the forest we have gained much knowledge of what is occurring in LeVara. It is true that the Unni desire revenge. But there are still many of my people who will not easily forget all the blood that was spilt in the name of Humans so many years ago. As such, I will give ye an opportunity te prove yer worthiness, Esra daughter of Great Keepers. I had heard rumors that there was a child, so now ye must live up te yer heritage. "

A stunned silence hung over the crowd as the Unni-se stood and announced to Esra in a thunderous voice, "The Valkor people te the south of Fira Nadim are persistent enemies who war with us at every opportunity. We have recently captured a scout and brought him te Shadow Glenn. Ye will duel with this man te the death. And if ye win, I will come with ye te the Stronghold."

XXIX

Shouts of opposition and agreement rung in Esra's ears as she stood in shock before the Unni-se. Duel to the death? This can't be right. She was supposed to convince him with her wise words, not her two weeks' worth of battle training. Baelin hastily stepped forward with a pained look.

"Great Chief, Esra has only begun her training a few short weeks ago. She is not yet an official Keeper nor trained fer battle. Let me fight in her stead."

"No," Zakai stood, gesturing to his guards nearby. "She must fight herself or ye will have no chance of leaving with my company. And may I also make it clear that no magick shall be used te aid or protect her, or the duel is forfeit. The daughter of Great Keepers must prove on her own that ye deserve our allegiance once more."

Esra's eyes darted around in panic as she felt herself being pulled away from her friends and towards what appeared to be a sparring ground. Baelin pushed his way through the throngs of warriors to her side. "Ye don't have te fight, Esra."

Every inch of her body begged her to agree. Let them be dragged out of the forest and sent home empty handed. It was not worth her life. It was absurd to think that she could stand a chance against any weathered warrior, especially a Valkor. This was no sparring practice with a wooden sword. She knew from her studies with Cane that the Valkor were a people who lived for the thrill of battle, even if there was no purpose for it.

"But this is my first test," she tried shakily to convince herself. "Nor and Cane believe in me, so do my parents. There must be a reason I've come to this point. If only I could win, as faint as that chance is, it might change everything."

"Esra, please," Baelin pleaded. "Let me try and speak with him

194

again."

"No," Esra said to her own surprise as she tried to swallow the lump that was quickly growing in her throat. "I will fight."

"But..." Baelin began to argue, quickly realizing from the look on her face that her mind was already made up. "Alright, well remember what we taught ye. Stay on yer toes and anticipate his movements. Fight smarter and ye needn't be stronger or bigger than him te win."

Esra nodded nervously. She suddenly realized that in order to stay alive she would have to kill someone else. She had never injured someone on purpose, let alone ended a life. Even trapping animals for food made her feel guilty. Trying to ignore that part of the bargain, she turned to the Unni who brought her Baelin's handcrafted sword and shield. The buckler seemed so small now, she wondered how she had ever used it to protect herself. The sword, its incandescent hues reflecting in the sun, felt familiar in her hands as she swung it twice to remind herself that she indeed knew of its form.

An Unni with greatly shortened horns appeared in front of her with outstretched hands, offering her a helmet. A large orange stone hung from a leather string around his neck, swinging towards her as he leaned down. She reached for the armor with gratitude. Although Baelin had worked on various pieces of her armor before leaving for Fira Nadim, it was nowhere near complete. The others had brought theirs along, but when she had tried on a few pieces it felt more uncomfortable and distracting than anything else. Baelin told her that sometimes armor was like that, made for a specific person, and no one else could grow truly accustomed to it.

Touching the cold metal of the helmet, she was jolted with a memory of Yarmon, the young Keeper of Foresight she had met just before their departure from the Stronghold. He had warned her about this.

Esra tentatively took the helmet into her hands as the warrior smiled at her with smug satisfaction and stalked away. She motioned to Baelin, who once again pushed his way through the hordes of people to her side.

"Good, ye've got a helmet at least."

"I can't wear it."

"Why not?"

She gestured to the Unni who was quickly disappearing from sight. "Yarmon warned me about a bad man who would offer me a helmet. He said not to wear it."

Baelin rubbed his chin thoughtfully and shrugged. "I hate te see ye fight without one, but I trust Yarmon. He's young but his powers are strong. Very well. I will see if I can find ye another."

"No thanks. I've been fighting without one so far, it would just be a distraction to change now. I won't be able to see."

"Alright," he conceded reluctantly. "Just remember te use yer shield and stay low."

The crowd continued to pack into a circle around the practice ring, the Unni men, women and children roaring and stomping in anticipation. Baelin took the rejected helmet and went to stand by the other Keepers, who looked equally worried. Esra gave them a forced smile, more for herself she knew than anyone else.

Across the sparring ground, which was roughly fifty feet in diameter, appeared a pale, strange looking man. His face and bare chest were covered with a red and white paint and he wore only a short tattered rag, covering from his waist to the top of his thighs. He was completely bald and appeared to be twice Esra's age. Although he was older, the long muscles in his lean frame were hardened, and as they untied his hands he snarled towards her with malice. There were only a few broken teeth remaining in his mouth. *What was I thinking? Maybe I can still say no.*

Before she had the chance to change her mind, the Unni-se approached the center of the practice field to announce the start of the contest. "My people will bear witness te this duel and the honor of my word. If the Valkor from the south wins, he will be allowed free and no further harm shall come te him. If Esra of the Stronghold wins, I will journey with her and the other Keepers te the Jade Gardens fer a War Council."

Cheers rang out as the Valkor grabbed the sword that was offered to him, refused the shield, and sunk low in preparation of the duel. Esra bent her knees and assumed the defensive stance that she had been practicing, buckler held in front of her, sword poised at the ready behind her.

"Let the battle begin!" Zakai roared.

The Valkor slinked slyly around the circle, waving his sword at her tauntingly. Swinging the blade easily around his shoulders, Esra noticed with disappointment how comfortable he seemed to be with his weapon. She tried to remember that she too felt at ease now with her sword, and swung it in a reciprocal display. They both stared at each other for a long moment, neither willing to make the first move. Finally the Valkor lunged forward and stabbed at her forward leg as Esra deflected the blow with her shield. He swung from the right and she countered him with her sword, their weapons singing with the impact. He continued towards her, unaffected by her defensive maneuvers. *Left, right, right,* she counted in her head as she anticipated his attacks. She watched his movements as if they were in slow motion, the sound of metal humming in her ears.

Suddenly he feigned left and jabbed quickly over her buckler, piercing deeply into her left shoulder. Esra cried out with pain and surprise as she watched the blade retreat from her skin, a slow gush of blood beginning to trail down her shielding arm. She could hear the Valkor laughing triumphantly as her eyes became speckled with intense bursts of light from the pain, and she stumbled backwards. Clenching her teeth, Esra retreated to the far corner of the sparring ground to recover. She adjusted her grip on the buckler, left arm slick with warm blood, and bent lower. Strangely reenergized by her injury, adrenaline moved her onto the offensive as she attacked him with a fierce determination. Even without a shield he countered her, and spun to take a wide swing at her head. She ducked quickly, clipping a small chunk out of his calf with a well-aimed jab. He howled, just as much from anger as pain, and backed away slowly. Esra took advantage of his withdrawal to catch her breath for the next stream of attacks.

There were bursts of ringing as their swords collided again and again, a strangely musical sound. Esra darted about, trying to keep ahead of his quick swings. Growing more confident in her abilities the longer she was able to avert disaster, Esra made two quick jabs, one causing a shallow scratch on his left side. The Valkor hissed in annoyance and took a wide sweep at her legs. Esra jumped over the blade just in time to see it reappear next to her head. She felt a stinging at her cheek as the sword lightly dragged itself across her face. The metallic taste of blood entered the corner of her mouth as she lunged forward powerfully with her buckler, knocking him to the ground. She took an overhead swing but he rolled over and onto his feet swiftly, jeering at her with his few crooked teeth.

Pacing the circle, Esra took the defensive stance that was quickly becoming a habit and continued to deflect his attacks. Gritting her teeth against the pulsating pain in her left shoulder, she tried to focus on all the defensive maneuvers she had learned. Sensing that the Valkor was becoming impatient, she hoped to wear him down by letting him attack. He lunged and stabbed at her furiously, growing exponentially more agitated with each deflection. After a few long minutes of sparring, he guessed at her game and retreated to the other side of the practice field.

"Oh no ye don't," she breathed. Not wanting to allow him recovery from his weakened state, Esra took the offensive and swung at him with controlled fury. He countered, but in his exhaustion the force of the blow knocked him off balance and he stumbled. Esra punched quickly with her shield at his sword hand and watched with relief as the blade tumbled to the ground.

She pointed her sword straight at the Valkor's throat and held it there, his raspy breath wheezing in and out heavily. She could hear the people around her, shouting for Esra to end his life. In her fury, she wanted to push the blade through his skin, this man who so desperately wanted to kill her. But instead she took a step back and lowered her sword, turning to bow to the Unni-se. Cries of disappointment traveled through the crowd as Zakai stepped forward.

"I respect yer mercy, but this was te be a duel te the death."

"Great Chief, I…"

"Esra!" At the sound of Baelin's panicked voice, Esra turned just in time to throw her sword out in front of her as the Valkor ran into her blade. The sword which he had retrieved to attack her from behind dropped heavily out of his raised hands. There was a sickening gurgling sound as Esra pulled the sword from his midsection and he crumpled over into a heap, a red stain spreading quickly over the dry earth. She looked towards Baelin with overflowing gratitude at his warning, which was followed abruptly by an intense wave of nausea. She bent over to vomit, a tear streaming down her bloodied cheek. The crowd of Unnis shouted and beat their weapons together in a cacophony of applause.

Baelin came to her just before she fell over, lowering her slowly to the ground. "Well done, Esra. Ye did it."

Arland and Fynn grasped each other's hand with relieved smiles as Nadia approached with a look of concern. "Ye had to, Esra. Don't be upset. He would've stabbed ye in the back, even after ye spared his life."

Zakai stepped towards her and stuck out a large hand. Esra felt dazed as she looked up at his looming form, almost as if she were in a dream and not quite in control of her own body. With much effort, she reached out with her good arm and he pulled her up so that she was standing right in front of him, her head barely as tall as his chest. He gave her a nod of approval before addressing the crowd.

"People of Fira Nadim, I am true te my word. Esra has proven herself this day as a Human with courage and honor. I will make ready te leave fer the Jade Gardens, where I will attend the first War Council in hundreds of years. I will represent the great Unni warriors in this gathering of the races. Before I leave we will hold our own council, where any man or woman may speak as they like upon the issue of war against Tallen. I promise te hold yer opinion in mind as I go te the Stronghold, but in the end know that I will decide what I think is best fer our people."

Esra blinked back the wetness that formed over her eyes as she looked up at the sun filtering dimly into the Glenn. She could hear the excited cries of the Unni crowd that surrounded her, but they seemed distant in her ears. A whipbird flew low over her head, and she could see the animal's chest swell gently as it breathed, it's wings framed in a graceful bow. It was so alive. Yet how quickly things could change. Esra had claimed a life, but she felt as if it were her own life that were ending. It was if she could feel the steady breath leaving the Valkor's lungs for the last time, sensed the irrevocable end to the beating of his heart as his body surrendered its fight to survive.

Barely aware that her face was streaked with tears, she lowered her head in defeat and felt darkness close in on her soul. An old tavern ballad from Sorley came to mind, and she felt momentarily confused about all the songs she had heard about the valor and glory of war, of a battle swiftly claimed. She had taken a life, and there was nothing triumphant or glorious about it. Like the Valkor, she now had the urge to lay down and succumb to fate, to submit to this strange world that had such indiscriminate rules. She put her face in her hands and let out a great heaving sob that shook her body violently. *I'm sorry, I'm so sorry* she began to whisper over and over, rocking gently back and forth. *I'm sorry.*

Baelin stood looking wide eyed at her sobbing form before slowly coming to put his arms around her. Esra let herself be held for a moment, cursing the world and all of its bitter ways. Cursing the Elite soldiers and Tallen, LeVara's indifferent King, the stubborn Unni-se, her estranged parents, everything that had brought her to the brink of this moment, of her needing to kill someone. What saddened her more than anything was the thought that this was just the beginning, that she would feel the sensation of bone and flesh on her sword again, or else be on the other side of someone's blade. And she felt guilty at the thrill she now felt at her aliveness, her gratitude that it had been her opponent, and not her, that lay broken and bleeding on the dry ground. Baelin held her steadily until the sobs slowly left her body and were reduced to small gasping breaths.

When she was too exhausted to cry anymore, Baelin stepped back awkwardly and lowered his gaze. The Unni that helped her in the forest came marching up and indicated in a rumbling voice that Zakai requested Baelin's presence. He glanced worriedly at Esra, who stared at him blankly.

"Go, I'll be fine," she said scratchily, her throat raw.

Fynn suddenly appeared next to them and Esra gratefully leaned onto his steady frame. Without another word, they parted from her blacksmith friend as the Unni guided them towards a tent where she could sit and rest. By the time they reached the tent, Esra's knees buckled and she slid downwards until she was sitting awkwardly next to the fire. Fynn began to unload a bag full of herbs onto a folded blanket. "Jumpin' jig, Es. Serves him right, being skewered like a noonmeal rabbit. Ye did great. Nasty gash he gave ye, though."

She turned her head to look blandly at the dark, thick blood that was still flowing from her left shoulder. She felt nothing, the horror of the event of death had reduced any physical injury to a mild irritation, like a fly buzzing about a horse's mane. Fynn cut the sleeves of her shirt and she barely flinched as he tenderly felt the wound. He wiped the skin and placed a clean cloth over her arm, taking her hand and directing her to apply pressure to the bandage.

"It's too bad he told us we couldn't use magick. We were all waiting te cast some fantastic spells."

"It wouldn't have been fair," she whispered distractedly.

"Aye, well neither is a poisoned helmet."

"What?"

"That helmet someone tried te give ye. If ye would have put it on ye would be dead. There were a few small thorns in the top covered in the juice from a hethro plant. It would have made yer muscles weak, vision blurry, ye wouldn't have been able te fight. And if the Valkor didn't finish the job the poison would have killed ye within minutes. There is a cure, but not one easily found. I doubt even with all my skills as a Keeper, a spell te slow its course and the fastest skycatcher in the Kingdom, that I would have been able te save ye. "

"Oh my," Esra took a jagged breath, stunned by this revelation. Yarmon was right. She owed him her life. The realization seemed to bring her halfway back to the present, and she winced in pain. "Too bad I don't have an Earring of Recovery."

"Aye," Fynn nodded, absentmindedly touching the small silver hoop that was his fourth Gift. "But remember, although I can heal from any physical wound and I am immune te disease, I can still be attacked by magick. Now I know ye've had a rough day already, but I think it's a perfect time fer yer first lesson in restoration magick."

"Wait," she grasped his hand before it touched her shoulder and lowered it slowly into his lap. "Don't heal me."

Fynn cocked his head to look at her with concern. "The cut is deep, Es. We must stop the flow of blood and repair the muscle, else ye may not be able te use it again."

She looked up at the sky for a long moment before replying in a low whisper. "I have taken a life today. Ye and the others may have done it before, but I have not. I will remember what this foul deed has cost. If I choose to heal this hurt without ever being submitted to the irreversible pain of battle, I fear it will make me cold. Ye will do whatever healing is necessary using plants, as any apothecary would, but no magick."

They both sat in silence as Fynn absorbed her request. Then he reached over to snatch a small satchel from the ground beside them dumping the contents on the ground. He quickly began taking pinches from the small pouches, mixing the powders together in a bowl. "I admire yer courage, Es. And I realize that ye are feeling some things that are very foreign te ye. Killing someone, no matter how justified, is not something te take lightly. None of us do, and I respect ye fer it. However, I have two requests. One is that ye let me cast a simple spell to ward off infection, as that will be a most difficult thing fer me te cure later on, magick or no. Infections are complex, wicked things that penetrate the entire body, and they can be fatal. I promise that the spell will not lessen yer physical pain. Two, after the wound has healed the best it could on its own, ye must let me use magick te repair the muscle. Otherwise, ye may not be able te fight properly."

Esra contemplated the wisdom of his words before nodding weakly. He rubbed some type of oil over her shoulder, numbing it slightly before starting to pack the wound with the mixture from the bowl. Esra writhed in agony as he gently held her still and whispered the words of the spell to stave off infection. *Moro nuur trivia.* There are two components te restoration magick; one is physical and the other mental. The physical element is what ye see here, the herbs and ointments, the various mixtures I use when healing someone. It sounds simple, knowing which plant te use fer what ailment, but the truth is that it depends on the person yer trying te heal. And mixing different things together can prove te do more harm than good if ye don't know what ye need."

He continued packing her wound as he spoke and she tried to focus all her attention on his words. She had a feeling this was an attempt to distract her from the pain more than it was a lesson, knowing that she would probably remember little of what he told her. "The second element is the magickal side of healing. This is also fairly complicated. There are various spells that one can use te promote healing or cure an ill. Although I'm afraid there's no cure fer what ails me. It seems all women are indisputably attracted te me. Short of beating 'em off with a stick, it's a hopeless case."

He held his hands over his heart as he looked at Nadia, who had approached with a bucket of water. Esra laughed weakly as her Elf friend dropped the bucket on the ground, sloshing some water over the side and onto Fynn's pants.

"That should cool ye off a bit," Nadia scowled. "Esra, how are ye feeling? Ye look a little pale."

"I feel...awful, but not from the wound. From something much deeper.. Fynn is trying to teach me a little about healing."

"Well, the bleeding's stopped. Still, no heavy fighting or lifting fer at least a week," Fynn directed.

"No lifting?" Nadia stared at him in confusion. "Was there something that didn't allow ye to heal the wound properly?"

"Aye, miss Esra here wouldn't allow it," he said. "I will explain her request te ye later. Right now I think we need te put a little something on her face fer that cut, and then she should probably take a nice rest."

Esra nodded as Nadia unrolled a blanket and helped her to lie down. She had always known there was a violent element in her being, that she may be capable of such a thing as killing. But she still couldn't accept that this aggression had become a part of her, even out of necessity. She felt both empowered by this anger and appalled by it. How strange that one could both fear and respect something at the same time.

Esra was barely aware of Fynn's fingertips on her cheek as she closed her eyes to welcome the darkness of her eyelids. She let her mind fill with it, until blackness covered everything, leaving no room for thoughts or visions of what had just transpired. She had taken a life, and there was no going back, no matter how much she wished it were a dream.

XXX

Eventually Esra would fall asleep, bruised and aching and sick with grief but with the bitter sweet knowledge that she had successfully completed her first test. As she rested, the Unni-se held a village commune where people could come speak their minds and be heard by their chief. Her Assembly wanted to attend, but Zakai suggested that it may not be a good idea.

"Can we perhaps walk around Shadow Glenn? I would love to see more of it," Nadia asked hopefully.

"I think not. Ye have caused quite an uproar here, and even with guards I can't ensure yer safety while wandering about. I hope my people would act with honor, but this is a long-standing feud and unfortunately I cannot predict some people's actions. As ye have already seen from the poisoned helmet. Feel free te stay here and rest and eat, and I will post as many guards as possible around ye."

By the time Esra awoke from a hot and restless sleep, she was disappointed to learn that they could not walk around Shadow Glenn. She longed for a distraction from the reality of her situation, from the memory of her blade piercing the midsection of the Valkor. But a hot throbbing in her shoulder reminded her of the dangerous nature of their visit, and she said no more. Fynn tried to distract her by introducing all the herbs in his pack, and she focused on his words with a comforting intensity that blocked out all other thoughts. She was grateful that her mind was disciplined enough to allow her a brief respite from her mental torture.

Zakai returned to their camp at midday with a few other Unnis trailing close behind him. "These are some of my most trusted commanders, and they will accompany us te the Gardens. It's as much fer yer protection as mine. I find it hard te believe that ye haven't encountered any Elites on the journey down here, so my guess is that we'll find some on yer way back."

The Unni also rode skycatchers, as they were the largest horses in the Kingdom, and, Esra guessed, the only ones who could possibly support their weight. She watched as Roja and the other horses in her group greeted the Unni skycatchers. It was at this interval that Meshok trotted out of the forest and across the open field to Esra.

"There ye are!" She rubbed the Great Wolf's head briskly. "Ye missed all the excitement! I battled a Valkor and completed my first test."

Meshok licked her hand in response before sauntering up to one of the Unni guards, who turned to look her with wide eyes. "What's this, a Great Wolf?'

"Aye, that's Meshok."

He bent down so that he could scratch behind the Wolf's ears. It was a comical sight, this massive Unni warrior petting her furry head with great care. He appeared to be younger, at least by Unni standards, and the hair covering his body had a dark orange hue to it. "We've not seen one of her kind in a very, very long time. They were an ally in our fight against Rïvan all those years ago. Brutal warriors, the Great Wolves are, but they don't usually take te non-Wolves. How did ye ever stumble upon one?"

"Meshok was a gift from my parents. I believe they've somehow befriended a pack of them. She's been with me since she was a pup. And Fynn, the Keeper of Earth, can speak to them."

He nodded, impressed. "I'm Hadvi."

"I'm Esra. Pleased to meet ye. Do ye know who else is coming with us?"

"Two other commanders, Mox and a woman named Shova."

As if on cue the other two guards approached to introduce themselves.

"The name's Shova, and this 'ere is Mox," a middle aged woman offered with a crooked smile. "I'll be keepin' all these menfolk in line. Nice bit with the Valkor, by the way."

"Err, thanks." Esra was surprised that a woman here could be a commander. There were no such women in the King's Human army. Seeing that Shova's arms were as big around as any of the other Unni men, Esra in no way doubted her abilities as a fighter.

Mox looked older, which Esra deduced from his long horns and the dotting of silver hair that peppered his body. Although Shova seemed simultaneously as fierce as she was jovial, he seemed more stern and less talkative than the others, as he hardly acknowledged their introduction except with a terse nod of his head. But after getting used to Baelin's quietness, this did not overly disturb Esra.

By the time they had finished loading up the horses it was dinner time, so the group ate a quick meal of flatbread and dried vernok before mounting their steeds. Zakai and the others bid farewell to their families as they turned towards the darkness of Fira Nadim. It surprised her to see that the Unni-se had three children and a beautiful wife, Kinci, although exactly what made her beautiful, Esra was unsure. Only a short day ago she could not imagine thinking any Unni was more or less attractive than another.

It was much quicker riding out of the forest than it was walking into it, and after only an hour they were back into the sparse, flat fields north of Fira Nadim. Without the massive trees to wind around, their pace intensified and they rode hard through the night, stopping only once for a short rest.

It looked as if they would maintain the same pattern of traveling at night and hiding for sleep during the day. Esra had grown accustomed to the strange hours and found that the night air indeed made for more pleasant traveling than the burning sun. She also found that she was now able to doze lazily on Roja's gently rocking back. Over the next few days the flat terrain would become rocky, rolling hills and Esra found herself chatting comfortably with Hadvi and Shova while Mox sat quietly beside them.

"So Hadvi, do ye have a family?" Esra asked.

"I just had me first daughter with me new wife," he beamed proudly. "I'm young, only eighty. Although by yer standards I'm already a dead man. Heh."

"That's true. Congratulations! I'm sorry ye have to be away from them now."

"Aye, me too. But I've dedicated myself te training young warriors in the hopes that one day I may be called upon te protect my people."

"A noble calling. What weapon do ye use?"

"Twin axes, but only when absolutely necessary. I prefer the use of me horns, which is considered one of the most difficult and highly respected battle skills of the Unni."

"Bumbling huckfly. I certainly wouldn't want to get skewered by ye."

"I promise not te try," Hadvi chuckled.

"Shova, do ye have any children?" Esra turned towards the woman warrior.

"Aye, seven young boys. I grew up with all brothers and alas, now I'm surrounded by men again. Before I left I convinced em that if they didn't listen to their father while I'm gone their horns would fall off. Ha!

All them rowdy boys, it's one of the reasons I'm so patient, I suppose, in training the warriors in Shadow Glenn. Have done that fer almost all my life. I love it, getting the young ones te find themselves, their strength. It's very rewarding"

"Soon ye'll be training my daughter," Hadvi added.

"Ye jes can't wait, eh," Shova chuckled. "I've hear ye've already commissioned a tiny axe fer Pixa at the blacksmith."

"Aye, te the frustration of my wife. She'll be pleased when Pixa becomes a warrior, but it's a bit too soon fer her, I think. We hope that someday she'll be as great a leader as ye, Shova."

"I'm sure she will be, if I 'ave any hand in it."

"What's yer weapon of choice?" Nadia asked interestedly.

"The war hammer. Normally considered more of a man's weapon, which is why I chose it," she added with a wink. "Never could stand being told I shouldn't do somethin'."

Esra noticed that she had almost as many notches in her horns as Mox, who was the most seasoned veteran. "What about Mox? He seems to be a quiet one."

"Aye, he's always been reserved, but much more so as of late," Shova explained. "He lost his wife and only child some years ago when they were killed by Valkor scouts. He'd never admit it, but he respects the fact that a young Human woman with little training could kill one in a duel. I daresay he might not 'ave agreed to come if it wasn't fer yer boldness. A crying shame, it was, when his family died."

"That's terrible," Esra said sadly. She looked over Mox who sat whittling a small piece of wood with a furrowed brow. "What does he fight with?"

"A mace. Don't let his age fool ye, he's still bloody good with it."

Zakai continued to say little and avoided most of the others, preferring to sit in solitary meditation by the fire for the first two nights. Hadvi and Shova would join in the Assembly's conversations with proud tales of the Unni people and funny stories of their families. Esra's shoulder throbbed with a hot pain as she laughed at Shova's tales about her seven sons.

"Ruka, my second youngest, jes got his head stuck in a bucket trying te lick sugar from the bottom. Left 'em in there, I did. Cut two holes where his eyes were and made em walk around like that fer a whole day as punishment."

Even Mox grunted with approval as Hadvi told a short tale of the great chiefs that had come before Zakai. Esra slowly grew more comfortable around the Unni, finding that their piercing yellow eyes were more inquisitive than aggressive, and their horns more intimidating for other foes than dangerous to her. Bu she silently worried that the Unni-se was not open to the War Council after all, and maybe he would avoid the others for the duration of the journey. She wished that he would at least try to talk with his nephew Baelin. On the third night, her worries were slightly relieved as the Unni-se approached Esra an hour before they were ready to depart.

"Esra, soon te be Keeper, I would like te assist in yer training, if ye would like."

Startled, she looked up at Zakai and gave him an open mouthed nod.

"That would be wonderful," she said earnestly, curious at his sudden interest in helping her.

He walked Esra over to a small board he had laid out on a blanket, which looked hauntingly similar to the strategy practice boards and stones in the War Room at the Stronghold. Although she had not yet had a proper lesson in strategy at the Gardens, this board looked significantly more complex, with many new markings and stones. As they sat down, Zakai made no move to describe the board to her.

"Why did ye decide te become a Keeper?"

Esra sat for a moment as she contemplated his question, wanting to answer it as truthfully as possible. "Because I want freedom fer myself and fer all the people of LeVara. And because I believe in the Keepers and what they are doing, how they live their lives. Before I came here, Baelin showed me the Five Laws of Keepers, and I greatly respect these guidelines."

"But why not fight with yer Human King?"

"King Keridon is not the most...dedicated... ruler, and he is ill prepared fer war. The Keepers are ready and willing to lead a fight against Tallen. And besides, a King is still a King and is in command of his people. The Stronghold requires nothing of its members except commitment to their quest fer the freedom and happiness of all creatures. Most rulers of LeVara have not been unjust, but they are still the sovereign and law of the Kingdom, and we must do their bidding in the end. I am not suggesting that LeVara doesn't need a King or that I don't want one, I just never knew there were any other options. I have lived this way all my life, as have the generations before me. Now that our freedom is in question I realize what it truly means to have it."

Zakai nodded, apparently satisfied with her answer, and began to explain the basics of the board and its various pieces. Three people or an army, high ground or low, full sun or dark of night, there were endless scenarios to cover. Almost every other sentence she had to stop him with a question as if he were speaking a foreign language. She recalled her lesson with Cane when he told her that Zakai was a strategist like no other. She fully believed that now. He seemed not only to be a mastermind in war preparations but knew exactly how to adapt to the many different situations that a battle could morph into. Esra could hardly do anything but gape open-mouthed at his instruction and occasionally sputter out an incredulous question.

On their journey the Unni-se would continue this lesson at each break, taking out the board for a short time to give her something that she could think about during her ride, a battlefield riddle to solve. She was not sure if Zakai had simply gotten bored or was sincerely interested in her training, but she was grateful for the help either way. He seemed not only to be a mastermind in war preparations but knew exactly how to adapt to the many different situations that a battle could morph into. And since she could not physically fight as her shoulder healed, this was the next best thing.

Esra's Assembly eventually began to practice their defensive and offensive maneuvers, intending to brush up on their battle skills as well as help pass the time with some friendly rivalry. The two races seemed eager to assert themselves as the master of their craft. For one lesson Shova stepped in showed them how to use a war hammer. Esra could hardly hold the heavy thing as her one shoulder still hung painfully in a sling and the other was weak from fatigue. She had been having trouble sleeping since leaving the forest and her dead foe behind. But she watched the sparring and studied the way the weapon was used and how to better defend against it.

The Unni marveled at the craftsmanship of the weapons Baelin had made and especially liked the creativity of his staff with the unbreakable Knife of Piercing and spiked ball at opposite ends. They looked impressed when he told them about the Hammer of the Shendari at his shop in the Stronghold, the only blacksmithing tool capable of forging Shendari scales.

Esra even got to hold Arland's Greatsword of Narajuv, but she knew from the moment it touched her hands that it was not meant for her. It was an instinct similar to riding the same horse for years and suddenly trying an entirely differently shaped saddle. But it was more than that, almost as if the sword had an aversion to her. She was awkward, more awkward than usual, and could not seem to wield the sword hardly at all.

"Don' worry," Arland assured her. "The sword was intended fer only one warrior, who will enjoy greatly improved skills. Anyone else who tries to use it will have the opposite effect."

"There is much more te all of ye than meets the eye," Shova acknowledged with respect.

They were almost halfway through their journey to the Jade

Gardens when Nadia stopped her horse mid-stride and cocked her head to one side. Esra and the others halted immediately, craning their necks to look at the Elf woman, who appeared to be deep in thought.

"Err…is everything alright?" Esra finally asked, breaking the silence.

"Elites," Nadia spat with vehemence, rocking to take the Stone of Awareness out of her left side pocket.

"How many? How far away?" Baelin asked quickly.

She held the small grey stone in her hand and rubbed it gently between her fingers, closing her eyes. "Maybe a day ahead and heading towards us from the North. There are many of them. Dozens upon dozens, I think."

"Fynn, can ye talk te Meshok?" Baelin turned towards the archer, who sat with alertness atop My Lady. "She should be traveling ahead of us. Find out the details, we need te know exactly what's coming."

Fynn too fumbled briefly to find his Listening Stone and held it between his palms. Esra felt slightly paralyzed with panic as she waited for her friend to reply.

"She's far ahead of us, as usual. She says that she can continue forward and scout the area a bit, let us know more when she can."

"Alright," Zakai nodded. "We should wait here until then, get a few bites te eat and take some rest, make preparations. We don't need te meet with them any sooner than we have te."

The group dismounted as Fynn communicated their plan to Meshok. Esra pictured the Great Wolf running at full speed towards the north, her grey flanks shining with sweat. Fynn began to pace back and forth, clutching the stone in a tight fist. My Lady whinnied nervously, nuzzling towards her disturbed rider. Suddenly Fynn made a turn and came straight at Esra, with a determined look on his face.

"It's time te heal yer shoulder," he continued before Esra could open her mouth to protest. "I know that ye have dealt with the pain the last few days, and it has been admirable. But we are about te meet with some nasty fighting, and ye need te be at yer best fer everyone's sake. We will need every ounce of skill at our disposal."

He stepped forward and placed both hands on her shoulder, murmuring a low incantation. Esra's shoulder suddenly filled with light, and she opened her mouth to scream in agony when the sensation subsided, leaving her breathless. Fynn removed his hands and untied the sling. She stretched tentatively at first, cautious that the prior days pains would come rippling back through her muscles. When nothing happened, she luxuriously rolled her shoulder through its full range of motion.

"Thank ye," Esra said sincerely. "Someday, ye'll have to tell me how ye did that."

"Someday, aye," Fynn agreed. "Yer lessons have been more random and unpredictable than an injured brengard surrounded by a hunting party, but I promise that one day we will explain the concept of magick te ye."

Esra thanked him again before walking over to Roja and grudgingly pulling out her sword. Unnerved by the prospect of battle and not quite ready to eat, she wanted to attempt some quick sparring practice, do something besides sit around and wait. She looked at the pearlescent blade and turned it over in her hands. Baelin had secretly cleaned it for her after she killed the Valkor, and she was grateful for it. He probably knew that she didn't want to see the blood on her sword, evidence of the life taken.

The next hour was full of nervous anticipation as everyone waited in stunned silence. Fynn made no attempts to sing or make jokes, even Shova was not quite as jovial. Esra swung her blade around in the slow, practiced movements of her lessons, attempting to reacquaint herself to the motions of battle. Her shoulder didn't give her a hint of pain, although it was somewhat stiff from lack of use. It seemed like a full day would go by before they would hear anything. Esra wasn't sure she wanted to know the truth about what was coming, but not knowing seemed even worse.

"I've got some bad news," the archer finally gathered everyone together. "The Elites are almost upon us. They are burning small villages as they go. Meshok tells me that they will meet with us in less than a day."

"How many?" Zakai asked.

"About a hundred, and all on horseback."

"A hundred! That's greater than ten times our numbers. And they're all trained sorcerers and warriors," Esra said bitterly.

"They're burning villages?" Nadia asked.

"Meshok says that they're slaughtering everything in their path, including women and children."

"They should still be at Kiran Brae," Esra wondered aloud. "Why are they already east of The Naduri River and moving south? Are they headed fer Hals Arün already?"

"No, a hundred Elites could never capture a great city. They probably have special orders te ambush us as we come back from Fira Nadim. Somehow they guessed at our plan te recruit the Unni-se and aim te catch us on our return."

"We should ride up and meet them," Hadvi growled. "Give them a little surprise ambush of our own."

"No," Zakai said forcefully, turning to Fynn. "Where's the next village?"

He quickly summoned the Tur on his arm, glancing over the map. "There are a number of very small villages that we'll be passing in the next couple days. But a town called Wilspry which houses a few hundred people is a half day ride northwest. My guess is that the Elites will be heading there. Plenty of people te kill and houses te rob. They will be able te restock their food and supplies."

"We should ride up and meet them."

"No, we should try and warn the town."

"Maybe we can get them out and hide them."

"We'll never have enough time, we need te fight."

"If we stay here we'll have more time to prepare."

Zakai silently twisted his long, braided beard as the rest of the group argued back and forth. Holding up his hand, everyone looked to him in silence.

"We ride hard and reach Wilspry by morning. This will hopefully give us time te warn the townspeople about the attacks. We will then have a few hours te set some traps and make other preparations, perhaps barricade a part of the town. Out of a few hundred townspeople there have te be some that can fight, so any that are willing and able should join us. With any luck our traps will take care of half of the soldiers and we can take care of the rest. I daresay the Elites won't expect us rallying a town."

Everyone nodded in agreement and quickly mounted their horses, not wanting to waste any time. Esra thought again of her friends and family back in Sorley and hoped that they were safe. *This could be my village, my grandparents.* The suggestion of it made Esra shake with anger. How could someone just kill for the joy of it? Because they believed that the people they were murdering weren't worth anything? It disgusted her, disgusted everyone around her. She could see the fury on their faces. They were going to fight. They were going to defend Wilspry and kill every Elite that dare cross its border. They were going to fight.

XXXI

With Fynn as their guide they made it to Wilspry as the orange light was barely peeking over the horizon. The sight of the small town made Esra wince in homesickness and she touched the bread beater tucked in Roja's sidesaddle.

"Good people of Wilspry, we bring news of a danger that comes to yer town!" Arland cried loudly as they rode past the farms and small houses. "Awake from yer sleep, leave yer plows in the fields. Come meet with us at the town center!"

Women and children came onto their porches to see who was making such a fuss, and the men raced towards their families with the threat of danger ringing in their ears. When the people of Wilspry saw that it was not just a man who had called to them but a group of Humans, dark skinned Elves and large hairy beasts upon larger horses, they thought it a dream. But it could not be a dream, for there was their neighbor and his dog, and there was old man Jaspar. So they followed each other, whispering and wondering what these strangers meant by such a peculiar, dramatic entrance.

They rode past the low wooden gate that bordered the town, the skycatcher's hooves beating loudly on the dry ground. Wilspry was smaller than Sorley, with only a general store, feed mill, small smithing area, and an old alehouse that included a few small boarding rooms. Upon reaching the stables, Esra dismounted and thrust Roja's fake reins into the hands of the only stable boy in the town, who stood open mouthed at the skycatchers and four towering Unnis. The young lad took note of the various weapons that hung from the saddle and asked no questions as he took the horses away immediately to be watered and fed. As the crowd gathered, Esra worried about their reaction to such news, especially from such an odd seeming group.

"What if they don't believe us?" She asked nervously. "Would we have to continue forward and try to stop the Elites before they reach the town? Or maybe at least a few of the townspeople will join us."

"Don't worry, Arland is very convincing." Nadia assured her. "He is the Keeper of Charm, after all, and speaking to crowds is one of his skills."

The murmurs gained in volume as the crowd swelled and curiosity rose to an uncomfortable tension. Looking around, Esra could see that people seemed just as unnerved by the race of their visitors as they were with anticipation of this unexpected news. The youngest children were crying at the sight of the Unni and some of the men had even brought weapons. Esra hoped they were for use against the professed danger and not her new friends.

"Good people of Wilspry! I bring news that yer town is in danger." Arland announced from the porch of the boarding house. "I know that we must appear to be a strange lot, but we mean ye no harm. We are Keepers of LeVara and these are the Unni of Fira Nadim Forest. Many of ye have heard tell of us, whispers passed down from yer mothers and fathers from their mothers and fathers. Stories about the mystical Unni warriors who live far to the south of our realm. Of sorcerers that can bend elements to their will, do strange and magnificent things using only a few words. Or perhaps ye've even seen Keepers passing through here, sensed briefly the strength of magick that surrounds them. Well, we appear in front of ye now, as true as the light of day, as allies in yer hearts. If word has not yet reached yer town, our Kingdom is under attack from a foul sorcerer named Tallen. The great city of Kiran Brae has already fallen under his control."

Esra had expected the crowd to erupt in panic at the news, but instead, they stood silently, waiting for him to continue. It was as if they were completely mesmerized. Arland was taking every care to sound and appear as calm as possible, but she had not realized the full extent of his skills until then. He truly was a powerful Keeper.

"Tallen's army of Elites is slaughtering people throughout the Kingdom and there are a hundred of them headed right here. They will be upon this town within a few hours, so we will need yer help in defending it. Any person who is able to fight, please join us. If ye cannot fight but wish to help, we will see that ye are put to use. There will be barricades to build and traps to be set. Children and anyone else unable to aid in our resistance will be concealed in the safest place possible. We promise to do what we can to defend ye and yer families."

Listening to him oddly gave her a sense of hope, and looking around she knew the townspeople felt the same way. It was a complete contradiction of Human nature. To be able to deliver such news without causing a riot was truly amazing. Even in the face of such absurdity, such imminent danger, you couldn't help but believe him with a confident fervor.

Arland began shouting out instructions and there was a flurry of motion and sound as the people of Wilspry scattered into groups. There were no questions, no objections, just organized movement.

"This is unbelievable," Esra marveled. Those who wanted to fight came to the front of the crowd while the children and elderly made their way to the back. Many of the women and children too young to fight gathered to the side, willing to help set the traps. Out of a few hundred townspeople, it appeared that more than half were able and willing to assist in the defense in some way, which greatly relieved Esra. The more people helping the better everyone's chances.

Esra had to steer a few young children, probably only five or six, away from the group of those willing to fight. They held up their small sticks and pocket knives like brave swords, poised to prove that they were indeed battle ready. She smiled inwardly at their earnest protests.

"It's Arland's special request that ye be the warriors dedicated to taking care of the women and children. It's yer job to protect them, and a great responsibility," she convinced them with a serious gaze. Satisfied with that response, the young ones bounded back to their families with renewed vigor.

A master of communication and efficiency, Arland spoke briefly with Zakai and began to assign tasks to all of the groups present. The farmers retreated to their houses to gather all the supplies and arms they could. Esra watched as Baelin ducked behind the general store to head for the small blacksmith shop, hoping to fashion at least a few spears and shields in the limited time before the Elites arrived. Nadia disappeared, attempting to use her stealth to locate a place where the small children and elders could hide undetected. Shouts rang through the crowded streets as people darted about, trying to prepare for a battle too soon coming.

As some of the townsfolk arrived with their arms, it was clear that virtually none of them owned a real weapon besides a bow for hunting. Most stood ready with hammers, shovels, and other various farming tools.

"These *weapons* are better suited fer barns and fields," Mox grumbled.

"It's all they have," Shova countered fiercely. "At least so many are willing te fight. Besides, I use a hammer and it crushes skulls jest as well as yer fancy mace."

Fynn was able to seek out the few woodworkers in the group and took them to Baelin, who had set up shop in the smithing area, to begin making as many bows and arrows as possible. Since Shova, Hadvi and Mox were commanders back in Shadow Glenn, they quickly took on the task of teaching the men and women who arrived with weapons. Pairing townsfolk up for some practice sparring, they began to give basic instructions on offensive and defensive maneuvers. Esra looked to Arland, feeling useless in the scattered chaos of preparations.

"Esra, I want ye to go help Zakai with planning the defense and setting the traps," he instructed, gesturing towards the alehouse. She nodded and took off towards the building, taking the entry stairs two at a time. Bursting through the front door, the room was packed full of people whispering low and passionately about the defense of their town. The center of focus appeared to be towards a towering frame at one of the large round tables. Esra began to push her way through the people to the Unni-se until Zakai caught sight of her and motioned to let her pass. A townsperson was tracing his hands about on the table, trying frantically to describe the layout of the town and surrounding landscape.

"Wait, I can help with this." She put both her arms on the table palm up and called upon the Tur to show her a map of the town. "*Orro Wey Sim LeVara Wilspry.*"

Loud gasps erupted in the room as the dark lines began to take their illuminated form. Zakai picked up a smudge of charcoal and began to trace a basic outline of the town on the face of the table, mirroring the image on Esra's arms. In usual Tur style, the map replicated the different elevations of the rocky town, like a perfect miniature version.

"Thank ye, that was very useful. Forgot ye Keepers could do that," he gruffly admitted, finishing his sketch. "It seems that the town is set atop a long sloping hill, which is good fer us. We will be on the higher ground which is easier te defend. There are very few trees surrounding the area, which will mean that we should be able te see the Elites coming, depending on what kinds of magick they decide te use. It also means we have te be more creative in setting traps. Now, is there any town north of here that we need te warn?"

"There's a small village about an hour's walk from here," a young farmer said as he approached the table. "About fifty people live there."

"Alright. Well then take a few others and some horses te go warn them. Bring them back here as soon as ye can."

"Couldn't we try and hide them?" Esra asked.

"I wouldn't take the chance, the Elite sorcerer's will feel strange coming upon an empty village and use magick te find them. It's just as good te get them back here, we can protect them or they can join the fight. And make sure they don't try te bring anything with them," he said to the young man. "They need te travel as fast as possible back here. Put the old and young on the horses ye arrived on, and the rest will have to run. We cannot spare any more steeds, unfortunately."

"I'll take my sisters. We'll go now." The farmer grabbed a couple of women next to him and they made their way quickly out of the tavern.

"The first thing we need te address is making this place defendable," Zakai asserted. "The farther the houses get from the center of town the more open space between them. I say we begin by barricading off just a small portion of the buildings in the center. It will be better te have a small area fully protected than a large area that is only halfway secure."

Esra nodded as Zakai pointed towards a few of the young men near the table. "I need ye te find a few more Humans te help barricade the town center. Focus only on filling in the gaps between these buildings here, here, and here. We want te create a circle that is impenetrable fer their soldiers, or at least something that will make it very difficult fer them te get past. Gather whatever heavy items ye can, bags of grain, furniture, bales of hay, and stack them in the gaps between the houses and buildings. This will also give our archers some places te safely shoot from. Once yer finished with that, make a second blockade here and here, in case we need te fall back."

The three men nodded vigorously and swept out of the room to complete their mission. Zakai leaned forward and ran his hand down the long, dark braid on his chin. "Now, we need te find ways te stop some of them before they reach the town."

"What about digging trenches? We could disguise the ground so that the horses would not be able to see the holes and they would charge right into them," Esra suggested.

"I'm glad ye've been listening during our lessons," he nodded approvingly. "However, there is not enough time te dig trenches, at least proper ones. They will be riding in from the north, approaching here. We can dig some shallow holes scattered around the back of the town where most of them will hopefully come. At least the holes will slow them, perhaps break the legs on some of their horses. That will shake them up a bit, make em' nervous. And it will give our archers an easier time te pick off some of the Elites. Make sure the archers go here and here, I want them protected and at a good vantage fer shooting."

Esra felt a familiar tingle on her arm that meant someone was trying to send her a message in Tur. "*Alor Etta,*" she whispered, lowering her arm under the table to view the script in private. Fynn's name appeared in the top left corner. *Spoke with Meshok. Three hours left.*

Esra looked up at Zakai. "Three hours."

He nodded and pointed at some other people near the table. "Ye two, get together with some others, find shovels and start digging. The holes should be scattered about this area, and as wide and deep as ye can make them in the couple of hours before they arrive. Dig like yer life depends upon it, because it does. Have a few people set as many snares and foothold traps as ye can around the field. I assume people have plenty of those here fer catching rabbits fer their soup pots."

The Unni-se bent over the table, brow furrowed in concentration "This isn't nearly enough. What else am I missing...what else can we do? Well, there is much we could do if there was more time. Think Zakai. There has te be more."

Cane had said that the chief was a master strategist, so if anyone could pull this together, Esra believed he could. She was touched by his frustration, his drive to defend the Human town. Suddenly the shimmering shape of Nadia appeared brightly next to Esra, causing her to jump completely out of her seat.

"Nadia! Are ye trying to kill me?" She scolded, readjusting in her chair. The Elf woman let out a trickling laugh, placing her hand on Esra's shoulder in apology.

"I've come to help. The children and others that could not fight are hidden as safely as possible. As long as we can keep out most of the Elite sorcerers they should stay undetected."

The crowd parted as Arland stalked up to their table and collapsed into an empty seat. He stretched his neck from side to side before sighing deeply. "Fynn is taking care of all the archers and communicating with Meshok to track the Elites' progress. The Unni guards are training the townspeople fer battle and Baelin is furiously making as much of everything as he can. How are the preparations fer the traps coming along?"

"I have some Humans working on snares, pitfalls and barricades. It will stop a few of the soldiers but not nearly enough. I wish we had more time. Arland, as Keeper of Charm ye are skilled in Influence Magick, correct?"

"Aye," he answered. "I have the ability to influence objects and people, to a certain degree of course. I would not be able to do anything substantial to a hundred of them at once, but I am fairly skilled when I focus on just a few people, even more so with one."

Zakai sat for a moment, dark brow furrowed in concentration. "Alright, I need ye te pick three of the soldiers spaced at various locations in their formation. Do ye think ye could get them te attack their own when they charge?"

"Aye, I think I could," Arland nodded enthusiastically.

"It will catch them off guard and each of them should be able te kill at least a couple other soldiers before they are taken out themselves. That takes care of ten of them. But first things first, of course. I would assume that all of the soldiers will be protected by some kind of spell that will prevent us from casting anything upon them. We will first need te have someone remove that before Arland can work his magick."

"Baelin," Arland stated confidently. "He is the best at removing spells. He is the only one who will be able to expose all of them at once. And he is resistant to influence magick because of his Amulet, his third Gift."

"Good. Let him know our plan, then. He should wait until the Elites get close te the town, just before they attack. We can't remove the protective spells too soon or the sorcerers will have an opportunity te counter and recast."

They all stared again at the drawing of Wilspry on the table, racking their brains for another way to defend against attack. Nadia turned to the towering Unni-se, a small shadow against his looming frame. "Is there anything I can help with? I am the Keeper of Stealth, ye know. If there are any traps that need to be set off in close proximity, I'm yer girl. I'm also more than capable in resistance magick."

Zakai pondered this statement, absentmindedly stroking his chin. "Yes, if ye are willing, that would be very helpful indeed."

He leaned over the map and narrowed his yellow eyes, his fingers tracing the table in an excited fashion. "Yes, that will most certainly help. Do ye think ye could use a spell that will prevent some of the sorcerer's from using magick?"

"Well," she frowned, "I've done it before but only fer a few sorcerers at a time. And I doubt I will be able to prevent an entire group of advanced sorcerers like this from casting spells, at least fer long."

"But the ones that captured me from Sorley, there were only two sorcerers in that group," Esra interjected. "And I didn't know resistance magick could be used to prevent someone from casting spells. I just thought it was defensive, preventing harm from spells once they were already cast."

The Unni-se turned to answer her. "There will be many more sorcerers in this command, I assure ye. If I had te venture a guess, I would say they'll be a dozen. Tallen will take care te send some of his best followers, especially since he misjudged ye the last time. That mistake will not happen again. And resistance magick has many different forms."

"Can't we also cast a protective spell fer ourselves?"

"We could, but protective spells have te be maintained, and we would need multiple people casting them te protect everyone. Which would mean we'd lose some of our best warriors. I think we're better off having them fight."

"How do ye know so much about magick? I thought there were no Unni sorcerers?"

"There aren't," he made a deep raspy sound like a laugh. "But in order te be a master strategist, one must know everything he can about his friends and foes. I am more than familiar with magickal abilities, even though I possess none. I would not be very good at defending my people otherwise."

Esra nodded in agreement as Zakai continued. "Nadia, ye should choose the few sorcerers that ye feel are most powerful and jest focus on them. I would assume that they will be located in the center group and that there will be a couple of the lower level sorcerers on the flanking sides. It doesn't seem like much, but trust me, keeping a few powerful sorcerers at bay will be much help indeed. And as soon as ye feel ye cannot hold them anymore, come join the fight. Yer Necklace of Stunning will be of good use there."

He paused for a moment, pouring over the charcoal drawing on the rough wood. Hope was growing in Esra's chest as she watched the great Zakai weave a manageable defense of Wilspry. They just might stand a chance.

"What about Meshok?" She offered. Although she hadn't consulted her friend on the issue, she was more than sure that the Great Wolf would want a chance to bite at some Elites.

"No, as much as I would love te have her fighting with us, that's a secret that's better kept. At least fer now. Something tells me that the surprise of her kind being alive will be much more useful at a later moon. Can ye show me that Tur map of the town again?" Esra did as he asked, and the Unni-se scoured the dimensional form on her arm. After a moment his eyes lit up and he poked the table in excitement.

"Here's what I'm thinking. See these two large hills on either side of the northern field, here and here? They provide good cover, as they stretch all the way te the edge of town. The Elites will probably come right in between the two of 'em and send two smaller groups around the hill te flank us."

"How do ye know?" Esra asked, studying the Tur map. The hills seemed to be a couple of hundred feet across, narrowing as they neared the town.

"They would hope that the shadow of the hills will keep them fairly cloaked and avoid detection for the flanking groups. At least that's what I'd do, and they are sure te come prepared with some strategists of their own."

"We could set a trap at the top of one of the hills," he continued. "The left one would be the superior choice because of all the rocks scattered on the side and top. We could cause a landslide without having te carry anything te the top. Good fer our lack of time. That would take care of one of the flanking groups, so we only have te worry about the center and the other side. Arland, that means ye have te choose yer three soldiers from the center and right side, mind ye. All we need is someone te spring the trap, start the slide."

"I'll do it," Nadia offered. "I can work on the resistance spell fer the sorcerers right afterwards."

"No, we will need them te be taken care of from the very beginning. It's too important te put off. Especially if Baelin will be removing all of the protective spells right before."

"I can do it," Arland jumped in. "I have to wait until Nadia and Baelin complete their spells anyway."

"That could work," the Unni-se leaned back in his chair, staring at the map.

"No, let me do it," Esra interjected. "I don't have anything else to do, and it will require no magickal skill to push some rocks."

"That's brave of ye, but I'd rather have ye safe in the town, Esra." Nadia said with a worried look. "It's not that I don' think ye can do it, it's jest that if something goes wrong, ye don't know any spells to protect yerself."

"But we need to have Arland in the town, not on the hill," she argued. "The townspeople are going to be very frightened and he will be the only one that will be able to give them comfort and the courage to fight."

"Can Arland start the slide from the town with a spell?"

"Aye, but if he's casting a spell fer that, he's not using his magick to calm the townspeople. And ye'd still have to post someone on the hill or use insight magick to see when they approach, which further distracts someone. We need Fynn's archery skills in the town as well. Honestly, I can do it."

Zakai pondered this, frowning slightly. "She's right. Arland would be most useful here. Esra, ye will be in charge of the trap on the left hill. If everything goes well and the landslide takes care of the whole command, ye can come down the hill and get back te the town using this path. They will know that yer there after the trap is sprung, so if there are still soldiers try te stay hidden until it's safe. We will send out a few of our soldiers te pick off the remaining few Elites and ye can return back te the town barricade with them as quickly as possible. The worst thing that could happen would be that ye don't hit anybody but at least

220

we block off that route te avoid being flanked on both sides. Bottleneck the center command and force them te have te come at us only a few at a time. Go talk te Fynn, he's the Keeper of Earth, correct? He should know if we can cause a landslide and what's the best way te do it."

"Alright," Nadia conceded as they all stood to leave. Esra made her way out of the inn, knowing there was little more than two hours left before a hundred Elites were upon them. She just hoped with all her might that their plan would be enough.

XXXII

The chaos that the town experienced over the next couple of hours was like nothing Esra had ever seen. There was a nervous fury to everyone's movements, and she was glad they had convinced Arland to stay near the townspeople. It seemed to be the only thing holding them together. The barricade was set, the elderly and children safely hidden, and as many snares that could be set and holes that could be dug scattered the fields north of the small town.

Meshok appeared in the distance, the final signal that the Elites were approaching, and everyone gathered behind the barricade. Baelin came to Esra and gave her a worried nod of encouragement, gently touching her shoulder before she began the swift climb to her place on top of the hill, her white sword sheathed at her side. She could hear nothing but the occasional shuffling from the town, silent in nervous anticipation. Her friends and a few of the townspeople mounted their steeds and stood behind the rows of earth bound volunteers. Esra had given Roja to one of the townspeople, hoping the horse may help save the life of its brave rider.

The Unni perched upon the skycatchers were a sight to behold, towering twice as high as the others. Shova had told Esra before she left for the hill that although they began each battle atop a horse, most Unni preferred to fight on solid ground and dismounted before the first contact. It was an intimidating show to the opposition, especially to see how massive they still were even without a horse.

Zakai stood atop the five foot tall barricade at the front of the town, one leg resting on a crate and the other on an overturned cart. He wore an intricate helmet inlaid with sapphires that had razor sharp barbs about two inches long protruding from the thick metal surrounding his horns. Esra shuddered to think what would happen to someone who met with a thrust of his barbed head. His solid breastplate gleamed in the sunlight, a picture of a yanquor tree regally sprawled in its center. The other Unni wore similar breastplates, although they all forewent the need for bracers, greaves, or other such armor, and none wore a helm like that of their chief. Zakai towered over the town with his flail swinging in his right hand tauntingly. His narrow yellow eyes looked with hatred upon the field in front of the town, and Esra thought that anyone with half a brain would never attack such a fierce and determined commander. She hoped the Elites would be so stupid.

The minutes ticked by slowly as Esra waited at the spot that Fynn had determined the best chance for a rockslide. Earlier he had moved a few large rocks around with influence magick and sent her to find a strong stick that she could place under the biggest boulder to start the slide. All she had to do was push down on this stick, and hopefully this one boulder would start the rest down the hillside. She realized this was a crude method, and one that they could have easily used magick with, but at least this left her Assembly free to do more important things.

Nadia and Fynn had taken to organizing the archers and luckily there were quite a few hunters that were already more than skilled at hitting a moving target. More than a dozen of them took their place on rooftops and in between makeshift battlements in the wall of carts and bags of grain. Shova, Mox, and Hadvi had been vaguely successful in training some of the townspeople the basics of hand to hand combat, but that was a greater challenge. Most of the people had still never swung a blade or weapon before in their life, so everyone hoped there wouldn't be many Elites that made it far enough to test their new skill.

A dark line appeared in the distant horizon to the north of Wilspry. Elites. They were approaching the two large hills, just as Zakai predicted. *Orro Ken Baelin.* Esra sent a message to her blacksmith friend, indicating that she had spotted the Elite soldiers. She could hear Arland in the distance, speaking words of encouragement to the frightened villagers. The faint rumble of horses grew slowly louder as she crouched down beside the boulder, keeping a steady eye on the approaching army. She accepted a Tur message from Fynn. *Try not te squash yerself.* Esra laughed as she replied, *Glad to see yer confident in my ability to push a stick.*

The Elite horses were running full speed towards the town. As the shapes came in to view, Esra noticed that the soldiers were wearing dark metal armor with a red stripe down the front of their helmets and breastplates. The mark of Tallen, just like the ones who had captured her in Sorley. Esra was able to pick out the ones that appeared to be sorcerers by the lack of armor and weapons. *Ten.* She sent the message to Nadia, silently impressed that Zakai was so close on his guess.

The rumbling grew louder as the sound of hooves beating the dry ground came upon the town, menacing and powerful. Just before reaching the hills, a soldier in the front lifted his arm and the charge stopped abruptly, dust clouds rising from the sudden halt. They stood there, unmoving, as Esra's heart beat loudly in her ears. She wondered what it was they had stopped for. With only a few hundred meters between the town and the Elite army, the tension in the air was thick. Back at the barricade there were murmurs of questions floating in the air.

"Why did they stop?" A farm girl asked Zakai.

"They sense something is very wrong. They knew the Keepers would be here, of course, but I daresay they didn't anticipate the whole town being ready fer them. And I don't think they had any idea there'd be Unni with ye."

"Wouldn't they have sent a scout?" A young townsman with a scythe asks.

"No, not the Elites, not fer this. They have too many sorcerers in their midst. They would have used magick te see that the Keepers were close and wouldn't care fer much else. Never would have assumed that they should look fer others, that the Unni might be with them. Arrogance is certainly their flaw."

Baelin was standing a few steps away from the townspeople, holding his staff firmly in between his hands, feet planted shoulder width apart. Suddenly the Elites lurched forward, two groups of a dozen soldiers breaking off to either side of the hills, accompanied by two sorcerers. The remaining six sorcerers lingered behind the army as the rest of the warriors pushed forward. Baelin closed his eyes as he began to murmur the words of the removing spell. A moment later he nodded towards Nadia and Arland to indicate that he was finished.

A few of the horses suddenly stumbled or were yanked to the ground as their feet were caught in the snares and holes. Some of the riders could not avoid the fallen soldiers in time and were thrown from their mounts as the horses collided.

Nadia came to take Baelin's place as he went up to the front line. Focusing her attention on the six sorcerers in the center of the field, she wondered if she should risk blocking all of them at once. *Six is quite a lot, but here goes nothing.* Casting the resistance spell, she stood in silent meditation as Arland looked towards the galloping onslaught of warriors.

Only a hundred meters away now. Selecting the first one, Arland whispered the influence charm that would turn their will and swords against their own. *"Yasir monverra pasu fehwar."*

One of the dark armored warriors suddenly threw his horse towards the rider next to him, knocking him to the ground. Spear raised, he began stabbing frantically at the Elites around him, knocking another off his horse to be trampled and stabbing another. Suddenly realizing what was happening, an archer shot an arrow towards the rogue soldier, piercing his chest. Arland had already chosen another rider from the other side of the hill, who felled four more Elites before being taken down by a morning star.

Nadia fell to her knees, the weight of the resistance spell growing heavy. She was unsure if she could continue holding all six back, their combined strength was more than any other sorcerer she had encountered before. If she could just hold them a few seconds longer…

By the time Arland had cast upon the third soldier the Elites were ready for it, killing the possessed rider before he injured anyone else.

"Damn," Zakai spat, raising the flail at his side. He jumped down with abnormal ease from his menacing perch on the barricade, which did not belittle his stature in the least. "Archers, ready!"

Esra's eyes darted around from her spot on the hill in anticipation as the flanking group rounded the curve of the hill. *Patience*, Esra reminded herself. It was important that she wait until the Elites were practically underfoot to start the slide or she would miss them. If she was too early they would be able to turn right around and rejoin the middle command. Too late and they could still flank the town. A loud whistling sound carried through the air and Esra knew that the archers had released their first volley. She watched as a handful of riders were pierced with the townspeople's arrows, falling underfoot.

"Fire at will!" The Unni-se's voice boomed as the archers rained a fresh wave of arrows upon the field.

The violent force that Esra had felt within when dueling the Valkor began to bubble up to the surface of her skin. Instead of fearing the rage this time, she decided to embrace it, and gritted her teeth with the desire to harm those attacking an innocent village. It was an emotion unlike anything she had ever felt, one ready to overwhelm her at any moment, and a flicker of panic pressed on her chest. She ignored the sensation and refocused her attention on the grip of her hand on the rough bark.

Taking a ready stance over the heavy branch, Esra watched as the first rider approached her position. Counting slowly to three, she leaned with all her might on the branch, struggling to start the slide. The colossal boulder shifted slightly, causing the branch to sway violently to the left. She watched in horrified slow motion as the wood snapped off at the base and the boulder shuddered lightly before settling back into place.

XXXIII

Oh no, Esra panicked. She threw herself into the boulder forcefully but it didn't budge. *What do I do?* Her eyes darted around the hill top, searching frantically for another branch, something she could wedge underneath the stone. The Elites were almost underneath her now. Nothing. She couldn't see anything. In a few moments they would pass and the chance would be gone.

She thought furiously of the words Fynn had used to move the stones earlier. If they had taught her more about magick, perhaps she could have recalled the spell. But it was too late for that now. Closing her eyes, she tried to picture him standing there, remember exactly what he said.

"*Yasir brey novallo!*" She screamed as the boulder lurched forward fiercely, smashing into the rocks Fynn had strategically placed ahead of it. She watched with sickened relief as the slide gained momentum and force, gathering a hillside in its descent upon the soldiers. A thunderous roar erupted as the rocks met with the ground, a cloud of debris and dust rising from the impact.

Crouching low, Esra scanned the valley as the dust settled, searching for survivors. Satisfied there were none, she stayed low and ran to the side of the hill near the town, sliding down it quickly. She was met by two of the townsfolk and Hadvi, who plucked her off the ground and half carried her back to the barricade.

"Well done!" Hadvi congratulated, slapping her on the back. "Get ready fer more!"

Esra caught a glimpse of Nadia, who stood shakily up from where she had been sitting in her resistance spell reverie and slinked wearily towards a nearby rooftop to continue with her throwing spears. There was a deafening crash of metal and wood as the Elite army reached the barrier. Most of the horses leapt easily over the wall, trampling a few of the slower townspeople. A couple of the Warhorses stumbled and were crushed against the barricade by the fierce onslaught of soldiers.

"To arms!" Zakai roared, swinging his flail into an Elites skull. The chaos of battle erupted in Wilspry, the clash of weapons and armor rising above the town like a heavy fog. Esra quickly unsheathed her sword as an Elite came towards her on foot. Before she could react Baelin had lifted him off the ground, piercing him through the stomach with his staff. She turned as another Elite came towards her on horseback, his whip snapping through the air. Rolling underneath the horse to the other side, she came up swinging and felt her sword sink deeply into the flesh under his knee. The soldier gripped his leg but didn't cry out as his horse panicked and bolted, throwing him to the ground. He stood up, leg bent at an awkward angle, and growled fiercely as he came slowly towards her, his foot dragging lifelessly. Esra recalled Cane telling her that the soldiers had a dulled sense of pain and heightened aggression as a side effect of Tallen's twisted spells. It was disturbing to see how right that was. Not wanting the foul creature near her, Esra threw her sword towards the injured Elite and winced as it pierced his chest with a low thump. He crumpled over stiffly and she pulled her sword quickly from his body before he fell to the ground.

Fighting the urge to be sick, Esra looked towards a young towns girl that was dueling with an Elite, her small club deflecting feebly off his greatsword. She appeared to be a few years younger than Esra, and the top of her tunic was already soaked with sweat as she tried frantically to defend herself. Running up from behind, Esra cut into the soldier's side with a mighty swing just as he stabbed the girl in the leg. She quickly grabbed the young girl by the collar and dragged her into a darkened corner, going back to snatch a dagger from the now dead Elite. The girl writhed in pain as she tried to tie a strip of her skirt around her leg.

"Hold on to this dagger and stay here," Esra yelled, turning back to the fray.

She spotted Arland and Shova fighting back to back, a circle of death for the oncoming soldiers. Even on horseback, the Elites were still within comfortable reach of the Unni. Shova swung her war hammer as if it were a toothpick, the muscles in her strong arms bulging with the force. She turned to Esra, giving her a wink as she crushed the thigh of an oncoming soldier. "Now that's how ye use a hammer. Should've been a carpenter!"

Fynn was on a rooftop, notching and firing three arrows at a time. Had it not been so chaotic she would have loved to stop and admire the way the arrows arched incredibly in three different directions. It seemed an impossible task. She supposed that was why it was a Gift from a Great Keeper, the Bow of Many.

Even with their expert fighting, the Elites continued to pour over the front of the town. Esra watched as three of the townspeople fell, then a young boy, and another. There was blood dripping down Baelin's arm as he whipped his staff around deftly, surrounded by four soldiers on foot. Most of the Elites had dismounted or been thrown from their horses once inside the cramped quarters of the town center. She made her way to Baelin, watching as Mox was caught in the side with a small dagger by a dark armored Elite. Grabbing the culprit's throat with one hand, he pulled the soldier's helmet off with a grunt and threw it to the side. Still clutching his throat, Mox pulled the Elite close to him and drew the dagger slowly out of his side, stabbing the Elite through the eye with a ferocious howl.

Esra gasped in disgust at the reminder of what was underneath the red striped helmet. The revelation of the Elite faces from her kidnapping were still fresh in her memory, but for some reason in the light of day it was much worse. The greyish skin with no eyelids, no hair, just ears and a nose that seemed to be melting off their face. A distorted, abnormally large mouth underneath their black, sunken eyes.

Esra turned from the horrific face in repulsion just in time to see Hadvi spear an Elite with his horns, tossing the soldier off his horse with a quick flick of his head. He held his twin axes mockingly at his side, obviously a second choice to his natural weapon. Letting out a fierce cry, he ran towards the next soldier with his head down, fueled by adrenaline and fury. The Elite, who was busy overpowering a young farm boy, tried to lift her shield in a last moment of panicked awareness, but Hadvi was running at such speed that he pierced right through the metal and into her breastplate.

Transfixed by the Unni warriors, Esra hardly noticed when an Elite suddenly appeared in front of her, swinging her large shield into Esra's midsection. She fell back onto the ground as the breath left her body in one large gust, and she clutched frantically underneath her ribs, trying to get air. It was a terrifying moment, not being able to breathe, and Esra was momentarily unaware of where the Elite was, but knew she needed to move. Rolling to the side, she heard a loud thump as a club came down next to her head. Her lungs finally opening, she inhaled greedily before throwing up her shield against the next swing. Scrambling to her feet, she swung blindly towards her attacker, landing a lucky but shallow hit on the top of her opponent's thigh. The Elite hissed towards Esra, throwing down her shield in a furious show of confidence, grabbing her club with both hands.

Suddenly the right side of the barricade collapsed as the flanking group reached the town. Pouring through the opening, a fresh wave of mounted soldiers attacked as another group of townspeople quickly fell.

"Fall back!" Zakai thundered as he wrapped his flail around a soldier's leg. With a quick jerk he severed the leg at the knee, then swung the barbed metal with inhuman strength into an oncoming soldier's helm. "Regroup at the second barricade!"

Esra abandoned her injured soldier and ran back to the center of town, stumbling over the bodies layering the street. She caught a glimpse of the young girl she had helped earlier, dead with an arrow piercing her midsection. There were still so many Elites. She was exhausted and there were still so many.

She passed a townsman, whose homespun sword appeared to be bouncing wildly around his Elite opponent as if it had a mind of its own. He watched with wild eyes as he tried to tame the dancing metal in his hands. Esra turned and watched as everyone's weapons began to deflect off an unseen shield. A couple of Elites were wandering around as if in a fog, no weapon or shield. They must have been victims of Nadia's Necklace of Stunning. Even in their defenseless stupor, the townspeople could not fell the dumbfounded soldiers. Esra realized with sickness that the sorcerers had recast their protective spells. The Elites were now unstoppable, and there was nothing they could do.

XXXIV

"Esra, come with us!" Nadia pulled her against a street barricade and hastily began to scale the wall of carts and grain bags. Esra followed clumsily, an Elite grabbing at her ankle as she swayed backwards, almost losing her balance. She kicked violently out of their grasp and clambered eagerly over the top of the blockade. They jumped down into an alleyway where Fynn was already waiting.

"The sorcerers, we have to get to the sorcerers," Nadia panted. "They're casting new protective spells over the soldiers and I think if we can take care of that, the Unni will be able to finish them off. We need to come around the side of the hill, get close enough so that Fynn and I can cast striking spells."

"What do ye need me to do?"

"There are still a couple soldiers guarding the flanking sides. Fynn can't shoot an arrow and I can't throw a spear until they come around that curve. If we aim too high the sorcerers will see us. We need a straight shot. Can ye get them to chase ye back towards the town a little?"

"Ye want me to be the bait?" Esra asked incredulously.

"No," Fynn jabbed her teasingly with his elbow. "We want ye te be the distraction so that the ugly mongers will chase ye while we shoot from a protected, safe distance."

"Oh, well in that case..." Esra rolled her eyes.

"B'sides, yer much prettier than some worm on a hook. Although maybe the foul Elites would prefer a slimy, stinky... "

"Alright," Nadia interrupted, slinging the quiver that held her throwing spears over her shoulder. Esra still couldn't get used to the idea that this tiny shimmering woman could launch a spear almost as far and fast as any bow and arrow. "We need to move now. Fynn and I are going to wait by that barricade. Esra, go find Roja and wait fer our signal to approach. And make sure that ye get all of the soldiers tc follow ye. Otherwise the rest of our plan will be much harder tc accomplish."

With that Nadia turned and sped from the alley and towards the side of the hill to hide, Fynn close at her heels. Esra stared for a moment before turning around with a resigned sigh.

"Where *did* I leave my horse," she mumbled, darting back towards the street. She climbed halfway up the barricade and whistled shrilly. Not able to make out much from the clamor of weapons on the other side, she pulled herself up to the top to get a better view. Scanning the crowd hastily, she caught sight of an Elite archer whose sights were set directly on her. Diving quickly off the barricade as the arrow whizzed by her head, she landed hard on her feet, a sharp pain shooting up her right leg. Grimacing against the sting, she whistled again.

This time, she only caught the attention of an injured Elite, who came at her with a stumbling swing. Caught off guard and with her sword hanging helplessly at her side, Esra did an impromptu jump and roll to the right, unsheathing her sword and stabbing at the soldier as she sprung up. Instead of piercing his skin, the sword wobbled unsteadily and pushed away.

Stupid defensive spells, Esra cursed as she danced in a wide circle, noticing now that most of her allies had abandoned the offensive and were practicing the same evasive maneuvers. Out of the corner of her eye she saw a skycatcher rear loudly and come down upon an Elite. The soldier was uninjured but lay pinned from the weight of the horse, which hovered almost a foot above his body. It was Fariel, her grandparents' great grey steed that Baelin rode. She continued to maneuver around the soldier, who was quickly tiring of her avoidance as she scanned the crowds for her blacksmith friend. The Elite was breathing heavily, spittle spraying out of his brown crooked teeth. He stabbed at Esra and she jumped backwards, throwing her hands sideways to avoid his blade. He raised his sword overhead to deal a final deathly blow, but Esra anticipated his move and dodged out of the way, and he stumbled on the uneven street. Taking advantage of his momentary lapse in the offensive, she took three great, staggering steps towards Fariel and leapt upon his back.

The skycatcher whinnied loudly in surprise, then recovered in the next instant as he recognized his rider. Fariel turned and jumped easily over the barricade as Esra directed him down the narrow lane. Turning out of the side street, the noise of the town grew more muddled as she galloped towards the hillside where Nadia and Fynn were waiting.

"*Allor Etta*," she breathed, picking up the sleeve of her arm to accept the Tur message from Fynn.

Ready, wormie?

Esra managed a tired smile as she gently pushed on Fariel's shoulder, urging him to run along the long, low side of the flanking hill. Unlike the other hill where they had set the trap, this one was much shallower, with Esra almost visible sitting atop the skycatcher. There would have been no way to shoot an arrow that far without going over or around the knoll, thus alerting the sorcerers. She forced Fariel onward at full speed and kept low to his back, knowing that every second wasted was another moment her friends and the people of Wilspry had to try and defend themselves against unattackable foes.

Trying not to think about what lay around the curve, she reluctantly forced Fariel to slow until he was only lightly cantering around the bend. Suddenly an Elite soldier sitting atop a horse came into view, and then another, and another. No longer hidden by the hill's shadow, Fariel reared aggressively, neighing so loudly that the sorcerers that hadn't spotted the pair spun in their seats towards the source of the noise.

Two of the soldiers immediately came towards her, their dark metal armor clicking dissonantly as the horses began their charge. The third soldier remained frozen in his spot, unwilling to abort his defense of the sorcerers. Esra only had an instant to make a decision, knowing that she needed to get all of the soldiers to follow her. She lunged forward just before the two soldiers reached her, and to her surprise Fariel leapt cleanly over one of the horses, landing gracefully on the other side of both Elites. Stunned at the skycatchers great feat and her inability to plan beyond that impulsive move, Esra paused briefly before urging Fariel towards the lone holdout.

What am I doing? She panicked, knowing she was heading straight for six powerful Elite sorcerers like a suicidal madwoman. The one slightly amused soldier gave his opponent a sneer as he began to gallop towards her. Suddenly there was a commotion from behind and a familiar voice called out to Esra.

"Preyn huvvi raghn!" The voice shouted just before she reached the soldier, releasing the defensive spell that was protecting him. As the soldier was not prepared to defend against any attack, she cut easily through the skin beneath his helmet. Turning towards her rescuer, she watched as he knocked an Elite off her horse with a staff to the face, stabbing the other soldier underneath his dark breastplate.

"Baelin!" Esra called to her friend. But suddenly the sorcerers who had been uninterested in the lone demented opponent now looked at the three dead soldiers with disgust. Four of the enchanters continued focusing their attention on Wilspry as the other two turned towards the intruders with fury.

"*Yasir brey jianka!*" One of them shouted as a wall slammed into Esra's body. She knew logically it could not be a wall, that they did not in fact throw a wall at her, but the sensation was real nonetheless. In one swift movement Esra was lifted off the skycatcher and smashed violently into the ground. Gasping fiercely, she barely had time to draw a painful breath before the other sorcerer looked at her warily and with a small flick of his wrist lifted her off the ground like a ragdoll, her feet dangling a hand's breadth off the grass. Paralyzed by magick, Esra watched with sickening fear as the sorcerers turned towards Baelin.

She could not see anything but the furious face of the enchanter in front of her, but she could hear the low rumblings of Baelin as he cast his best defensive spells. She thought frantically of any spell that could help her release this grasp, but she had learned little defensive magick and no offensive spells at all. Racking her brain, she thought of the words she could use to send a Tur message to one of the others, but it kept escaping her mind. It was as if her head were becoming foggy, no slippery, an effect of the strange magick she now felt encompassing her. Her mind as well as her body seemed to be weaving in and out of a dream state.

Unable to speak aloud in her paralyzing state, Esra had a sudden memory of a crisp fall night when she was a small child. She had found a dead whipbird in the forest, and thinking it was just asleep and too cold to move, Esra decided to make a nest for it so that she could carry it inside by the fire. She spent an hour gathering things she thought the bird would like for a temporary home, soft, dry leaves and plump twigs of bright berries. Tenderly placing the bird on his new bed, she carried it carefully back through the trees, trying not to wake it. When she found her grandmother in the kitchen, she was crushed to find out that the bird was not asleep and would sing no more. It was her first glimpse at mortality.

A loud crackling sound brought Esra back to the present, and she saw an Elite sorcerer murmuring with open arms towards someone behind her. She focused all her panicked energy into thinking about Tur, remembering the day with Cane in the library. *Orro Ken Fynn*, she finally remembered. *Help.*

She wondered how long the sorcerer was going to hold her there and toy with her. He certainly could have killed her by now. It was obvious that they already thought the takeover of Wilspry a success, even with the unexpected rebellion. The four enchanters who faced the town seemed to be relaxed in their saddles, eyes open and lips barely moving in their chants. She hoped that Baelin was alright, for she had lost sight of the other sorcerer. And her eyelids were growing very heavy…

Esra was unsure of how long her eyes had been closed, but a sound like a gust of air snapped them open just before she hit the ground for a second time. She rolled over as a shimmering form glinted past her. *Nadia*, Esra thought with relief. The Elf twin made her stealthy way on foot towards one of the unsuspecting enchanters facing the town, her body a hazy blur in the landscape. Fynn remained on horseback as he engaged the sorcerer battling Baelin, allowing the blacksmith to turn his attention back towards the one that had been holding Esra hostage in the air.

Still muddled from being hit by the wall of imprisoning magick, Esra rolled onto her knees and stood with trembling legs. Three of the enchanters were already slumped over on their horses or on the ground, from a physical or magickal attack she couldn't guess. Then she tried to unsheathe her sword, intending to make her way towards her friends, to help them, but she collapsed before taking a step. Rolling over to stare up at the sky, Esra noticed what a clear, beautiful day it was. Clouds were rolling by, light and fluffy, apparently unaware of the jarring chaos that ensued beneath their tranquil watch.

Baelin appeared over her, whispering something she could not understand. No, shouting perhaps. It was as if he was very far away, but Esra knew he was right here, could see his face hovering before her. It was such a bother, him blocking her view of the beautiful sky. Esra tried to read his lips but she seemed to be unable to focus on one particular area of his face. She felt herself being gently lifted up, and Baelin's strong arms cradled her tall frame against his broad part-Unni chest.

"Ye sure are hairy," she whispered to him half deliriously, feeling the dark, coarse fur rubbing on her arms and legs. The look of worry on his face was replaced by relief as he laughed at her brazenness.

"Aye, that I am," she heard him say faintly, and she smiled up at him, wanting to thank this man who was her friend, her Keeper. But instead she closed her eyes and relaxed against the gentle sway of his walking. She had the sense that Nadia and Fynn were close, wondered if they had noticed the beautiful clouds above. She couldn't quite remember what they all had been doing. Was it time to travel again? Or perhaps she was late for noonmeal?

Baelin let her slide in and out of consciousness as he carried her back towards the town, where he did not need to be told that Arland, Zakai, and the other Unni were now greedily devouring the last of the Elite warriors. He pitied the few that had remained alive long enough to invoke his uncle's wrath. Although many had fallen, the town of Wilspry had survived. He hoped with all his heart that it was a sign of things to come, but knew that this small victory would be just one step in the long road of war. But he was a Keeper, and he would protect the freedom of the people of LeVara at any cost. No matter what.

XXXV

It had been a long road back to the Stronghold, filled with the mixed emotions of the victory at Wilspry and the knowledge of all that had died to make it so. They spoke little on the three days journey, burdened with this truth and haunted by the faces of the dead townspeople. All those in their party had survived, not without some scars of their own. Fynn was the only one who escaped seemingly unharmed, as his Earring of Recovery healed all his wounds before the sun could set that day.

The people of Wilspry did not seem to begrudge Esra's group their escape from an ill fate and thanked them with all sincerity, knowing that they would have been slaughtered without the strange Unni-Elf-Human Assembly's help. Some even tried to give gifts to their protectors, which were respectfully declined. In fact, Esra saw Arland leaving behind many of their own supplies to help the townsfolk as they tried to rebuild. Her friends walked around casting various spells to ease the suffering of the townspeople, and set some traps to alert them of any oncoming danger. Esra hoped that Wilspry would not see more trouble anytime soon. They had been through enough. She wished that they could've stayed longer, but knew they had to return. They could not even help bury all the dead.

The one thing they did end up taking with them were two orphaned children. Everyone had been strictly against this, knowing that the journey ahead needed to be made as quickly as possible, especially with more than a day's worth of a delay. And the Stronghold was no place for orphaned children. It was only after much discussion and insistence by the townsfolk that they discovered these children had certain "gifts". The presence of a mysterious rash on their arms confirmed any suspicions and Esra's party agreed to take them along.

Jaar, a young boy of about ten, had hardly spoken since they left the town, his eyes wide with surprise at his new surroundings and sadness at leaving his old. Shova worked her good humored magick with him and he seemed to always be near her, although he still did not speak. The silence in his unmade answers seemed to matter little to her, and she talked to him as if he spoke back. Esra guessed she knew exactly how to deal with young boys, having seven of her own, and spoke just to comfort him.

Jaar's talent seemed to be the ability to heal animals. When his older brother had brought home a large kelvar he had found with a broken wing, Jaar took the creature in his hands and whispered, stroking its feathers gently. Suddenly the bird stirred violently and the young boy released the newly whole kelvar to the wind. From that day on the townspeople sought him out whenever a horse was lame or a pig or brengard took sick. And many people spoke fondly of a time when Jaar healed a beloved hound or favored animal of their family. They had hoped that perhaps his skills could be applied to Human illnesses, but his talent seemed restricted to other creatures.

Immediately after the successful defense of Wilspry, Esra had noticed a young boy walking around, touching all the horses, stroking their sweaty flanks. She assumed he was in shock, maybe stricken with grief over the small rivers of blood that ran through his home land. But it was not until later that it was noted that with all the dead and injured soldiers on both sides, there was not one horse that had presented itself with so much as a scratch. When the townspeople spoke of his gift, they knew then to take the boy aside and look for evidence of Tur.

Fynn admitted he was excited that the boy had such a talent, for he hoped that he could combine his skill for animal-speech with Jaar's healing abilities. Sometimes, when the boy wasn't near Shova or visiting with the skycatchers, who seemed to love his touch like a fresh spring of cool water, he could be found by the fire with Fynn.

The Keeper of Earth would try to cheer Jaar by describing the Stronghold and the process of becoming a Keeper, hoping to get him excited. Fynn knew that they could never replace his home, his real family, but at least they could offer a new place among a welcoming people, people as diverse and skilled as Jaar was.

Esra was able to add her experience here, explaining to Jaar that she too was someone who had never really left her town and had recently become fully aware of the Keepers and all of their mysteries. She attested to the beauty of the Stronghold and the truth of Fynn's words that it really was a wonderful place. She also took him aside and told him the story of her childhood, of growing up without parents or siblings and how it affected it her. Jaar listened to her without a word, his head sunken into his chest, and she grieved for him. Esra was not typically so open about herself, but she remembered her conversation with Baelin about his family not so long ago, and wishing she had known that there was someone else to talk to about these things. So she tried to confide in Jaar her fears and struggles without restraint, so that he would know he did not have to pretend to be strong all the time.

Meshok also took a liking to the young boy and he to the Great Wolf. Although Esra knew that Meshok did not like being touched while she was sleeping, she gently guided her to lie near Jaar. The boy was thrilled to nuzzle against her fur on the cool nights, thinking that this was indeed a very special treat, wishing he could tell his friends that he *knew* a Great Wolf. Seeing the resigned look on Meshok's face, Esra laughed to herself that her friend was being so reluctantly generous. Although the Wolf loved to be petted and attended to on many occasions, she remained in her very nature an independent beast, as Esra knew herself to be. The reason they got along so well was because they both understood this. But they were also kind, and Meshok was willing to lay aside her proud sleeping habits for a few nights to comfort a child in need of a friend. Meshok had confessed to Fynn that when she awoke in the morning after a night with Jaar cuddled against her fur, she felt more refreshed than she had in many moons.

Where Jaar was reflective and internal, the young girl, Toddy, was vibrant and talkative. She held up four fat fingers to indicate her age at every opportunity, her beautiful long red hair splayed down her back like a river of fire. She was jovial, having less knowledge than Jaar of what had just occurred, only occasionally crying for her mother but easily distracted by anything shiny or shimmering, especially Nadia. Toddy's squeals of laughter would cause a stern reproach from Mox as to the noise when Nadia played hide and seek with the youngster.

Toddy's talent was a little less direct than Jaar's in that she seemed to radiate heat. She could not manipulate flame as a Keeper of Fire could, yet it burned brighter and hotter when she was near. Her family also claimed that they had no need for a lit stove in the wintertime, for wherever Toddy was, the warmth followed. It was actually slightly uncomfortable at times, enough so that they had to open windows or go outside to eat. And if she threw a tantrum or got in the least bit upset over a broken toy or inattentive parents, the house temperature would rise so high that they would have to take the girl outside for fear their home would start aflame.

Esra could only let the small child sit on her lap for a few moments at a time before the heat would overwhelm her. Even Toddy's skin was hot to the touch, although it never bothered the girl. She seemed to be gloriously unaware of the fiery waves that emanated from her core. The one thing she did mind, however, was her inability to play in the Snow with her friends. The area around Wilspry and Sorley east of The Naduri River did not get Snow like The Frost Grounds, but enough that children could enjoy a romp or two every winter with Snow fights. Any Snow that had settled on the ground would melt in a radius of fifty feet around Toddy. Sure enough, the few times she did get upset her body glowed as if a fire raged in her body and surges of heat would pulsate through the air, the beating almost perceptible.

The townsfolk had given Jaar and Toddy a horse to ride so that they would not burden the other riders on their journey, but the steed would not tolerate Toddy's warm weight on her back. Esra found that her skycatcher Roja seemed to be able to bear the girl's heat, but Esra could not stand to ride beside her. The other option would have been Meshok, who also seemed immune to the girl's fire. But Esra knew that there would be no chance that the Great Wolf would allow herself to be ridden like a common field horse, so she didn't dare ask. It was enough that she let the child poke at her fur and pull her tail without nipping. And occasionally, when Toddy lay asleep with her thumb in her mouth by the fire (how she needed to sleep next to a fire, Esra would never understand) Meshok would come up to the girl and lay next to her for a time, licking and cleaning her long red hair as if she were one of her pups.

So Esra gave her great horse to the little girl, insisting that Baelin fix the youngling a proper saddle so that she would not fall, which he wholeheartedly agreed to. Jaar would go with Shova and Esra would ride the small field horse. She was grateful for the townspeople's generosity in offering her a simple but well cared for steed. At least now the town had more horses than they could ever want, since Jaar had healed all the Elite steeds. Esra hoped that maybe it would help rebuild the town that had lost so much.

When Toddy asked why she had to ride alone, Arland explained with his convincing low voice that in time she should be able to control the level of heat she radiated. Toddy, not quite understanding but accepting the handsome man's answer, would continue making her rounds with her four chubby fingers, reminding everyone of her age. Even Mox would force a smile and pretend that she hadn't told him twenty times already.

Hadvi thoroughly enjoyed the presence of Toddy, missing his own baby daughter at home. Zakai would look at the children pensively, but never approached or spoke to them. This was just as well with them, because even though they were a little scared of the other three strange Unni creatures that traveled with them, the leader one with the swinging weapon seemed best left alone. It wasn't that he was ever unkind to either of them, it was just a sense that he preferred his space to be unbothered.

When they arrived at the Jade Gardens a few days later, Esra's awe was undiminished. In fact, she laughed as she watched their new young charges take in the sights and smells with open-mouthed wonder, knowing that she had looked just the same a fortnight ago. Arland once again told the story of the creation of the Stronghold, of the Unni's great woodworking skills and how they brought the massive yanquor trees. He told of the Shendari and their plated scales that later became the roofs, and his people, the Elves, and how they were great stoneworkers. Esra told some of the stories from Cane's earlier lessons about the other races, and Jaar nodded silently in reverent appreciation while Toddy squealed with delight. There would be many more people that didn't know how old she was, and she planned to let them know.

Despite the last-minute preparations for the War Council, they were greeted in front of the Great Hall by a large party of people, including Talitha and Adonis. Esra's parents came to embrace her before turning to meet Zakai, who had dismounted his skycatcher but still looked as tall and broad as a tree. Undaunted by their new guest, the first of the Unni race to cross this border in decades, they bowed deeply to the Unni-se and his three guards. Mox, Shova, and Hadvi nodded courteously in turn as Zakai bowed respectfully but somewhat awkwardly. Esra guessed these were gestures they did not make often.

Adonis stepped forward in greeting. "Welcome, honored guests of the Jade Gardens. The Keepers have long awaited a reunion of our races. As ye are most certainly tired from yer long journey, we will show ye to yer quarters so that ye may rest."

In answer to Talitha's subtly raised eyebrow at the young Jaar and Toddy dismounting, Esra went to her mother and quickly explained the circumstances of the two children and the town of Wilspry.

"Attacked at Wilspry?" Her mother exclaimed breathlessly. "Yes, I would expect they were looking for you, but a hundred Elites? I suspect that Tallen certainly didn't think you'd get a town to fight with you, though. Especially with four Unnis. I have a feeling Arland had something to do with convincing them all of that."

Nor, the Great Keeper of Strength, stepped out from the crowd and approached Esra. She watched his small form approach, bent over slightly as if he were chilled or had an aching back.

"So I see you have completed your first test." Nor smiled at Esra, grasping her hand in congratulations. The wispy white hair on his wrinkled scalp danced with a sudden breeze. "Although there is still much to do in preparation of the War Council, the Elves are already here and Prince Bronnen will arrive tomorrow. We plan to send Fynn to Fire Lake to escort the Daughter of the Shendari, so they will be here in a few days' time. Now that you were able to bring the Unni, it looks like the four races will be together soon after all."

Esra beamed at their good fortune. A War Council of the four races: some formal introductions, short discussions, and then it would be time to attack Tallen and defend her home. She pictured an awkward but happy reunion of the races, one that hopefully would resolve these conflicts of old. Maybe within the week they would be marching towards the liberation of LeVara. She knew that this war would not be over quickly or easily, but she longed with nervous energy to finally do something about it. The faces of the dead townsfolk of Wilspry lingered in her dreams, especially the young girl that she had tried to help. And how many more were there? How many more had died in Kiran Brae? In other towns?

"Tell me, how did you convince Zakai to come?" Nor pulled Esra out of her reverie as Cane approached.

"Well, I had hoped to convince Zakai with my wisely chosen words when we arrived at Fira Nadim, but it seems I needed to provide more, err, tangible proof of my worthiness. So I agreed to a duel to the death with a Valkor. I still can't believe I actually agreed to it, but it seemed my body took over the terror screaming against it in my mind. Although we had worked on battle skills during the fortnight traveling, I was nowhere near an accomplished warrior."

"In fact, I was so afraid and shaken that I thought I wouldn't be able to fight. Somehow I found the courage, and the Valkor stabbed me in the shoulder almost immediately after we began. But I just kept going, and eventually he tired and I was able to knock the sword from his hand. I tried to show mercy, I didn't want to kill him, but he picked up his sword and came at me from behind..." her voice trailed off and she shuffled her feet uncomfortably. "Anyway, I turned around and threw my sword out, and he ran right into it. I was sick with grief, I've never felt so awful in my life. I will mourn that moment fer the rest of my life. But Zakai agreed to come with us. Oh, and Yarmon warned me about accepting a helmet, which turned out to be true, as it was poisoned. Fynn said I would have died. So I owe him my life."

The Great Keeper of Strength nodded solemnly as he turned to the rest of the Assembly and called for quiet to make an announcement. All around people hushed in anticipation for his declaration. "The night after tomorrow we shall have Esra's Gifting in the Ceremonial Room. It will give you all a day to rest and relax and await the Prince to be in attendance. I am sorry to hear of the struggles on your journey and the irreparable damage to Wilspry. But know that I am proud that you have accomplished so much already and take it as a sign of good things to come. We shall soon see who our new Keeper is and what skill she will bring to her Assembly."

XXXVI

Arland had explained to her about the Gifting Ceremony on the way back from Wilspry, so Esra had a general idea of what was going to happen. There would be a welcoming, probably something different than the normal speech from years past, considering the Prince, the Elders and the Unni-se would be in attendance. Arland said she was lucky, for only a few of the Keepers currently at the Stronghold had anyone from the other races at their Gifting, so this was a great honor. And Cane did not attend many of the ceremonies, since he was mostly in Sorley the last decade, unless he was the Gifter. Not that the Gifting Ceremony was less magickal with the other Great Keepers, for they were a sight to behold on their own.

After the welcoming speech by Nor would be a brief description of the task assigned to Esra. Then a member of her Assembly would explain how she had accomplished this feat. Nadia snickered and said that they always picked Arland for this part, since his charm seemed to make everything you did seem that much more wonderful. You could've shoveled manure all day and everyone would cheer just as loudly as if you'd single-handedly killed Tallen himself after Arland was done telling it. Esra was just grateful that she didn't have to speak. Her legs were going to tremble enough being in front of all those people. Finally, Nor would say some words about the Gift she was receiving and then present it to her. This is when she would officially become a Keeper, a One.

It was also when Esra would learn what she was the Keeper of. The ceremony would be directly followed by a rather nice feast. She was devastatingly curious to see where her affinity lay. She had mulled over the different options in her mind, but none of her natural talents seem to be strong enough to warrant becoming the Keeper of such a thing. For most people it had been clear, like Baelin or Nadia. But she really had no idea what she could possibly be that clever at, although she was good at many things. She certainly had nothing as amazing as Jaar, the healer of animals, or Nadia, who could disappear as if she never existed.

Esra thought about this again as they entered the foyer to the Great Hall, pushing through the Naduri River doors that still amazed her. She kept thinking that one day she would put her hands up against them and splash into water. "So then who spoke fer Arland when he completed a test?"

"Actually, Fynn. He has a way with words himself, although he is more entertaining than charming."

"What happens if no one sees ye complete a test?"

"Well that does happen on some occasions. Especially with me, since many of my tests involved stealth. In these cases the Keeper with the best insight magick would recall the event."

"Ye can do that?"

"Aye. None of our Assembly is particularly affluent with it, but we all can do it te some degree."

As they entered the open doors of the Ceremonial Room a wall of sound and energy hit Esra in the face, a brutal reminder of just how many people were in attendance. Practically every Keeper came to Giftings, especially the first ones. She also realized that no one would miss a chance to see the Unni-se, Elves, Prince Bronnen and the daughter of two Great Keepers.

It was common knowledge in the Gardens that you could tell how powerful a Keeper would be by the strength of the first Gift. This would be what they had all been waiting for for twenty years. To know if Esra would truly be the hero they needed against the Elites, or if she would not possess any special powers after all. She tried not to think too much about this, about being judged. Besides, every time a Keeper receives their first Gift they are judged to a degree, and that's not necessarily a bad thing. Seeing that Baelin, Nadia, Arland, and Fynn got unusually powerful Gifts were how they became her Assembly, and she was certainly grateful for that.

The empty chairs in the front row had been reserved for Esra and her friends, although Fynn's would remain empty as he had been sent to escort the Daughter of the Shendari to the Stronghold as soon as possible. He had stopped to see Esra before leaving, giving her a great Bear hug and swinging her around until her head ached. Kissing her on the cheek, he bragged that "a kiss from a man as handsome as Fynnigan is known across the land to be the best of luck." She smiled and gave his cheek a playful kiss back as he feigned a swoon.

The noise rose exponentially as Esra and Nadia made their way to the front of the room as everyone took notice that the guest of honor had arrived. The hall was enormous; large enough to fit hundreds of Keepers, and it looked as if almost every seat was occupied. The room was decorated with soft flowing fabrics in beautiful hues of blue and gold, the high ceilings and long windows letting in the final light of the day.

As she passed the rows and rows of carved wooden benches, the long aisle seemed like a march to her death. Esra didn't understand why she was so nervous on what was supposed to be a joyous occasion. She turned to Nadia.

"What if the Gift I receive isn't what everyone had hoped fer? What if it isn't enough to help in the battle against Tallen? Then again, what if it is? Do ye think I'm really ready fer that kind of responsibility?"

"Don' worry, Esra. Yer gift will suit ye perfectly, it always does."

Arland smiled at her encouragingly as she reached the front row, and she took a seat between him and Baelin. Esra stared at the low marble steps leading up to the open platform and the now empty seats. There were five golden marble chairs bordering each side and a larger, more elaborate one in the middle. She knew from her tour with Fynn that the eleven chairs were for the five Great Keepers, the three Elders, the Unni-se, the Daughter of the Shendari and the King. The speaker or host of the event sits in the middle, so Nor would be center chair today, as the Gifting Great Keeper.

Baelin placed a soft hand on her arm and she sighed heavily, not realizing that she had been holding her breath.

"Don't worry, Esra, Keeper of the Unknown. Yer Keeper is here, and I shan't let anything happen te ye." He gave her a reserved smile and in that moment she could not think of anyone else she would rather have with her on this day. She carried the Great Wolf knife he had given to her faithfully, and the feel of the small blade at her side gave her comfort, made her remember her life before all of this. Her simple life with her grandparents, her Wolf, her teacher, and her blacksmith friend.

As if on cue, Meshok sauntered up to the front of the aisle, licking Esra's hand in greeting before plopping down on a large blue pillow placed at her feet. In her worried state, Esra hadn't noticed it.

"Meshok!" She exclaimed, rubbing her hands greedily down the long, dark grey fur.

"I asked fer them te have a 'seat' fer her, too. I knew ye'd be nervous enough and would be glad te have another friend near," Baelin admitted, stroking the Great Wolf's head.

The crowd hushed suddenly and Esra looked up to see the Great Keepers walking down the aisle towards the platform. She recognized

Cane, Nor, and her parents Talitha and Adonis, so she assumed that the fifth was Tayen, the Great Keeper of Magick. She was surprised to see that he was dark skinned, obviously an Elf. He was much older as well, older looking even than Cane with his baldness and Nor with his white wispy hair. The Great Keeper of Truth, her old teacher, nodded solemnly at her as he passed. Esra's father looked at her with his rosy cheeks and gave a generous smile while Talitha flicked her wrist in a small wave of encouragement as she continued to move up the stairs towards their seats.

The Great Keepers were followed by a group of four dark Elves in regal purple robes, walking proudly and nodding this way and that as they passed the rows and rows of Keepers. The Elders.

Arland leaned towards her and whispered quietly, "The one in front is Kered. He is the oldest and wisest of the Council. Although he is quieter than the others, when he says something, everyone listens. He knows much about the history of the Council and the ways of the Keepers. Kered is light hearted and well liked."

Esra stared at the grey haired Elf, whose eyes twinkled with the glimmer of youth despite his age. He smiled walking past her, revealing a mouth full of straight white teeth.

Kered's tall lean frame and long strides contradicted the two middle aged Council members behind him, who were shorter and rounder with hastier, bouncier gaits. Their heads came together at frequent intervals as they whispered hurriedly back and forth, scowls flickering briefly over their faces.

"Those two are rarely seen apart, as ye can probably tell. The woman is Danya and the man is Isak. Although I must admit that they are very knowledgeable, they are often blinded by self-will. They consider themselves to be "Keepers of Elvish prominence" or some such nonsense and are always talking about "preserving the old ways". I think sometimes they are only trying to preserve their own power. Convincing people to fear what they should not, to gain support. Danya and Isak will be some of the most difficult to convince of our cause at the War Council. I am sorry to tell ye that the Elders are not always made up of the most generous of our people, but they are chosen carefully, so we must make do with what we have."

"Elders are elected every ten years, correct? I remember from my studies."

"Aye. So although it's a long term, it's not forever."

Esra nodded gravely as she watched them both mount the steps with heads held high, making a large show of sweeping their robes before sitting delicately. Behind Danya and Isak was a rather plump young woman with a beautiful plait of hair that reached past the small of her back and was interwoven with shining silver ribbon. As she reached the front row, the woman turned directly towards Esra, although none of the others had done so, and gave her a grand sweeping curtsy. Her round freckled face gave a mischievous wink and she stomped gaily up the stairs to a bench that had been set for her beside the Council, ignoring the slightly raised eyebrows of her two middle aged companions. Esra guessed that her greeting was not something customarily done at a Gifting.

Arland laughed quietly at Esra's stunned face. "That would be Linae. She is the youngest, an Elder in training, but she has a fierce heart, as ye can see. Nadia and I used to enjoy spending time with her before we came to the Stronghold. She is witty and playful, almost an exact replica of Fynn, if he were a woman. The people choose her to be Kered's apprentice a few years ago. She can be very outspoken against Danya and Isak, a dangerous road to tread fer an apprentice, but she always maintains sound arguments. Linae does not argue fer sport, she has a purpose and is determined to resolve issues, especially if she feels it is in the best interests of our people. Ye can imagine that she rubs them both the wrong way quite often, especially since she can be very convincing. I daresay that Kered is secretly amused and glad at her spirit, as I hear he is often trying to hide an outburst of laughter in meetings by pretending a cough."

Entering the back of the room behind the Elders was a young man in his early twenties, the son of King Keridon. He was slowly making his way past the benches, pausing every so often to shake an outreached hand or touch the head of a small child. He was wearing a tunic of muted green edged in simple silver lines over earth colored trousers. Although his dress was not flashy like the King's, it was very well made and in a modern cut, and he carried himself with confidence. His face remained calm as he looked around the grand Ceremonial Room, taking in the wonder of the space; the lavish benches, high ceilings, dark blue marble floor and pale golden walls shimmering with sunlight from the tall windows. Esra imagined that even the son of a King had not seen anything quite like it.

"Prince Bronnen, of course," Arland whispered. "Thank goodness he takes after his grandfather. Yer Human King has a great liking fer ladies and hunting, but not much else. The youngest son, Samuin, seems to be heading in the same direction as his father, unfortunately. Quite lazy and careless. Prince Bronnen is the real ruler of this Kingdom, although King Keridon would never admit it. LeVara would be in much worse condition by now if it weren't fer the eldest son. It is a good thing that the King saw fit to send him, especially amidst all the upheaval of struggling to find him a match. His parents are both trying very hard to get him married off, but I hear he will have none of his suitors. But that seems to have been put aside for the moment. I was worried that King Keridon's curiosity would get the best of him and he would try to come himself, but alas he probably could not fathom to take such a long trip and be expected to wake up before noon every day."

Esra knew that what he spoke was true, all the people of LeVara knew it. She wondered how someone from another race could know so much more about her own rulers than she did. Watching Prince Bronnen approach the front of the Ceremonial Room she now knew with her own eyes why everyone had faith in him. Something about his manner projected strength and proficiency, but with a sincere warmth. As he reached the front of the room, he bowed respectfully to the Great Keepers and Elders before proceeding up the long, low marble stairs to the platform. His chair was the closest to Esra, and as he turned to sit she was surprised to see that he was also very handsome. He had fair skin, light eyes, and blonde hair that fell casually around his head, the hair on his chin markedly darker. He had strong shoulders and arms that sloped flatteringly into a slim waist. He didn't have the overwhelming air of charm that Arland radiated, nor his devastatingly attractive face and body, but he was certainly handsome nonetheless.

The clinking of a metal chain brought Esra back to the present and she didn't need to turn around to know that Zakai was approaching. She had spent the last few days listening to the intimidating ring of the flail at his side. The Unni-se strode heavily and quickly up the long aisle, followed by Mox, Shova and Hadvi, who took their seats directly behind Esra. A great warmth suddenly overcame her as Toddy stumbled up to her Unni friends and slid into the same bench, Jaar close behind her. Meshok groaned wearily as she got up from her comfortable pillow to give sloppy kisses to her traveling children, who giggled with pleasure at the Great Wolf's gesture.

As the Unni-se was seated and only the Daughter of the Shendari's chair remained unoccupied, Nor stood from his center seat as Gifting Keeper to address the hall. The small, withered Great Keeper of Strength took a few feeble steps forward and the crowd immediately hushed. Nor was quiet for a long minute, in no hurry to begin despite the barely contained excitement of all those in attendance. *Although if I were immortal I would probably have no need to hurry either,* Esra thought. The frail old man in front of her suddenly opened his arms in greeting and spoke in a great booming voice so unexpected that Esra jumped in her seat.

"Honored guests of The Veiled City, Fira Nadim Forest, and The King's Hold of LeVara, we welcome you. Your presence marks this day as a wondrous and glad occasion. Keepers of the Stronghold, we welcome you. Esra of Sorley, we welcome you. Today is the celebration of a first test completed." He paused here to take a sweeping gaze around the room. "The first test of Esra was to travel to Fira Nadim Forest and then continue on to Shadow Glenn, where she would find the Unni-se and bring him back to the Stronghold to attend the War Council."

Here he nodded to Esra and Arland, which she knew meant that they were to come forward for the telling of the test. Arland had informed her beforehand of all that he was to say, as the speech was meant to be only a brief account of what had passed. Her Assembly had already met with Nor earlier this morning to give him and the other Council members a detailed account of what had transpired, including the defense of Wilspry. Arland grasped Esra's shaking arm to escort her up the long marble steps and then gently guided her to turn back towards the hundreds of people who sat with hungry expectancy. She was sorry that she did not have more courage and wondered if maybe that meant she was not quite worthy of any reward after all.

"Bring the Unni-se to the War Council," Arland began. "Although this test came from the Great Keeper of Strength, this was not to be simple test of muscle. One could not just fetch the chief of the Unni and carry him back to the Gardens over their shoulder, as ye can see." Ripples of laughter wove through the crowd as he gestured towards the massive Zakai, who gave as much a smile as he could muster.

"After a long and arduous journey to the Jade Gardens, followed directly by another long and arduous journey to Fira Nadim, ye would think that this alone would be proof of strength. Here is a young woman who knew not of our ways, who was far away from all she knew as a home, who still agreed to do whatever was asked of her to bring peace to this land. We trained and instructed her mercilessly on our journey, hoping she would gain the basics of defense and offense with her newly forged sword and shield. Upon arriving at Shadow Glenn, she was challenged to participate in a dual to the death with a Valkor, to prove to Zakai she was worthy of his audience. She would fight a seasoned warrior with little more than a week's worth of battle training."

The crowd broke into excited murmurs at this and Arland had to pause briefly before continuing. "Esra, despite all odds against her, agreed to fight the experienced warrior to win the favor of the Unni-se. The battle began, with Esra receiving multiple wounds from her opponent, including a deep stab to her shoulder. Things did not look well fer Esra of Sorley. One armed, under practiced, and weary, she fought bravely, using every piece of muscle and training to defend herself against his blows. Eventually she managed to overcome her foe with determination and skill, knocking aside his weapon and showing mercy by refusing to land a fatal blow. As she turned to accept her victory, the devious Valkor came again, intending to fell her from behind. At the last moment she turned and slayed him, allowing the Unni-se to fulfill his promise to return to the Jade Gardens. This is the account of Esra, daughter of Talitha and Adonis, and the completion of her first test."

The room erupted into cheers. Arland smiled generously and bowed deeply, opening his arms to present Esra to the hall. She smiled meekly and performed the best bow she could to the now standing crowd.

Nor nodded to her again, indicating that she should kneel before him for her reading. She had trouble understanding this part when Nadia had tried to explain it to her earlier. It had something to do with measuring her beyond the story of what she did, beyond her actions. A Great Keeper could lay their hand upon the shoulder of someone and know exactly what Gift was right. Esra had assumed that the Gift was chosen beforehand according to how the test was accomplished, but that was not so. It was a reading of one's intentions, their heart and mind. Nor would be able to see her strength from the inside, be able to know exactly what she needed to aid herself in becoming a better Keeper.

Esra shakily knelt on the hard marble step, bowing her head humbly to the Great Keeper of Strength. She held her breath as Nor closed his eyes and placed a hand on her shoulder. A shiver ran down her spine at the first hint of his touch, and the crowd was so quiet that Esra could hear every breath she took as if it were a strong wind rattling an old shack. She had no idea what he was sensing from her, or if it were good or bad. Maybe because she didn't have any extraordinary skills and he couldn't sense anything. She tried to control her trembling body under his small but steady hand.

Suddenly he pulled his hand back from her as if he had been burned. Recovering his composure quickly, he smiled openly at her and gestured for her to stand at his side so that he could present her Gift and Title to the hall.

Before addressing the crowd, he turned and spoke quickly to her under his breath, so that only she and the people on the platform could hear. "Your strength is very great, greater than you can imagine. It is something I have not felt in a long time, Esra of Sorley."

She didn't have the opportunity to be appropriately surprised by this revelation as he stepped forward and continued in a thunderous voice.

"Esra, I give you The Bracelet of Fortitude. In your darkest moment, when your heart and body tires and all seems lost, this bracelet will give you and all who fight with you, a powerful surge of renewed energy. This is the Gift I grant you."

He opened his palm to reveal a small, flat silver bracelet that had not been there a moment ago. It shone like Tur, radiating with some inner life. Aside from the glowing, it appeared to be a simple piece of metal, unadorned and without carving. She held out her arm to Nor, noticing that the bracelet was much too large to stay on her slender arm. She hoped that Baelin would be able to adjust it for her, if that would be allowed. He slid the metal onto her arm and there was an intense burst of light, filling the entire hall with a blinding whiteness. Esra heard the crowd erupt with gasps behind her. When her eyes recovered and she looked down, the bracelet now fit snugly around her wrist. A few words in what appeared to be blue Tur scroll were carved into the metal. Esra blinked to clear her eyes so that she could make out the words. It looked to be her own name, followed by Keeper...

"Esra, I give you The Bracelet of Fortitude. And I present to you, honored guests and citizens of the Stronghold, a new Keeper. I give you Esra, Keeper of Peace."

XXXVII

The shocked silence which hung over the hall like a heavy curtain lasted for only a few brief moments, but to Esra they were a lifetime. As the room broke into a frenzy of excitement, Esra could do little more than stare at the new piece of blue and silver metal that was now almost a part of her flesh. *Esra, Keeper of Peace*. There it was. Undeniably so. But she couldn't be a Keeper of *Peace*. How does one keep peace? It is not something like Toddy's fire or Fynn's herbs or even Arland's charming nature. Peace was, well, peace.

Her father rushed over and gathered her up in a fierce hug as everyone began to surround her, shouts of congratulations ringing through the air. Faces were spinning around her so fast that suddenly she thought she might become ill. Esra closed her eyes to avoid the nausea that was about to overcome her and bent forwards tentatively. People continued to press in around her, a swarm of well-wishers about to engulf her. In her confusion she hardly noticed when a strong set of arms lifted her off her feet and carried her towards the back entrance of the hall. Once through the doors and into the refreshing cool air, Esra felt herself being set gently on the grass.

"Are you alright?" An unfamiliar voice spoke to her from seemingly far away, and she opened her eyes briefly to see where the sound was coming from. Prince Bronnen stood over her with a worried look, his pale cheeks slightly reddened from the exertion.

Esra sat up gingerly and propped herself up on her elbows. "Aye, I think so."

He gently put a hand to her clammy forehead, brow furrowed with concern. She could see now that his eyes were green, a nice contrast to his light hair. Embarrassment suddenly washed over her, and she was confused at the intensity of the feeling. For a moment Esra wished vehemently that she had paid more attention to those stupid girls in

Sorley and their social dramas. She had never been in such close proximity with a man she hardly knew, let alone a noble, and had no idea how to respond. The Prince of LeVara was leaning over her so closely that a leather string with an emblem of the royal crest briefly caressed her cheek. "You feel a little warm. I've heard that Gifting Ceremonies can be very draining. You should rest a bit."

"Esra?" Baelin called loudly as he burst from the door, followed by Nadia and Arland. They rushed over to her and bent down, examining her as if she were about to perish from The Cough.

"I'm fine now, really. Just got a bit too excited or something," she mumbled, brushing off their offers to help her stand. The nausea was subsiding, although her body was now covered in a cold sweat. She glanced at the Prince, who had moved to the side once her Assembly had arrived.

"Jumping jig, Es," Arland stated proudly. "Nice Gift."

"Oh, yes. Well, I guess so. I'm not quite sure what it does. Renewed energy? I was kind of hoping fer a sword that wouldn't miss when I swung it or the ability to fly. But I guess some extra energy is fine."

"Some extra energy?" Arland asked incredulously. "Some *extra energy*? Is that all ye think that is? Bumbling huckfly! Do ye know what kind of a Gift that is?"

"It's true," Nadia agreed. "That is an amazing Gift. Ye have to understand that usually when a Keeper receives a Gift it's fer their use alone. On rare occasions it is something that can be used fer yer Assembly. But to have something to use fer an entire army, now that's powerful."

"But did he say I could use it fer an army?"

"Yerself and all who fight with ye, to be exact," Arland explained. "That means that if yer fighting a battle, everyone on yer side will be included. It could help thousands."

"Oh," Esra acknowledged sheepishly. Prince Bronnen stood patiently off to the side, unsure of if he should take his leave. "Thank ye, Prince Bronnen, err, Yer Highness."

"My pleasure, Esra Keeper of Peace." He swept her a quick bow and hesitated for a moment, looking as if he intended to speak further, but then turned and started back towards the Great Hall.

As soon as he was out of sight, Nadia leaned in close to Esra. "Oh, dear. I think that I might pretend to faint just so he can carry me off somewhere."

"I'm tellin' Fynn," Arland teased.

"He is...handsome," Esra admitted shyly. "I didn't think that a

Prince would look like that."

"Well, what'd ye think he would look like?" Arland laughed as he helped her to her feet. "An old vernok?"

"I don't know. I just didn't think he's look like *that*."

"How are ye feeling?" Nadia looked her over with concern.

"Better."

"Let's get back to our dwelling, ye can lay down fer a bit. Arland will go tell yer parents yer alright, they're worried but wanted to give ye some space. If ye feel alright later, Baelin and Arland can give ye a lesson on magick this evening before the feast."

"I'm fine," Esra insisted, dusting off her skirt. Looking around for Baelin, it was only then that she noticed he was already gone.

XXXVIII

Baelin showed up for their lesson an hour late and sat quietly while Arland spoke about influence magick. Not that Baelin's being quiet was anything new, but Esra couldn't help but feel uneasy about his silence. It was too purposeful, not like the natural pensiveness she was used to. But Arland's charm seemed to soothe her nerves enough and after a while she went back to focusing on her lesson.

That night Esra ate dinner with her parents in the Hall, where she told them the full story of their journey to Fira Nadim and back. Her father's face showed emotion at every turn; surprise, fear, anger, while Talitha's demeanor remained fairly constant, although she asked questions here and there.

After dinner, Nadia asked her how things were going with her parents. "Are ye feeling any more comfortable with them yet?"

"It is getting a little easier to be in their presence, now that the initial shock of their existence has worn off," Esra admitted. "Not comfortable yet, but easier. Talitha is harder to read than Adonis, though she is very kind and gentle. My father is like an open book, sharing his thoughts and feelings without reservation, but my mother seems more inclined to privacy. Nevertheless, I can't forget my first night here and the woman who allowed herself to cry upon seeing her long lost daughter."

That night Cane called Esra and her Assembly to his personal chamber, which was piled high with shelves upon shelves of books and oversized reading chairs, not unlike his house in Sorley. Indicating that she should take a seat directly across from him as he began packing his pipe, Esra happily recalled their spirited lessons not so very long ago. She tried not to think too much of the aching loneliness she still felt being away from her grandparents.

"I'm glad everyone is here," Cane began solemnly, rubbing his balding head. "We may need yer help with the War Council."

"Are we supposed to attend?" Esra ventured a guess.

"No, no one outside of the eleven leaders may attend, with the exception of Linae, who is in training." He leaned forward to tap his pipe briskly on the side of the table, looking in and tapping it again. He repeated this process in silence a few more times as Esra tried not to show her impatience.

"Ah, yes." Cane relaxed back into his chair after a final tapping, apparently satisfied. "As I was saying, we may need yer help. Although ye cannot attend the Council meetings, I think that ye still have a fair amount of influence over the members. We need yer help to unite them in any way ye can."

"Unite the War Council?" Esra was slightly relieved. At least there were no swords or Valkors involved. "Well, that can't be too hard. What happens at a War Council anyway? I imagine just some lengthy meetings and long-winded speeches, if ye'll beg my pardon. I know that there have been deep seated resentments among the races, but how can they stand apart in a time like this, when the right path is so glaringly obvious? What more could we do?"

"Well, that's a valiant viewpoint to have, but utterly wrong, I'm afraid. As to what ye can do to help, believe me when I say that it's no small undertaking to unite these races. In fact, some say it may be impossible, given these times. The walls that have been built between the races over the last generations will not crumble easily. War Councils are difficult even when everyone is in relative harmony. Each person has a certain set of beliefs, and the beliefs of the people they represent. Different ideas on how and when things should be done. And there are some times ye will find they are simply unwilling to negotiate. The Elders are divided in their sentiments, the Prince is sympathetic but faces limited resources, namely a lack of trained soldiers, and the Unni-se, well...Zakai will be difficult. Ye won over his favor in a duel, and he led the defense of Wilspry, but don't think fer a moment that his cooperation extends much beyond coming here. That was all he had promised, after all. But ye've all fought beside him, and ye have gained more of his trust than anyone else here, besides myself and the other Great Keepers. And while he may respect us, trust is another matter. The Daughter of the Shendari seems to be the only one capable and willing to forge an alliance, but only time will tell."

"But how can LeVara possibly face Tallen divided?" Esra interjected. "If we don't come together all will be lost. We cannot fight this war alone."

"That is precisely what ye must make them see. Trust me, it will take all of the skill and wit in yer Assembly's possession. And mine."

Everyone was gloomily quiet leaving Cane's chambers and the silence extended on the walk back to their dwellings. It pained her to think that all their hard work may be for naught. Esra had a hard time getting to sleep that night, plagued with worry over their new assignment. And Meshok had decided to sleep at the foot of her bed, which was hardly comfortable even with its generous size. Esra absentmindedly petted her friend's stomach with her foot.

"How can we get people that have not mingled fer hundreds of years to agree upon something so important in so little time? Arland told me that the limit on a War Council is eleven days, representing one fer each of the members. After that a decision has to be made and a vote taken. It's like one moment I believe with confidence that they will have to see the truth it's so plain. But then the next my mind is filled with dread that this will be much harder than that, and I'm as unprepared as trying to fight an Elite with an Acorn."

Meshok murmured in either agreement or pleasure over the belly rubbing, and Esra tossed and turned into the night. After a troubled sleep, she rose earlier than usual at the first hint of the orange glow of morning, exhausted from the restless night. She pulled on her pants and cloak, figuring she may as well go to the Council Hall and see if anyone was already there.

Her steps echoed on the dark blue marble floor as she entered the foyer to the Great Hall. Finding it empty, she took a seat on a bench against one of the walls, unsure if she should wait or try to find the rest of her Assembly. Deciding she was too restless to sit and wait, Esra got up to leave but was halted by the sound of footsteps coming down the corridor.

Suddenly nervous at the anticipation of meeting a Council member alone, she had a panicked moment trying to decide whether she could sneak out and pretend she never heard anyone approaching. She did not have long to scold herself as a figure stepped out into the sunlit foyer.

A small gasp escaped Esra's lips as she looked at the… woman…across from her. If woman was the right word. The figure in front of her made a motion like a bow as Esra stood frozen. Although it resembled the structure of a Human, the being was only about three feet tall, practically half of Esra's height. Her body was covered in a hardened type of flesh resembling fish scales in varying hues of dark orange and hints of red. There was not a speck of hair anywhere on her body, nor was she wearing clothes, and all her facial features seemed to lie flat on her face. There were no ears that Esra could see, but there were two small black eyes and a Human-like mouth. Three small slits where the nose should be flared very subtly at each breath. Intuitively

Esra understood that this was her. This was the Daughter.

Attempting to recover her composure, Esra was finally able to make an awkward bow towards the Shendari woman. She opened her mouth in greeting but a strange gargling sound came out instead. "Grrrsshhhiiimmmfflllaa."

Now it was the Daughter's turn to be surprised. Then again Esra was not sure what surprise would look like on a Shendari face. Or any other expression for that matter.

"Hello, I am Shakti." Although those words are what translated in Esra's mind, the noise that came from the Daughter was the same gurgling sounds she had just made. Was it possible that Esra understood the Shendari language?

"Bbbuurrvveerraannn eeesssrraa." What was going on? Had she heard Fynn speak this before? She didn't think so, but her mind was still sluggish with shock.

"Pleased to meet you, Esra."

Rooted to her spot, she stared at Shakti in disbelief. The orange-red woman came towards her with small elegant steps and took Esra's hand in hers. "You speak Shendari very well, Esra Keeper of Peace. I did not know."

"Wwhheeyy Ppphhaayylloonnnqquu." *Me neither.*

Shakti smiled largely and made a sound like trickling water that seemed to be her way of laughing. Esra thought back to her lessons with Cane, trying to remember what he had said about the Shendari. They were orange when newly hatched and grow darker red with age, which meant that this Daughter seemed to be fairly young. They were also practically immortal, so age might be irrelevant. They are a community driven people who do not have a natural leader, unless it is a time of war. The women are the warriors and men do not go to battle. What else? Oh, and their language is virtually indecipherable to the Human ear. Which meant that Esra definitely should *not* be able to talk to one.

They were interrupted by the entrance of Nor, who swept in quickly and quietly, giving a garbled greeting towards Shakti. They stood and exchanged muddled conversation for a moment as if Esra were not there, until the Great Keeper of Strength turned to her with surprise.

"So, you speak Shendari quite well Shakti tells me."

"Umm...well I guess so. I mean I wouldn't really know, I've never spoken it before. I thought that Humans weren't able to understand it?"

"Usually they can't, only in very rare cases. All of the Elves can speak it in moderation, although the Great Keepers and Fynn are probably the most fluent. I guess it is another Gift you have, and a very unusual and precious one at that. Now if you'll excuse us, we must head to the Council Room to begin preparation for our first day of discussions." Nor nodded at Esra pleasantly and walked with the small orange figure towards the door. Shakti turned to give Esra a shy smile before disappearing into the Council Room.

Walking back towards the bench in stunned silence, she fell heavily into the seat, grateful for the hard stone to support her. Glancing up to see Fynn walk into the foyer, she met the curious look on his face with a blank stare.

"Dumbfounded by my beauty, I see. Don't worry, it happens te ye all." He plopped down next to her and gave her leg a playful swat "Trouble sleeping? I did as well. Almost thought about going te see yer father about knocking me out with a turnip."

"Aye, I had a hard night," Esra laughed quietly, trying to shake herself from her stupor. "I just met the Daughter. And found out that I can speak Shendari."

"Speak Shendari? Jumping jig, Es," he whistled loudly through his teeth. "What did ye say?"

"Just hello and my name. Oh, and that I didn't know I could speak her language. It's funny though, I can't remember any of the words now, but they were so clear when she was standing in front of me. Is it like that with ye?"

"No. But ye have te remember that my first Gift was the Ring of Tongues. What a conundrum. Ye seem to be full of those, my dear Es. Either way, Shakti is an impressive woman, three feet tall or no. I was glad te see that she was the one chosen."

"I agree. She seemed...kind. I'm not quite sure why, but she did."

"Aye, she has a gentle nature. Except on the battle field. Definitely don't get in her way then or ye'll be sorry," he shivered dramatically. "Well, there's not much we can do here, seeing as how we can't actually get into the Council Room. Baelin and I were discussing last night how we think it may be useful te find some information on past Councils, see if there is anything helpful. We were going te meet in the Library after breakfast. Care te come?"

"Sure. Not much else I can think of to do."

Arland and Nadia joined Fynn and Esra for a quick meal of oats and berries before they all made their way across the foyer to the Library. Walking past the rows and rows of dark bookshelves, they found Baelin waiting at the back of the room by the large stone fireplace. He was so involved in what he was reading that he barely noticed as they approached the round wooden table.

"Find anything?" Arland asked, sliding tiredly into the seat beside the blacksmith.

"Not yet," Baelin mumbled, looking up briefly.

"What exactly are we looking fer?" Esra inquired as she peered into the thick dusty volume with small print that lay open on the table.

"Well, anything relating te prior Councils," Baelin answered. "We were hoping that maybe there is some evidence of prior disagreements. War Councils were held often enough, usually te decide in defending some part of LeVara against an outside Kingdom or peoples. Or sometimes te intervene in skirmishes within the Kingdom. It's not likely that they were always in agreement. So maybe if we can find out how they handled their differences back then it will help us te know what te do now."

"That and there's not much else we can do directly since none of us are allowed in the Council Room," Arland admitted. "So we are going to have to wait fer the scarce opportunities when they are not meeting. The attendees will probably be in session from dawn till sundown every day, so they will be tired. This means that we should probably make what we have to say powerful, short, and to the point. We will have limited time to make our argument, so we need to make it good."

"Alright, then. What books do we need?" Esra asked, scanning the countless volumes lining the rows upon rows of shelves.

"I already have some here," Baelin pointed to three dirty, large stacks of books on the table. "These are the accounts from all the War Councils that have ever taken place at the Stronghold."

"There have been that many?" She stared incredulously at the heavy volumes. "So who wrote them all?"

"Err…it's not really a who," Arland explained. "One of the Great Keepers simply casts an influence spell over a pen and it takes an account of everything by itself as the meeting is conducted."

"Oh." Esra tried to imagine a phantom pen swirling about on parchment like a ghost while it wrote down everything that was being said. "How strange. I wish I had known about this spell when Cane had me writing scrolls upon scrolls during my studies."

"Indeed. Arland and Fynn, ye stay here with me te start going through these," Baelin delegated. "Nadia and Esra, see if ye can find anything outside of the meeting records that could be helpful."

"Well, I'm not sure what we'll find or where it will be, so I think that going row by row will be easiest," Nadia turned to Esra as the men took a seat. "Would ye prefer I use the ladder first?"

Esra looked up at the rolling ladders four times her height that bordered the room. "No, I'll start with the top row and maybe we can switch after a while."

"Deal."

For the rest of the day Nadia and Esra scanned the titles of books in the history, philosophy and poetry sections. A few names had appeared promising, but upon further investigation it was clear that whatever was in these pages was not what they needed. By the time their growling stomachs alerted them it was far past lunch, they made their way towards the back of the room, eager to see if the rest of their Assembly had better luck.

"How'd it go?" Arland looked up hopefully.

"We got through quite a bit but haven't found anything yet. Ye?"

"Nothing."

Everyone was quiet for a moment in disappointment before Baelir stood and stretched. "I say we get something te eat, come back fer a few hours, and then see if Cane can tell us what happened today. After that we'll head home an' see if we can start fresh in the morning. We only have ten days left te convince four very different races that the only path te freedom is te work together."

XXXIX

Although they would all shuffle back across the hall to the Dining Room and later wait outside the Council Room far past dark, they would not catch sight of Cane nor anyone else for the next six nights. Their pattern would be the same; waking, eating, searching the Library, eating, searching, waiting, finally resigning to sleep. Esra's hope was diminishing a little every day as she watched her Assembly comb through countless volumes without a hint of anything that could help them. And she was wrought with curiosity and frustration that neither she nor anyone in her Assembly had any idea of what was going on behind the Council Room doors. If Cane had wanted them to help, he was certainly making it difficult.

"Why have we not gotten word?" Esra groaned aloud.

"Maybe the reason fer the long days is because they've already agreed to unite and are formulating a plan of defense." Arland offered hopefully. Esra appreciated her friends attempt to be optimistic, but she couldn't help but think that someone would have told them by now if that was the case.

Finally, at the end of the seventh day, Esra was roused by Nadia in the middle of the night and told that Cane had summoned them to his quarters.

"About time," she grumbled under her breath as she leaned over to lace up her boots. When they met with the other three Assembly members and arrived at Cane's personal chambers they found him pacing the floor.

"Sit, sit." He motioned towards the overstuffed furniture and wooden chairs dotting the room. "I'm sorry that we have been unable to speak until now, but the Council discussions have been going much longer than any of us wish. And I daresay they're going worse, too."

He continued before any of them had a chance to ask why. "Prince

Bronnen has made it clear that he supports our cause but he lacks resources. He is painfully aware of the position LeVara's army is in, which is that it's non-existent. There simply is no army. King Keridor hasn't seen fit to train one. He may be able to hand over materia support, namely gold and supplies, to aid our fight. But that only helps if there are people willing and able to fight. We can't throw gold at the Elites. I think that this is the only reason the Prince is hesitant to fully commit to a war. He worries that he will not be able to hold up his end of the bargain, and he seems to be an honest and realistic young man.

"The Daughter of the Shendari, luckily, believes fully in the importance of uniting against Tallen. She is small but I can assure ye that the other members hear her position loud and clear. She is already aggressively on our side without question. The Elders are divided in their sentiments. Kered, the eldest of the three members, is also an ally to our cause, although he shows it more quietly than the Daughter. Danya and Isak, however, say that they are *doubtful about the outcome of such a war and cannot in good conscience commit their people to an uncertain battle.*"

"Heh!" Arland spat. "How did I know those two would be a problem? Doubtful about the outcome fer an uncertain battle? Well the only certainty is that not joining us would result in death and oppression."

"I absolutely agree," Cane's eyes narrowed as he pulled on his already long chin. "Danya and Isak are very proud. They want to be the hero, the center of attention. They are not the type to make hard decisions, to be depended upon to do the right thing like Kered. They are more concerned with being popular, having power. Very dramatic and arrogant. Although I have to say Linae has made it interesting."

Esra thought about the bold young woman who gave her a great sweeping bow at the Gifting Ceremony, to the disapproving glares of Danya and Isak. It didn't surprise her that Linae was creating some waves among her more conservative group members.

"She has a feisty spirit, that girl. And she has no problem letting the other two know her opinion, whether they've asked fer it or not. I believe the term she used once was *bumbling, frightened fools who are so self-centered that they wouldn't know a good idea if it kicked them in the...* well, let's just say she has been very vocal. Kered has done his 'pretending to cough' laugh more than a few times already. The difficulty is that Linae cannot vote, so the Council is opposed two to one."

"What about Zakai?" Baelin asked.

"The Unni-se has surprisingly grown slowly more supportive of our cause. As a great strategist, I think he knows the odds of beating Tallen and his massive army if we do not unite. Unlike Danya and Isak, he certainly is no fool. The problem he is facing is that the Unni are still in constant battle with the Valkors to the south of Fira Nadim. And there is also the issue that if he does make the decision to align with the other races, it may stir up some deep-seated resentments in his tribe. However, I think he knows that either way, this decision will not make everyone happy. His first concern is for the safety and freedom of his people. But like Prince Bronnen, he faces a more material obstacle. How many warriors can he send north and still keep his lands protected? Will the Valkor see this as an opportunity to attack unrestrained? He may put his people in danger while trying to avoid other perils."

"There are already seven Council members in favor and four opposed," Esra pointed out. "Won't a vote mean that the majority wins? Won't the others have to yield?"

"In other matters, yes, the majority would win. In cases of war, however, that is not the case. It was decided long ago that because this Council decides the fate of an entire race of people, their chosen leaders would select their own fate. This means that if the Shendari vote opposed, then none of the Shendari come. If the Unni-se votes in favor, then all of the Unni are committed. For the Elves, two out of three of the Elders that vote alike prevail. This is also true for the Great Keepers, who need at least three out of the five."

"So we may get one race but not another?"

"Correct. In a smaller battle, this may not present a problem. In fact, many Councils concluded with split votes. But when it comes to Tallen, there can be no separation. It is imperative that everyone unites. We cannot defeat such large and powerful forces without each and every one of our allies."

"What can we do?" Esra asked. "Can we help protect the Unni from the Valkor? Or maybe we can negotiate a truce?"

"A truce, I fear, would be impossible. The Valkors do not care much fer reason. They are fueled by their aggression, not logic. As fer helping to protect them, I am afraid that is also not an option. We would be depleting our own resources, which we need fer our own defense.

"As fer Danya and Isak, I would leave them fer last. Hopefully by then ye will have gained the support of the Unni-se and the Prince, which ye can argue certainly gives us a better chance of a favorable outcome. We only need one of the Elders to change their minds fer the Elvish vote to pass. If ye could find a way to convince them, find out what it would take to get them to change their position, that's all we need. But these are all a lot of 'ifs'. And only four days left to do them."

Baelin looked up at the pacing form before him and rose from his heavy wooden chair. "Well then, we won't waste any time."

XL

The next afternoon Esra's Assembly had a stroke of luck. It was an insightful observation by Nadia that as the Keeper of Charm, Arland had good fortune. So maybe if they weren't finding anything, it was because he was looking in the wrong spot. So they recruited Arland to join them in scanning the high rows of books for helpful titles as the other two continued looking over the meeting accounts. Less than an hour later, Arland had wandered away from his sister and came back with a hint of excitement. He explained that he felt it important to go over a mercantile section previously examined by Esra and Nadia on the third day.

"I just feel there's something there."

"But we've already been over that section," Nadia argued. "We didn't find anything except a bunch of old ledgers and lessons on trade improvements. Not exactly what we need, some logbooks about how many copper pieces a barrel of grain was worth two hundred years ago."

"Something's there, I know it."

Nadia shrugged and continued looking over a row of agricultural books. "Alright, well yer the lucky one. And ye've found some stranger things in stranger places. Go get us a book, Charm boy."

A few minutes later Arland came rushing past them, ushering them towards the back of the room where Baelin and Fynn looked up in surprise.

"There," Arland said breathlessly, tossing the book in the middle of the table.

"*Adventures of a Chicken Trader: The Tales of Whippleton Humgard*," Fynn read.

"Whippleton Humgard? Adventures of a Chicken Trader? Ye can't be serious," Nadia groaned. "Yer saying that this is the answer to a hundred years of intolerance between the races?"

"Aye," Fynn interjected. "Either that or he thinks he can appeal te

Tallen's humorous side. Maybe try te offer him some Chickens ir exchange fer conquering LeVara. Might jest kill him with laughter. Or perhaps we could train them some Hens to peck out the Elites' eyes."

"Very funny," Arland chided, giving the archer a hard punch in the arm. "I'm incredibly serious. Most of the book is utterly useless, I agree. But chapter four details Whippleton's encounter with a small tribe of isolated people to the far northwest of the Kingdom. They did not keep many material possessions, as they were modest people. Most of the items they kept were simple and useful rather than decorative, but they were very interested in this Chicken creature that the traveling man had brought with him. Since the people had nothing of value he wanted, Whippleton decided to eat noonmeal in exchange for a few eggs and be on his way. But when he sat and ate the bread and stew he was served, he was amazed. It was the most delicious bread he had ever tasted. Asking the man who had baked it what the ingredients were, he found it was not much different from the usual flatbread he made for himself. He then asked the man to detail the process, which was vastly different than his current method. So the answer lay in the preparation.

"Whippleton decided that he would indeed trade with these people. Since he ate on the road so much, it would be a great achievement if he could find out how to improve his simple bread making skills. He asked the man if he would teach him how to bake his special bread in exchange for three Hens and a Rooster. The man eagerly agreed and the trade was made. The tribe now had access to a good they had not possessed before, and Whippleton had learned a new skill. Both sides had gained."

"Alright, but isn't that the basis of trade? Each side exchanges different things so that both can improve?" Nadia pointed out.

"Aye. In this case one side traded a good and the other a service. We can apply the same principle to the Council members."

"Ye mean give them Chickens?" Fynn asked.

"No," Arland laughed, "give them each something they need in order to fight."

"He's right." Esra's excitement was growing. "So what does each side want that they don't have? The Humans need trained soldiers and the Unni need help defending against the Valkors if they are to send their warriors. I can't believe we haven't thought of this yet! So we get the Unni-se to agree to send some commanders to train the Human army. That's their specialty, as we have seen firsthand from Mox, Shova, and Hadvi when they taught the townsfolk of Wilspry in record time."

"But what can the Humans give the Unni?" Nadia asked. "They have no warriors to send. That's the exact predicament we're trying to solve. Both sides need soldiers."

Baelin nodded his head enthusiastically. "We need something te aid in the defense against the Valkors besides more soldiers. What about a wall? Something much too tall fer the Valkor te climb over and too strong fer them to breach. A stone wall. It could run the entire border of Shadow Glenn. The Unni are good with wood, but not very skilled with stone. We could convince Bronnen te send stoneworkers te build a wall fer protection in exchange fer training his soldiers."

"But wouldn't a wall that size that take a very long time and a whole lot of people?" Esra asked. "Stone work is slow. Ye must wait fer the mortar to dry between layers, and the border of Shadow Glenn is quite a big area to cover. Zakai's people will still be exposed while it's being built. Not to mention I didn't see any stone in Fira Nadim, so it would be a huge task to bring all of that into the forest."

"Not if we use Prion and Humi to move things along," Nadia looked over at Baelin, who nodded slowly.

"I know Humi is the Keeper of Speed but who is Prion?" Esra asked.

"Prion is the Keeper of Growth," Nadia answered. "He can take any object that isn't living and make it larger or smaller."

"Jumping jig. So he can just make a stone into a wall?"

"No, it doesn't quite work that way. He can make something multiple times its normal size, either bigger or smaller, but he can't change the structure of that thing. Prion couldn't take a kernel of Corn and grow an entire ear. But he could make a really huge kernel of corn as big as your fist."

"We often use his skills in the pantry," Fynn chimed in. "It's very helpful te feed a large group of people with a much smaller amount of food when Prion's around."

"Ah, so that's why the food is so enormous here," Esra acknowledged. "So we get Humi to help build a wall with the stone workers sent by the King. She can set the stones quickly or do whatever the masons ask in a much shorter time. But instead of trying to make it fifty feet tall, which would still take a long time even with the Keeper of Speed, we make a short section of a wall in intervals around Shadow Glenn. Once each section is dry and ready, Prion will use his powers to 'grow' it."

"Exactly," Arland clapped his hands together in excitement. "So hopefully this will solve the problems both the Unni and Humans are facing."

"Arland, ye prove te be a lucky bloke, as usual," Baelin grinned. "Let's not waste time, we need te let Prince Bronnen and Zakai know our idea as soon as possible. We can split up and approach them tonight after the Council ends fer the day."

"I say we send the ladies te the Prince," Fynn leaned forward eagerly "He seemed te take quite a liking te our Esra, here. And having another beauty like Nadia certainly can't hurt. I'm not afraid te use looks te help sway his mind, and certainly no man can resist these two."

Arland interjected quickly as Baelin flushed slightly at the suggestion "Besides, we'll need the nephew of the Unni-se to try and convince his uncle. The three of us men should be able to handle that. And I'll use my charm as much as possible to help things along, although I fear it's something I dare not use too much, since Zakai will surely notice if he is being influenced."

"Alright," Baelin conceded. "Let's see if we can find Cane, Humi and Prion te discuss our proposal. I'm sure they'll be more than happy te help. Then we can get some dinner and hopefully go convince two very independent races that an exchange of services is in order."

XLI

Cane's subdued smile and Humi and Prion's eager enthusiasm told the Assembly that their idea was a good one. Hopefully the Prince and Unni-se would think so, too.

Even with Cane's encouragement, Esra was beyond nervous as she approached the private chambers of Prince Bronnen that evening. She tried to remember the kind face and soft green eyes that took such attentive care of her a few days earlier, but the fact remained that this risky proposal was their only chance. After tonight there would be only three days left before the final Council vote, and they still needed to figure out a way to convince the Elves.

Esra also had a suspicion that she was nervous for another reason, and her limited dealings with handsome young men made her feel quite unprepared for a somewhat social visit. Mingling was not her strong suit, and she was glad to have Nadia with her.

A tall young man with dark skin and hair answered their knock and gestured for them to enter the sitting room. He exited briefly to the next room and exchanged a few mumbled words with the Prince, who came out into the sitting room to greet them. The King's son wore a more casual dark leather suit with boots fit for riding, and his blonde hair was freshly combed, although dark shadows covered his face where he had not shaved.

"Ladies," he swept towards them with an eager smile, making a respectful bow and then coming to take their hands in a more personal gesture. "It is an honor and joy to see you again. And Esra, you are looking well. I hope that you are feeling better?"

"Much, thanks to yer quick thinking, yer Highness." She smiled back at him openly, feeling some of her nervousness melt away at his warm reception.

"Please, sit." He motioned towards a few stuffed chairs surrounding a gold marble fireplace.

"Would you like a glass of mead? My first attendant and I were just about to share one as well. Or would you prefer something else, perhaps some wine?"

"Mead would be nice, thank ye Cailean." She turned towards the tall young man that had greeted them at the door, who was standing quietly at the entrance to the sitting room. He raised his eyebrows unexpectedly at the sound of his name.

"So ye've met Cailean?" The Prince leaned forward with curiosity.

"No, I've just been taught the names of all of the foremost people who live or work in The King's Hold, including the eldest son's most trusted attendant," Esra replied shyly.

"I'm most impressed. Then again I'm not entirely surprised, considering you've been studying with Cane."

"Aye."

They were quiet a moment as Cailean left the room and returned a moment later with a tray full of handsome silver goblets. Prince Bronnen approached the woodless fire burning in the hearth, studying the dancing flames that gave off heat and light but required no kindling. "I still can't get used to this, this place of magick. I mean, I've often thought of it, the Stronghold and its Keepers, what it would be like. But I have to admit it's better than I could have imagined."

"You'll have to excuse my fancifulness, sometimes I think too much aloud," he apologized, sitting across from them and taking a goblet. "I'd love to think that this is just a friendly visit from two gracious Keepers, but I must say I am curious. To what do I owe the presence of such beautiful and influential guests?"

"Well, we'd like to think it is fer both friendship and business," Nadia spoke with ease as her form flickered slightly. Although Esra had decided to wear a more simple dress of pale blue, Nadia had chosen a dazzling dress of lavender, which was a perfect complement to her dark skin and long, flowing curls. She was stunning with little effort, as usual.

"We have a proposal to make, yer Highness, if I may be so bold." Esra leaned forward eagerly, setting the half empty silver goblet on the tray. "Something we think will address the concerns ye have about an army."

"It is no secret that my father has left me in a difficult position to help the Council, if *I* may be so bold. Any ideas would be greatly appreciated, although I'm not sure how much good it would do at this late hour."

"Baelin, Arland and Fynn, the others of our Assembly, are meeting

271

with Zakai as we speak. We are proposing an exchange of services to accomplish two goals fer both races."

"Indeed?" Prince Bronnen raised one eyebrow questioningly. "Please then, continue."

"The Unni are fierce warriors, as ye know," Nadia explained. "They train their people from a young age and are known fer their skill at instruction as well as battle. We would like ye to consider allowing some of the Unni commanders to help train a Human army. Ye have the necessary supplies to outfit an army and ye can recruit the people, especially after news of Kiran Brae reaches the rest of LeVara, but the problem is organization. Ye need skilled soldiers and commanders accomplished in the way of battle tactics, defensive and offensive maneuvers, not a jumbled array of people with weapons they have little understanding in. And we've seen firsthand in Wilspry that the Unni are more than capable of accomplishing this."

"You're right. I admit it is tempting to think that they would be willing to help. They are beyond skilled in all aspects of war. Getting people to follow an Unni commander, however, may be a bit of a challenge. But the bigger question is, what would the Unni want in return?"

"Stone workers."

"Stone workers?" There was such a mixture of surprise and confusion on the Prince's face that Esra had to bite her lip to keep from laughing. "What could they possibly want with stone workers? Do they not prefer the craft of wood?"

"Yes, but as ye know the main concern of Zakai is that he is in constant battle with the Valkor's to the south, and he worries that sending warriors north will leave his people vulnerable. We would like to ask ye to send stone workers so that we can build a protective wall along the border of Shadow Glenn."

Prince Bronnen was silent for a moment as he took in this information. "I see. But won't this take a very long time? A wall that large would take years to complete. I do not have that many stone workers in the Kingdom, so I fear it will not be an effective means of protection, at least not right away."

"That's exactly what I thought," Esra admitted. "Until they told me that Humi, the Keeper of Speed, and Prion, the Keeper of Growth would be there to help. All ye need do is send as many stone workers as possible. Humi will be able to set stone at speeds beyond what ye could imagine, she will be worth a hundred workers. They just need to tell her what needs to be done. And after a short section of the wall has been set and finished, Prion will use his powers to grow it to ten times its height and width."

"Unbelievable," he whistled, rocking back in his seat. "That is the craziest, most absurd plan I have ever heard in all my time as Prince. I absolutely love it. We would get one of the best trained armies the Human realm has ever seen and the Unni get a permanent solution to their Valkor problem. I do have one concern though that keeps me from fully agreeing, and I do think it will pose a significant threat to your plan How to get Humans to allow themselves to be trained by an Unni and how the Unni would feel about training us. Not to mention there would be a group of Humans they don't know in their forest. These are two groups of peoples that have not mingled in generations. It will not be an easy task to introduce one another."

Esra had known that this would be a problem; her Assembly had already discussed it over dinner. She tried to picture the people of Sorley being told that the army of the King would be trained by eight foot tall Unni commanders. There would be apprehension and fear if they were fortunate, but a few would be downright offended. "Ye can leave that to us. Arland, our Keeper of Charm, will be able to help ease those tensions, and there is another Keeper, Lara. She is a good friend of mine and an expert at the art of Tranquility. We also have plenty other spells of influence magick that will help. With any luck after everyone gets acquainted it won't continue to be a problem, the focus will be on Tallen. People just need the opportunity and time to get used to the idea of it."

Prince Bronnen stood up and began to pace back and forth, stroking his chin with a pained expression. Esra thought back on all they had said and wanted it to be enough, for she knew she could not leave until he agreed. Many lives depended on it. Suddenly the Prince stopped his pacing and turned to face them. "I hope you're right, Esra, Keeper of Peace. If the Unni-se will agree to it, then I think we have a deal."

XLII

Things had gone similarly well for Baelin and the others. Zakai had voiced many of the same concerns but in the end had agreed to the exchange. He could not deny that such a wall would be the greatest thing to happen to his people in generations. Even if there were some of his people that didn't like working with Humans, it was a small price to pay for freedom from a lifetime of senseless battle. They also brought in Prion to show an example of his "skills". The twenty pound carrot now sat prominently on the Unni-se's bedside table. In a show of good faith, Zakai designated Mox and Shova from his own personal guard to be the first two commanders to train the Humans. Hadvi would remain at the Stronghold and help with the development of strategy. His wife and child were to be sent for so that they could have their own dwelling here. Hopefully this would begin to rebuild the relationship between the Keepers and Unnis.

As Cane performed a sight spell to communicate with Hadvi's wife in Shadow Glenn, Hadvi admitted he was concerned that she would not agree to such a drastic move. But she graciously accepted the challenge and set about to pack so that she could leave as soon as possible. The look on Hadvi's face when he found he would soon be reunited with his wife and infant daughter Pixa was irreplaceable.

"Things are really looking up fer the first time since I've started this treacherous journey," Esra said hopefully to Nadia. "Or been kidnapped into starting it, anyway."

There was no denying the thorn that remained in the side of her Assembly, the small barb that could be the undoing of all this progress. The Elders. Tomorrow was the last day of the War Council and the final vote, but Esra's Assembly had come no closer to finding an answer to the riddle of converting Isak or Danya. Arland and Nadia had spoken with Kered the night before and although he expressed support for their cause he was just as certain that the other two would vote against it. Everyone seethed that Linae could not be an official Elder yet.

"It's no use," Esra moaned in resignation as her group sat in the Dining Hall during supper, eating little. "They're too stubborn."

"I agree," Fynn smashed an enormous Grape into a pulpy mess on the table with his fist. "Maybe we can capture one of them and hide them in a closet, claim they were eaten by a brengard. Heck, maybe we can even really feed them te one. Although I feel like that would be offensive towards the poor animal. Either way they'll have te let Linae vote."

"We need a better plan than kidnapping, tempting as it is," Baelin sighed. "We still have one day. Come on, think. All we need te do is convince one of them, not both."

"But how can we? Danya and Isak claim that they cannot 'in good conscience' commit their people to slaughter in an uncertain battle. Obviously we've gone beyond the point of trying to reason with them. Cane talked about how arrogant they are, how they are more concerned with having power and prestige than making the right choices."

"Maybe we can use that te our advantage," Baelin said slowly.

"What do ye mean?"

"Well, they're both overly concerned with appearances and praise. Maybe we can convince each of them that the other is going te turn on them tomorrow. That they will vote te support the cause so that *they alone* will be the ones who receive all the recognition and power. Then they can go home and tell the Elves that *they* are the reason the races united, that history is being made."

"But won't they lose certain powers by joining us? They would have to share decisions with others regarding the war."

"They will, but if they feel they were betrayed and would lose out on doing something popular, jealously will be their only concern."

"So how do we pull this off?" Nadia shimmered darkly.

"We go te each of them separately. Convince Danya and Isak that we have learned that the other one has secretly decided te vote with Kered, that we are there as a 'friend' te let them know. That the opinion the other has been voicing all along was just a trick te get the other te look weak so they can claim all the glory."

"Do you think that would work? That they would be so foolish?"

"I don't know but at least we can try and use their arrogance against themselves. Does anyone have a better idea?"

"Arland," Esra turned to her friend, "do ye think ye can make them dream something about this as well? Maybe make what we're saying into a reality in their head. Play a scene where the other person votes with Kered against them and receives all sorts of praise and power. I remember how real that dream ye gave to me felt. It was very powerful."

"Great idea, Es, the Bracelet of Dreams," Fynn bounced up and down in his chair vigorously. "It seems so silly, but then again we are proving te be masters of the impossible. We just won't tell Cane the specifics of it all. If anyone ever found out we used magick te sway a Council Member, even an idiot one, we'll have our britches te pay. This might actually work. And we only need one of them te believe it."

"Let's do the same thing as before," Nadia suggested. "Send a woman to Isak and a man to Danya. Should we go in groups again?"

"No, I think it better that someone goes alone," Baelin asserted. "Make it seem like we are taking a big chance te go and tell them, that it's our secret. And we don't want te give the impression that our Assembly is conspiring against them, they might get suspicious."

"Then I think I should go," Nadia offered. "I can make up a story about how I was using my stealth when I 'accidentally' stumbled upon Danya talking with Kered about voting together."

"That's good. And Arland, maybe ye can go te Danya. Use some of yer charm te help the situation a bit. We can work on the dream bit later."

As her Assembly dispersed, Esra felt more at peace than she had in the last couple of days, even after hearing that Zakai and Prince Bronnen had joined with them. Maybe this plan was crazy, but it was something. And like Baelin said, they only needed one of them to believe it.

She waited up all night, knowing that Nadia and Arland had made sure that the "secret informant" trips had happened well beyond the guise of darkness and any spying eyes. It also gave them less time to think things through and more of an opportunity for their anger to gain impulsive momentum. Hopefully, by the time they fell into a restless sleep, Arland's dream would be the final straw to their jealous frenzy.

"How did it go?" Esra bolted upright in her bed and staggered to the entrance of her bedroom at the first creak of the front door.

"I figured ye'd still be up," Nadia chuckled, shimmering towards Esra's room and taking a seat at the desk. "I actually think it went fairly well, Isak seemed pretty upset. *That slithering snake of a woman dare betray me,* was the way he put it."

"What about Arland, did ye see him?"

"No. Let's see if he's done."

Esra sent a Tur message and a short moment later a reply appeared on her arm.

Went well. She didn't believe me at first, her pride I believe. But then her face got so red I thought she may burst into flames right before me. She didn't say much, but I know she was beyond angry.

They both laughed at the picture of the short, plump Elf woman's face growing redder than a huckfly as Nadia sent back a message describing her encounter.

"And they both should be having some very interesting and vivid dreams tonight, don't forget."

"Aye. Do ye think that they will suspect Arland? Could he get in trouble?"

"Not likely. They have no idea that's one of his Gifts, and even if they did there's no way to prove he had anything to do with it. Besides, they will probably be so focused on each other that a dream will be the least of their worries by tomorrow."

"Well, I suppose we've done all we can, haven't we," Esra sighed.

"Aye, that we have." Nadia patted her shoulder reassuringly and shimmered towards the door. "Whatever happens tomorrow, I'm proud of all our Assembly has accomplished. Everything the races have accomplished. At least fer now we have three of the races and the Keepers standing together against Tallen. We'll figure everything out one way or another. We have to. The future of the Kingdom depends on it."

XLIII

Esra awoke in the early afternoon, both surprised and grateful that she had been able to sleep so long. Nadia had risen just before her and they both headed towards the Dining Hall for some noonmeal-breakfast, followed directly by a trip to the Library to meet her Assembly. Esra was attempting to read up on the history of the Stronghold, but after reading the same paragraph five times she defeatedly put down the book and began to pace back and forth. Everyone was on edge, speaking little and lounging about in nervous contemplation. Even her calm blacksmith friend seemed a little uneasy.

When it was finally time to walk together to the Great Hall, Esra was almost sick with fear. They marched in silence up the long, low stairs and through the Naduri River doors. The Council was still in session, so they took a seat next to each other on the marble benches in the foyer. The space slowly filled with other Keepers, all anxious to hear the results of the vote.

Long minutes passed and still no one spoke. Everyone seemed lost in their own world of reverie, the air hanging thick with tension. It seemed to Esra that the Council would never leave their room, that they would be waiting outside forever. When the heavy wooden doors finally swung open, everyone sat up with a start, eyes wide in anticipation.

Zakai and the Daughter swept past so quickly that Esra couldn't even catch a glimpse of their faces. The rest of the Council members exited the hall slowly, speaking in low, tired tones. Danya and Isak seemed slightly bewildered, wandering in silence as if they had just been hit by Nadia's Necklace of Stunning. Esra caught sight of her father as Adonis lurched towards them, a grin spreading to his rosy cheeks.

"The vote passed," he said breathlessly. "It was unanimous!"

A great gust of air left Esra's lungs as she deflated back into her seat. The dread that had been slowly building in her chest finally released and she felt noticeably lighter. Talitha joined her husband with a look of contained excitement. The vote had passed. The races would unite in a war against Tallen.

"Jumping jig," she muttered, standing to give her mother and father a strong hug. Cane swept over to where they were gathered and took her hand in a rare show of affection.

"Both Danya and Isak voted in favor of an alliance. I'm not sure how ye did it, but ye did. Then again, I don't think I want to know. No, I don't. Please don't tell me."

"Well, we didn't threaten them if that's what yer thinking," Esra laughed. "Not that we weren't tempted, believe me. We just outwitted them."

"I'm very glad to hear that. Tomorrow we begin to make preparations fer the defense of LeVara and determine the details of our strategy. Prince Bronnen will be sending his first attendant Cailean back to The King's Hold by skycatcher to gather as many stoneworkers as possible. The Prince remains behind to assist in the defense planning. Mox and Shova will also be leaving immediately fer Fira Nadim to enlist more commanders to train the Humans. Although he is needed here, Zakai will go with them since he feels it is greatly important to tell his people this news in person, and I must say I agree. The Daughter will return to Ember Isle to prepare her army of women warriors and Pura beasts. The Elders will send their attendants back with all haste to The Veiled City. Isak and Danya have volunteered to join them, although this is certainly fer the attention they will receive upon arrival. Linae and Kered will remain at the Stronghold."

"I can't believe it," Esra whispered in astonishment. "This is really happening. The races are uniting. We are going to war."

"Aye, that we are," Cane stated proudly, turning to look over Esra and her Assembly. "That we are."

It was a long time before the excitement died down in the foyer and everyone reluctantly but joyfully parted ways. Esra left the Great Hall slowly, stopping at the top of the marble stairs. Baelin, Fynn, Nadia and Arland silently joined her as they watched the last slice of an orange sun sink into the quiet earth. Esra had a fleeting thought that maybe this would be the last peaceful moment she would have in a long while. A long and treacherous road lay ahead. This war was going to be unlike anything the Kingdom had ever seen. She didn't even want to think about all the people that we going to die, that already had. But for now, Esra stood tall next to her new friends, her people, and knew that they would not be alone. For the first time in generations the races had been united. The people of LeVara were going to fight for freedom, and they would stand, or fall, as one.

The End
of
Book One

ABOUT THE AUTHOR

I am proud to be a self-proclaimed nerd with a lifetime love of reading. You can find me in the beautiful countryside of Northeast Ohio with my husband, son, and two dogs. I'm currently working on book two of the series.

There is no better feeling than escaping into the alternate reality of a good book, and so I was inspired to create a reality of my own. Not an easy thing for someone with a literary resume equivalent to that of a grapefruit. After a few crazy years of writing in any spare moments I could find, and doing practically everything they tell a new author not to do, this piece has finally culminated into something I can be proud of.

I welcome all comments and questions (NicoleMBurr@gmail.com) so feel free to give me your two cents. Or more if you can afford it. I am a struggling writer, after all…

For LeVara!

Nicki

Nicole Burr

www.ingramcontent.com/pod-product-compliance
Lightning Source LLC
Chambersburg PA
CBHW021217250626
47155CB00008B/2842